Son of Winter

ANNA KATE LOGAN

Copyright © 2020 Anna Logan

All rights reserved.

ISBN: 978-1-7343904-1-4

For my parents. You guys are awesome, for so many more reasons than I could ever list.

CONTENTS

1 - Leader 1
2 - Kill or Enslave 21
3 - Heir 34
4 - Dragon 57
5 - Separated 68
6 - Blending In 82
7 - Prisoners 94
8 - The Key 105
9 - Rikky 116
10 - Surrender 130
11 - Water 141
12 - Wards and Wardens 156
13 - A Game of Two 176
14 - Arrows 190
15 - Iron 206
16 - Casualties and Candidates 220
17 - Drifting 238
18 - Guilt 244
19 - Tessa 257
20 - Miracles and Nightmares 270
21 - Infiltration 283
22 - Kings and Orphans 300
23 - Grrake 314

24 - The Village	327
25 - Queens and Questions	350
26 - Handler	365
27 - Letters and Doors	382
28 - Captain	394

1
Leader

"There it is."

Talea squinted against the sunlight to see the haliop nestled in the woods below them. It was almost identical to her home, back in Vissler. The haliop with its single door and a few windows, a shed, an outhouse. The standard dwelling of a lower class family in a laborer's village. A year ago, she never imagined she'd be anywhere else...let alone the unbelievable places she'd been in the past month.

"Right." She crossed an arm over her chest, toying with a strand of hair. "Remind me why it's me that has to go talk to her first?"

Yhkon and Ahjul exchanged a glance. It was just the three of them, standing on a forested hilltop overlooking the haliop. The rest of the group was at a safer distance from the village. *Uh oh, an exchange of looks. Generally a bad sign.* Yhkon answered haltingly. "There's multiple reasons...we'll discuss it afterwards."

She gave him a frown. *And now you're sending me in there already anxious about this coming discussion.* "How evasive." When all he did was shrug, she sighed and faced the haliop again. "Okay, so...how, again?"

Ahjul gave her a reassuring smile. Smiling was what he did best. "It'll be a breeze. You're just going to have a conversation with her, that's it. And she's a kind girl, I think she'll take it well."

Yeah, because everyone takes being told that they're destined to lead a war well.

"She's coming out. Best go." Yhkon nodded his hooded head to indicate the figure that had just left the haliop, going into the shed. From that distance it was hard to see much, but she was tall, with long, straight hair.

"Alright." Talea took a few tentative steps in that direction, before glancing back at them. They both wore their masks and hoods since Yhkon said it was best to keep their identities concealed when close to civilization. Each had a sword on his hip, Yhkon's hand resting on the pommel as it often did. An assortment of other weaponry, the pauldron and gauntlets. When she thought about it, Yhkon looked downright scary. Ahjul not so much—he somehow managed to look both the part of the impressive warrior and the part of the kind, joyful young man beneath the armor and weapons. "Maybe take off the hoods and masks when I bring her back, though? You're not too bad," she grinned at Ahjul, then turned to Yhkon with raised eyebrows, "but you're kind of terrifying."

Since she was already walking down the hill, she didn't get to see his reaction, but she did hear Ahjul's muffled laugh.

Terindi Vegn. That was the name of the unsuspecting girl she approached. Ahjul's ward. One of the Eight. *Another teenager with a freakish ability like me, lucky her. How on Kameon am*

I supposed to tell her about all this, again? Stopping a few paces from the shed Terindi had disappeared into, Talea called softly to the open door. "Terindi?"

The girl stuck her head out, a slight pucker of confusion in her brow. Upon seeing Talea, the pucker deepened, and she stepped out of the shed. Up close, she clearly wasn't fully Zentyren, having a cool tan complexion, small eyes, and a face that was softly contoured. Not to mention the coloring of her hair—it was dark brown, but with streaks of honey-blond. "Yes? Do we know each other?"

"Um, no, not exactly." *Come on. Not too blunt, not too cryptic...* "But we have something in common. That's why I'm here." *Yep. Definitely not cryptic.*

Terindi just waited for her to explain.

"Is there anyone else around?" she asked, lowering her voice. At Terindi's growing frown, Talea inwardly slapped herself. *That doesn't sound suspicious at all...* "I mean, sorry, okay...I'm not sure how to say this, so..." She raised her hand, forming a sizzling sphere of electricity in her palm.

Those small, pale eyes widened briefly, then returned to normal. After studying the orb a moment, Terindi turned her attention back to Talea. When she spoke, her tone hadn't changed pitch at all. "That's certainly something in common."

Don't get excited easily, do you? "Yeah, I know." She offered a smile and let the sphere die out. "So, obviously, that's why I'm here."

"Alright..." Terindi was chewing on her bottom lip. "Then do you know more about this whole thing than me, or are you here in hopes of finding out more?"

This had to be one of the more unusual conversations she'd had with a stranger. Then again...maybe not. She'd had some even more peculiar discussions with Wylan and Yhkon in the early days of knowing them. "Well, a few months ago I was found by one of the others—" Noticing a flare of puzzlement in Terindi's pale green eyes, she backtracked. "There's eight of us. You can't see the others' lightning pillars, they're too far away, I couldn't either. Anyway, one of them found me…and we…well we went and found two others who are twins, and…" *Oh bother. How am I supposed to explain this?* "It's complicated."

Terindi's expression barely changed. It was almost as if she were missing some of the muscles necessary for facial contortions. "Okay, well, do you know why? Why we have the ability, I mean?"

Talea stifled a moan. This had to be the hardest part for her to explain. "Well we're San Quawr, you know that, right?"

"Yeah."

"Okay, so all eight are…and there's these guys that joined us, they're called Wardens, they're our guardians basically, and according to them…" She frowned. "Maybe I should just let them explain this to you."

"They're here?"

"Yeah, not far. Just on top of that hill."

The girl was clearly wary, even if her demeanor remained calm. But when Talea started toward the hill, she followed.

As instructed, the Wardens removed their hoods and masks as the two girls neared. Ahjul was already smiling. He looked even more boyish when he smiled. Talea had liked him from their first meeting that night in Jalkiva, and in the month of traveling since, she'd only come to like him more. "Terindi, this is Ahjul. He's your Warden. As in…uh, he's the Warden assigned specifically to you." *Yhkon, remind me your reasons for why I had to be the one for this job? It clearly wasn't that I was the best orator in the group.* "And this is Yhkon, he's the lead Warden."

Yhkon greeted Terindi politely, Ahjul with more warmth and a sort of shy friendliness. Terindi seemed to have relaxed some. After the two Wardens had made their greetings, she turned back to Talea with a hesitant look. "And...what was your name?"

Talea's cheeks flushed. "Talea." *I'm an idiot.*

"You didn't even introduce yourself?" Yhkon's amused smirk only made her blush grow hotter.

From there on, the task of explaining their story to Terindi fell on the Wardens. That was fine by Talea—as far as she was concerned, having her be the first person to make an impression on Terindi had been one of Yhkon's less-than-brilliant decisions. Besides, Ahjul was way better than she ever could be. He probably could have claimed to be a murderer on the run and ask for help on his next assassination, and still make it hard to refuse.

On top of that, Terindi fulfilled Ahjul's expectations: she took it well. All of it. Even the crazy bits about prophecies and wars and the Shadow Region.

Since she'd already heard the story multiple times, Talea lent her attention to a study of the new ward. What ethnicity was she, anyway? Not Zentyren, not Irlaish, and not Sanonyan. Must be Canadise, then. Though hadn't Larak said he was Canadise? Yet he didn't share any of Terindi's distinguishing features. He had chocolate brown skin like Alili, much darker than Terindi's.

The bracelets on Terindi's thin wrists caught her eye. She wore several, simple rings with colorful beads. She toyed with them as she listened to the Wardens and asked an occasional question. She was a pretty girl, even if somewhat exotic looking to Talea. Not a stunning beauty or anything, but there was a grace and a serenity in her countenance. Everything about her was composed. No matter how bizarre what the Wardens were saying was, she listened quietly—with interest, with surprise even, but always calmly.

All considered, Talea decided she liked her already.

They had been talking for several minutes when a tired female voice came from the haliop below. "Terindi! Where are you? What's taking so long?"

Terindi spun one of the bracelets around her wrist a couple of times, glancing back toward the haliop. Fortunately, they were concealed from whoever had called by the incline of the hill and the trees. "I better go. I'll talk to my parents about all of this. Perhaps you might come back, this evening? Seven o'clock?"

"We'll be here," Yhkon agreed.

After nodding, Terindi looked at each of them in turn a moment. "Well…until then."

Talea smiled at her, as did Ahjul. She returned the smile modestly before walking back down the hill to her haliop.

The three of them started in the other direction, back to where the other Wardens and wards had been left to set up camp. Talea ended up walking between Yhkon and Ahjul, feeling rather dwarfed by the two men who were both at least six feet tall. "So uh, what ethnicity is Terindi? I mean I assumed Canadise, but that's what Larak said he was, yet they don't look at all alike."

"She is Canadise," Yhkon answered. "Canadi is split into two regions, the Northern half and the Southern half. Or at least that's what they think. The rest of us just think that the two halves squabble but are in fact the same region. Either way, the people of either half don't share the same physical traits. Terindi's mother is half Northern Canadise, while one of Larak's parents was Southern Canadise."

"Oh." She smirked. "Is being a giant a normal Southern Canadise trait, or…?"

Ahjul chuckled. "No, that's just Larak."

They walked in silence for awhile. Talea shoved her hands into the pockets of her skirt. Since they'd been re-entering civilization—almost, anyway—she'd had to go back to wearing a dress, rather than the pants and shirt that had become her new normal. "Well anyway, I like her. Think her family will take it as well as she did?"

"I doubt it." Ahjul's smile had dimmed. It brightened again, however, and he added, "But I'm glad you liked her."

Arriving at where they'd left the celiths, all three mounted, Talea riding behind Yhkon. That was a new normal, too. While their travels through the mountains to get to Jalkiva had been mostly on foot, they'd ridden for most of the return journey. Yhkon had said it was a little risky to ride celiths in mountain terrain, but it was worth it to him to make the trip shorter. Once they'd left the mountains, they'd continued on celithback and at a faster pace. The Wardens were clearly used to all the riding. Wylan was at least somewhat accustomed to it. But to Talea and the twins, the first couple weeks had been a constant battle with soreness and stiff muscles.

Now, after a month of it, she rarely felt sore. Yhkon had often let her ride front, to give her practice at celithmanship, something he said she ought to master sooner rather than later. That was fine by her—she had come to enjoy it.

It took a little less than half an hour to get to the campsite. They'd picked a spot a few miles from Terindi's home and village, to hopefully avoid anyone noticing their presence. Especially anyone wearing the maroon dragon that was Kaydor's insignia.

She'd been learning more about this Kaydor over the past

month of travel, too. Yhkon didn't divulge much about the new king, though he made it plenty clear that he quite disliked him. She got the feeling that perhaps Yhkon had some sort of history with Kaydor, and not a good history. The other Wardens told her and the wards about him, though. He was a military man, they said. He had convinced the Leadership to start the Eradication in Zentyre almost two decades ago, and had been a primary figure in its execution. But the Leadership had changed their minds after about a year. Kaydor had remained in a top rank of the military. After that he'd become one of the Leaders, and then, somehow, he'd convinced everyone that Zentyre needed a king and that he was the perfect candidate.

They rode into the camp at a trot, coming to a stop and dismounting. Yhkon and Ahjul tied their celiths, while Talea walked forward to meet the twins as they moved to greet her.

"So? How'd it go? What's she like?"

"Did she think ya were crazy?"

Talea smiled. "Actually, no, she didn't seem to think that. She took it well. She's uh, well, she's nice. Quiet. Canadise, apparently. She's going to talk it over with her family, and we'll go back tonight."

The Wardens and Wylan meandered their way closer for a report too, though they got theirs from Ahjul, since Talea had already turned back around to stalk Yhkon as he unsaddled his celith, Eclipse. "So, why did I have to be the one to talk to her? You going to tell me your *reasons* now?"

His narrow eyes scrutinized her, while something like reluctance tugged at the corners of his mouth. "Maybe, maybe not."

"Hey, that's not fair. You already said you would." She crossed her arms. "You can't back out now."

Yhkon scowled at her, though she could tell he wasn't actually irritated, and was perhaps even in an unusually decent mood. "Fine. But *you're* going to learn to handle a sword, while we're at it." Before she could respond, he raised his voice to address everyone. "Let's do some training, plenty of good daylight left. Gustor, perimeter check. Larak, Resh, Ahjul, see if there's any game to be had. Wards, with your Warden for a lesson on swordsmanship." He faced Talea again, and jerked his head in a beckoning motion. He was smiling just a bit. "Come on, get over here."

Giving him a suspicious grin for no reason, she edged forward and crossed her arms again, this time expectantly. He, meanwhile, withdrew his sword from the scabbard on his hip. It was certainly not the first time she'd seen the weapon, yet she still admired its beauty. It wasn't a mere chunk of metal hewn into a blade, it was more like some sort of magnificent masterpiece of art that also happened to be a deadly tool.

Yhkon's gaze traveled over the sword as well, a look of satisfied pride lighting his features. He grabbed the flat of the blade and extended the handle to her. "Here. Ever held a sword before?"

What do you think? Haven't you been shadowing me most of my life? "Uh, no…" She gingerly wrapped her fingers around the pommel. It was sleek, black, the top and bottom embedded with bits of crystal in hues of silver and blue.

"Go on, then." He pushed it more firmly into her grasp. "It's not going to whip around and kill you on its own accord. Just think of it as an enlarged kitchen knife."

Talea took the weapon fully, smirking at him, and trying not to let on that the thing was astonishingly heavy. "An enlarged kitchen knife, huh? You know I'm going to call it that from now on. 'Hey Yhkon, can I borrow your enlarged kitchen knife?' 'Hey Yhkon, can I use your enlarged kitchen knife to chop these onions?'"

"Hilarious." He started adjusting her hold on the pommel, prying her fingers off and moving them about. "You know, in Canadi, they name their swords. It's quite a serious matter. A sword is practically an entity to them."

"What do they name them? Is there some sword named Lady Talea the Arm-Cleaver?"

He rolled his eyes, grinning. It was rare to see him grin. "You're impossible. Now spread your feet, a little past shoulder-width. There. Toes pointing out a bit. Weight on the balls of your feet, not your heels. Bend your knees. Not that much. Better." He stepped back, examining the stance he'd instructed her into. "Good. This sword is rather big for you," he pulled her wrists up, so that she held it higher, "but it'll work for practice. In Calcaria, you'll get a real, custom sword, like this one."

Always dreamed of having my own custom sword. Not. But hey, sounds kinda cool. "Right, but why do I need a sword if the whole point of all this is me having magical abilities?"

Yhkon shook his head. "You may not always be able to use your ability. You may be in a fight where you don't want your opponent to know you can throw lightning, see? If a bunch of Kaydorian knights were to swarm the campsite this minute, I'd rather you not inform Kaydor of our greatest asset."

"Fine then." She delicately poked his arm with the tip of the blade, light enough that he probably barely felt it. "Teach this *asset* how to not be helpless without her ability that makes her so valuable to you, and while you're at it, remind me why I had to be the one to go talk to Terindi?"

Those ice-blue eyes squinted at her. "Are you being irritable and demanding, salqui?"

"Are you calling me names in some language I don't even know, Silquije?" She raised an eyebrow at him coyly.

"Salqui. It means *ward* in Calnec-Arayn, which I intend to have you fluent in within a couple of years. Now." He grew more serious. "My reason is…you're the leader of the Eight."

The what? Leader? You're kidding. Talea blinked. "Uh…what?"

Yhkon put his hands in his pockets with his thumbs out, reminding her of Wylan's trademark pose. "I suppose I should have told you earlier. Didn't you ever wonder why you were assigned to the lead Warden? It's because you're the lead ward."

This is just dandy. "Nuh-uh. Come on. Why? I mean, shouldn't the leader be chosen or elected? How do you know it's me? *Why* is it me?"

Yhkon removed his hands from his pockets, and slid one through his dark blond hair. "That would be a question better suited to Grrake." When she only looked at him expectantly, he frowned and averted his gaze. "Narone chose you. There. That's why."

Despite the more pressing issue of her being the leader of the Eight, Talea looked at him until he made eye contact again. "Why does that bother you?"

He was scowling again. "What, and you're perfectly amicable towards the subject of Narone?"

"No, but you know why I'm not. I don't get why you aren't, considering your position and all."

The scowl turned into a glare, that made her want to retreat a step. "And that became your concern, when?"

Talea flinched, lowering the sword.

He took the sword from her hands. "Let's work on a few basic maneuvers," he said, quietly, though not so angrily. "I'll show you, then you can try."

He did an exceptional job of acting like nothing had happened, simply demonstrating the movements before guiding her through them. She didn't do quite as good a job. Every time he leaned in or grabbed her arm to move it into the correct position, she wanted to shrink away. The only responses she could make to anything he said was a nod or mumbled answer.

They practiced until Ahjul returned with a strange creature she'd never seen before slung over his shoulder. To her relief, Yhkon returned his sword to the scabbard, told her to help Ahjul clean and cook the game, and walked away.

Talea folded her hands behind her back as Ahjul approached, managing to return his smile. "What's that?"

"This," he knelt, depositing the animal on the ground, "is a merkil. Good for eating, not so good for carrying around, because I'm sure I'll smell like it for days." She'd been about to wrinkle her nose at the stench, but forced her expression to remain neutral instead. He looked at her with a twinkle in his eyes. "I can see you trying not to make a face."

A smile, as well as a wrinkled nose, came more easily that time. "Good grief, it does smell."

"They always do." He pulled a knife from his belt. "They're known for it. They usually live on riverbanks in burrows they dig in the mud, so you would think the water would have a bathing effect and take away the smell…no such luck." He poked the tip of the blade into the merkil's throat and moved it down, cutting a slit all the way to its belly.

Once he was convinced that she wasn't upset by it—which was only partially true—Ahjul showed her how to properly skin the creature and get the usable meat. After her nose became accustomed to the powerful stench, it wasn't so bad an occupation. With the mess cleaned up and several slabs of raw, slimy meat, they worked together to start a fire and cook the fresh game. By the time the pieces were sizzling, Larak and Resh had returned, with three barbsits between them. Gustor also came back from his perimeter check, with nothing to report.

It might as well have been a feast. There was enough meat for everyone to have a satisfactory amount, and Ahjul was right—merkil was good for eating, if not for smelling. Talea noticed after a while that she was the only one sitting anywhere near Ahjul, and realized it must have been because his clothes reeked with the odor, but she had gotten used to it.

Sure enough, Haeric shook his head with a chuckle. "You'd better change your clothes before you go back to the Vegns, or we'll never get the chance to convince them of anything."

"Amen to that!" Tarol scooted even farther away from the youngest Warden. "You smell worse than a carcass baking under an Irlaish sun."

Ahjul smiled sheepishly. "I know, I'm going to change."

"Still." Larak gave him a nod. "Good kill, lad. A merkil isn't an easy catch."

"Hmph," Resh smirked, "I'm the one who taught him to hunt. Of course he's catching merkils."

Ahjul's brow puckered. "Um, Grrake taught me to hunt."

Resh rolled his eyes. "Yeah, well, I took you out once. Close enough. And we all know I'm a far better hunter than Grrake."

No one argued that. Even Grrake just shrugged. Tarol, however, laughed. "Yeah, just like we all know Jewels is a better hunter than you, Resh."

While Resh scrunched up his face in protest, Ahjul's cheeks flushed slightly and he ducked his head. "Not really."

They kept going from there, but Talea tuned it out. As discreetly as possible, she observed Yhkon and Gustor, the only two Wardens not participating in the jovial conversation. They sat together, as she'd noticed that they often did. Gustor was sharpening one of his knives, the blade scraping against the stone in a drawn-out whine. Somewhere along the way, she'd picked up on the fact that he had actually been an assassin before he was a Warden. When or for whom, she didn't know. Either way, it wasn't hard to believe. At the beginning of their journey back into Zentyre a month ago, she'd been undeniably intimidated, even frightened, of the man.

Not anymore. He was a daunting, intense individual—but he wasn't someone to fear. If any of the Wardens were to be feared…it was Yhkon.

He, unlike Gustor, wasn't doing anything in place of joining the discussion. He just sat there, staring at his hands, a distant look in his eyes.

Talea looked away, down to her own hands. Whatever had happened to him, whatever made him bitter toward Narone…it was something she should try to help him with, not resent him for. He was willing to be friends, to build trust and appreciation, she was sure of it.

As seven o'clock drew near, Ahjul left to change his clothes. When he came back, Ki got up and approached him with a suspicious look, inhaling loudly through his nose. "Nope." He shook his head, recoiling with a grimace. "Ya still smell like it. Or d'ya alwees smell like that?"

Grrake got up, rolling his eyes and giving Ki's arm a whack to shoo him away. "Come on." He nodded Ahjul toward the Warden's tent. "Let's find some soap, and you can wash up in the creek. That should get the smell out."

"Make it quick, though." Yhkon finally broke the silence

he'd held for almost two hours. His tone was remote, abrasive, even if she guessed his gloom wasn't directed at Ahjul. "We leave in fifteen minutes."

Grrake frowned, before he and Ahjul disappeared into the shelter. When they came back out, Ahjul left jogging toward the nearby creek, while Grrake returned to the group where they sat around the fire.

"You could take it easy on him, you know." Tarol was glowering at the lead Warden. "Unlike the rest of us, he's too naive to realize you're just an irritable bully and that he shouldn't be bothered by you—"

Yhkon was instantly on his feet and towering over Tarol, who was still sitting on the ground. "That's enough out of *you*." He said it so vehemently that Talea was surprised Tarol didn't cower.

Even if he didn't cower, he did close his mouth and keep it that way.

Yhkon stormed off. Grrake followed him warily. The rest of them sat in stunned silence.

Tarol crossed his arms and glared at the fire, shoulders hunched moodily. Talea had gotten the feeling that something had happened between him and Yhkon early on in the trip, or even back in Jalkiva. They hadn't spoken much, and Yhkon had been harsher with him than with the other Wardens. It seemed as though her suspicion had been correct.

Yhkon came back moments later, looking angrier than before. Ignoring all of their stares, he started saddling Eclipse and Ahjul's celith with jerking movements. The poor celiths shied away from him with the whites of their eyes showing. Grrake reappeared too, with a countenance similar to that of the celiths.

Talea caught Kae's eye, seeing her concern mirrored there.

Larak got up and walked away with what sounded like an exasperated sigh. *Well.* She rubbed the back of her hand with her thumb. *Our trip to the Vegns ought to be interesting.*

Ahjul came back trying to wring out his hair that was just too short to grab. He'd been remarkably quick, but Yhkon was still waiting beside the celiths with arms crossed and jaw set. Ahjul hastily returned the soap and towel to the tent and jogged the rest of the way to the celiths. Talea joined them, probably just in time to avoid having Yhkon snap at her to hurry up.

He pointed her to Eclipse's saddle. *Yay. Can't wait. Nothing I'd like more than to be in close quarters with you when you're practicing your murder-glares...*

"Yhkon? Could she ride with me, actually?" Ahjul spoke up tentatively. "If not I understand, I just was going to tell her more about Terindi, and it would be easier if—"

"Fine." Yhkon brushed past her to mount Eclipse, not even waiting for them to mount Ahjul's celith before trotting away, in the direction of Terindi's home.

Ahjul let her climb into the saddle, before getting in behind her. At his gesture, she took the reins and cued the celith into a trot after Eclipse, keeping far enough back that Yhkon would be unlikely to hear them talking. "I can't believe that worked. Thanks."

A backwards glance showed that Ahjul was smiling, but sadly. "You're welcome...though I did it for him, too. Sometimes when he's in one of these moods, he just needs a little time to himself."

"So hopefully by the time we get to the Vegns', he'll be better?"

"Hopefully." A pause. "You know he doesn't mean to hurt you, whenever he snaps or seems annoyed?"

She craned her neck to look at him. "How did you know

he had…?"

"I didn't." Ahjul shrugged. "I just guessed."

Facing forward again, Talea watched Yhkon's back as he posted, up and down, in rhythm with Eclipse' gait. "So in the future, when he's in a mood like this, I should just leave him be for awhile?"

"No." Ahjul shook his head. "Usually he actually does better with company, I think, so long as it's just one or two people he feels comfortable with, which you qualify as."

He was beginning to remind her of Grrake. It seemed that they had a respect and even affection for Yhkon that the other Wardens did not. Though, in different ways. Ahjul admired him, Grrake…well, he seemed to feel protective of him. "How long have you known him?"

"Three years, since they started training me to replace the original Silquije Hyrru. But I've known *of* him for more like six years." He was smiling. "The Wardens are pretty much famous in Calcaria, especially Yhkon and Grrake."

I'm sure Yhkon loves being famous. Can't you just see him, smirking and waving to the cheering crowd and adoring young ladies? Shaking her head at herself, she gave the celith another light kick when it started to slow down. "What happened to the first Silquije Hyrru?"

"I don't know the details…I think he was caught doing something illegal, or at least immoral. Not sure why they decided to have me replace him, but they did."

Talea gave him a smile over her shoulder. "Well, I'm glad they did."

Yhkon had stopped and dismounted ahead of them, so the only response Ahjul made was to reflect her smile. They caught up and got down, Ahjul tying his celith next to Eclipse.

Talea eyed Yhkon as he finished tying Eclipse. In the dark,

it was hard to tell much about his demeanor. Still, his shoulders didn't look as rigid, his head was up instead of down. It was confirmed when he turned to them upon finishing. "Ready?"

Nicely done, Ahjul. "Yep." She gave Yhkon the same smile she'd given Ahjul. "Ought to be fun, right?"

They went the rest of the distance on foot, until they were standing at the door of the Vegns' haliop. It was larger than most haliops. No wonder, since Ahjul had mentioned that Terindi had several younger siblings.

It was a stern-looking man with none of Terindi's Canadise features that opened the door when Yhkon knocked. Where Terindi's face was soft and smooth, his was hard, with hooded eyes and a firm mouth.

"Jasib Vegn." Yhkon extended his hand. "I'm Yhkon Tavker, lead Warden."

Jasib shook his hand, though not particularly happily. "And you're Terindi's Warden?" he asked Ahjul, with a skeptical frown, as if he didn't like the notion of his daughter having a "warden". *Which he probably doesn't, and I can't really blame him.*

"Yes." Despite the unfriendly address, Ahjul smiled kindly. "I'm Ahjul Rye'Shan."

Finally, those critical eyes landed on her. "And you're one of the others with the ability."

"Yes sir." Talea dipped her head to him. "I'm Talea Andul." *Leader of the Eight, apparently.* She waited to make sure he wouldn't try to shake her hand. He didn't. Most adults didn't, when introduced to a lower class teenage girl. Yet she could have sworn that irritation flashed across Yhkon's features. What did he expect? *A red carpet rolled out before my feet?*

Jasib let them into the haliop. They entered into a cramped living room.

It reminded her of home...painfully so. A year ago, would

she have entered the haliop and thought it felt cramped? No, she would have noticed how it was more spacious than her own. This had been her life for fifteen years. A laborer's life.

Terindi was standing beside a thin woman with nervously flitting eyes, and the Canadise features, except even more distinct.

The introductions were repeated with Terindi's mother, whose name was Adashi. Talea saw a couple of young faces peek out from a doorway down the hall, but they must have been instructed not to interrupt, because they disappeared back into the bedroom.

From there, Adashi and Jasib, mostly Jasib, peppered the Wardens with questions. They wanted Talea to demonstrate her lightning for confirmation, and asked her a little bit about her connection with the Wardens. Jasib seemed leery, even resentful. Adashi, mostly scared. Terindi, meanwhile, appeared to be gaining enthusiasm…in her calm, withdrawn sort of way.

"How are we supposed to trust you?" Jasib's frown hadn't softened at all. It had hardened, if anything.

"You already asked that." Yhkon was hardly *soft* either. Whatever patience he'd entered the haliop with had been sucked dry by Jasib's distrust and skepticism. "So all I can tell you is the same thing I did last time—what reason do you have not to? We are the only ones with an explanation for Terindi's ability. We know more about it than anyone. We're San Quawr, that in and of itself counts for something."

"I've heard better reasons to trust someone," Jasib retorted. "And what reasons don't I have? How about that you're complete strangers. That you supposedly came from the Shadow Region. That you're—"

Ahjul stepped forward. Unlike Yhkon he didn't look impatient, just anxious. "You have to understand how important this is. Terindi, Talea, and the other wards were given this ability, by Narone Himself, for a very important task: stopping the Eradication." He looked at Jasib, then Adashi, searchingly. "Don't you want that?"

"You're asking to drag her off and into a war!" Jasib's fists were clenched. "You think I'm going to agree to this? This is all ridiculous. You can't just—"

"Enough!" Yhkon said the word forcefully enough that Jasib fell silent. "This is getting us nowhere. The fact is, unless you manage to change Narone's mind, she's going to end up doing what He made her to do. It doesn't matter whether or not you like it." He took a deep breath. If it had been meant to calm him, it didn't work. "So I'm done arguing with you about it. We'll be back tomorrow. Hopefully by then you'll see some sense." With that, he was marching out the door.

2
Kill or Enslave

Talea was beginning to understand.

Watching Tarol glare daggers into Yhkon's back as soon as he turned away, or Larak's occasional exasperated sigh that was otherwise inexplicable, Haeric's shadowed frown that often followed one of the lead Warden's irritable outbursts or silences…it all made sense now. She understood how they felt, and why they felt that way.

Excluding perhaps Ahjul and Tarol based on lack of experience, and Resh based on questionable character, any of the other Wardens could have taken Yhkon's place and filled the role with more wisdom and patience. She doubted any of them—well, except maybe Gustor—would have so quickly lost patience with Jasib the night before. And the fact that Yhkon had lost patience and spoken so harshly would probably make their job of convincing the Vegns to let them take Terindi all the harder.

It was no surprise that there was a sense of resentment

between the Wardens. No doubt they looked at Yhkon, at his shortcomings, and wondered why he had been made leader over them.

She wondered the same thing. And she wondered what sort of a leader she would make.

"Yhkon?" Talea looked up from the dress she was mending, to where he sat a few feet away, polishing his sword. "How old were you when you were made lead Warden?"

He held the sword up, squinting at a smudge. "Almost nineteen." His eyes flitted briefly to hers, before returning to the smudge as he began working at it with a damp cloth. "I know you probably don't feel ready to be a leader. I didn't either." Under his breath, he added, "I still don't."

Technically, those words weren't exactly comforting. Yet somehow they were. "And you're *sure* it's me? Why not…" She observed the twins, laughing as they practiced their lightning with Terindi. Though their visit to the Vegns that morning hadn't accomplished much, they had convinced them to let Terindi come to camp with them and meet everyone. Wylan was watching them practice too, from where he stood by himself. "Why not Wylan? He seems a better candidate."

"Why?" Yhkon gave her a meaningful look.

She resisted the urge to roll her eyes. "For several reasons. Mainly, the reason that I'm *not* a good candidate."

Ignoring that comment, he shrugged. "Actually, Wylan is the marshal. Your right-hand-man, basically. The way Grrake is for me."

Oh. This is news. Good news…bad news? "You didn't mention that."

One of his eyebrows rose. "Is it a problem? You just said he'd be a good leader. Why not a good second-in-command?"

Okay, good point. While she'd rather have Wylan be leader

and *she* be marshal, if that wasn't to be, perhaps this was the best alternative. "It's not. I just…this is all rather…it's kind of weird." *Everything about all of this is weird.*

He didn't contest the point. In fact, he seemed to agree with her. It wasn't much of a surprise when he put the sword away, stood up, and walked off without a word.

Terindi remained at camp with them late into the afternoon. By the end of it Talea could tell that Terindi would settle nicely into the group, and make a pleasant addition. Everyone liked her and she had become more relaxed with them as time went on.

Unfortunately, Jasib was not similarly softened over the course of the day. When Talea, Yhkon, and Ahjul brought Terindi home, they were given a curt nod and a closed door. Yhkon had glared at the door irritably enough to wither a forest.

Yhkon's fists were clenched at his sides. "There isn't time for this useless bickering. Kaydor is actively seeking out San Quawr, even in villages, to capture them and probably kill them. You're not safe here."

Talea wondered if Jasib Vegn was *that* hard headed and stubborn, or if he genuinely didn't believe them, or if he just didn't want to let Terindi go. Because here he was, still frowning, still shaking his head. "How do I know we'll be any safer with you?"

Yhkon looked to be somewhere between utter astonishment and an explosion. By the way his usually golden, Sanonyan complexion was turning to crimson, he was teetering dangerously close to the explosion. Talea touched his arm soothingly before it could take place, and faced Terindi.

"Terindi?"

Terindi's small, pale eyes widened. Clearly she understood Talea's silent question: what did *she* think and want? Would she choose to join them? Did she trust them?

She could imagine—as well as see in his expression—Jasib's indignation at her for bypassing him to ask his daughter instead.

But Terindi didn't defer back to him, like Talea worried she might. She straightened her slouched shoulders and answered quietly. "I think you're telling the truth. I think…" at this, she sent a nervous glance her father's way, "I think I'd like to join you."

Talea could have sworn Yhkon gave Jasib a smug look, nigh on a sneer.

It was Jasib's turn to redden with anger. After seeming unable to speak, he just went to the door and gestured them out.

They obeyed the gesture, Ahjul with a meek smile at the rest of the Vegn family, Yhkon with a glower. Outside and back at their celiths, he released his breath in a snarl. "I'm not sure I've ever met anyone as hard headed as Jasib Vegn."

If Tarol were around, Talea was pretty sure he would have smirked and said something along the lines of, "Except for yourself, of course." Since Tarol wasn't there, it wasn't said. Ahjul probably didn't think of Yhkon as hard headed, and Talea knew better than to point it out and risk irritating him further.

The ride back to camp was a quiet one. What now? What more could they possibly say to win Jasib over? Or…would they resort to force, if he refused to be persuaded? They couldn't just give up and leave without Terindi. Talea knew that. But she didn't feel as though they could tear her from her family and whisk her off, either.

In any case, they couldn't remain camped outside of Luriville forever, waiting for Jasib to give in. A San Quawr scout had arrived the day before with news that the Eradication really was sweeping the region, and that there appeared to be a force of Kaydorians approaching Luriville. Yhkon had relayed the information to Jasib, expecting him to be more easily persuaded under the looming threat of the Eradication...while Terindi and her mother Adashi were swayed, Jasib was not.

Back at camp, Yhkon took care of Eclipse before seeking out Grrake. Talea could hear their lowered voices. Not the words, but the tones—Yhkon impatient and hostile, Grrake trying to calm him.

"What now, do you think?" She shadowed Ahjul as he fetched a bristle brush from his pack to groom his celith.

"I'm not sure," he was wearing one of his infrequent frowns, "but we have to convince them, we can't leave without her, nor can we stay much longer. Narone will provide a way. I guess we just have to wait for that."

The only times Ahjul ever annoyed her was when he made references to Narone, in his innocent, trusting way. Yet this time, it didn't bother her. It was admirable, really; his sincere and unwavering faith. Like Grrake's. Sure, they didn't have the logic, reasoning, or discernment that Yhkon did, which was also admirable. But she was beginning to think that perhaps what Grrake and Ahjul had was preferable between the two.

Yhkon joined the group somewhat mollified by whatever Grrake had said, if only to a grumpy demeanor instead of an angry one.

The rest of the day passed as usual: training, lounging about with nothing to do, a few chores. The discussion arose at supper of what to do next, in regard to the Vegns. The only conclusion the Wardens came to was to sleep on it and decide tomorrow.

Tomorrow came, and made the decision for them.

"Mr. Yhkon! Mr. Yhkon!"

The high-pitched voice of a young boy startled all of them in the middle of their morning workouts. A boy with the distinguishing Canadise features came running into their campsite, face red with exertion and eyes bulging. It was one of Terindi's siblings, nine-year-old Avten.

Yhkon was on his knee in front of the boy in an instant. "What is it?"

"Kaydorian knights," he panted out, wiping his perspiring forehead. "I saw them while I was on a walk and I ran home and Mother said to get to you and—"

Yhkon briefly put a hand on Avten's shoulder. "You did fine." Standing up, he raised his voice. "Grrake, Ahjul, Gustor, you're with me. Talea and Wylan too. Tarol, Larak, Resh, you and the twins pack up the camp and catch up to us in Luriville. Haeric, you ride to the station and tell them we'll be needing Elikwai. Let's go!"

In a blur of activity, the designated group mounted up, Avten riding with Ahjul. Talea had barely settled into the saddle when Yhkon kicked Eclipse into a canter. "Talea, Wylan," he shouted above the rumble of their celiths' hooves, "no lightning unless I say otherwise! We'll take care of the knights, your job is to protect Terindi's family."

Um, right. She took a deep breath, wishing it would slow her rapidly increasing heart rate. *How are we supposed to do that without lightning?*

They reached the Vegns' home just as ten knights did.

Yhkon practically shoved her out of the saddle, already

charging Eclipse toward the soldiers, with his sword brandished. Grabbing Avten's hand, Talea darted with him into the haliop, nearly running into Terindi and Adashi as they came to the door. Wylan was on her heels, locking the door behind them.

Adashi pulled Avten into her arms and held him, crying. She was whispering something, over and over. Instinctively Talea moved forward to hear. "Not again, not again, not again…"

Had she experienced the Eradication before?

There was a pounding on the door, and the knob rattled. Adashi gasped and cowered away from it, bringing her younger children with her. Terindi remained with Wylan and Talea, as they faced the door, waiting…the rattling stopped, there was a grunt, a thud, a gargled yell. Through the window, Talea could see the Wardens with only three more opponents to go. No, now only two. "It's alright." She turned to Adashi, after seeing Yhkon cut down the final knight. "The Wardens won."

On cue, the door rattled again. "It's me," came Yhkon's voice.

Talea unlocked it, letting him in. His bloodied sword was still in his hand, but otherwise, he appeared unharmed, not even winded. After glancing at the Vegns that were present as if to satisfy himself that they were fine, he stepped back out. Talea followed, as did Wylan, and shortly Terindi. "Ahjul, you stay here with them."

With a nod, Ahjul took up his place beside Terindi.

"The rest of you," Yhkon led Eclipse over to Talea so she could mount, "we're going into the village."

No questions, no objections. Everyone got on their celiths and set them at a canter toward Luriville.

Talea had to swallow the constriction in her throat to get

out the question that was nagging her. "What will they do to the San Quawr they find, if we don't stop them?" Her voice was nearly drowned out by the din of hooves.

Yhkon must have heard anyway. His shoulders were rigid. "Kill or enslave."

"But we'll stop them," Grrake called, from where he and Wylan rode to their right.

Yhkon lowered his head, pulling his hood more securely over his forehead and balling his fist tightly around the reins. "This time."

Her throat only became even more constricted than before. *All the times we can't stop it...how many will die?*

They broke from the trees into the clearing of the village, where knights were gathering up villagers and restraining any that resisted. Eclipse lurched, nearly throwing Talea from the saddle, as Yhkon wheeled him around to avoid the sword of one of the Kaydorians. She gripped his waist tightly as he engaged with the soldiers, her eyes locked on the villagers. There was a sort of calm, a lull, about the situation. There should have been shouting and confusion, instead it seemed the laborers were too stunned to put up much fight. It was the Wardens who were disrupting the strange tranquility. Among the villagers, a little boy stood between an even younger girl and a knight. He tried to shove the man away, to dodge him and move his sister from harm's way. Instead, both children were grabbed and torn apart from each other. The girl's screams shattered the serenity of the scene. The stillness was gone. In its place, chaos.

"Go for the celiths!"

Talea heard the shout of the commanding knight, a moment before Yhkon was leaping from the saddle. He hit the ground already moving, attacking the nearest Kaydorians. The other Wardens had dismounted as well, leaving two riderless celiths, Wylan on Grrake's mount, and Talea still on Eclipse.

The knights trying to subdue the villagers were becoming more aggressive toward their hostages. They were threatening women and children in an attempt to get someone to betray any San Quawr in the group.

"Talea!" Wylan had moved Lenjeya, Grrake's mare, to Eclipse's side. "Let's go!"

She blinked. "Go where?"

He was already kicking Lenjeya into a gallop, straight toward the villagers and the knights surrounding them. Surely he knew they weren't supposed to use their lightning. So what was his plan? Trample them? Wouldn't the knights just kill the celiths out from under them?

Yet for some reason, she was urging Eclipse after him.

The soldiers directly in their path drew their swords, backing away. The celiths' hooves left a wake of dust, stinging Talea's eyes and clogging her throat. She was coughing and blinking rapidly as they reached the knights, and she still had no idea what they were supposed to be doing.

Wylan didn't hesitate. He drove Lenjeya straight into a soldier. Clearly the man hadn't expected such a bold move, which was what made it work. He was sent sprawling by the impact, but before he fell, Wylan somehow managed to snatch the sword right out of his hand.

Now there was just the minor problem that she was still aboard a galloping celith, with about zero seconds to decide what to do. Her hands decided for her, guiding Eclipse to the right, toward the little boy and girl, and the soldiers that held them.

"Talea!" Yhkon's voice. "What the—"

He probably finished with a curse and an inquiry as to what

exactly she was doing. Oh well. Too late to stop now. Eclipse was already thundering down on the soldiers who were hauling the children, writhing and screaming, away from each other.

Well what good was all that training Grrake and Yhkon had been making them do, if it couldn't help her out here?

She jumped from the saddle while Eclipse was still running. He kept going, knocking a few knights down and one unfortunate villager, while she ended up flying straight into the man holding the little girl. Her shoulder hit his armor painfully, sending all three of them down in a tangled heap. She was already grabbing the girl, fingers prying her loose from the soldier's hold. Freeing her suddenly, Talea stumbled backwards, with the girl tight between her arms. Her balance was off. It was either fall, or drop the child. Her back met the ground with a jarring thud. Instinct sent her rolling, getting to her knees, her back between the little girl and the men still standing around them.

A hand closed around her upper arm and yanked her to her feet. The shouting and general pandemonium around her had increased. She looked up and sure enough, the Wardens had caught up, and were making quick work of the remaining Kaydorians. Tarol, Larak, Resh, and the twins had ridden into the village too, and were soon using their mounted advantage to force the knights away from the villagers, before finishing them off.

Wylan let go of her arm as soon as she was steady, a hint of a sparkle in his dark eyes. "Did you have a plan for getting out of that, or were you just counting on me saving your neck?"

Her stomach twisted at the same time as she gave him a dazed grin. "You think I had a plan to begin with?" She set down the little girl, who looked at her for just a moment before fleeing back to her brother.

Another hand grasped her arm, tighter. She spun to face the owner: a tense-looking Yhkon. "What on Kameon were you two doing?"

She couldn't quite tell if he was legitimately angry or only pretending to be. It rather looked as though he wasn't sure himself. "Um, well, we were…"

When she didn't come up with some sort of an excuse, he finally rolled his eyes and released her arm. "You did good." His expression relaxed. "I prefer to be asked, though, when you're going to perform dangerous heroics, is all." After giving them a slight smile, he left to rejoin Grrake and Larak, who were addressing the nervous villagers. Among them was the rest of the Vegn family. Jasib wasn't making eye contact with any of them.

While Grrake had been trying to reassure the people, Yhkon took a different approach. "Alright. We've dealt with these Kaydorians, but more will come within days to finish the job. We won't be here to stop them. If you're San Qawr, and they find out, they will either kill you or take you prisoner." He let the words hang for a moment, in the tense silence. "One of our men will be returning shortly with some Elikwai, an elite force of the Calcarian military, who will escort any San Quawr to Calcaria. If you don't want to go, that's your choice, but there will be no protection for you here. If you're coming, pack enough food for two weeks, the materials for a shelter for your family, and only whatever else you absolutely need. Any questions?"

"Um," a middle aged man with a thick beard spoke almost instantly. "Who are you people?"

Larak grunted from a few feet away, giving Yhkon a disapproving glance.

Yhkon, meanwhile, just looked impatient. He backed up,

gesturing Grrake forward. Mumbling an "If you would," he left Grrake to answering questions, while he approached Tarol and the twins, telling them to go to the Vegns' home and let them know what was happening.

Talea tuned in to the discussion between Grrake and the San Quawr villagers. He had given an abbreviated account of who they were and why they were there, without mentioning anything about lightning-wielding teenagers or impending wars. *Probably wise.* The people appeared more receptive to what he had to say. Not much of a surprise there…Yhkon was the type that would get respect and submission. Grrake was the type that would get trust and amenity. Since they'd been on the verge of execution or enslavement by knights only minutes ago, it was probably the latter that would be more helpful.

Still, not all were to be so easily convinced.

"So what you're suggesting," a younger man with a scowl spoke up. His shoulders were thrown back, head held high, eyes sharp. "Is that we—any of us that are San Quawr, anyway—up n' leave everything we've ever known, on nothing but the five-minute speech of a few strangers with shiny swords? And who make some dandy-fine claims 'bout the Shadow Region and San Quawr armies?"

Grrake was about to reply, with that usual gentle, patient expression of his, but Yhkon marched forward and spoke before he could. "That's exactly what we're suggesting, and if you'd been listening to our *five-minute speech,* you wouldn't be questioning it. Do you know what those knights were going to do to you, if we hadn't intervened?" He gave the briefest of pauses to allow for a response before barging on. "They were going to kill any of you who caused trouble, enslave children that were an ideal age, or adults who were healthy and submissive. The rest of you would have been put into some mass prison full of other San Quawr laborers who Kaydor thinks are useless but aren't worth digging a grave for."

Silence.

Yhkon must have realized his hand was gripping the pommel of his sword and that he was in a threatening stance, because he swallowed and relaxed his posture slightly. "We're not forcing you to go. But I can tell you from personal experience that if you stay, you'll last a week at the most."

More silence. The people exchanged glances and shuffled their feet. A few whispers. It was Jasib Vegn who stepped forward, turning to face both his fellow villagers and the Wardens. "You all know me. You know I wouldn't lie to you. So, I want you to know that I trust these men. I've had previous interactions with them, and have been given cause to believe what they say. Especially since they warned me that this would happen, and now it has." He made eye contact with Yhkon. There was a sort of grudging reluctance in his features, but he gave the lead Warden a nod. "My family will be going with their Elikwai to Calcaria. I hope all of you will choose to do the same."

3

Heir

Zoper gave the laces of his boot a sharp tug, pulling them tight before crossing and knotting them. The strings were frayed, worn down from years of use. There was a gradually widening tear in the leather-like fabric of the right boot. In all, it was getting past time for a new pair. Not that that was an option.

He was just getting up and grabbing his canteen when a melodic, female voice distracted him. His nine-year-old sister stood in the open doorway that led to a room decorated in bright shades of yellow and peach. Her wispy blond hair was ruffled, no doubt from recently being against her pillow.

"Yaila!" He shook his head at her with a smile. "What are you doing up, silly bird?"

"Can't sleep," she mumbled, rubbing bleary eyes with her fists.

"Oh." He gave her an understanding nod. "And getting out of bed is a guaranteed cure. Good choice."

Either not catching the sarcasm or choosing to ignore it, she moved forward to curl up on the sofa he'd just gotten up from. "Won't you read me a story?"

"I have to go to—"

"Yes but before you go to work," she said, as if it were quite sensible.

With another smile and shake of his head, Zoper returned to the sofa and sat down next to her, picking up a stack of children's books. She snuggled against his shoulder, scanning the titles. All of them were books intended for kids younger than her, but she still cherished them. Probably because they were the books their parents had read to her when she was little. "The one about the fluffy barbsit." She pointed to one of the covers.

He set aside the other books and inspected the chosen one. The cover featured an illustration of a furry barbsit with a human-like expression. The edges of the book were far more worn than his boots. He could remember his mother reading the very same story to him, over a decade ago, before Yaila was even born. "Alright, let's see what happens to this fluffy barbsit."

Five minutes later, he'd said "The End" and closed the book. Yaila made no move to untangle herself from his lap. "Okay little bird, now I really *do* have to go to work."

"I know," she sighed. "I wish you didn't, though."

"Well, just think how sick of me you'd get if I was here all day to pester you?" With that, he set to tickling her waist and bare feet, until she leaped off the sofa, giggling. He pretended to chase her, and she darted away with a squeal. She fled back into her bedroom, diving into the bed and burrowing under the covers. Grinning, he pulled them up around her chin, smoothing her disastrous hair out over the pillow. "Alright little bird, time for you to get some rest. We wouldn't want you falling asleep in class."

She blew out of her lips in exasperation. "But arithmetic is *so* boring."

"Okay…" He put on a contemplative expression. "Well, I reckon you'd best sit behind someone fat and tall, then. Maybe Ms. Daws won't notice you snoozing."

Yaila laughed, girlish and chirp-like, hence her nickname. Everything about her reminded him of a bird, from her dark brown eyes, to her pointy nose, but especially her singsong voice. "Axlem ought to do nicely. I'll sit behind him. He brings at least two sandwiches for lunch everyday!"

Zoper gave her a decisive nod. Just one sandwich would be a luxury, he was feeling rather envious of this Axlem boy. "Perfect. It's a plan." He retreated to the door. "See you later."

"Bye, Zoper."

Outside the house, the cold air burned his lungs, the breeze cutting through his clothing. *Having an all-day, completely outdoors job will be even more delightful in a month when it's winter. Not.* Smirking to himself, Zoper set out at a jog away from the house. Leaves, recently fallen from the bare trees around him, crunched under his boots. A couple weeks ago the forest around his house had been a gorgeous palette of autumn golds, oranges, and mahogany. Since then most of the leaves had been blown off by the wind, leaving the trees stripped, and stealing the beauty of the place. But, winter would bring a different kind of beauty. Really, the spot was pretty no matter what time of year it was.

Which, of course, led him to more depressing thoughts about whether or not it could be their home for much longer.

Enough of that. It was too early for gloominess! Zoper kept up a steady pace for the entire three miles to the sawmill.

Reading to Yaila had put him behind schedule, and he couldn't afford to be late. Besides. Nothing like a good run to invigorate a person for the day.

When he arrived at the mill, there was only one other person there. *Bossman.* "Hello Restir! Fine morning, isn't it?"

"Hmph," the man grunted as he checked machinery. "Well, it's morning alright. You nearly beat the sun up, lad."

"Early bird catches the worm, I'm told."

"What good's a worm unless you're going fishing?"

Zoper joined him in assessing and preparing the equipment. "Well, who says I'm not?"

Restir glanced disinterestedly at him. "Ain't many fish 'round here, boy. If you're so eager, then get to it already."

With a shrug, Zoper complied, moving to pick up a section of log small enough for him to carry alone. "Someday I'll be fishing. My father was a sailor, you know, before—"

"Are you talking to yourself over there, greenhorn?"

Another shrug, and a smile. "You weren't offering much conversation."

Restir rolled his eyes. "I'm not here for conversation. And," he jabbed a finger Zoper's direction, a hint of an exasperated smirk toying with his lips, "neither are you. Now help me with this hitching."

"My pleasure, boss." Zoper winked. Restir just muttered grouchily. Together they lashed a thick rope around a few logs on one end, then the other. After connecting the two bindings to another set of ropes that attached it to two yuley harnesses, they moved to the next pile of logs.

The other men began trickling in. Jobs were assigned. Zoper ended up on one end of a handsaw, dragging it back and forth through log after log, with a grumpy-looking fellow on the other end. They went on, for awhile, no sound but the rhythmic grind of the blade through the wood. Why not have some conversation, to liven up the job? "It's Evres, right?"

The man looked up at him with a skeptical, dull furrow in his brow. "Right."

"I'm Zoper." He smiled. "I don't believe we've met, officially. I—"

"I know who you are, kid. How about less talking and more sawing?"

Zoper paused, just for a moment, in the back-and-forth drag on the saw. Then he nodded and averted his gaze. He wondered when, if ever, people's opinions of his father would stop affecting their opinion of him. And when, if ever, people would look past their negative assumptions of politicians to realize that his father had in fact been a kind, fair, faithful man. Not just a politician.

Flexing his back muscles a little, he hunkered down to the work with renewed resolve. It didn't matter. What they thought of his father, and of him, was their problem. He couldn't let it bother him. Because he knew the truth, even if they chose to ignore it.

Still, sometimes he couldn't help thinking how nice it would be to not have his father's reputation attached to his name. Most eighteen-year-olds didn't get frowns and gruff voices the moment they said their name. Zoper Veserron. Son of a member of the late Leadership. Who, like any leader, could never please everyone with his decisions. It didn't seem to matter that the man wasn't even alive anymore, nor did they seem to realize that Zoper was his *son*, not him.

Though of course, to be honest, he did want to be like him. Zoper couldn't think of anyone that he admired more than his parents...which made it all the harder, now that they were gone.

The hours passed slowly, with little to no distraction. Just the saw moving back, forth, back, forth. Occasionally a different task, usually of a similar nature and level of dreariness. The only entertainment offered by his coworkers was their sporadic banter. That, and their colorful vocabulary. Growing up among nobility, and raised by parents who believed in respectability and courtesy, Zoper had never been exposed to the sort of profanity and slang used at the mill. Most of it he didn't know the meaning of originally, but now that he'd been hearing it for a few weeks, he was catching on. Though he probably shouldn't have, he found it to be entertaining, listening to them string together the different curses and profanities in surprisingly elegant rants. He'd even tried out a few of the words himself.

Finally, it was lunch break.

Zoper gratefully got up, sore from kneeling to saw the logs, and extended his hand to Evres. Warily, the man took it. After helping him to his feet, Zoper smiled briefly, and left to find Restir. The other men were already plopping down on the grass or logs and digging into their lunch sacks. Restir looked up from his sandwich as Zoper approached. "Gallivanting off to play with the kiddies, again?"

He shrugged cheerfully, despite the growing soreness in his back. "Yes. I'll be back—"

"Before break is over, I know." Restir shook his head at him with a sort of begrudging amusement. "Get on with ya, then."

Offering a grin, Zoper nodded and left the mill at a jog. At this point in the day, he wouldn't have chosen to run simply for the fun of it—rather, he would need to in order to get to the school and back in time. Not that he'd ever been late. He went almost every day during lunch break and so far had always made it back before break was over, in the three weeks since he'd started working.

The running increased the slight rumble in his stomach to an uncomfortable growl. By the time he arrived at the main entrance into the city, there was a shaky feeling in his limbs and an empty ache in his gut. Oh well. That was becoming commonplace. He threaded his way through the stream of people coming and going. While to him it was the main entrance, to most everyone else, it was the *only* entrance, other than the gate behind the castle that was for military use only. Zoper's father had shown him the other small gates that could be used to get in or out of the city wall in an emergency.

Since this wasn't exactly an emergency, the main entrance it was.

The guards recognized him and waved him through without asking the usual questions or requiring identification. Fortunately, unlike many citizens, the soldiers that had known his father had respected him, and treated Zoper kindly.

Also fortunately, the school his brother and sister attended wasn't far from the gate. The school they used to go to, when their parents were alive and money wasn't a problem, was much farther, in the eastern section of the city where most of the upper class lived. Now they went to the middle class school, only a few blocks from the city wall. Most orphans became lower class, but because of their previous rank, they'd landed somewhere between lower and middle.

As he neared, children's high pitched voices and laughter could be heard over the usual noises of the city. Aydimor, as the capital city of Zentyre, wasn't exactly a quiet place.

It didn't take long to find his brother and sister in the schoolyard—they sat by themselves, unlike most of the students, who sat in large groups. Still, Yaila was cheerful as he approached, jumping up to give him a hug. No such cheer from his brother, Jakkit. "Why do you bother coming every day?" he muttered.

Sitting down beside Yaila, Zoper gave his brother's arm a whack. "Maybe because I want to make sure you guys are okay and spend time with you when I can, you larrikin."

"What's a larrikin?" Yaila looked up from her sandwich.

"A, mmm…" Zoper bit his lip and squinted, searching for a word she would understand. "A delinquent, sort of."

She copied his squint. "I thought that was a criminal. He's not a criminal."

"No," Zoper agreed, amused, "but he's a troublesome fellow, so I was just teasing him."

"Oh." Yaila brightened with a smile his direction. "Anyway, I'm glad you came. I wish you still went to school with us."

"Sometimes, so do I." He winked at her. "But, I'm an old man, now. No more school for me, I'm afraid!"

"But," she went back to the perplexed squint, "Father always said you'd go to the advanced school, that they have for the older kids, after normal school."

He sucked in his breath discreetly. "Things are different now, little bird. I have to work."

He could tell she was about to press the topic. She wasn't easily dissuaded once she got going, and often managed to reason him into a corner. Usually a corner of, "But *why* is it that way?" It was his stomach that saved him, by rumbling loudly.

She giggled. "Sounds like an angry dog."

Relieved, he grinned and leaned forward to tickle her. "Do you know what you sound like?"

"A bird!" She proved the point with her high, singsong

voice.

"Exactly. And little birds shouldn't mess with angry dogs!" He tickled her until her eyes watered with laughter. It made any anxiety he had been feeling melt away. When he finally let her go, he was laughing too.

Jakkit did not pick up on the mirth. "You didn't pack yourself a lunch, *again*?"

Zoper simply smiled at him, shaking his head. "You have a remarkable talent for turning concern into an accusation. Bravo. I'm not sure many can—"

"Zoper, I'm serious."

Serious. The word echoed in his mind. It was serious. Being in as much debt as he was was extremely serious, and it couldn't be fixed by Yaila's melodic laughter. "Not now, Jak," he whispered, sending his little brother a pleading look. *Not in front of Yaila. She doesn't need this burden.* Though even Jakkit didn't know just how great their debt was. He didn't know that much longer, and Zoper wouldn't be able to afford for them to pack a lunch, either. *What then?*

"What does he mean that you didn't pack yourself a lunch, again?" she asked. So much for not letting her catch on.

"Nothing." He poked her nose playfully, earning another giggle. "You see, it's just that angry dogs are often hungry enough for *two* lunches. I only had one, so…" He shrugged, as if wistful. "Alas."

While Yaila was diverted, Jakkit wasn't. He extended half of his sandwich to Zoper. "Second lunch," was his mumbled offer, without eye contact.

Zoper tried to ignore the way his stomach clenched, desperate for a lot more than half a sandwich. "No, Jak, come on, you—"

"Oh just take it." Practically flinging it into his hands, Jakkit hunched his shoulders and finished the rest of his lunch in a moody silence.

No use arguing further. Zoper gave his genuine thanks, and did his best not to swallow it in two ravenous bites. When he stood up to leave and dizziness made the ground sway beneath him momentarily, he knew that half a sandwich was barely going to get him through the rest of the day. How much longer could he continue doing strenuous labor at the mill on only two light meals a day?

Instinctually, Zoper glanced west. Though it was blocked by hundreds of buildings, the castle lay only a few miles away. One visit, one plea, and all his problems would be solved...As quickly as the temptation came, it was stamped out by his father's dying words echoing in his mind. *"Don't...trust him, Zoper. Don't rely on him for anything...you have to take care of your siblings...don't trust him."*

And yet, his father's warning wasn't as convincing as it used to be.

Zoper forced the matter from his mind as he finished the meager half-sandwich. After telling his siblings goodbye, it was time to make the trip back, again at a jog. About halfway to the mill, he slowed to a walk, body trembling. All he could do was take a swig of water and force himself back into a run as soon as the weakness abated slightly.

The rest of the day passed even slower than the morning had. The men he worked with weren't any friendlier than Evres, but he didn't have the energy to make conversation anyway. He didn't really have the energy for the work, either. Twice he stumbled and dropped something. The first time, Restir snapped at him. The second time, he asked if Zoper was okay. With a forced smile, he nodded.

Finally, finally, it was six o'clock: time to go home.
Home for how much longer?

By the time Zoper was walking through the woods toward his house, he had given up on keeping his posture straight, and on ignoring the stress that he'd been dodging for so long. It had caught up to him. There was no more avoiding it. He was in debt, he was so physically exhausted that he could barely work. Without any hope of paying back the money through a middle-class job at the mill, he would have to sell the house. The only home he and his siblings had ever known.

Jakkit would probably want to kill him. Yaila would cry. He knew her tears would hurt him far more than Jakkit's anger.

On the porch, he opened the door, stamping his boots half-heartedly on the rug. "Yaila, Jakkit, I'm home." No delicious aroma of supper, like there always was when their mother was alive. Jakkit and Yaila occasionally worked together to cook something up after school, but mostly supper consisted of simple things; some bread and jam, cold meat from the cellar, cheese and canned fruit.

Except, the table was bare of even those items. And there were no voices to answer him, no Yaila scampering out to greet him.

"Yaila?" He ventured further into the house, checking the kitchen, her bedroom, Jak's bedroom, his bedroom, their parents'. Nothing. Swallowing, Zoper turned and went back outside, searching the yard. "Yaila, Jakkit! Come on guys. Let's play hide-and-seek after some supper, alright?"

His voice rang out, only to be absorbed by the stillness of the evening. Nothing stirred.

Dread stabbed his chest like a knife. Sprinting back to the house, he went inside and scanned every room again, this time for their school books.

Those weren't there either.

They never made it home.

Zoper tore out of the house and back down the path he'd just come from. Panic-driven adrenaline overcame his exhaustion, lending speed to his legs that got him the three miles to the city gate in record time. Panting, sweating, and shaking with both fear and fatigue, but there, just in time.

"Hey, that you, Zoper?" one of the guards hailed him. "You look a sight, kid. What's—"

"I need to go in." The words came out hoarse, between ragged breaths, as he started forward to pass them.

"Hey, wait," the man caught his arm, "we close this gate at sundown, which is in ten minutes. You know that. Whatever business you have in the city can wait until morning, surely."

"No it can't!" He brushed past the man. Frenzy was leaking into his voice. "My siblings didn't come home. I have to…please just let me in."

They backed up, allowing him passage. He sped up to a run again, knowing he wouldn't be able to hold it much longer. He stumbled into the schoolyard, gasping for breath. There wasn't a soul in sight. No response came to his croaked calls. Where could they be?

An image filled his mind, shoving out everything else. His father and mother, lying in a pool of their own blood, in the forest not far from their home. Attacked while out on a walk. His mother's eyes already fixed on nothing, lifeless. His father only able to get out a few garbled words past the blood in his throat, before he died. Murdered by a band of ruffians who didn't like his policies.

What if he found his siblings the same way?

His vision was blurred, whether from weariness or tears, he didn't know and didn't care. Calling his brother and sister's names every time he could manage enough breath, Zoper started backtracking, checking alleyways and side streets along the route they would have taken to get home. Multiple people shouted out of windows or doorways for him to be quiet. He just staggered on, voice cracking with each yell, weakness dragging at every muscle in his body. "Jakkit...Yaila! Jakkit!"

"Zoper?"

He jerked his head toward the raspy, familiar voice and mustered a fresh burst of energy to sprint into the dark alley it had come from. Yaila's pale face appeared, tear streaked. A flood of relief brought him to his knees, enveloping both of them in a tight embrace. Yaila cried something he didn't hear before burying her face in his shoulder. Even Jakkit hugged him back. Zoper couldn't bring himself to let go of them. So he held them close, one of the curse words commonly used by his coworkers slipping off his tongue. When he spoke, his voice was wobbly. "What happened? You two had me scared to death!" He repeated the curse word again, as if it would somehow calm his frazzled nerves and cure the weariness in his body. "Why didn't you come home?"

Jakkit leaned back, against the building wall behind them. His voice was just as wobbly. "We were on our way...some men stopped us...thieves. Thought we'd have money." He gulped. "They left when they found out we didn't, but Yaila sprained her ankle badly, and I couldn't...I couldn't..."

Zoper grimaced, setting a hand on his brother's shoulder. Jakkit had never been healthy—he lost his breath easily, couldn't lift anything heavy, didn't have the energy that most boys did. It wasn't his fault. But it was easy to imagine that it upset him that he, as a thirteen-year-old boy, wasn't able to carry his little sister. "It's not your fault, Jak." He rubbed his temples, wincing at the throbbing ache that was building there.

"It's my fault." If he'd gotten them new clothes, that were those of lower class rather than upper or nobility, they wouldn't be mistaken as wealthy by thieves. But it was that very reason that he hadn't—they *weren't* wealthy, so it hadn't made any sense to not use the clothing they already owned, even if they no longer belonged to the class that it did.

He gently pulled Yaila back so he could look at her. "Sprained your ankle, huh, little bird? Well," he kissed the top of her head, "it's a good thing birds use their wings. Let's get out of this alley, shall we?"

Blackness crowded his vision, legs wavering, the second he stood up with Yaila in his arms. Jakkit must have noticed, because he got up too and gripped Zoper's arm as if to steady him. "You don't look to be in great shape yourself. And where are we going to go? The gate will be closed. No one's allowed to leave the city after sunset."

All too true. Well, they could use one of the other entrances, but technically that was rather illegal, so probably not a brilliant plan. There were inns around…not any that would take three kids without a cent among them, however. It was awfully cold to spend the night outside, not to mention hardly safe—Aydimor had its fair share of criminals. Otherwise…

Otherwise, there was an obvious solution, if not an ideal one. He'd been keeping himself and his siblings away from the castle for months, but this was different. He couldn't keep his siblings, cold and hungry, on the streets all night. Not when there was such a better alternative. His father's words replayed in his mind…but hadn't he also implored Zoper to take care of his siblings? Surely their father wouldn't prefer them cold and hungry on the streets. "Do you know," he brushed back a lock of Yaila's wispy blond hair, "we have an uncle in the city, who has quite the respectable establishment. What do you say we spend the night with him?"

Yaila was already smiling and nodding her approval. Jakkit quirked an eyebrow. "Sure he'd take us?"

Zoper nodded decidedly. "Of course. Are we even thinking of the same man? Come on, Jak, if he knew we were out here he'd likely have us escorted to the castle by the royal guard."

His brother only shrugged.

They set out, moving deeper into the city. The farther in they went, the nicer their surroundings became, from houses to mansions, from dirt paths and alleyways to cobblestone streets. This was the part of Aydimor he was familiar with from his childhood. Their family had always lived in their cozy home outside the city, but as a child, he'd attended one of the best upper class schools, shopped and dined at all the nicest stores and restaurants, and visited his uncle and other nobility in and around the castle. He'd never spent time in the poorer parts of the city, let alone stepped foot in a sawmill. Until being an orphan had lowered him and his siblings to the status of lower class.

Unfortunately for his tired body, the castle was at the very back of the city. There was nothing to do but trudge on. Jakkit must have been tired also, or grouchy, as he lagged several paces behind for the entire trip. Zoper looked back frequently to make sure he was alright, and asked Yaila how she was doing occasionally, but he didn't have it in him to try and have a conversation.

As they reached the main gate of the towering castle, Yaila had fallen asleep in his arms, Jakkit was trailing him with head down, not even looking where he was going, and Zoper felt certain that as soon as he let himself stop and sit down, it would be some time before he could get back up.

"Hold." One of the sentries at the gate stopped them. "Name and business?"

"Zoper Veserron, we're here to see our uncle."

"Uncle?" A confused pause. "Oh. Veserron. Oh, um, okay, go ahead, or I mean, I'll escort you."

"Thanks," was all he managed. If he hadn't been so tired, he might have been amused. As it was, they silently followed the guard into the castle, through the courtyard, through halls full of life-size statues and portraits of nobles or historically significant individuals. To a set of double doors with golden knobs. The man knocked, then spoke to the closed door. "Excuse me, Your Majesty, your uh, your nephews and niece to see—"

The door flung open, the guard barely having time to dodge it. "Well I'll be!" In the doorway, Kaydor Veserron, king of Zentyre. Or, just Uncle Kaydor. He smiled broadly. "Look who finally decided to visit me. But," now he frowned, scrutinizing their battered state, "what happened? Is everything alright?"

"Well, no." Zoper found the smile he'd lost an hour ago. "I'm sorry to barge in like this, of course we would have let you know ahead of time, except—"

"The day you have to apologize for *barging in* is the day I'm no longer fit to be your uncle. Come, come in!" Kaydor practically dragged him into the room, which happened to be the throne room. "Yaila, dear, what's the matter? Are you alright?"

Eyes puffy from her nap, Yaila gave a timid smile. "I hurt my ankle."

"Oh," Kaydor took her hand to kiss it, "we'll just have to get that fixed up, won't we? You there," he addressed the soldier standing awkwardly in the doorway. "Have three bedchambers prepared for my nephews and niece. Send a medic to her room."

"Yes, sir." The man bowed and was gone.

"Now." Kaydor took Yaila from Zoper, carrying her into the room, and setting her on the throne. "What do you think of this seat? Will it do?"

She grinned up at him. "It's actually quite comfortable."

The man laughed, resonating and husky. "I'm glad you think so." He turned to face Zoper and Jakkit, who hadn't moved far beyond where he'd left them. "My dear nephews, please, relax. Consider yourselves at home. Now tell me, what happened?"

Zoper did his best to adopt a more informal posture. It wasn't that he felt particularly nervous—to him, Kaydor was his uncle first, king second. And he'd grown up visiting the castle, so that was nothing new. It was more the weakness in every muscle and bone of his body that made relaxing difficult. "Jakkit and Yaila were set upon by thieves on their way home from school. She sprained her ankle, I found them in the city, and since we were unable to go home…" His voice wavered. How early could he get his siblings to go to bed so that he could talk to their uncle alone, and stop pretending he wasn't utterly spent?

Kaydor considered him, head tilted slightly, gray eyes keen. Everything about his aging, but attractive, features was keen. Finally, he nodded. "I'm so sorry to hear it. The crime in the outer parts of the city is appalling. Well, it won't be happening again. Come, let's get you all to bed. Have you had supper? How does hot soup sound?" At Yaila's eager nod, he smiled. "Settled, then. Come along Princess, let's get you to your royal chambers!" He swooped her into the air and charged from the room in a heroic fashion. His rich laugh and her chirping giggle could be heard moving down the hallway. Zoper mustered a smile and shrug for his brother, and followed, Jakkit on his heels.

When they caught up, Kaydor had already gotten Yaila into a huge, luxurious bed in an equally huge, luxurious chamber. A maid was bringing in a tray with steaming soup, bread, and what appeared to be some sort of dessert. Kaydor was much the same as Zoper remembered him from his own childhood: affectionate, fun, and prone to spoiling them. A medic was in the room as well, waiting quietly for an opportunity to wrap Yaila's ankle.

Kaydor kissed her hand again and bid her goodnight, before leaving to take Jakkit to his room. Zoper could already tell she was content and well taken care of, so he kissed her forehead and followed them.

Until finally, with Jakkit and Yaila both taken care of, Kaydor showed him to his room. Just the two of them, now. Zoper was still deciding how to start the discussion, when his uncle faced him with a serious look and sat him down on the bed. "Zoper, tell me what's going on. I haven't seen you three in months! I'm told you're working at the sawmill outside the city. You know that's not the type of job you should be at. And how long has it been since you had a decent meal, lad?!"

Apparently the weight he'd lost had become more conspicuous than he'd realized. Well, he had always been broad-shouldered and sturdily built, and no longer fit that description, so it shouldn't have come as a surprise. "I am working at the mill. And, forgive me Uncle, but that *is* the type of job I should be at." He ducked his head. "We're not nobility anymore, or even upper class. Not since they died."

Kaydor's heavy hand came to rest on his shoulder. "Your parents' death does not change the fact that you are of noble blood. Yes, most children become lower class when orphaned, because that's the only way for them to effectively fit into the system. But that does not apply to you three! Zoper…" With a gentle, intent expression, he gripped his other shoulder as well, turning Zoper to face him. "Look at me. You are *not* lower class. You're the prince of Zentyre."

His gut clenched as a weight settled into the pit of his empty stomach. "What? I don't think…I mean…"

His uncle smiled patiently. "Now, don't go accusing me of lying. And for goodness sake, let's get some food in you, lest you pass out before me." Leaving him sitting on the bed speechless, Kaydor left briefly. He returned, followed shortly by another maid with another tray of food that smelled so unbelievably incredible. Taking it from her, Kaydor brought it over and set it on his lap. "Go on, then. Enough formality. I will always be your uncle first and foremost, lad."

There was no point trying to deny his desperate stomach. He didn't have a clue what to say, anyway. Zoper nodded his thanks and picked up the spoon, trying to let the savory liquid flood his taste buds rather than just gulping it down. His success was limited. Kaydor sat down in a chair across from him, considerately perusing a book he'd picked up rather than awkwardly watch him eat.

But Zoper was still uncomfortable. How could he not be, after what the man had just said? Finding himself unable to address it, he pretended Kaydor hadn't said it. "So, um," he put down the tray, the bowl empty and bread gone, forcing himself to leave the dessert for later, "I was hoping to get your advice, on some things." Kaydor didn't say anything, so he drummed his fingers on his leg and continued. "Well, I'm in debt. You know I couldn't start working until I turned eighteen a few weeks ago, so for months we were living off Father's savings, and it just didn't last. The only thing I know to do now is sell the house, and move to something cheaper, in the city, then I—"

"Zoper!" Kaydor wore a chiding smile. "Did you not hear me? You're the prince of the whole region. Don't you think that comes with some perks? No more worrying about debt, no more working at a sawmill, and certainly no moving into one of those decrepit lower class houses!"

Zoper swallowed, trying to loosen the tightness in his jaw. "But I'm not...I just don't think...that I should be the prince. I'm not..." His father's words echoed in his mind again. *Don't trust him.* Had his father had any idea that Kaydor might make Zoper his heir? Did that have anything to do with his dying plea that Zoper stay away from the king?

"You're my heir, there's nothing for it. Arineema and I are sure now that we can't have children of our own." There was some sadness in his tone. Zoper knew that his aunt and uncle had been gradually becoming more accustomed to the possibility that they were unable to have children. Apparently, after five years of marriage, they had officially resigned themselves to it. Kaydor leaned forward, catching Zoper's gaze and holding it. "My throne goes to you."

Without meaning to, Zoper whispered one of the milder curses that Restir used often.

Kaydor just laughed. "I know it's a lot. But it's not as if I'm expecting you to help me run the region starting tomorrow. For now, all it means is that you and your siblings will live here. You don't need to sell your house, I know you're attached to the place. I'll take care of the debt. And you won't be setting foot in a sawmill ever again."

This was ridiculous. Him, prince of Zentyre? Sure, it made sense, if Kaydor couldn't have children of his own. But what sort of prince would he make? And…how could he rightfully be prince, if Kaydor wasn't rightfully king?

The thought made him wince. It was a glaring reminder of why he hadn't come to his uncle for help months ago, before he ran himself into the ground with debt, before selling their home became his only option. Kaydor had wanted to take them in immediately, when their parents died. Even after Zoper had declined, saying that for the time being he thought it best for Yaila and Jakkit to be home, their uncle had tried to help financially. Zoper had declined that too.

Because his father had warned him to stay as far away from Kaydor as possible. It had been his dying appeal. Zoper hadn't understood why then, nor did he now…but he'd trusted his father.

It was different now. Surely his father wouldn't still want them to decline Kaydor's help, if it meant his three children starving and homeless? Perhaps whatever had occurred between the two brothers…perhaps his father had overreacted. Surely it wasn't so drastic as to necessitate Zoper, Jakkit, and Yaila living in destitution.

He met his uncle's expectant look. "If you're sure…then all I can say is thank you." Yaila and Jakkit came first, and this was what was best for them. Besides, while Kaydor couldn't be held up as a shining beacon of perfection to humanity, what founding had Zoper's father really had to not trust him? Zoper knew only a man who loved his family, who believed in justice, who was brilliant as well as a skilled warrior. He had no reason not to trust him.

Kaydor smiled widely. "Of course I'm sure, lad!" He moved back to the bed, sitting beside him. "I've wanted you three to live here for years. Your brother and sister can have the best tutors, or, if you think it's better, they can go to the finest school in the city. You can continue your education too, and you certainly won't be skipping meals anymore. I've never seen you so gaunt, Zoper; I wish you'd come to me earlier."

"I should have." He managed a slight smile. "And truly, thank you. Won't you at least let me keep working, some job, so I can pay off the debt myself? You shouldn't have to—"

"Oh, enough about the debt! Don't you think I have a few spare silvers lying about?" Kaydor laughed, only to grow more serious, and place his hand on Zoper's shoulder again. "But, there is one thing I would ask of you. I want you to begin elite military training."

He probably didn't do as good a job of hiding his consternation as he should have. "What?"

"Remember that training you did with your father and I? You were a natural, Zoper! You were born to the blade, trust me. And the best leaders have not only knowledge and experience in politics and laws, but also the battlefield. The best leaders earn the respect of their fellow warriors and citizens long before they take on a role of authority. I want you to have that opportunity. One day, you may even be the captain of the elite military group I'm putting together, the Tarragon."

"But…" He grimaced. "I don't think I'm a natural. I enjoyed training with you and Father, but to be in actual combat, I'm not sure—"

"Zoper." Kaydor's hand became a little heavier on his shoulder. "I'm asking this because I believe it's what's best for you. And, because I need someone I can rely on out there. Won't you trust me on this?"

Zoper drew in his breath. This man was offering him a castle to live in, stability and education for his siblings, even to pay off his debt. And he certainly knew better than Zoper how to best prepare him for his role as prince. The steady pressure of Kaydor's fingers around his upper arm made him nod jerkily. "Of course. I'm sorry, I shouldn't have argued."

"No need to apologize." The hand released his shoulder, the smile returned. Kaydor got up. "I'm glad you'll stay, Zoper, I've missed you three. Get some sleep. And," his eyes sparkled merrily, "enjoy your dessert."

4

Dragon

"Nakelsie was talking about her?"

Talea rubbed her thumbs against her fingers. "Um, well, no, I think it was Ki who mentioned her name...then, I mean, Nakelsie said they shouldn't talk about her, and so did Haeric..." She tilted her head sideways slightly, trying to get a glimpse of Yhkon's expression. Behind him in the saddle, she couldn't see much. "I was just, well, curious. I thought maybe—"

"Didn't Nakelsie and Haeric tell you it would be better not to talk about it?" his voice came low, icy.

Her tongue felt clumsy, making her stutter on a reply. "Well, yeah, I just—"

"I don't want you to bring it up again."

She flinched. "I'm sorry." Whispering the apology only made her feel pathetic.

Yhkon stopped Eclipse and dismounted without another word. "Everyone get off and walk, give the celiths a rest." It was hardly a friendly command. All scattered conversation ceased. Leather creaked as everyone obeyed, but no one spoke until the lead Warden had gotten a ways ahead, leading Eclipse with his shoulders rigid and head down.

Talea hadn't moved from where she'd landed when someone tapped her softly on the shoulder. "Talea?" It was Ahjul. He and Terindi had stopped beside her. "Are you okay?"

She blinked, turning again to look at Yhkon's departing back. Grrake had jogged to catch up with him. A brief exchange, in which Yhkon looked like a snarling dog ready to bite. Grrake cringed, as she had, and didn't try to talk to him again.

"Yeah…" She pursed her lips and nodded. "Yeah."

"Want to walk with us?" he offered. Terindi didn't say anything, but her pale eyes were both concerned and welcoming.

Another nod. She fell into step with them, Ahjul leading his celith by the reins. He gradually started talking, not consistently, just enough to distract her. Neither she nor Terindi responded much, but he didn't seem to mind. Wylan joined them, silently. Hands in pockets with thumbs out, eyes on the ground. His tread hardly made a sound beside her, despite the tall, swishing grass they walked through. Something about his presence was calming. His mute, moody presence. *Because why wouldn't that be calming.*

Talea glanced sideways at Terindi. It had been only two days since they'd left Luriville. A band of Elikwai was taking the rest of the Vegns and most of the other San Quawr villagers north, toward Calcaria, while the wards and Wardens traveled west, toward the next unsuspecting teenager with lightning at their fingertips. Rikky, was his name. Yhkon had said it would be easily two weeks before they arrived at his village, possibly more.

Despite having been uprooted from all she'd ever known so recently, and thrust into a group of strangers who already knew each other, to traverse the region collecting more strangers...Terindi seemed to be doing quite well. She remained composed and serene, as seemed to be her constant state. Even though she was reserved, she was also settling nicely into the group. Everyone accepted and liked her. There wasn't much not to like—she was easy to get along with. And, fortunately, she and Ahjul seemed to get along especially well. Talea could tell he was excited, perhaps a little nervous, and eager to be the girl's protector, mentor, and friend to the best of his abilities.

In some ways, she was jealous of Terindi.

Yhkon didn't currently seem eager to be her friend, after all. His goal appeared to be isolation. He was doing quite well at it—nearly twenty yards ahead of the rest of them, yet the anger practically radiated from him even at that distance.

To be fair, it probably hadn't been a brilliant move on her part to ask about Tessa, when Haeric had made it clear it was a touchy topic. But how were she and Yhkon ever supposed to have an open, trusting relationship, how were they supposed to be Warden and ward...*friends*...if they couldn't be honest with each other? If he wouldn't let her get to know him?

Somewhat to her relief, Yhkon didn't have them ride again for the rest of the day. They walked, and walked, until it was evening and time to set up camp. As the rest of them caught up to him and began their roles in getting everything ready, she watched him hesitate, clench his fists, then mount Eclipse and ride off, telling Haeric he was doing a perimeter check.

He didn't return from that perimeter check until well after

supper. When he did, it was completely dark, and they were all growing tired. He walked up, appointed the watches, and vanished into the Wardens' tent.

Talea sighed. He'd given her the first shift. Whether as punishment, or randomly, she didn't know, and didn't particularly care. The bigger issue was that it meant she had to stay awake for another three hours.

At least there was a fire, tonight. Often they didn't have one, or only had it long enough to cook supper, lest the smoke draw attention. But according to Larak, they weren't anywhere near any form of civilization, so there wasn't anyone near enough to notice. So, they could have a fire all through the night. It offered a slight diversion—add the occasional stick, stir it and watch the brilliant orange embers flutter into the night sky, or catch leaves on fire and let them burn almost all the way to the stem before stamping them out.

Every several minutes as her eyelids started getting heavy, she stood up and paced for awhile, trying to walk quietly to avoid disturbing any of the twelve people sleeping in shelters around her. *So if there's no one around to see the smoke...why do I need to stay up and watch for no one...* Yawning, Talea returned to the log that served as her seat and sat down. Yhkon. What to do about him and all his delicate topics. Would his mood be improved by morning? There was no guarantee. He'd been known to go two or three days straight without cracking a smile or speaking a friendly word.

"What good is being on watch if you don't even notice someone walking up behind you?"

Talea nearly jumped out of her skin at the unexpected voice. A mixture of a scowl and a grin was already taking over her face by the time she recognized it as belonging to Wylan, standing with hands in his pockets a few yards away. "Wylan

Cravei. You certainly could use a lesson or two in manners. I've lost count of the times I've told you not to sneak up on me!" She kept her voice low, as he had.

"And I've lost count of the times I've done so without hardly trying." He smirked at her.

Without anything else to say, she just gave him a "very funny" look and huffed, getting up to stir the fire again. "So what are you doing out here? It hasn't been three hours, has it?" She knew he had the next shift, but was sure it hadn't been that long already.

"No. I couldn't sleep though," he replied with a shrug, taking a seat on one of the logs that had been placed near the fire.

"Why not?"

Another shrug, before he simply changed the subject. "So do you know what's up with Yhkon this time?" He lowered his voice even more, no doubt in case Yhkon was awake. The Wardens did have an uncanny way of hearing everything, after all.

This time. Talea poked at a rock with the toe of her boot. "Remember when the twins mentioned someone named Tessa? Who we aren't supposed to ask about? Well…I asked about her."

He nodded slowly with brows raised. "Well. That was kind of stupid."

Grinning again without meaning to, she elbowed his arm. He smiled slightly, and didn't pursue the subject.

Though silence with Wylan wasn't particularly awkward—that was almost all there ever was, anyway—she found herself fidgeting. In fact, she'd felt more awkward around him ever since Yhkon revealed their…hierarchy. Maybe it would be better just to get it out there. "Um, Wylan?"

He looked at her expectantly.

"Has uh, has Grrake told you about our...numbers?"

"You mean our ranks?" he asked, head tilted and what was almost a scowl making his eyes glint.

She frowned at him. "No, I specifically didn't say that, because I don't like to think of us in *ranks,* with any one being 'higher' or 'more important' than the other."

Wylan seemed to consider her for a moment. At first she thought it must have been a look of distaste or irritation. When he simply nodded slowly and moved his gaze to the fire, however, she decided she'd imagined it. Especially when he replied quietly, "Well if that's really how you feel about it, I admit I'm feeling better about the whole thing."

Okay, then. She watched him, trying to figure if she ought to be hurt, annoyed, or appreciative. For both their sakes, the last would probably be best. And honesty was good, right? "I guess...I guess that's good. I mean...I didn't choose it. And I wouldn't...I think you'd be better at it than me."

Now he eyed her almost quizzically in the orange light of the fire. "I don't...mind, if that's what you're worried about." A shrug. "I wouldn't choose it either."

Since they were apparently striving for candor, she gave a sheepish smile. "I might have been *sorta* worried about that..."

Wylan responded with one of his rare, sincere smiles, even if it was as much a smirk as a smile. "I guess you and I will have to try and get along, anyway."

Grinning, she nodded. "Guess so. Might be difficult."

"Might be," he agreed, with mock thoughtfulness.

She barely remembered to soften her laughter less it awaken the others. He was grinning back, and she didn't feel awkward at all as they fell into an easy silence.

Since it was his shift next, Talea stayed out for a little while longer, then left him at the fire and retreated into the girl's tent. It was nice, having another girl in the group. At least she and Kae weren't quite so outnumbered as they used to be...though, they were still plenty outnumbered.

Crawling into her makeshift bed, she got as comfortable as was possible on the ground, and let out her breath as she relaxed her muscles. It would have been even nicer to have Brenly there with her, or her mother, or Alili. Or even if they wouldn't help with the outnumbering problem, her father and brother. It had been over a month now since she had come with the Wardens and wards to Zentyre, and they had gone to Calcaria, to return to "normal" life—as much as was possible—among the San Quawr.

Talea woke with surprise, feeling as though she'd only just fallen asleep. The Wardens were waiting for them outside, as they stumbled out still rubbing sleep from their eyes. Time for training.

Training was, in general, challenging. Today especially, since she was tired from having the night shift, and Yhkon's mood showed no improvement from the night before. He was putting more effort into hiding it, at least, making it possible for them to pretend nothing had happened. It didn't quite make it possible for her to pretend she wasn't slightly frightened of him.

Afterwards, it was the chores necessary to pack up camp, breakfast, and they were on their way once more. Since they were riding, it was back to close quarters with the gloomy lead Warden. He wasn't talkative, to say the least. But, at least he wasn't intimidating the others out of conversation as he sometimes did, so she distracted herself by listening to or even participating in their exchanges.

Part of her said she ought to try and talk to Yhkon. Try to resolve the issue, or get him to open up about it, rather than just brooding and drawing deeper into himself.

A larger part of her said never in a million years.

So, she didn't.

~ ♦ ~

"Sire, you don't have the funds."

"I don't have the funds?" Kaydor echoed, glaring at the man. His treasurer only retained his usual sleepy countenance. "Why not?"

"It's not that you don't have funds, Your Majesty. You have plenty. But to hire out Irlai's army? Forgive me, but that's ridiculous."

Forgiveness wasn't exactly in his nature. But unfortunately the dull-eyed, strangely-dressed noble beside him was useful to him. "Fine. Then I need more money. How do I get it?"

"It will take time, Sire."

"I'm not asking for it tomorrow. Just answer the question."

"Very well." The treasurer straightened himself, only to slouch in his seat again. "Raise taxes, first off. I'll get reports of current living conditions and finances through the region so we know how much we can get away with taking. Second, command an increase in production of resources. More stone, more wood, more minerals, more materials, more grain. We can increase trade with other regions for more income."

Kaydor nodded contemplatively, rubbing his thumb up and down the bridge of his nose. "Fine. But not of lower class, their conditions are poor enough as it is. We can tax upper class, maybe middle, as well as try and raise support from nobility. Doing all of that, how soon can I buy Irlai's armies?"

The man shrugged. "Depending on circumstances,

anywhere from a few months to two years. Probably a year."

Kaydor drummed his fingers on the arm of the throne. "That will do. You are dismissed, go get those reports. Have Commander Dejer sent in on your way out."

"Yes, Your Majesty." The treasurer slunk out of the chair and into a bow, before continuing to slink until he was out of the throne room.

Shortly after, Dejer came in. He went immediately onto one knee. "Your Majesty."

"Up." Kaydor yanked his hand upward. "What news with the rebels?"

"Nothing yet, sir. Still searching for them."

"Do better. How many men are you employing?"

"One hundred. Five groups of twenty hunting them down."

He stroked his jaw. "Send out a hundred more. No more than that, though. I'm limited on manpower, and I need the brunt of my men working on the new base and defending. Actually, you know what...get a few dragon riders searching from the air, too."

"Yes, sir."

He waved his hand toward the door. "Dismissed."

Dejer faded out of sight.

That left Kaydor alone in the empty throne room. The walls and floor of dark stone cast the room in a shadowy dimness, eerily contrasted by splotches of bright light from the two windows. Dust glittered in the illuminated margins only to vanish in the gloom. *Raise taxes to build the army...and improve living conditions of laborers...it'll cost but benefit in the end.* With his military limited to what men were already drafted in Zentyre, he couldn't continue with the Eradication very well...which meant more time for the miscreants to escape and find somewhere to hide or join the rebels. But once he had Irlai's armies, perhaps other mercenaries, he would find them out and strike the final blow. *Once the new base is built, and the army doubled or tripled, the San Quawr won't stand a chance.* "Just need to bide my time..."

~♦~

Talea reached down to pluck a blade of grass, rubbing her fingertips over the scratchy tip. The short bristles that made up the end pricked her skin and gave off a summery fragrance as she ground it between her fingers. The same tall grass crunched underfoot and swished against her pants as she walked.

She'd been walking beside Wylan for a few minutes now. Why not strike up a conversation? "So were you ever this far west? I mean, since you traveled around and all."

"No, I stayed along the eastern side. I didn't actually travel very far ever, just often."

"Ah. And you never got caught by knights?"

"Had to run away from a few of them once. That's it."

Terindi caught up to them, brow furrowed as she poked a needle in and out of a torn shirt.

Talea glanced at her, then the shirt. "Ahjul can't sew, I take it."

Terindi shook her head with her lower lip between her teeth. "Nope. He was trying. It was so pathetic I took pity on him."

"Sewing and walking probably isn't all that easy."

"Not really." She dropped her hands and abandoned the work for later. "Beautiful day, isn't it?"

"Yeah," she agreed, scanning their surroundings. Clear blue sky, amber fields, warm weather, a light breeze. And, she noticed quizzically, a growing black dot in the sky. "What do you think that is?" She pointed.

Terindi squinted. "I don't know. Some sort of big bird, off in the distance."

Wylan shook his head. "Definitely not a bird."

Talea frowned in agreement. It didn't seem like a bird. Maybe—

"Hey." Someone gave her a side hug, and she turned to see Kae's bright smile. "How's it going?"

"Hi, good…does that look like a bird to you?"

Kae peered in the direction Talea indicated, and her smile vanished. "No, not really…Yhkon?"

The lead Warden was walking at the head of the group. His head was down and he strode forward, looking secluded compared to the other Wardens and the teenagers who all traveled in pairs or trios. He rotated his head toward them without actually looking up. "Yes?"

"What's that? Up in the sky, coming toward us?"

Now his head jerked up. He took one survey of the sky and stopped walking. "Mount up!"

Everyone scrambled into action, jogging to their assigned celith and mounting with their riding partner. Yhkon was already aboard Eclipse when Talea reached him, so he grabbed her arm and practically lifted her into the saddle behind him. *So impatient.* "What is it?"

"A dragon."

5
Separated

"Around here, the only dragon riders are Kaydorian." Yhkon kicked his heels into Eclipse's flanks, sending the stallion into a gallop. The other Wardens and wards' mounts thundered along beside and behind them.

Talea squirmed deeper into the saddle and put her arms around his waist for additional stability at the break-neck speed. The wind whipped pieces of hair from her braid and brought moisture to her eyes. "So, is it like, a...a patrol, or something?"

"A scout, probably looking for us."

"*This* is why I said Luriville was a bad idea," Larak yelled over the noise.

Yhkon spun around abruptly to glower at him, making Talea want to back up, which wasn't exactly an option. "Why don't you say that to Terindi? Go ahead, tell her that you think we ought to have left her village to be enslaved and executed!"

"Don't even try that with me, you're not—"

Grrake tried to jump in. Unlike Larak and Yhkon, he wasn't very good at raising his voice enough to be heard in the commotion. "Larak, let's—"

"Quit defending him, Grrake, he—"

"Both of you," Gustor's impatient voice silenced them, "shut up and focus on the real problem."

Though his jaw was still clenched and eyes ice cold, Yhkon faced forward again and said nothing.

The thirteen of them, spread over nine celiths, raced over the prairie. Their rapid pace didn't stop the dot in the sky from growing into the distinct form of a dragon just above them, massive wings beating the air. Having never seen a dragon in person, Talea peered up at it curiously, until it was close enough that she could see its glinting talons and teeth. Then she decided her curiosity was quite satisfied.

The beast and its rider kept pace with them for several minutes, keeping just high enough that Yhkon grumbled he couldn't shoot the rider down, and low enough to be an intimidating presence. It was a frightening sense of helplessness, having a dragon overhead that could swoop down and engulf them in flames, or pluck them from the ground, at any moment. Then, the dragon gave a snarly bark, and beat its wings with renewed vigor, bringing it up and away from them. Soon it was out of sight.

Yhkon slowed Eclipse. She leaned in to whisper, as if the dragon might overhear. "Why'd it leave?"

He was frowning, with a sort of grave annoyance. "Because it was just a scout. A scout's job is to find the prey and let the real force know where they are, then the hunt begins."

Talea blinked. "Oh."

Yhkon maneuvered Eclipse to the right, bringing them alongside Grrake on Lenjeya. Wylan, riding Ash, was just behind. "What do you think?"

"They'll probably bring that dragon back," Grrake twisted in the saddle to look the way the dragon had gone, "in which case we'll be wanting some cover."

"Right. Forest it is," he agreed, and stopped Eclipse. The others halted around them, quickly aligning their celiths so that they could converse. Larak's heavy features were still etched with a scowl, while Gustor looked impatient with him. Yhkon glared at the massive Warden, but didn't address the issue. "Listen up. Since a Kaydorian force will no doubt be on our heels within hours, and potentially a dragon, we're going into the woods for some cover from air attack. When they do arrive, we'll play the situation by ear. Wards, no lightning unless I tell your or your life is in danger."

She barely kept from smirking. *Um, aren't our lives in danger basically the moment the dragon appears over our heads?*

"Understood?"

She nodded along with everyone else, even though Yhkon couldn't even see her. "Good, then let's go." They stayed in the lead as the group trotted on, toward a distant treeline.

The serene prairie with its open skies and uninhibited view wasn't so pleasant anymore. Talea was sure they were going to be ambushed at any moment. She kept peeking over her shoulder, half expecting to see a dozen dragons in the sky just behind them. But they made it to the woods without an enemy in sight. Under the cover of the trees, Yhkon had them all slow the celiths to a walk. That felt unbearably slow to Talea, even if she knew it was best to have the mounts energetic, and that it was dangerous to gallop them in the forest anyway. Too much underbrush.

She was thankful to be out of the exposed grasslands. Now, though, they were seemingly trapped in the dense woods with almost no visibility. Adversaries could be waiting just over that rise, or sneaking up on them from all around, and they'd never even know until it was too late...

She didn't realize how uptight she was until Larak sneezed and she nearly jumped out of the saddle. Though of course, Larak did have an incredible sneeze. And it helped lighten the mood as Yhkon raised an eyebrow at her over his shoulder, then chuckled a little.

On they went, the only sound the celiths' hooves on twigs and leaves. If ever someone thought they heard something, everyone stopped and listened. It was never anything more than imagination or a bird or a kip cackling at them from the treetops. Sometimes Talea would spot movement out of the corner of her eye. Yhkon would always feel her tense up and would check what had caught her attention, but it never amounted to anything either; a branch swayed by the wind, a few deer startled by the presence of humans.

Yet for all their surveillance, the predator still caught them by surprise.

A noise like that of a wind gust filling a sail, only with a certain *clapping* quality and a greater volume, startled them all. When Talea jerked her chin skyward, the movement she saw was no tree branch: a shadow passed above the overhead canopy of foliage, then disappeared. Her arms tightened around Yhkon's waist. "What was that?" she breathed.

He regarded the treetops with a sigh. "Oh, just a dragon."

The noise came again, multiple times. She realized it must have been the dragon's wings. That seemed a trivial revelation, however, as one of the trees that provided their cover shuddered and creaked. Leaves showered down on them, along with small branches and bits of wood. The top of the tree bent with a long groan, creating a hole in the leafy roof, and revealing the dragon that perched only a stone's throw above them. Talea's mouth was dry. Probably because it was hanging open.

"Time to go!" Yhkon squeezed his knees into Eclipse's rib cage, sending the animal forward at a canter. A high-pitched roar blasted Talea's eardrums and widened her eyes. Even over the din of hoofbeats, she could hear splintering wood and crashing underbrush. The din only grew, until it enveloped them, as if the entire forest had come alive.

In a way, it had. Knights with the maroon insignia—a dragon—of Kaydor, mounted on coliyes, were pouring through the trees toward them like a flood of iron. That flood was in for a hunt.

Yhkon growled something she didn't catch, and kicked Eclipse into a gallop. "Grrake, take the lead!"

Talea watched Lenjeya streak to the front of the group. A weight gripped her chest and stomach as Yhkon applied steady pressure to the reins, forcing Eclipse to shorten his stride, and gradually bringing them to the back. With each ward and Warden that passed them, her panic rose. Soon, they were between their friends and the embodiment of Kaydor's fury. All she could do was clutch Yhkon desperately and wonder how long before fire or teeth as long as her forearm became her demise. Apparently being Eun required being the first to be eaten by a dragon.

"Talea! Switch places with me!"

Yhkon's words shouted back at her made her fear give way to confusion. "What?!"

He was shoving the reins into her hands. "Switch places with me," he repeated, already grabbing her by the shoulders to drag her forward while he leaned out and pulled his legs up, so that he was somehow crouching in the saddle instead of sitting in it.

"What are you doing?!" she shrieked, even as she went along with the insane endeavor by scooching forward to Eclipse's withers, where Yhkon should have been, rather than balancing there like he had a death wish. Yet balance there he did, maneuvering as soon as he was able so that he was behind her. Only then did he get into a sitting position. Except...he was backwards. "Yhkon!"

"Just keep him following the others," he replied as calmly as if they were on a pleasure-ride in his backyard.

What else was she going to do? Turn Eclipse around and run him right into the jaws of the dragon?

Talea gripped the reins with white knuckles and leaned forward the way she'd seen the Wardens do when galloping. Until Yhkon elbowed her back. She looked back to see what he needed—*maybe instruction on how to properly sit in a saddle?*—only to be whacked on the head by his bow as he lifted it over his head. That was when she realized what he was doing. Bow. Quiver of arrows. Sitting backwards. He was going to try and take down some of their pursuers. Well, at least she didn't have to worry that he'd completely lost it.

Which was perhaps a good thing, because those pursuers were catching up. Being in charge of directing Eclipse, she could only catch glimpses over her shoulder, but it was obvious that the knights mounted on celiths were gaining, and so was the dragon. The only reason the beast hadn't already devoured them, she figured, was because its flight was hindered by the trees. That would only protect them for so long, by the looks of it. And how long before one of their celiths caught its foot in the underbrush, or stepped in a hole and broke its leg?

Talea caught brief glimpses as Yhkon knocked an arrow and drew back the string, and let it fly. The arrow skimmed the armor of the dragon rider. Didn't penetrate.

"Come on Yhkon, what was that?" Tarol called over the chaotic cacophony. Talea nearly gawked at him. What did he think, that this was a game?

Yhkon was scowling. "Well if you can do so much better, then get back here!"

"Challenge accepted!" Tarol's celith soon raced beside Eclipse, with Ki at the reins and Tarol backwards behind him. He and Yhkon continued with the archery.

Yhkon was successful in taking down the dragon rider on the second try...except the dragon wasn't dissuaded even after its master toppled off. Yhkon muttered just loud enough for her to hear. "This is why I hate dragons."

"Why don't you just shoot it, then?" she let the wind carry her words back.

"Can't. Their scales are too thick for arrows."

Typical.

Next thing she knew, Yhkon was snarling out another inarticulate sentence and slapped Eclipse's hindquarters for more speed, before turning back around so he faced forward. She whipped her head around to see the dragon descending on them in all its fury, its fangs bared and an orange glow building in its throat. At first, that didn't make sense. Then, it made all too much sense. Eclipse lunged into full stride. The dragon released a burst of angry flames from its jaws. Instinct made her duck as low as she could to the celith's neck. Yhkon inclined so far forward that his body shoved her down anyway. Heat enveloped her, but no pain. And then it was gone, though the flapping of the dragon's wings was not.

Yhkon sat back up, allowing her to do likewise. He had wrapped one of his arms around her and she could feel the tension coming from him like a physical tide. It settled around her like a sinister fog, creeping up her spine and bringing frenzy to her mind. Half of her was grateful for his protective hold. The other half had a wild desire to be free of his grasp. She could only satisfy the first half. He, meanwhile, shouted just behind her ear. "Grrake! Get us out of here!"

"Almost there!" came the wind-tossed reply from ahead of them. It was nearly drowned out by the constant, impending sound of the dragon's wings moving through the air.

A high-pitched roar came terrifyingly close. Yhkon's arm tightened around her and he leaned forward again, pushing her lower as well. "Hold on!" he exclaimed, just before the dragon dove.

Something else wrapped around her as Yhkon's arm had. Only this was harder. It was sharp, lifting her from the saddle. It was the arm-length talons of the dragon. She screamed. Yhkon yelled. Air separated her from Eclipse while the pressure increased, squeezing her breath away and clamping her against Yhkon. A tremor traveled through the gigantic claws that imprisoned her, and the dragon screeched, so close that it left her ears ringing and paralyzed every muscle in her body. Yhkon yelled again and she could feel him moving against her. Then, the dragon dropped them.

Another scream tore from her lungs as they plummeted. Eclipse rushed toward them in a blur, and they collided painfully. Talea's mind was blank but her limbs scrambled for a hold, somehow realizing that if she fell she'd be trampled. Yhkon's arm was still around her. He grunted, then shouted as if in pain, before yanking her into the saddle. She found her balance and straddled Eclipse's sides as tightly as she could. But Yhkon wasn't in the saddle behind her. He was clinging to her with one arm, to Eclipse's barrel with the other, precariously clasped to the galloping stallion's side. Talea grabbed his arms and pulled with all her might. Eventually he was astride the celith rather than dangling. Both of them were panting. Yhkon still clutched her, even more rigidly than before, and now she clutched him right back with trembling hands.

"Grrake!" Yhkon's voice was unusually strained.

"Almost!"

As if on cue, the forest they raced through suddenly opened up to a city. They galloped straight into it. The celiths' hooves went from making a dull thunder to clattering sharply on the cobblestone. *What about the dragon?!* She turned enough to see it. The beast had lagged behind considerably. One of its feet was mutilated and bloody, and she realized Yhkon must have hacked at it with his sword to make it drop them. The creature seemed to be regaining its fervor and speeding up to catch them, while the Kaydorians were trying to stop it. She could hear their muted shouting as they slung ropes and spears at it. Finally, they brought the enraged dragon down.

That was hardly the end of their troubles. She faced forward again to see that they were about to run straight into another group of mounted knights.

Yhkon had taken the reins from her and was tugging on the bit. Eclipse planted his feet, hooves drifting roughly over the street to a halt. "Split up!" He eased the pressure on the reins and instead swerved the stallion left, sending him galloping again. Talea caught glimpses of the other Wardens driving their mounts in every direction, before the Kaydorians flooded the area they'd just been in and obstructed her view.

Under Yhkon's hand, Eclipse carried them deeper into the city. Almost a dozen knights were still on their tail. Yhkon kept veering off and changing directions so often Talea soon had no idea where they were in relation to where they'd started.

Everything looked the same. Cobblestone streets, wooden houses and shops, startled townspeople that scrambled to get out of their way.

On and on they went, yet they couldn't shake their pursuers. And then, they rounded a corner, and were met by more knights.

Something like nausea clenched Talea's stomach. Eclipse came to a clattering halt. For a moment, no one moved. Her eyes groped for an escape route, and she had no doubt Yhkon's did as well, but they were caught on a street snugly lined with buildings. A person could run down the alleyway behind them and slip between the two houses at the end, but there was nowhere for a celith to go except through one of the groups of knights.

The Kaydorians started to advance. Yhkon began pushing her out of the saddle. "Talea, run!"

"What?!" She fought his prodding hands. "No! I can't—"

He grabbed her waist and shoved her off. She stumbled onto the damp street, palms stinging as they scraped against gravel. The sound of the soldiers' mounts moving closer got her to her feet and retreating backwards, eyes wide and on Yhkon. "Go!" he ordered. "I'll catch up to you!" With that, he withdrew his sword from its scabbard, and wheeled Eclipse to face the knights.

What choice did she have? Before she could stop them, her feet were bearing her down the alleyway, just as the clash of combat rang out and echoed after her.

~♦~

Talea peeked out from behind the corner of the house, hand gripping the wall tightly. She immediately ducked behind it again, as male voices reached her ears from a dozen yards ahead.

"Should we keep looking this way or go back?"

"You idiot, Ulmre and the other boys went the other way, why should we? We're probably close, there's only so many places she could have gone."

"I dunno, man...these San Quawr, they're slippery."

"They ain't mythic, man! Come on, already. Go check that alleyway."

Unsure if "that alleyway" was in fact the one she currently occupied, Talea turned and bolted. Stopping in a shadowy alcove to catch her breath, she listened to hear their voices again. Nothing. Next, she eyed the alcove—nope, bad idea, there was only one exit, she would be trapped if they appeared. Still panting, she moved on, more slowly since there was no sign of Kaydorians.

It wasn't much of a question, whether or not Yhkon had escaped the predicament she'd left him in. It had probably been ten soldiers, a number she felt confident he could defeat. Well. Mostly confident. What if he hadn't? What if he'd been captured...or killed?

No. He hadn't. There was no sense worrying about it.

What she did have to worry about, were her own circumstances. Was she supposed to hunker down and wait for him to find her? Or keep going and try to find him? How long would it take? She was already growing thirsty and hungry, and it had only been a couple hours since she and Yhkon had been separated.

What about the rest of the group? Had they fared better, or worse?

Stop it. You're not doing yourself any good. Focus. Without any clue as to Yhkon's whereabouts, it was probably best to let him do the finding. She'd just work on staying away from

Kaydorians.

The nature of the town she'd been stranded in made that relatively easy. It was no laborer's village. It was similar to the twins' home, Castown, so it must have been a middle class town. No haliops, just wooden houses…everywhere. Lining the streets, often with only a few feet between them. And, the streets were all gravel. Not a dirt path overgrown with weeds anywhere in sight.

What the town did not make easy, was staying away from other people in general. They were everywhere. Apparently, they weren't restricted to working all day every day except Eunday. While they didn't pose the threat that the soldiers did, she thought it better to avoid them all the same, considering she was dressed strangely and probably looked like a thief or tramp.

Talea kept going, meandering between buildings and down passages. As time passed, evening brought gloom to the entire city. It made her task of staying out of sight easier, though it also made her uneasiness grow. To add to it was the discomfort of a sore, bruised body from the dragon's claws and being dropped onto Eclipse; scraped hands from Yhkon pushing her to the ground; and an empty stomach. Would she be alone and lost out here all night? Longer? How long would it take for Yhkon to locate her when knights were combing the town for both of them? And the rest of the wards and Wardens…were they even alive? All separated like her, or had they regrouped?

Something clicked and shuffled repeatedly over the cobblestone. She froze, heart beginning to race. Any light from the sporadic torches along the streets was blocked by buildings on either side, and her gaze could barely penetrate the murkiness. She couldn't see anything amiss. What had the sound been, then?

More clicking and shuffling. Silence. The noise again, drawing closer to her. *Run!* Her mind screamed, while her body refused to move. A shaft of dull orange light lay between her and the sound. She waited breathlessly for some predator to come sailing through it and attack her. Instead, more clicking, and a dog appeared in the illuminated area.

Talea released her breath through her mouth, mustering a smile. "'Bout scared me to death, boy."

The dog observed her with its head tilted. One ear was erect, the other flopped over and had an ugly scar on it. Then the dog licked its chops, turned, and disappeared with its nails still clicking on the cobblestone.

It wasn't until the sound faded away that she kept going. Where, she didn't know. Gradually she stopped thinking about it. Stopped wondering how and when Yhkon would find her, stopped straining her senses to hear nearby knights. Simply plodded through the dark streets, head down, shoulders hunched, body heavy with weariness. And stomach growling.

Talea's heart leapt into her throat as a door unexpectedly swung open only a few feet in front of her. The creaking of the wood and the low squeak of the hinges grated on her nerves, seeming extremely loud in the stillness of the night. A man stumbled out from the golden glow of the house into the darkness. The light reflected off a glass bottle in his hand. Talea remained rooted in spot, even as he marked her presence and faced her. "Hey..." His voice was slurred. "Wha you doing here?"

She blinked, jaw slack and tongue refusing to cooperate.

The man staggered toward her, waving the bottle around. "Come here, girl. What yer name?"

Only as he neared did she regain mobility. Talea spun away from him and bolted.

"Hey. Hey!" he bellowed after her, though she heard no following footsteps.

Didn't matter. She kept running. Heedless of where her feet took her. She could still hear him yelling for awhile, until it gradually died away as she distanced herself. But in its place came another sound: the clanging and jingling of armor. Her lungs burned, her feet ached from the hard stone, and her muscles felt like lead. That didn't matter either. She just kept running. It wasn't until she was so lightheaded and her legs so exhausted that she stumbled, sprawling into a stack of crates, that she stopped. Chest heaving for each breath, head pounding painfully, Talea curled up in a ball and hugged her knees to herself. She vaguely noted that she was partially concealed by the crates and the shadow of a building, before squeezing her eyes shut and letting her mind sink into a troubled sleep.

6
Blending In

Talea woke with a start. After dozing in and out of consciousness, between a frightening reality and terrifying nightmares, she expected to be greeted by the same darkness that made her shrink farther behind the crates, shiver, and try to go back to sleep. Instead, bright sunlight made her squint and shield her eyes with her hand. Finally. It was morning. She grabbed one of the wooden crates beside her, only to recoil at the stinging in her hands. Inspection proved that both her palms were red, tender, and smeared with dried blood. Massaging her forehead with the back of one of her hands, she gripped the crate again, ignored the discomfort, and heaved herself upright.

The ground swayed a bit as she did. Black dots invaded her vision like a thousand flies. She floundered for the wall of the building and steadied herself against it. Gradually the dizziness abated. In its place came a wave of hunger. And stiffness, the moment she took a step. *Oh, and let's not forget how dry my throat is...*

All considered, she was feeling cheerful compared to her despondency the night before. With the sun up and exposing her surroundings in its warmth, she didn't feel nearly so nervous.

There were still problems to be considered, however. Primarily, how she could reunite with Yhkon. By the way her hands shook with fatigue, that would require food and water. How was she to come by those? There was probably a well nearby, though she'd have to be careful about being seen at such a public, frequented place. But food? She didn't have money to buy anything. *Probably should stay out of shops anyway.*

Well, first thing's first. Find a well.

Talea set out at random. She remembered seeing a well last night, but she didn't remember when or where, and no doubt had done too much reckless running to find her way back. So she wandered. The longer she walked the hungrier, thirstier, and wearier she felt, but there was no way to solve that except to keep going. It was necessary to be ever alert, with knights still patrolling the town, more thoroughly now that it was daytime. She was even more conspicuous, since at this hour almost everyone her age was at school, not traipsing the streets.

Time dragged along with her feet. How could there not be a well for such a long way? Or was she walking in circles? Was that man eyeing her suspiciously? Had she been on this street before? Where was Yhkon? Wait, wasn't that girl carrying a bucket? She must be going to a well!

Talea followed the girl at a distance. And to her abundant relief, the child did indeed lead her to a well. It took restraint to remain hidden while the girl filled her bucket. The moment no one was in sight, she moved at an awkward jog and came to a fumbling stop beside the well. Grasping the rope to lift a bucket from within the reservoir made her palms smart even worse. She did it anyway. Until finally, the pail was up, and she cupped her raw hands to ladle the cool water into her mouth. It moistened her dry gums, soothed her sore throat, and made her otherwise empty stomach rumble all the more.

"Miss?"

Talea jumped at the unanticipated voice. She scrambled so that her back was at the well, allowing her to see the middle-aged woman that regarded her with concern.

"Dear, are you alright?"

"F-fine," she mumbled, standing and backing up.

The woman didn't appear convinced. "Are you sure? Looked like you hadn't had water in some time. Do you have food? Are you hurt?"

She retreated further, until the well was between them. There was nothing untrustworthy about the woman's demeanor. Still, better to be safe. "I'm...I'm lost. I got separated from my friends."

The lady cocked her head to the side. "And the blood on your, um," she eyed Talea's unconventional garb, "clothes? How long have you been lost?"

"I scraped my hands, is all." She scanned the clearing that held the well, lest anyone else approach. "And...since yesterday."

Comprehension flooded the woman's eyes. "You're one of the fugitives they're after!"

Talea's muscles tensed. She surveyed the area again, planning the best escape, already poised to run.

"No, wait!" The stranger extended her hand in a calming gesture. "Please. I mean you no harm. Why are they chasing you?"

Did she dare trust her? "I'm San Quawr."

A sad frown melted the woman's countenance. "That's no reason for them to terrorize a defenseless girl." She extended her hand again, this time in invitation. "Come. Please, let me at least get you some food and a moment's rest."

The exhaustion that weighed her down overcame hesitation. Talea cautiously edged forward. When she was within reach, the woman put her arm around Talea's waist and they left the well.

"My name is Lerese. What's yours, dear?"

"Talea."

"How old are you, Talea?"

"Fifteen."

"Ah, poor dear. You should be in school right now, not running from knights."

She lowered her gaze. For middle and upper class and nobility, children didn't leave school until they were eighteen. "I'm a laborer, ma'am. I don't live here in…well, I don't know what town this is, actually."

Lerese eyed her curiously. "It's called Boroe, dear. How is it you came for refuge here, then?"

Talea laughed dryly. "Long story."

The woman didn't question her further as they navigated the twists and turns of Boroe. Eventually she led Talea to the door of a rickety-looking house and brought her inside. There she pointed Talea into a chair, while she bustled about the kitchen, and continued the conversation. "How come so many knights are after you? I know they persecute San Quawr, but why so many for so few of you? How many friends are with you?"

How much should she disclose? "I uh…I can't explain everything. But there are twelve others in our group. And some of them are trained warriors, and got into a skirmish with some knights a while back…it's uh," she laughed again, fidgeting in the seat, "quite the mess."

Lerese gave a hum of compassionate agreement as she brought Talea a slice of bread and an apple. "I'm sorry, dear, I don't have much to offer." She gave her the food and took a seat beside her. "My husband was recruited to Kaydor's army a couple months ago, and things are tight."

Talea's eyes bulged just as she bit into the bread. A lump formed in her throat. She hastily chewed the bite and gulped it down. "I'm…so sorry. I mean, I don't…" What could she say?

Lerese shook her head with a kind, pained smile. "Don't you fret. Certainly isn't your fault. It does put us in a bit of an awkward situation since you're on the run from Kaydorian knights and it sounds like your friends killed some…but I bear you no ill will. And I want you to know that my husband would never have chosen to serve the king. He had no choice."

She cringed with sympathy for the woman. "Of course. And, well, I don't hold it against him at all. My brother was almost taken to serve as well. It's not fair, the way Kaydor rips men from their families and forces them to do his bidding."

Her hostess nodded jerkily. "Quite right, my dear. We've both suffered at Kaydor's hand. Now, please. Eat the food, however meager. Sounds to me like you'll be needing your strength."

"Thank you," she murmured, and obeyed the request. Upon finishing the piece of bread she instantly went for the apple, only to stop at the last moment. Fool! While she was in here, Yhkon was out there looking for her! She had to get back outside. And when he did find her, no doubt he'd be hungry too. She set the apple down on her knee. "Do you mind if I save this for later?"

"Of course not. And here," Lerese got back up and

returned to the kitchen, "let me get you a canteen."

Talea stood as well, and accepted the canteen, reluctant to take anything else from this woman but realizing she'd probably need it. "Thank you so much. I can't stay any longer, my friend is looking for me, and I need to be where he can find me. But I...I greatly appreciate your kindness."

Lerese smiled at her in a motherly fashion. "You're very welcome, Talea. I wish you luck."

"Thank you," she said again. Then she stuffed the canteen and the apple into her pockets, and left the house.

She hadn't made it ten steps before another voice startled her. "There! There she is!"

Talea broke into a sprint at the sight of several knights. They weren't far behind, heavy boots thudding and armor clanking. It struck her that their burdensome armor was probably the only reason they hadn't outran her already.

Her heart raced in tempo with her feet. She forced her weary, frazzled mind to stay sharp and vigilant, watching for possible hindrances or opportunities rather than running heedlessly. That alley was a dead end, don't turn there. That street was open, go that way. There was a fence over there that she could easily jump, while their armor might make it difficult for them. Someone was coming out of that shop, don't run into them. There were more knights to the left, swerve right. On, and on, until her breath came in ragged gasps and her muscles were on fire.

A nearby stable caught her eye. A small corral was right next to it, holding several male yuleys. Bulls were far more irritable than cows, and they had horns. They were dangerous enough that they were almost never used for anything other than breeding, unless they were castrated. The roof of the barn was just above their pen, within reach of the top of the fence.

And from there, a housetop was close enough to jump to…the knights were far enough behind her that she should have time…

Did she dare enact the bold idea? It had plenty of potential to end poorly. Then again, so did being captured.

Talea directed her path toward the corral. She came to a panting stop beside it, just long enough to unlatch the gate with trembling fingers and swing it open. Then she darted through, praying none of the bulls would get angry yet, and went to the back of the enclosure. There she touched the nearest yuley and exerted electricity from her hand into its hide.

The creature bellowed and swung its huge, horned head savagely. She mounted the fence just as it went berserk, ramming into anything in sight: other bulls, the barn wall, the knights that had entered the corral after her. Soon an entire stampede was in motion. The soldiers gave up on her and instead focused on escaping the raging yuleys that charged from the pen and trampled anything that got in the way.

Talea, meanwhile, had hoisted herself from the fence up onto the barn roof. From there she ran toward the opposite edge and jumped, sailing over the small gap and crashing into the house. Picking herself up, she kept going, scurrying along rooftops with arms outstretched for balance and gut contracted with anxiety.

Gradually the noise of the pandemonium she'd caused by freeing the bulls ebbed until she could no longer hear it. Without a Kaydorian in sight, she warily crept to the edge of the rafter she was currently atop. Could she hop down from here? It seemed awfully high. It should be alright though, right? She sat down and wiggled forward until she was right on the rim. *One, two, th—*

"Talea, wait!"

She jerked her head up, a grin already forming. "Yhkon!"

He materialized from seemingly nowhere, grinning back. "I thought I'd never find you. Now don't jump, you might hurt yourself."

Okay, just stay up here indefinitely? Until the knights catch up and can fetch me a ladder?

The Warden moved forward until he was standing directly under her. "*Now* jump."

"Wait, what?" She scrunched up her face and leaned away from the edge.

"I'm going to catch you," he said as if it were foolish of her to question him. "Oh, come on. I just watched you run into a pen of bulls, zap one, and climb onto a roof while they trampled your pursuers. And you were about to jump off and sprain an ankle, but now you won't jump and let me catch you?" He smirked.

Talea puckered her lips. "Fine." She squirmed forward again, examined the unnerving amount of empty space between her and Yhkon's open arms, took a deep breath, and slid off.

He caught her easily and set her down. "See? What'd I tell you." Before she had a chance to respond, he was already pulling her down the street. "Come on."

They jogged through alleyways, undisturbed by knights. It was necessary to avoid confrontation with the citizens, and stay out of sight, but conversation was possible. "What happened to Eclipse?"

Yhkon's lip curled in something between melancholy and venom. "Those bloody knights took him."

"Oh." She sucked her cheeks in. "Sorry."

"Anyway." He shook his head as he stopped at the corner of a building, peering out from behind it to scout the next open square they'd have to pass through. "I wanted to say, you did well. I never intended for you to have to spend the night by yourself. But then when I finally found you," he sent an amused look her way, "you seemed to be doing just fine."

She beamed and ducked her head.

Yhkon turned back to observing the square. "Too bad all my gear was on Eclipse, or I'd have some food to offer you."

"Oh! I completely forgot—food!" She pulled out the apple and the canteen, holding them out to him with a smile. "Because as it is, I have food to offer *you*."

His eyebrows lowered with skepticism even as he eyed the apple hungrily. "Where'd you get that?"

"A woman met me at the well and let me come back to her house for a bit. Don't worry, I didn't trust her right away. But she was really nice. And I already had some bread, so the apple is yours." She moved it up and down in an enticing gesture.

The Warden paused only a moment before accepting the fruit. He crunched away at it while they strode across the square. Probably made them blend in more anyhow, she figured. *Well, okay, not so much.* The tall, broad-shouldered man with an assortment of weaponry, an unusual pauldron and gauntlets, and a hood that shadowed his face did not blend in—whether or not he was eating a crunchy apple.

~ ♦ ~

"Yhkon..." She closed her eyes and stopped walking, reluctant to complain, even more reluctant to keep forcing her exhausted body on. "Can we take a break?"

The Warden kept up his constant scrutiny of their surroundings, only casting a brief glance her way. "Just a little farther."

So Talea trudged on after him. *A little farther until what?* Her gait was more of a stagger than a walk, but at least he had slowed down considerably, no doubt to accommodate her. Muscles were sore and stiff, her palms stung, her stomach was past growling and instead just hurt, and her head pounded with a dull ache. Keeping her feet moving in a straight line was more and more difficult. Still, the eerie shadows of the coming night made her increase her efforts to keep up with Yhkon.

Her brief respite and bit of food at Lerese's that morning felt like days ago. They had been walking—and sometimes running or hiding—ever since. Yhkon wasn't very talkative, but he'd made it sound as though they would be out of the city soon, where they could rest more safely and hopefully find the other wards and Wardens. She wished *soon* would come a little sooner.

Even talking sounded exhausting, but she wanted a distraction. "How will we find the others?" As she asked, she thought she saw trees up ahead, between buildings.

"Theoretically..." Yhkon made a gesture for her to stay where she was, while he—for reasons beyond her comprehension—climbed on top of a shed, and then onto a higher roof beside it. From there, he peered through the darkness, toward the trees she'd seen. "We won't have to."

"What?"

He climbed back down. "You think this is the first time us Wardens have been separated in a big city? We always regroup on the northern side."

Please let us almost be on the northern side.

"And we're almost there."

She grinned, and they kept walking. To her delight, the buildings thinned out, revealing woods. Finally, they left the city behind and advanced into the forest.

And there they were...some of them. Ahjul, Terindi,

Larak, Tarol, Haeric, and Wylan.

Yhkon assessed the group with a frown. "Seen the others?"

Haeric's broad shoulders were slumped. He seemed anxious. Even Tarol didn't demonstrate his usual nonchalance and buoyancy. "Ki and Kae got cornered. We were going to go help them," he nodded toward Tarol, "but Grrake and Gustor were closer. They got there first, but weren't able to escape...we knew we wouldn't be able to defeat that many knights either...Grrake waved us off. They were taken as prisoners."

The lead Warden's features had hardened. Still enough to be a statue, he spoke quietly. "Are you sure?"

"Yes," Haeric confirmed, head lowered. "We followed them long enough to find out which direction they were going, then found everyone else and came here."

Yhkon's cold lethargy was shattered by an enraged outburst, starting with a string of profanities that would make Talea's mother gasp. "Curse that wretched tyrant and his..."

She didn't catch the rest of the words in his angry tirade. Perhaps that was a good thing. The way he balled his fists and paced like a caged forest cat, muscles rigid, made her retreat a few steps to stand beside Terindi and Wylan. Larak watched him with some of the impatience she'd often seen him display, but also with what looked like apprehension, even pity. Ahjul, worry. Tarol was glaring at nothing, arms crossed.

It was Haeric who spoke tentatively, when Yhkon stopped muttering curses. "Yhkon?"

"What?!" He whisked around to face him.

"Nothing, nothing." He raised his hands, soothingly. "What do you want to do?"

Yhkon took a long breath through flared nostrils. "No one knows where Resh is?"

All the Wardens shook their heads.

Yhkon began pacing again, more contemplatively than furiously. "Ahjul, you'll stay here with the wards, they need some rest. The rest of us go back in and split up. If we can't find Resh before sunrise, we'll assume he was captured as well, and leave to free them. Clear?"

Now the Wardens nodded. "Then let's go." He set back out toward the city without another word.

7
Prisoners

Yhkon launched the rock over a rooftop. It clattered against the cobblestone on a nearby street.

"Over there!" The prowling knights raced toward the sound, giving him the opportunity to cross the open square unseen and continue on at a jog.

Keeping away from soldiers who had nowhere near his level of training or experience, even while trying to find Resh at night in a large city, wasn't enough to distract him from his thoughts. It was impossible not to stray to the possibilities.

Or were they probabilities?

Stop thinking about it. It was pointless. Irrational. Either Grrake, and the twins and Gustor, were fine, or they weren't. It didn't give him any justifiable reason to fret about it. In any case, the sooner he focused and found Resh, the sooner he could find the others and get them back.

Before they were delivered straight into the hands of Kaydor Veserron.

He knew that they were alive. Grrake and Gustor were no fools, and they weren't reckless either. They would know when to surrender, and how to go about their actions from there, to make sure that—most likely—they and the twins were imprisoned, not executed.

But, as prisoners, they would be taken to the capital. To Kaydor.

Yhkon came to a stop behind a stone wall and leaned against it. Curse that wretch! Villainous, murdering…stronger language came to mind, and left his tongue in a snarled string of profanity. After all, Grrake wasn't around to either chastise or give him that disappointed look.

Focus. Find Resh, the idiot, then find Grrake, get him away from those miscreants, get the wards, and get out of this blasted region.

He'd been roaming the southern portion of Boroe for hours, in the rain no less. No sign of the missing Warden. There was the possibility that one of the other men had found him, of course. But there was just as good a possibility that they hadn't. While Yhkon made no pretense of having as much concern for Resh as he did for Grrake, the twins, and even Gustor, he still would be reluctant to leave the city without him.

So, he would search as long as he could, until it was time to rendezvous at sunrise. After that, Resh would just have to fend for himself.

His gaze swept the adjoining streets and buildings, and landed on one building in particular. Tall, made of brick instead of wood. Barrels and crates stacked along its perimeter. A man burst from the door laughing and swearing at the same time, on unsteady legs. A tavern.

Sucking in his breath, Yhkon gave his dripping hood and mask a tug to ensure they were in place, and strode forward.

For Resh's sake, he wasn't sure whether to hope that he found what he was looking for, or that he didn't.

He twisted the knob and pushed the door open quietly, just enough to slip inside. The hum of voices and a variety of other sounds contrasted the cold stillness outside. One voice caught his attention from among the rest.

"Sure do have the prettiest set of eyes I ever saw. What's your name, darling?"

"Enryda," came a feminine, giggling voice.

"Alright my good fellow, another drink for the lovely Miss Enryda, if you please, on me! A toast, my dear?"

"To what?"

"To—"

Yhkon had heard enough. "Resh!" He moved toward the voices, blood boiling, nearly knocking over a bystander who didn't move out of his way. He arrived to find Resh clinking glasses with a young woman, the neckline of whose dress would make a Canadise lady blush. If his behavior so far hadn't, the empty beer glasses and the stupid grin on his face made it clear that Resh had had too much to drink. "Yhkon! There you are. Been awhile since you've been in a tavern with me! Say, Enryda, have any pretty friends for my—"

Yhkon grabbed Resh by the pauldron and yanked him to his feet. A minute ago, it had been his intention to deliver a sound lecture. Now, he had an entirely different reaction in mind, and didn't bother trying to restrain himself from it. Holding the man with one hand, he pulled back the other to slam his fist into Resh's jaw.

Enryda shrieked. Resh floundered backwards, stumbling over chairs, though he managed to steady himself on a table without having completely fallen. "What in the devil's name was that for?!"

Advancing toward him, Yhkon took a vicious sort of pleasure in the way Resh cowered ever so slightly. "*Do not* play games with me. A little more spare time and I would give you a much more generous taste of my feelings regarding your complete idiocy." He narrowed his eyes, and pointed to the door. "Get outside. Now."

Resh straightened, if still a bit wobbly. "Yeah? And just what sort of moral high ground do you think you're on, to accuse me? I think your head has been inflated quite enough, *Silquije Eun.*"

That was it.

Yhkon grabbed Resh by the shoulders and pulled him down, while he drove his knee up. It made contact with Resh's stomach. He grunted, wheezing for breath as Yhkon shoved him toward the door. He sprawled on the floor instead, but clumsily scrambled into a more defensive position. His intoxicated body was entirely incompetent at dodging Yhkon's deft attack. Resh's jaw was soon swelling even faster, while Yhkon dragged him out the door.

Stumbling outside into the street, voices and movement immediately sounded to their right. Cursing, Yhkon jerked Resh to the left and broke into a sprint as the Kaydorians gave chase. Resh blundered about, knocking into crates and corners as they ran, but fortunately he wasn't so drunk that he couldn't keep up. Before long, the heavily armored soldiers fell behind. Yhkon maintained his pace, wanting to put as much distance between them as possible.

"Hold up, hold up!" Resh came to a panting halt in a dark alleyway. It was past midnight, and the entire city was in shadow. He was bent over, hands on his knees. "Give a fellow a moment…"

"You think I care that you need a moment?" Yhkon spun

to face him. Seething. "I don't. So I suggest you don't—"

"Oh, do you have to throw such a fit!" Resh sneered at him. "All I did was—"

He glared the Warden into silence. "You abandoned your post. Did you think we were on vacation?! While you've been enjoying your leisure time, Grrake and the twins are in the hands of the Kaydorians, and we've been unable to help them because we had to go looking for your sorry hide! Perhaps that was our first mistake."

Resh flinched.

Though his anger was in no way appeased, Yhkon clenched his jaw and didn't say anything more, pacing instead.

At length, Resh spoke, voice subdued. "Alright. I'm sorry. I didn't realize…I just thought I'd have a drink and then find you all…" He swallowed loudly enough for Yhkon to hear it. "I'm sorry."

The apology was a little too contrite for him to respond harshly again. "Let's keep going," was all he said, moving on at a walk.

By the time they made it out of the city and found the campsite set up by Ahjul and the wards, it was three hours to sunrise. The other Wardens weren't back yet, still in the city searching for Resh.

So Yhkon told Ahjul and Resh to get some sleep, while he kept watch. He was too uptight to sleep anyway. Which meant three hours of pacing and worrying.

In the morning, the other three Wardens returned, and camp was packed up quickly. The mood was more solemn than usual—of course, the twins' absence probably contributed to that. Haeric and Tarol told him where they'd seen the Kaydorians going, and they headed that direction.

Finding and following the tracks wasn't difficult in the least. It must have been a lance of at least a hundred, probably closer to two. Everything in their path was thoroughly trampled, the more so since they were traveling with coliyes and wagons. If that hadn't done it, the rain did—tracks were even more distinct in the mud.

They caught up to the lance in the afternoon. Leaving Ahjul with the wards at a safe distance, Yhkon and the rest of the present Wardens climbed a hill to the side of where the soldiers were taking a break. From there, they had a clear view of the Kaydorians.

"Toenail of a barbsit...that's a lot of knights."

Yhkon flashed a quick glare at Tarol. "Any other enlightening observations you'd like to voice?"

Tarol shrugged, as best he could while on his belly in the grass, propped up on his elbows. "They're pretty well set up."

"Do go on."

"Umm...looks like Grrake took a nice slug."

He glared again. The blood and swelling that was visible on Grrake's face even from this distance did not bode well for what sort of treatment they'd been receiving from the knights. How he hated Kaydorians. "Does anyone besides Tarol have some *useful* observations?"

Larak was squinting at the campsite, no doubt analyzing. He looked a bit strange flattened out in the grass, trying to hide. *Difficult to hide a giant.* "Tarol's right, their formation is tight. With Grrake and the others in the center and well guarded, it'll be tricky getting them out...but doable. I think it will require all of us Wardens and our swords, though. Not a sneak in, sneak out operation."

"Agreed." Yhkon ran his tongue along the roof of his mouth, surveying the soldiers that milled about the valley, stoking fires to keep the drizzling rain from dousing them, setting up tents, caring for celiths, guarding prisoners. "Except, what about the Kaydorians' tactic of killing prisoners at the first sign of outside interference?"

The men on either side of him frowned, remaining silent.

That left it up to him to continue the discussion. "They can all defend themselves, but they're restrained and potentially injured. And if the soldiers were to find out about the twins' abilities, that would cause us a heap of trouble down the road. We can't risk it."

"So, what, pack up and head home?" Resh retorted.

The only reason Yhkon didn't hit him was because movement could draw the knights' attention. Resh had been unusually docile ever since Yhkon had found him at the tavern the night before. Apparently he'd recovered from the remorse. "Another word I don't like out of you, Resh, and I might just consider it in your case."

Resh's cheek twitched as if he were fighting a negative reaction. His mouth, however, stayed shut.

"Now." Yhkon turned his attention back to the camp below them. "Here's what I propose."

~♦~

"Tarol, you better do as I say and—"

"Oh, please, I'll be an angel."

Highly doubting that, Yhkon gave him a skeptical frown, before advancing. They'd been over the plan multiple times. All that remained was to do it.

The campsite was shrouded in darkness, except for the crackling fire at its center. Two soldiers sat on either side of it, on watch. Luckily for Yhkon and Tarol, they were stupidly staring into the fire, ruining their night vision. "Okay, we're going to get within ten yards, then use the knives, got it?"

"Ah, but I want to tackle them!"

"Shut up and do what I say!" He rolled his eyes.

Tarol's teeth flashed in a grin, almost the only part of his face that was visible.

With an inward sigh, Yhkon lowered himself onto his stomach, put his arms out on either side of him with elbows bent, and flattened the sides of his boots against the grass. Pulling himself with his elbows and using his knees as the primary contact points instead of his feet, he began crawling forward, barely leaving the ground. It certainly wasn't the fastest mode of transportation. But it was quiet, and in the darkness of night, it would be invisible to the two knights staring at the fire.

On and on they went. Or so it felt. In reality, they'd only moved a few yards. The necessary stealth made even that much progress take several minutes. He could barely see or hear Tarol, only a couple feet to his left. It was a lie to say he wouldn't have preferred one of the other Wardens with him. But, Grrake and Gustor were his first choices, and they were hostages...not an option. Haeric, or Larak, would be next. However, it made the most sense to leave them—as the older, more experienced warriors—with the rest of the group to take authority in his absence. That left Tarol or Ahjul. In reality, Tarol was perfect for these types of missions. Except his infuriating talent for being an annoyance.

They made it to their mark unnoticed, neither of them having made so much as a leaf crunch. While ten yards was a little far for the type of knife throw they had to accomplish, any closer would put them into the light of the fire. Since Tarol would be unable to see a hand motion, Yhkon reached out and touched his shoulder to inform him they were halting. They both—ever so slowly—rose to their knees, eyes glued on the knights. The pair seemed quite oblivious to the world around them. If he were a little more slumped over, the one might have been asleep.

Yhkon slid his hand into his shirt and to the large belt around his waist. He pulled out a throwing star that gleamed in the minimal light. Tarol had done the same. With the blade between his thumb and forefinger, Yhkon drew back his arm, squinted at his target, and threw.

A slight grunt from the knight. The soldier Tarol had thrown at had already collapsed. Yhkon's victim, however, was still quite alive, the knife having hit just off the mark. Sure, the man would die soon enough, but not before he'd have the opportunity to raise an alarm.

"Blast!" He fumbled to pull out another throwing star, panicking, and further provoked by Tarol's muffled chuckles. The injured soldier was dazedly trying to stem the blood flow and just beginning to croak something out when Yhkon hurled the second blade. This one struck true, and the man toppled.

Tarol nudged his arm. "I thought you said it was imperative to kill 'em with the first throw?"

Yhkon growled under his breath and cuffed him over the ear. Tarol only snickered again.

They crept forward quickly and felt for pulses on the two men, removing the blades. No pulses, plenty of blood. That was the problem with going for the throat—it was a probable instant death, but it gushed blood and made a mess. A mess that would need to be cleaned up without a trace.

Having gone over the plan in detail, they both set to work wordlessly. The guards weren't wearing all their armor; what they were wearing was stripped off. They took the soldiers' extra garments off too and did their best to stop the bleeding.

Then they grabbed the bodies under the arms and dragged them away from the fire, into the surrounding forest. As soon as they were in the trees Tarol abandoned his load and returned to the fire, while Yhkon kept going. He towed the soldier along, cringing at the snapping twigs and rustling underbrush that resulted. Once he was deep into the woods, much farther than any of the other knights would venture, he found a thick copse of young trees and concealed the body in them. Then he went back and did the same for the other.

He sprinted back the way he had come, but slowed to a silent tread as he entered the camp. At the fire, he and Tarol swapped places—he sat down while Tarol picked up the armor and disappeared into the woods with it to wash off the blood. Yhkon sat motionless for a while, listening for any indication that they'd awoken anyone. When there wasn't a single noise after several minutes, he crouched on the ground where the two soldiers had died. It was hard to see in the flickering light of the fire, still, there were conspicuous blood stains. If anyone noticed those come morning, their cover would be blown. He tousled his hands through the grass and natural debris, pulling them away sticky and wet, having made little improvement. If only it were sand or even dirt, he could simply dig up fresh and cover it. Grass wouldn't work for that. How to remove the blood, then...

Movement.

Yhkon jerked his head up. Tarol wouldn't make that much noise.

A soldier had stuck his head out of a nearby tent, grumbling groggily. "Wha...oh, hey Ken—or, is that you, Kendon?" He peered quizzically at Yhkon.

Yhkon cleared his throat, trying not to fidget. He and Tarol had taken off their pauldrons and donned hooded cloaks that most of the knights would be likely to own. "Yep. Just a bit nippy out here." He gestured to the hood, wondering if he'd successfully covered his slight Sanonyan accent.

The man nodded understandingly. "Winter's on its way, true thing. Where's Martio?"

He shrugged. "Taking a leak." *Go back to sleep...*

Another nod. "Eh, think I'll do the same." He clambered the rest of the way out of the tent and wandered off toward the woods, thankfully in a different direction than Tarol had taken. Hopefully he hadn't woken any more men with his chatting.

Tarol returned with the armor and set it down, sitting beside Yhkon. He was about to lean forward to continue working on the blood stains, until Yhkon grabbed his arm. "One of them is awake. He'll be back any time," he explained under his breath.

The knight reappeared shortly, waving a greeting as he approached. "Ho, Martio! How's the watch treating you?"

Could you be any louder?

Tarol answered cheerfully. "Ah, not bad. Warmer would be better."

"Prisoners been making any racket?"

"No, silent as the grave." Tarol laughed and elbowed Yhkon's shoulder, as if to tell a joke. "That's where they're headed, after all."

The soldier chortled mirthfully, sounding more like a frightened pig than an amused man. He went back to the tent he'd come from, pausing outside. "Well, you boys got another couple hours, before sunrise, I'd say."

"Jendre! Get in here and stop your yammering!" came a grouchy voice from inside the tent. *Yes, please do.*

Jendre smiled good-naturedly and ducked into the shelter. Yhkon let out his breath in relief. Now, just to wait.

8
The Key

The sun was up. Finally. A man wearing armor that distinguished him as the commander marched out from a tent, put his fingers to his lips, and whistled. Then he strode to the fire and the two Wardens sitting next to it. "Alright, boys, up with you. Go get your armor on. You'll be guarding the prisoners again today."

"Yes, sir," they murmured in unison. Yhkon cast another glance at where the grass had been discolored to crimson. They had cleaned it up as much as possible, and they'd moved what remained of the firewood stock to cover it. Without purposely looking for it, he doubted anyone would notice.

He and Tarol left the fire and went to the tent they'd noted as belonging to Kendon and Martio, the men they were masquerading as. Inside, soldiers were busy packing up bedrolls and getting dressed, so it was easy to slip in and begin doing the same. They had to remove the hooded cloaks to put their armor on, but no one seemed to be paying enough attention to notice their dramatically altered appearances.

Except, none of the other knights were putting their helmets on yet. So the two of them would be suspicious to put on theirs. *Great. Just great.* They finished putting all their other armor on and packing their things, and left the tent. There were almost two hundred knights in the camp. Surely no one had memorized the faces of each.

They did their best to act casual while figuring out what to do. Everyone else apparently knew their designated tasks, leaving the two of them to scramble and hope for the best. The simplest thing to do at first seemed to be helping take down the tent that they had supposedly slept in. After that, they followed the other men that had occupied their shelter. Eventually, they improvised their way through feeding coliyes and eating a tasteless mush the Kaydorians called breakfast. Only then did the other men put on their helmets. They gladly did the same.

At last, the commander began giving orders. "Let's move it out! To your positions!"

Yhkon and Tarol went with everyone else to the coliyes, locating the two they'd observed as belonging to Kendon and Martio. Yhkon simultaneously located Eclipse, Ash, and Grrake and Gustor's mounts that had also been taken. If possible, he had every intention of getting them back as well.

Mounted, they rode the animals to the wagon that held the prisoners, replacing the soldiers that had guarded it through the night.

Up close and in the light, Yhkon was able to fully assess their condition. His focus was first on Grrake. As he'd seen from the distant survey yesterday, his friend had clearly taken more than one hard blow to the face. His cheeks were red, his lip was split, dried blood smeared around his nose. And the nose itself was another matter entirely. Crooked and swollen, it was cringeworthy.

Otherwise, though, Grrake seemed in good enough shape. No other evident injuries.

Gustor was in a similar state, minus the broken nose. There was a dark splotch on his sleeve. It couldn't have been too serious a wound, however, or the blood stain would be greater.

The twins appeared unharmed. Well, Ki had a black eye, and there was a bruise on Kae's cheek, but nothing else in their bearing suggested abuse.

Still, all of them were effectively restrained. The two teenagers were shackled at the wrists by chains that held them to the wagon. Grrake and Gustor had the same bonds, as well as chains around their ankles. Obviously they'd been identified as potentially dangerous.

That would make escape trickier. *Going to have to get a key from...well, who would have a key for the locks?* He rolled his eyes skyward. *Brilliant. For all your beforehand planning...you didn't think this part out, did you?* Oh well, it would be doable. If it came down to it, he could just hack at the wood that the chains were embedded in, and the four of them could get away still in shackles. By the looks of things, hacking was going to be the best option. Good thing he was using Kendon's rough, unpolished weapon instead of his own beautiful sword.

He looked back to Grrake, to find that the Warden was watching him. The Kaydorian helmets shrouded the entire face, with only thin slits for the eyes and holes to breathe through. Had the Warden still managed to recognize him? Or had he spotted him earlier, before he'd put the helmet on? Grrake's gaze remained steady, and the corners of his bloody lips curled up a little. That was answer enough—Grrake had indeed figured out the ploy. Yhkon grinned even if it was invisible and tipped his head ever so slightly to him.

Grrake smiled a little more, before turning away and leaning toward Gustor. A moment later, the other Warden looked at Yhkon with something like a smirk.

In better spirits now, Yhkon took to scanning the woods and hills they traveled through. He and Larak hadn't chosen a specific point for the rescue, both because it would be wiser to go by when the circumstances were best and because they had no way of knowing where exactly the knights were headed. As it was, this would probably not be an ideal area. The underbrush was too thick. Their mounts would be hard pressed to go any faster than a trot without stumbling, and they needed to be able to make a fast getaway. Their celiths were significantly faster than the coliyes the knights rode, but celiths weren't as sure-footed as coliyes. Galloping through thickets like this, coliyes would be more likely to take the lead. And aside from the brush, this part of the region was rugged, full of canyons and cliffs. Going at high speeds without thorough knowledge of the terrain was not only exhausting and difficult on the animals, it was also asking to run blindly over a cliff.

So, he settled into the saddle and tried to relax. With little rest and a lack of nourishment over the last few days, it wouldn't be sensible to spend energy being uptight.

The tightly-packed forest continued for some time. With the sunlight blocked by the foliage and clouds, and a cool breeze blowing that went right through clothing, it wasn't a warm day, despite the fact that they were in southern Zentyre. Clearly, autumn had arrived. Which meant it would be snowstorms and frigid temperatures in Calcaria just about now. Better to be there, joking with Grrake about their entrails freezing, than here, praying he'd be able to keep his friend alive when the fighting started.

And it did.

They left the forest and entered a valley. The woods on either side of them spewed forth attackers almost immediately. Larak, recognizable by his huge form and the massive celith he rode. The thing was so burly it could have been a yuley. Another Warden who wore the hood, but no mask. Ahjul. *That boy...never remembers his mask, no matter how many times I tell him.* Resh, whooping like an Irlaish tribe hunter. Haeric, who was dwarfed by Larak's immense size.

The knights were finally reacting to the celith riders that thundered toward them. The commander spun in his saddle to shout at the men surrounding the wagon, including Yhkon and Tarol. "Kill the prisoners!" He spun back around to deal out orders to his other soldiers. That was of little consequence to Yhkon, however. His only present concern was protecting Grrake, Gustor, Ki, and Kae.

One of the eight other knights guarding was first to yank out his sword and raise it above his head. Yhkon took out his own, the thrill of combat already fueling his muscles, and stabbed under the man's arm, where there was only chainmail instead of plate armor. It didn't penetrate deep, but deep enough. Yhkon was already wheeling his coliye to block the strike of the next soldier that went for the hostages. Commotion from nearby told him Tarol was doing the same. Commotion from everywhere told him all the Wardens had engaged.

"Kendon?!" a knight howled. Yhkon recognized the voice as belonging to Jendre, the noisy man from the night before. "You traitor!"

Yhkon tore off his helmet. It was obstructing his vision anyway. "Not a traitor. Just not Kendon." He smiled at the pure shock on Jendre's face, before attacking. Their swords clashed. Within seconds, Jendre tumbled off his coliye to the ground.

"Yhkon, back!"

At Grrake's call, Yhkon immediately raised his blade so that it covered his back. Sure enough, another sword crashed down onto it. With his arm bent at the unusual angle, he couldn't withstand the full force, and the weapon clanged against his armor. It did no damage. He whirled around and thrust his blade into the attacker's neck, where the iron plates didn't fully protect. That did plenty of damage.

"Y, get 'em free, yeah?" Tarol called as he dueled with another soldier. Dressed in identical armor, on identical coliyes, it was impossible to tell which of them was Tarol. "I've got these fellas handled!" As he fought he gave a short whistle. Larak would have left Tarol's celith somewhere nearby so it could respond to its rider's call.

"I'm supposed to be the one that gives orders!" he tossed back, even as he brought his steed parallel to the wagon, beside Grrake. "Get back."

Grrake leaned as far away as the chains would let him. Yhkon chopped down on the wood that held the fetters. Wood splintered and scattered as he hit it again and again, until…he hit metal. The shackles must have been attached to some sort of iron frame within the wagon. Cursing inwardly, he tried slashing at the metal, knowing it was pointless. Nothing.

"Plan B?" Grrake asked.

Yhkon worked his jaw as he scanned the valley that had become a battlefield. All the Wardens were locked in combat with multiple opponents. By the looks of things, they had a couple minutes before they'd start to get overwhelmed. "Any idea who might have a key?"

"The commander."

"Right. Excuse me a moment." He kicked the coliye into a gallop toward the commander. The man had several soldiers with him. Yhkon rode ride into their midst and started fighting. It was useless. The commander simply rode off while his men kept Yhkon busy. He tried to turn his coliye about to give chase, but they cut the animal down from underneath him. He barely managed to dive from the collapsing beast onto one of the other coliyes he'd just rendered riderless, and send it hurtling away. The knights were hot in pursuit. There was no way he could catch the—

"Yhkon! Speed it up!" Larak bellowed from somewhere close by.

Yhkon slammed his fist against his thigh. This was not working well. He saw Tarol in the wagon trying to free their friends instead of fighting, and directed his coliye back toward them. "Tarol! A little help?"

Tarol got back onto his celith and was ready when Yhkon brought the remaining five soldiers to him. Together they finished them easily.

Grrake was eyeing the rest of the battle uneasily. "Plan C?"

"Plan C..." Yhkon raked a hand through his hair and frantically scanned the valley. Couldn't get the key...couldn't break the chains...couldn't get them free...his eyes landed on where Eclipse and their other two stolen celiths were tied to another wagon that carted supplies. *It just might work.* "Tarol, stay here!" he yelled over his shoulder as he galloped forward again.

Meeting no resistance, he swiftly reached the celiths and jumped to the ground. Forcing the chaos and din of the skirmish out of his mind, he concentrated solely on untying the knots that held the animals to the wagon. When they were free, he got onto Eclipse, holding the reins of the other two, and went back the way he'd come.

Tarol was again, in vain, trying to get the Wardens and teenagers free. He glanced up with a frown. "How do you intend to get them on the celiths when they're chained to a wagon?"

"I don't. Shut up and help me." He dismounted Eclipse and led Lenjeya and Gustor's mount to the front of the wagon, where he began unhooking the two coliyes that pulled it.

"Ohhh," Tarol said with a grin, and leaped forward to assist.

"YHKON!" Larak roared.

Yhkon glanced up from his task of harnessing the two celiths to the wagon. A handful of knights were galloping their way. "Tarol, go throw them off!"

Tarol scrambled back to his celith and rode off.

Yhkon, meanwhile, cursed his clumsy fingers and tried to tune out the sound of oncoming hoofbeats. No doubt Tarol was unable to keep all of the Kaydorians distracted and away from them. *Come on come on come on come on come on…*

"Could you speed it up there, Yhkon…" Gustor's voice was tight.

"Working on it!" He yanked the final strap through its buckle. The harnesses weren't quite attached correctly, but they'd do. "Tarol!" he shouted as he moved back to Eclipse. Not before two knights on coliyes barreled toward them. He lunged out of the way, feeling a current of air as the hooves traveled only inches away from him. The confounded armor was slowing him down. By the time he was on his feet, one of the knights was coming toward him and the other was about to kill Grrake.

Not if Yhkon had anything to say about it.

He pounced, landing on the coliye's shoulder and neck and

clinging there like a bur. With the hand that didn't clutch the animal, he snatched the pommel of the sword that was about to murder his friend just as it went into the downward stroke. It was his one arm against the knight's two. For a split second, they were stuck there, neither giving or taking ground. Yhkon wrapped his other arm all the way around the coliye's neck and used it to swing his legs up and into the soldier, who lost balance and fell.

He didn't have even a moment to recover between losing his grip and realizing the other knight was driving his coliye forward to trample him. The beast slammed into him like a battering ram, sending him sprawling. Impact, pain, spinning, spinning...*thud*. Instinct took over as his mind seemed to retreat from the situation. The second he regained control of his body he hurled the sword he held at the grounded knight that was climbing into the wagon. With the blade protruding from his back, the man toppled off instead.

The other soldier was bringing his coliye back around. Out of breath and chest aching, Yhkon crouched, paralyzed, trapped in the moment as he observed the oncoming danger. No weapon. No way he could get up and out of the way fast enough. Coliye getting closer.

And then a celith appeared. It ran straight toward the other. The knight pulled his mount into a rear at the last moment, while Tarol took the opportunity to dispatch him with one blow.

"Yhkon! We have to retreat!" Larak's voice reached Yhkon despite the throbbing in his ears. In his everywhere, actually.

"Yhkon! Come on!" Tarol's strained voice.

His senses came rushing back. *Go!* He flung himself up and into the wagon. "Tarol, get Eclipse. The rest of you," he crawled over their legs and the rest of the wagon's contents until he sat in the driver's seat, "hold on." He slapped the reins over the hindquarters of the two celiths and whistled three sharp notes. They bolted forward like their tails were on fire. "Larak, retreat! Everyone, retreat!"

Thunder filled the valley as the hooves of eight celiths and almost two hundred coliyes raced over the ground. Blood still pulsed in Yhkon's ears and he could hear his heart beating wildly to add to the tumult. He flicked the reins over the celiths' rumps again before looking over his shoulder to search the mass of riders. There was Ahjul. Larak. Haeric. Resh. And Tarol rode beside the wagon, while Grrake, Gustor, Ki, and Kae, were all inside it. That was everyone. *Now just to get out of here.*

The valley narrowed as two forested hills created a bottleneck. The wagon, jostling along so bumpily that its passengers were bounced right out of their seats every few seconds and that Yhkon feared the wheels would fly off any second, reached the gap just behind Tarol and Haeric. The other Wardens closed in quickly, and they all galloped through the passage together. The Kaydorians weren't far behind, yet they were fading fast. The coliyes simply couldn't keep up with celiths, even those that were tied to a wagon. And the bottleneck forced them to slow, if only a little.

"This way!" Larak called, swerving his celith to the right. They all followed him. While Yhkon was only so familiar with this portion of land and its rugged terrain, Larak had grown up in southern Zentyre. Perhaps he had a trick or two up his sleeve.

Sure enough, he led them into a canyon created by two towering rock cliffs on the sides of mountains. Since going into a canyon was usually a risk, Yhkon knew Larak had some particular reason for doing so. That reason gradually became clear—the gorge narrowed the farther in they went. The Kaydorian lance had no choice except to group up in a line that was three-wide. The process of going from a madly rushing mob to an organized succession slowed them down considerably, while the Wardens kept going at the same pace. They came out the other side of the ravine while their pursuers were still trying to cram into it.

Larak directed them into another, wider canyon. They galloped along for awhile, until, just as the ravine was angling right, he abruptly veered to the left where Yhkon had not even realized a left was possible. He jerked on the reins to go after him, discovering a small outlet that had been impossible to see until they were already past it. The miniature gully was just big enough for them to travel through, and twisted and turned sharply, so that they had to slow to a canter. But he soon realized why Larak had taken it—the Kaydorians had raced right past the turn.

Under Larak's navigation, they retreated deeper into the stronghold of the hills and forests, until they were lost to their foes completely.

9

Rikky

"Rikky?"

The boy a few feet ahead of her spun around.

"Hi, can I talk to you?"

A dark blond eyebrow gradually rose, as did the corners of his mouth, until he nodded with a perplexed grin. "Sure." He moved forward. His gait was loose, flowing. Almost a swagger, except it was effortless and natural. *Does that make it better or worse?* Talea walked a short distance away, out of earshot of the other men in the forest. None of them appeared to notice, busy with their saws and axes. Rikky had left his embedded in a log.

"Have we met?" he asked as she stopped.

His village was at least twice the size of Vissler, Larak had told her. Still, she bet he already knew the answer. If she lived in his village, they certainly would have met, despite it having almost four hundred occupants. "No. I'm uh, I'm Talea. Talea Andul."

"Nice to meet you." He smiled. It lit up his sky-blue eyes.

"That's a pretty name. Is it Irlaish?" He extended his hand for her to shake.

She swallowed, not giving him hers. *Do you have to be so darn cute?* "Yeah, um, it is. Um, but about that..." She gestured vaguely to his offered hand.

His brow furrowed, as he looked down at his hand. With a sheepish shrug, he wiped it off on his shirt, and extended it again. "Sorry. Been working all day."

"Oh, no, not..." She inwardly slapped herself. *Why can't you do this, Yhkon?!* "I mean, that's not why I...okay." She took a deep breath. "Here, just don't...freak out." She tentatively slipped her fingers into his palm.

The spark of electricity brought a tingling warmth to her skin. Rikky jumped, surprise slackening his expression, but he didn't drop her hand or retreat. Instead, he held on, watching the glow spread.

Looking back the way they'd come from to see if anyone was observing, Talea pulled her hand away. "We don't want anyone to notice."

He nodded hastily. "Right. But..." His grin had returned. "That's incredible. How did you...I mean...?"

Smiling at his excitement, Talea folded her arms behind her back. "Well, it's a long story. But there are eight of us. Myself and four of the others came looking for you, along with..." *This is already getting old.* She jerked her head to where the other foresters were still working. "Are you able to talk now? Do you need to go make an excuse, or something?"

His grin faded, as he averted his gaze, rubbing the nape of his neck. "Oh, yeah, well..." He looked scared. "Yeah, I could, it's just..."

She watched him with concern. "What is it?"

"My dad," he finally admitted. "He'll be bloody mad if I

don't bring in a full day's wages."

His tone told her that *bloody mad* was something he really did not want his father to be. When she'd asked Larak for information about Rikky, he'd mentioned something about his father being a harsh man. *How harsh?* "Oh. Well, well that's okay, he won't have to know." She shook her head firmly. "Some of the people I came with will be able to pay the difference." *More like, if things go well, you won't be working at all by the time of your next payday.* But that would be difficult to explain so soon.

Rikky cocked his head. It made a strand of his tousled hair fall over his forehead. What Larak had failed to mention was that Rikayis Iserwood, the sixth ward, was charming enough to make any girl blush to her ears. "Really? These sound like generous people. What benefit is it to them to pay the wages of some laborer?" He was smirking, seeming to be somewhere between impressed and skeptical.

"They are generous," she wet her lips, "and you're not just *some laborer* to us." At the way his eyes lit up again, she had to duck her head while the heat in her cheeks dissipated. "So um, you don't have to worry about your father. Just go tell them you're not feeling well or something. I'll uh, I'll just wait over here."

He left and returned within minutes, clearly enthusiastic for her explanation. Yhkon and Larak had suggested that, in Rikky's case, it would be better for her to tell him as much as she could and gain his trust, before they made an entrance. So, she did her best to relay all the crazy details that had been brought to light since she'd first met the Wardens, months ago.

Rikky was a keen recipient. There were things he seemed skeptical of, but in an awed, tantalized sort of way. He became more animated the more she told him. The concept of being royalty, destined to live in the Shadow Region and lead a war, was received even more eagerly than the rest.

When she finished, there was a brief pause, before he laughed. "This is crazy. You're not just pulling my leg?"

"As if I could just make all that up? No, I'm afraid it's all true."

"I don't believe this." He was grinning again. She couldn't decide how to feel about that grin. *Irresistible* was the word that came to mind, and that could mean both good and bad things. "I mean I do. But...wow. Okay so these Wardens, and the other wards. When do I get to meet them?"

"Well, whenever. How about tonight?"

He nodded. "Dad usually heads out after supper, around six. Could you come to my haliop then? Do you know where it is?"

"I'm sure the Wardens do." She rocked from the balls of her feet to the heels. "We'll be there, a few of us, anyway."

"And..." His blue eyes locked on hers. "I can really go with you guys? To get the other two and then to Calcaria, and...all of it?"

"Of course." She smiled at him. "That's what I just spent twenty minutes telling you, isn't it? Though..." She broke eye contact. It was a little easier to be sensible and composed that way. "You should think about it. I mean, this is serious. And it won't be easy. Trust me, there's been some hiccups along the way. And this is a *war* we're talking about."

"I know." His enthusiasm didn't seem tempered in the least.

Alright, well, I'm gonna say "I told you so" someday. With something of a sigh, she just smiled again. "Alright, then. So, see you tonight?"

"Yeah. And, Talea..." He stepped closer, taking her hand

in his. The initial flash of sparks died away when he didn't release it, a soft aqua glow building where they touched. There was a chill on her skin but warmth within. Watching the glow gain strength, he shook his head with pleasant incredulity. "This is incredible. Thank you."

She was beginning to think she was going to have to be the one that ended the…*moment*…which was a bit of a problem because she was feeling slightly too paralyzed, and too tongue-tied. But Rikky let go of her hand, gave her a final smile, and walked away.

That left her standing there, still paralyzed. *What in Lamara's kingdom…*

"Um, Talea."

Yhkon's voice cured her paralysis. He snorted on a laugh at the way she jumped like a frightened barbsit. "You okay…?"

She glared at him as he approached from where he and Larak had been waiting in the forest. She might have glared at Larak too, if she didn't have to crane her neck so high to see him. "I think you could have given me some warning that he was so…so…"

"Well, yes," he made an acknowledging gesture, "he's a bit of a…charmer. But we figured if we told you that, you'd only be more nervous going into it."

Talea crossed her arms. "I think you should have let Wylan or Ki take this one."

Yhkon shrugged. "Talk to him." He indicated Larak. "I actually suggested that."

Larak took a deep breath and started talking as he walked back toward camp. They followed. "I said I thought you would be better because Rikky needed to hear it from someone he wouldn't feel threatened by. Any of us Wardens, or even Wylan or Ki, probably wouldn't qualify."

"Because Ki is so threatening?"

"No, because Rikky is easily threatened." He gave her a meaningful look. "His father has both verbally and physically abused him. The other boys at school disliked him because he was more popular with the girls. Most of his coworkers gang up on him too. The only people he's ever gotten validation from are his mother and...girls."

She bit her lip.

Larak's tone became more gentle, even if his voice still sounded like thunder. "I understand it puts you in an awkward situation, but try not to think too badly of him."

"I don't," was all she said.

There was a momentary silence, before Yhkon cleared his throat. "But I'll still be keeping an eye on him, don't worry about that."

Back at camp, the twins were on her in an instant, wanting to know how it had gone and what Rikky was like. Terindi and Wylan approached more calmly, waiting for the report as well. Talea did her best to satisfy their curiosity while avoiding the details of her interaction with Rikky that would be likely to make her blush.

Yhkon let them finish, then announced it was time for some training. Each ward worked with their Warden on whatever they deemed fit. Yhkon had her do some practice with his sword, then she and Wylan did some drills involving two people under the scrutiny of Yhkon and Grrake, the pair looking quite alike as they adopted their training stance: feet spread, arms crossed, chin lowered and expression stern.

After that, supper. As usual, it was a lively affair. Yhkon was in one of his better moods, even chuckling with the rest of them at some of Ki and Tarol's antics and tales. Ahjul and Resh ended up trying to sing a song in Calnec-Arayn together, fumbling over the lyrics and laughing almost as much as their audience. Yhkon told them with a smirk that they'd alert anyone within three miles of their presence, if anyone dared to investigate such a horrific sound. Though truthfully, she didn't think anyone could deny they could both sing surprisingly well…if only they knew the words.

Leaving the rest of the group to continue the merriment and clean up the meal, Talea, Yhkon, and Larak rode back to Rikky's village. They stopped a short distance from Rikky's haliop, just far enough to be invisible in the gathering darkness. All three of them dismounted, watching the haliop for movement. There must have been a candle inside, by the dim orange light coming through the window. Two shadows passed in front of it. His father must have still been home.

So, they waited. They had arrived early, anyway, it wasn't yet six o'clock.

A voice, muffled by distance and the dirt walls of the haliop. It grew louder and more aggressive, to the point of shouting. Talea stood up straighter, looking at Yhkon anxiously. It had to be Rikky's father…what if he was going to hurt him? If—

Yhkon put a calming hand on her shoulder and shook his head. "He's not drunk. He won't hurt him."

That was only so comforting. She could tell Larak was tense as well, but he remained quiet.

She wasn't able to breathe easily until the voice lowered, and a moment later, a man left the haliop and disappeared in the direction of the village.

They were just starting toward the haliop when Rikky slipped outside. His eyes landed on Talea and he smiled. They shifted to the Wardens, and he frowned. "Rikky," she stepped forward to meet him, putting on a cheery smile of her own in hopes of easing his uncertainty, "these are two of the Wardens. Larak, who's your Warden, and Yhkon, he's the lead Warden."

Yhkon and Larak both made their greetings and shook his hand. Rikky seemed to already be recovering from the initial wariness. He admired their armor and weaponry with unconcealed interest. "You guys look legit," he said finally, his grin slowly returning.

"I'll take that as a compliment." Larak was smiling more than he usually did. "Now. I know Talea told you quite a bit earlier, but do you have any other questions for us?"

"Um," he shrugged, "not really. I want to come with you guys."

"Are you sure?" Larak looked at him keenly, as if probing. "This is a serious decision. And it's not as though you can come with us, decide you don't like it after a few weeks, and come home. We want you to be certain."

Rikky's lips twisted into a sneer. "As if I'd have any reason to come home."

"Rikky," it was Yhkon who replied, to her surprise. "Don't be a little boy running from your father. Make your own decisions. Otherwise, you're letting him control you." His tone was brusque. And bitter. There was a pause, in which he seemed to shake off whatever had come over him. "So you want to come?"

Talea blinked, contemplating the unusual comment. The way he'd said it...she glanced at Larak. He was frowning at Yhkon, with some sort of dissatisfaction. Perhaps not directed at Yhkon, but at what he'd said.

Rikky's expression was a little offended at first. It quickly softened with thoughtfulness. Straightening his posture, he nodded firmly. "I want to come."

Smiling again, Larak clapped him on the shoulder. "We're

glad to hear it. Let's go get your things."

~ ♦ ~

Rikky's addition to the wards came with mixed responses. Ki found him to be great fun, and Rikky must have felt likewise—they were buddies within minutes. Kae and Terindi were neutral, though perhaps sharing in some of Talea's confliction simply due to Rikky's undeniable good looks and winsomeness. And then there was Wylan. He was Wylan-level polite, while Rikky made very little effort at hiding his own immediate and unexplained hostility. It wasn't long before Wylan abandoned common courtesy for indifference, peppered with some distaste. They were ignoring each other only minutes after the introduction. Though of course, Wylan generally ignored everyone if he could at all possibly help it.

The next morning, after training, the group set out as a whole, leaving Rikky's village behind. If Rikky felt any nostalgia or doubt, he didn't show it. He was enamored at the prospect of riding a celith. Talea couldn't help her amusement. *You'll be over that tomorrow, when you're so sore you can barely move.*

He had enjoyed the training, too. Though he had no experience with a sword, he excelled in the workouts and drills. Talea guessed he had some growing to do yet, but he was already tall, with an athletic build. The drills were not something he'd ever done before either, still, they seemed to come naturally to him.

As they continued on their journey, he became one of the primary entertainers of the group, not far behind Tarol and Ki. Except he wasn't simply goofy or witty the same way they were. He was more like a younger, pleasanter Resh. *Charming.*

By the time they set up camp at the end of the day, there was one more thing she concluded about Rikky: he had taken a special interest in her.

What she couldn't conclude, was how she felt about that.

She knew she wasn't the only one to notice. Larak seemed to be trying to keep the two of them apart. Terindi gave her a questioning glance when Rikky, wearing his handsome grin all the while, came to walk beside her when they were giving the celiths a break, asking her all sorts of questions about her childhood, family, interests. Wylan, she noticed, looked rather irritated by it.

The next morning, Yhkon asked her to go on a perimeter check with him. He let her ride front on Eclipse. She'd long since become a capable rider, even if she still felt a novice compared to the Wardens.

When they were approximately two miles from the campsite, she turned Eclipse to send him into a circuit around it. It was only then that Yhkon spoke up. "So…Rikky. If he ever causes too much trouble, let me know, alright?"

"Oh, well," she gave a light laugh, "I will. But, I mean, he doesn't seem that bad. Just a little…"

"Yeah." He cleared his throat. He didn't usually say *yeah*, he tended to use a more refined vocabulary, sticking to *yes*. "And I wouldn't be so easy on him, I suppose, except…well, his father, and having lost his mother…"

Talea wished they weren't on a celith, so she could see his face. Still, his tone told her plenty. "Yhkon…what happened to your parents? Did you lose both of them?"

His response wasn't immediate, but when it came, it was curt. "Yes, in a way."

As she wondered what to say next, he exhaled heavily and added, voice icy, "And I'd prefer that you didn't ask me about those types of things. It's not something I feel the need to discuss."

The difficulty of swallowing past the tightness in her throat told her his words had cut deeper than she would like to admit. It probably would have been best to answer, with a simple apology or just an acknowledgement. But it wouldn't come. She could think of more questions, she could think of a little speech about how it couldn't be helpful for him to bottle it up, she could even think of some retorts. But the apology, the simple acceptance, wouldn't leave her pursed lips.

So she said nothing. She realized she was leaning forward, as far away from his menacing presence as the saddle would allow.

Maybe, maybe she should make herself apologize, or just move past it. All he'd made was a request for privacy about what was apparently a delicate topic. So his tone had been a little cold. That was the case more often than not when he spoke to anyone, why should it bother her now? Why should she care if he wouldn't tell her about his family, or the other unknowns of his life?

But she did care. Logical reasoning couldn't change that.

She hadn't minded so much, leaving her family behind, all those weeks ago on the shores of Jalkiva. With Wylan and the Wardens and the twins…she was comfortable with them. Even if they weren't her family, weren't the constant love of her mother, the calm reliability of her father, or the protective, fun, sibling bond of her brother; there was something to be said for people who didn't just accept her unbelievable ability, they appreciated it, understood it, even shared it. There was something to be said for people who didn't see her as just a laborer, who in fact saw her as an equal, even a leader.

It was the friendships that made the absence of family tolerable. When it came down to it, specifically, Yhkon's friendship...and that was rapidly losing its benefit.

Homesickness had come and gone over the weeks away from her family, as could only be expected. Never staying too long, never too potent that it couldn't be fixed by time or by one of the friends she traveled with. Now it came as a violent wave. The presence of her *friend* only made it worse.

There was no way she was going to break down to him. He would probably only scorn her for it, or think she was being manipulative, or he might gruffly try to cheer her, but the real problem wouldn't be resolved. She knew if she tried to express her frustration instead, he would only become angrier, and her emotional defenses wouldn't stand up to that for long. Silence was the only option. Cold and deafening.

"Talea!"

She stiffened at his urgent whisper, splitting the raging silence between them. His hand grabbed hers...no, he was taking the reins, tugging them back, nearly hitting her stomach in the process. Eclipse's smooth gait stopped, the stallion's ears strained forward. Her gaze followed the direction of his focus, traveling past the trees, pinpointing to the glint of iron in the sunlight that filtered through the leaves.

Yhkon already had Eclipse turned around and fleeing the scene at a canter. How many knights had there been? Dozens? With only the flash of recognition, it had seemed like a whole swarm of them, riding their coliyes across the path she and Yhkon were on. Had they seen them? There wasn't a single noise, save Eclipse's lone hoofbeats, the crackle of underbrush, and her heartbeat.

Yhkon, still holding the reins, halted the celith much sooner than she was expecting. "Climb down," came his lowered voice in her ear. No longer icy. But closed off.

What, am I so vexing that you intend to leave me to be captured by the Kaydorians? "What? Shouldn't we—"

"I said climb down," he said it impatiently, though if anything, his mood seemed to have lifted. Once dismounted, he turned Eclipse so that he could face her. "Think you can get back to camp from here?"

"Um…" If he wasn't one of the most blasted confusing people she'd ever met, then she was a barbsit's tail. She wondered what his reaction would be if she were to verbalize the thought. If Seles were around, she knew she'd get a sharp look for using the word *blasted*. "Well, yeah. But—"

"Good. Then you need to run back there, as quickly as you can."

Oh, sure. Remind me why we can't just take Eclipse, the both of us? "Okay…what are you going to do?"

Yhkon looked back the way they had come from, an eager light flaring in his eyes. It told her what the answer would be even before he said it. It also told her that it was the prospect of a confrontation that had lifted his mood, and that worried her. "I'm going to go take care of that lance."

So, in all, her supposed new best friend thought their relationship excluded anything deep or significant about one another's lives, he found the opportunity to go kill a bunch of knights thrilling, and he didn't see any problem in making her run two miles back to camp. *A day of discovery.* All she did was nod. Her personal struggles would have to wait for later. "Right. But weren't there, you know, a lot of them?"

An unconcerned, even cocky shrug. Yhkon was not someone she would normally describe as being cocky. Apparently drastically uneven odds in combat brought it out in him. "Sure, most lances have at least a hundred men." He ignored the look she gave him, and continued on just as casually. "I'll draw them off. There's not much choice, they're headed straight for our camp. Eclipse can outrun their coliyes for quite a while. I'll either just escape them, or take down some," another shrug, "and then I'll come back. Now go. Tell Grrake what's going on, he'll know what to do."

When all she did was stare at him, he frowned, breaking eye contact. "I'll be back in anywhere from a few days to a couple weeks. See you then." With that, he gave Eclipse a kick, and left her standing there with a sinking feeling in her chest.

10

Surrender

It wasn't hard, luring the lance away from the trail they followed. As if they didn't realize that the single rider couldn't possibly have made so many tracks, as if they thought he could be the quarry they searched for. *Fools.* But, it served to his benefit, their foolishness. If they had been smart, and only sent a dozen or so soldiers after him, he would have had to devise some strategy to attract the rest of the lance. Then again, he could have just dealt with the dozen, then the next dozen they sent, then the next.

Well, what was the fun in that? It would be too easy. This way, he had a challenge—a lance of around seventy knights, all thundering on Eclipse's heels.

More importantly, this way he didn't need to worry about the wards and other Wardens. With the entire lance after Yhkon, Grrake would have plenty of time to get the group gathered up and moved out.

He'd also made it more difficult for the Kaydorians to

rediscover the trail later. They had been dumb enough to follow him as he had criss-crossed the trail multiple times before heading west, away from the group's direction. That way, the knights' coliyes would have trampled over a great deal of the tracks, hopefully obliterating the trail to an untrained eye.

Now, of course, there was the matter of "dealing" with the lance. Yhkon twisted to look over his shoulder, satisfying himself that they were still after him. Eclipse had been going at an easy gallop for nearly an hour, but was still fresh. He had at least a few more hours of energy, before he'd begin tiring. The coliyes, on the other hand, with lower speed but greater stamina, would be able to run for significantly longer than a celith; even a well-bred, excellently trained one.

Which meant, sooner rather than later, he would have to find a way to *deal* with them other than just outrunning them. Well, he had options, and they weren't so bad. Take on the force, cripple it, get captured and fight his way out—all sorts of fun ways to handle the problem.

The thought immediately brought a nagging stab of guilt. Oh, gods' end, why couldn't he go ten minutes without thinking, saying, or doing something that made him want to look around lest Grrake had noticed? He didn't give a dragon's hair what the council thought, what the other Wardens thought, what just about any other person thought of him. Why did Grrake have to be the exception? He wasn't even present, and the man managed to give Yhkon a guilty conscience.

He drew in a long breath. That didn't matter here. Whatever Grrake thought, the simple fact was that the lance had been about to find and attack them, and had to be stopped. Yhkon was stopping them. Simple as that.

~ ♦ ~

"So, how's he gonna find us, though?"

Rikky voiced the question that she had a feeling all the wards were thinking. The only reason she hadn't already asked it was because she didn't really want to talk about the lead Warden, just then.

Talea caught a murmur from Grrake, who was walking nearest her, that no one else seemed to hear. "Finding us won't be the problem." His head was down, hazel eyes tangibly pained.

Whatever her resentment, hurt, or disappointment directed at Yhkon was, it was clearly a laborer's living compared to Grrake's. It made it difficult to hold on to any bitterness, as if by doing so she was somehow hurting Grrake more. Ahjul was assuring Rikky of Yhkon's excellent tracking abilities that would make finding them easy, but she tuned it out to speak quietly to Grrake. "Don't you think he can deal with the lance?"

"No, I..." He closed his eyes briefly, pursed his lips, then mustered a weak smile for her. "I'm sure he can. Truly, I am, I know better than anyone how capable he is."

Somehow he managed to sound like he completely believed his own words, yet wasn't convinced by them. "Well, you trained him, right?" She gave an encouraging smile of her own. "And if he'd felt the lance was more than he could handle, he would have come back and gotten some of you Wardens to draw them off with him."

The way Grrake's expression sagged, adding years to his appearance, told her that had not been the right thing to say.

A tingling sensation crawled over her skin, sinking into her muscles. Connections, realizations, they all took place in her alarmed mind without her being able to quite comprehend their conclusions. She knew what Grrake's reaction meant. It explained things that had previously confused her—Yhkon's savagery in a fight, his bouts of apathy and vacancy, his eagerness to engage in a conflict where he was severely outnumbered.

Her voice snagged in her throat twice before she finally cleared it and spoke quietly, moderately. "What happened to him?"

Grrake shook his head, shoulders even more slumped than before, making her feel like she was just packing more weight onto the burden he was already carrying. "A lot of things happened to him, none of which he would want me to tell."

Yhkon and his secrecy. Did he not realize that if he was dealing with that much pain, it was probably past time he accepted some help with it? Or could he not see past the pain? Or, did the nature of what had happened have something to do with it?

"But..." Grrake surprised her by speaking again. His demeanor had changed, there was a spark of energy, or at least of desperation. "You can help him. He cares for you. If you could get him to open up to you...he needs someone, someone to help him. I think that could be you, Talea."

Her life hadn't been carefree, all sunshine and roses. But it seemed unlikely that she had any personal experience with whatever sort of grief Yhkon faced. How could she help him? All he'd ever done was shut her out when she'd tried. Unlike Grrake, she didn't even know what exactly she was trying to help. If Grrake hadn't been able to help the lead Warden, how could she?

Other than to look at him anxiously, trying to find the words, she didn't get the chance to reply. Larak, at the head of the group, stopped. "Grrake, what do you say to stopping for the night, even though it's a bit early? We can send two of us out to check for any signs of pursuit, but I imagine Yhkon has the lance well taken care of."

The baritone voice held a note of sympathy, of discreet support. Larak knew. He understood the details of the circumstances.

"Yes." Grrake straightened and nodded. He still looked weary, worried, but he obviously wasn't going to succumb to it yet. In Yhkon's absence, he was their leader. "Tarol, Gustor, you go. Three miles. Everyone else, let's set up camp. No fire."

Mechanically, Talea joined Kae and Terindi in performing their usual tasks. The entire group was lethargic, though the Wardens less so. After Talea had come panting and stumbling back into camp the previous morning, telling about the lance and Yhkon drawing them off, they had packed up and rode out. Through the day, into the night, and into the next, to put as much distance between them and the lance as possible. The wards had been able to sleep, sort of, riding behind the Wardens through the night. Except Wylan, since he rode Ash. She'd ridden with Gustor. Still, no one had gotten much rest, and during the day they'd done plenty of walking to give the celiths a break.

She could vividly remember Grrake's response when she'd delivered the news. His usually serene, gentle eyes had grown wide and frightened, yet not surprised. He had muddled through his concern well enough to take charge, with a little help from Larak. Since then, he had fluctuated between periods of calm, of flawlessly taking on his responsibility as temporary leader, and periods of nervous, distant silence, during which it was Larak who took charge.

Tarol and Gustor returned to report that all was well. With the camp set up, but no fire, everyone gradually drifted to a midpoint, gathering in a casual assembly, the dying, autumn grass their seating. Supper was smoked meat, and what the Wardens called trail mix, a mixture of long-lasting finger foods like nuts, dried fruits, and crackers. In some ways, the group was more lively than usual, in other ways, less so. Yhkon was not around to be in one of his moods that scared even Tarol and the twins into silence. So, they, along with Ahjul, Rikky, and Resh, were in high spirits. But for the rest of them, they were either engaged in their usual silence—*speaking of you, Sir Secrecy*—or, Yhkon's absence wasn't a cause for cheer. Without the distraction of travel, Talea could see that it wasn't just her, Grrake, and Larak who were worried, to one degree or another—Gustor was even more withdrawn than usual, and with less of an intimidating air than a reluctant one. Haeric kept casting questioning glances at Grrake.

Then Tarol threw a nut from his dry brew at Ki. And Ki threw one at him. An all-out battle ensued, twins and Rikky versus Tarol, all of them laughing and exclaiming and eating more of each other's brew than their own. It was impossible not to laugh at the spectacle, and even throw one of her own pieces at Tarol when a stray cracker hit her cheek.

Larak let it go on for a minute before stepping in, scolding in his thunderous voice, mostly directing it at Tarol. Haeric, watching with an amused smile like the rest of them, crossed his arms with a shake of his head. "This is what happens when Yhkon leaves you juveniles unsupervised."

"Hey, hey, hey now!" Tarol flung a hand to his chest. "*I* am one year superior to that youngster. And besides, all that's happening is that we're having some *fun* for once."

Gustor's aloof melancholy had lifted some, at least enough for him to direct a glowering smirk at Tarol. "And fun always involves a mess, when you're in the picture." Or, maybe he really was annoyed, and not just pretending to be. It was impossible to tell oftentimes, with Gustor. In any case, Tarol just shrugged and picked some of the dry brew that had previously been ammunition from the ground, popping it into his mouth.

Mirth already waning, Talea's gaze subconsciously moved to Grrake. Their eyes met.

The muscles around her ears tightened. She ducked her head. Some entertainment provided by Tarol and the other wards couldn't change the fact that he had implored her to *help* the lead Warden, the hostile young man that was supposed to be her mentor and trainer, who she was frankly afraid of. Who she didn't think she could help.

~♦~

Yhkon put a hand on Eclipse's neck, only to pull it away damp with the celith's sweat. His own body was clammy with it, making his shirt stick to his back uncomfortably. Of course it had to be today of all days that was hot, despite the lateness of the season. No doubt next week would be back to the cool autumn temperatures, but today had to be warm.

Dehydration wasn't helping. Unfortunately his canteen had only been half full when he'd started this crazy escapade yesterday morning, it had now been empty for hours. His parched throat was testament to that. Naturally with the lance hard on his heels, having gained as Eclipse's energy faded, stopping to refill hadn't been an option.

Which meant, it was time to choose from the options that were available to him. Simply outrunning the lance was no longer a possibility—Eclipse could barely keep ahead of them anymore, let alone leave them behind. That hampered things considerably. So, he could give up running, turn around, and fight. Well, even he had to admit that was foolhardy. One against seventy? Maybe spread out, but not like this.

That left only one other option. Capture. From there he could choose when to become uncaptured. For now, it was time to make a move. To make future escape possible, he needed to take down as much of the lance as possible now, for which he needed Eclipse to have some speed.

"Alright, you old nag." He gave the slathered, muscular neck a pat. Calling Eclipse a nag was about as accurate as calling himself a barbsit. Besides, it had actually been his nickname for Ash, who was more deserving of insult than reliable, obedient Eclipse. "Let's give 'em hell."

He guided Eclipse into a wide arch that brought them galloping straight at the lance. It apparently wasn't expected—several of the soldiers slowed or broke off as if to get out of his way. He heard the commander shouting orders, but couldn't make out what they were, over the commotion of so many hooves, and the wind in his ears. It was probably something to the effect of *"Back in formation, you cowards,"* because the riders that had reacted nervously rejoined.

The gap of peaceful grassland between them was rapidly dwindling away, trampled ground in its place. *One.* His gaze swept the front row of the lance, a line of twenty. He readied his sword. *Two.* He was toward the left of the line, giving him a perfect opportunity to sweep right across most of it. *Three.* The wild drumming of his heart felt like a rhythm for some ruthless, fervent key, to which every fiber of his body was tuned. Ready. Anticipating. Fierce.

Four.

A single tug took Eclipse into a sweep along the length of the line as Warden met Kaydorian. The startled coliyes responded in instinct, rearing to a halt rather than collide with him. Standing in the stirrups, wielding the sword single-handed, Yhkon cut down on every soldier that came within reach. By the time Eclipse had finished the span, five men and two coliyes were down. Without giving the lance time to regroup or otherwise react, he pulled Eclipse left, galloping along the right flank, sword wreaking further havoc. The lance was beginning to rebound by the time he reached their back lines. Yhkon drew Eclipse away, letting the stallion find his stride and the Kaydorians theirs, before he swung back.

It was easy, too easy, really. Gallop along a side and cut down as many as possible. There were over a dozen down before the commander managed to take control of his men and make Yhkon's goal trickier. "Split ranks! Engage!"

Fine then. It was his intention to be caught in the end, he could afford to accept the heightened risk and continue the endeavor. With the lance broken into halves, then quarters at the next order, they lost another seven to him, but they eventually seamed him in. Caught between four groups of a dozen was not a good place to be. By their actions so far, he felt relatively certain they wanted him alive. But in their frenzied charge, it could very well not work out that way by accident. Closer, closer, closer. He was trapped. Surrounded by thunder and glinting armor.

Yhkon kicked his heels against Eclipse's ribs, urging the exhausted celith into a final burst of speed, through the closing space between two of the companies. Coliyes and weapons closed in upon them halfway through, the coliyes' instinct to keep out of Eclipse's way the only reason they were still moving. A claw of fear gripped his body, squeezing the reckless vehemence out of muscles that had become rigid. A helpless, expectant, crazed fear—he was surrounded by this inferno of chaos and violence, about to be smothered at any moment…a sword nicked his leg. A rearing coliye's hoof struck his back. He noticed neither beyond dim recognition, hacking left and right at whatever his blade could reach, clearing as much of a path as he could.

And then, they were free. By some miracle, they were free.

The first breath he sucked in quivered, filling lungs that had been as clenched as the rest of him in those several seconds of brutal eternity. The second breath was resolutely steady, his fists tightening on the reins, eyes narrowing. He had escaped, now he would be captured, and later escape again. It was all going according to plan. An uncoordinated, poorly trained lance was nothing he couldn't handle.

Eclipse labored for every breath, and made no objections to skidding to a halt at Yhkon's cue. He spun to face the oncoming lance. Thankfully, they slowed, warily at first, then stopped fully a stone's throw away.

"Do you surrender?" the commander called.

"On certain conditions."

"Which are?"

Yhkon relaxed a little in the saddle. "You don't kill me, and you take care of my celith."

The man hardly even hesitated. "Agreed. Dismount, and step twenty feet away from the celith."

He swallowed. The lack of hesitation could just mean the commander thought his conditions reasonable, as they were...or it could mean he was tricking Yhkon into putting himself in their control, so they could kill him.

Some distant, restrained voice told him that this was idiotic. He had no proof that the Kaydorians wanted him alive, it was just a guess. For all he knew, they were going to slit his throat at the earliest opportunity. Or, if they didn't kill him, they would take him to Aydimor. There were still at least fifty of them, making his chances of escaping quite slim. And if they took him to Aydimor…

As always when he was about to do something arguably reckless, an image of Grrake came like a shackle to his mind. Grabbing him. Trying to talk him out of it. Even pleading.

Also almost as always…he ignored the nagging caution, and dismounted.

11
Water

Capture really was looking like a less and less brilliant plan, as it unfolded. Naturally, he had been stripped of his weaponry and minimal armor, and searched for anything hidden. Fortunately not thoroughly enough for them to find the knife lodged in his boot. After that, his wrists were bound tightly behind his back, he awkwardly clambered onto the coliye they directed him to, which was tied to two others. Eclipse, at least, was taken care of, as promised.

Well, at least he'd been right about them wanting him alive. Unless they were just waiting to kill him more creatively, later.

"Let's go!" The commander's sharp voice rose above the general buzz of the lance. They all mounted, moved into formation, and set out at a walk. Satisfied that the men were in line and in no need of further instruction for the time being, the commander turned lazy, yet cunning, brown eyes on Yhkon. A well-built man, average height, probably in his thirties or forties. Experienced. "I'm Commander Dejer, quarter of offensive infantry, eleventh platoon, of His Majesty's army. What's your name?"

"Quarter of offensive infantry, eleventh platoon"...fancy way of saying

the minimally trained, basic soldiers that Kaydor throws at problems in abundance until they eventually fix it by sheer numbers. "Commander of offensive infantry? You clearly didn't start with the rank. What did you do that so pleased *His Majesty* into promoting you?"

It was the lack of self-obsessed, snobbish ego that convinced him the man hadn't earned the rank for no more than a family name, or social standing. Still, Dejer showed his own sort of arrogance in his reply. "I'm the one who told him about you and your friends. Therefore," a cruel grin displayed perfect teeth, "I'm the one who gets to deliver you to the king."

"To him personally, is it?" Yhkon tilted his head as if curious. The last thing he wanted was for this Dejer to see that he was far from composed, actually seething. "He must feel quite threatened by just a few San Quawr."

The lazy eyes became more intent. "Are you going to tell me your name, or will I have to drag it out of you by other methods?"

"Well, I'm sure you're going to be trying to torture some sort of information from me before we're through, why don't I give you more to look forward to discovering?"

The cruel grin was hardening into a glare. Dejer's hand whipped out, yanking back the hood and mask Yhkon wore to expose his face. His smirk returned. "Ah, I wondered. You're nothing but a tadpole, talking like a man. Sanonyan, too."

Yhkon could have killed the man and enjoyed it thoroughly. At what point would men stop looking down on him for his age? When he was ninety? He was twenty-four, hardly a child. And he had the wretched imbecile by at least two inches, and twenty pounds. Though he knew there was restrained anger in his countenance, he kept his voice cool. "Says the man who lost a quarter of his force to me."

There was a brief flash of rage in the commander's face, before his fist slammed into Yhkon's jaw.

To say it didn't hurt, or that it wasn't difficult to keep his calm composure, would be a lie. But keep it he did. He met Dejer's gaze without so much as a wince, gathered up the blood in his mouth, and spat it to the side. It was tempting to spit it at the pompous Kaydorian, but he'd always felt that to be a petty, childish sort of gesture.

No matter. The collected, mocking expression he wore clearly irritated the commander plenty.

Dejer leaned back, recovering from his anger, even smirking again. "Have it your way, tadpole. As you say, it just means we'll have more to get out of you tonight." Obviously, he was looking forward to it. "Kaydor did insist you be brought in alive...but he gave me no other limitations."

I'm sure he didn't. So, the brilliance of increasing the commander's desire to torture him by being vexing was debatable. Not to mention, growing thirst wasn't a problem that would solve itself. Now he had little choice except to make his escape that night, before dehydration slowed him, and lest whatever pain-inflicting techniques they used debilitated him in some way. One thing was certain, he would *not* be taken to Aydimor, not alive.

Dejer straightened and kicked his coliye into a trot to move ahead. Yhkon waited till he was gone, before turning to one of the soldiers who rode as sentry beside him. "Don't suppose I could trouble you for a drink?"

When the man answered by snapping his riding crop over Yhkon's shoulder, he concluded that they were under no orders to pay him courtesy, and that getting some water would have to wait.

The day passed slowly. Nothing to distract from his growing thirst and lightheadedness. He kept his mouth shut and his head down, not wanting to dig himself even deeper into this mess, and not feeling much energy for sarcasm.

The lance didn't stop until it was already growing dark. By then, Yhkon was beginning to crave a feast, with a whole pitcher of water, maybe even some wine, and then a comfortable bed. That, he knew, was not at all what he was in for.

With his hands still bound behind his back, dismounting at the order of his guard seemed rather impossible. Would it be more humiliating to accept assistance, or risk falling on his face? Well, they weren't offering help, and he wasn't about to ask for it, so it would have to be the latter. He swung one leg over and slid down. He landed on his feet, only losing his balance and stumbling a little…until the nearest guard purposely tripped him. Unable to catch himself with his hands, he ended up on his side, coughing on dirt, with the Kaydorians laughing over him. Oh, what he wouldn't give to be able to jump up and snap their necks. No weapons necessary—he knew he could take the two sentries barehanded.

One of them grabbed him by the arm, yanking him to his feet. A wave of dizziness made the ground sway beneath him. They were already dragging him forward. It took a few seconds before his feet remembered how to walk, and he didn't have to lean into the soldier's grip. He stuck his tongue to the roof of his dry mouth. *Why bother torturing me? Just keep this humiliation up.*

They took him to the middle of the forming camp, and moved to either side of him, still acting as guards. As if he couldn't dispatch them both in seconds, even with his hands tied. As soon as an opportunity presented itself…

For the time being, he analyzed the scene. Most of the men were busy tending to coliyes, some were putting up shelters and starting a few fires. If he were to try now, there would be too many of them still near their mounts. *Not yet*...But it would have to be soon. The longer he went without water, food, or rest, the weaker he would become, and the more difficult the escape.

Dejer was approaching, backed by five soldiers. Either expecting trouble, or intending them to be his interrogators.

As much as he'd prefer to be as scornful and vexing as possible, that wasn't going to get him water. "So," he licked his chapped lips, looking Dejer in the eye but trying to keep any challenge or mockery from his demeanor, "since you have to keep me alive for the boss, could I have some water?"

The glint in his eyes, the sadistic smile...it made a sense of dread settle like a weight in Yhkon's stomach. Dejer untied Yhkon's wrists, then flicked his hand in a gesture to some soldiers that must have been behind Yhkon. "Get our guest some water, boys."

Yhkon had only a moment to guess at what was about to happen, before boiling water was dumped onto his back. Like liquid fire it spread over his skin in a burning, caustic wave. He gasped on a scream of pain that wouldn't come, dimly feeling his knees and palms hit the ground. The inferno that seemed to be eating away at his flesh saturated all his senses, throbbing in his ears, blurred red in his vision. Pain overwhelming everything. Dejer was saying something. Laughter. He let his forehead fall against the cool dirt. Every muscle in his body clenched as if to resist the pain, yet only made it worse. A groan slipped past his lips. The scorching heat didn't abate. No relief. No moment of freedom from its smothering grasp.

At some point he realized Dejer was kneeling beside him,

leaning in to speak closer to his ear. The words grated on his agonized senses. "Now. Let's have it. Your name?"

Yhkon opened his fist, closing it again around a handful of grass, squeezing until tiny pebbles and his nails cut into his palm. He heard himself inwardly pleading for relief, as if a spectator in his own clouded mind.

Dejer said something else, distant. Then a whip cracked, bringing a flash of pain like a razor across his raw back. A strangled cry escaped his gritted teeth. Dejer's voice, sneering, just beside him. "Your name?"

"Y-Yhkon." A cough wracked his body, bringing with it a spasm of fresh torment. Dust settled in his nose and mouth, only making him cough harder and groan again. "Yhkon Tavker."

"Good," Dejer leaned back, "I see we understand one another now. So, Yhkon, who are you and your friends? Where are you from?"

Oh, gsorvi...he couldn't give them anything. Not if they whipped him until there wasn't a scrap of skin left. He couldn't..."We...we're just..." Nothing would come. The haze left him blank, unable to think of a single excuse or lie. Jumbled words floated about, none of them helpful, some of them harmful if spoken aloud. "Just..."

"Better speak up, tadpole. I've got any number of riding whips, if this one gets too worn out we'll find another."

He snatched every curse his fogged mind could come up with and silently repeated them, willing his body to recover to functionality. Water. He needed water. If he could...maybe...the thoughts wouldn't stay aligned, always ending up scrambled as the raging pain engulfed everything else. "Water..."

"Alright," was Dejer's only response. Yhkon cringed,

muscles tightening again, waiting lest it be another bucket of boiling water. Not until a half-full canteen was thrown at him did he relax, grabbing it with fumbling fingers. The seconds it took for him to get the cap unscrewed were torture in and of themselves, before he finally put it to his lips and gulped down every drop.

"Now. You've had your water. I want my answers."

He set down the canteen, remaining on his hands and knees, but lifting his head enough to survey the campsite. His vision was still blurred, the pain still excruciating. His mind, however, was clearing. There were nine men around him. Fifteen near and alert enough to be a threat. The rest, occupied or absent, or at least distant. His weaponry and Eclipse weren't too far off or inaccessible.

"Answer!"

Yhkon closed his eyes. Drew in a long, deep breath. The pain was lessened just enough, that he could push it back, long enough to get away…just maybe…He had to try. Hand ready, he kept his head lowered, and waited. Waited…

The whip cracked. His hand shot out toward it, catching the leather just as the tip snapped over his upper back and shoulder. Ignoring the sting, he tightened his hold and jerked. Unsuspecting, Dejer lost his balance, stumbling forward while Yhkon lunged upward, knee rising to meet the commander's abdomen. The man fell aside with a grunt. Yhkon leaped at the nearest guard, taking him by the neck while he kicked the knee out of another. Wrapping his other arm around the first guard's head, he twisted, hearing and feeling the spine snap. Taking down the remaining five was equally simple, if a little time consuming and torturous to his back. By that time, however, an alarm had been raised. His opening was quickly vanishing.

Yhkon grit his teeth and sprinted for the coliye that had

been packed with his armor and weapons. The fire that still clung to his blistered flesh raged hotter with the exertion and movement. Each heartbeat pulsed through his entire body, bringing with it a stabbing ache to his temples. Knights were closing in, forming obstacles between him and his goal. Blast Kaydor and his stupid minions. He would get out of this alive, or he'd take them all down with him.

Injured and unarmed except for the knife he'd had in his boot, he attacked the armored soldiers as if the circumstances were reversed. Perhaps there was a time in his life when he would have hesitated to use whatever brutal tactics were necessary to get it done, try to spare the lives he could, avoid dealing out gruesome injuries. If there had been such a time…it was gone now. By the time he was past the opposition, he was splattered with blood, most of which wasn't his. Many of the Kaydorians had received not a clean death, but one that was sure to take its time.

He took his sword from the gear, left the rest. Grabbing the coliye's reins, he continued his sprint to where Eclipse was tied with some of the other mounts. There were more knights, making a chaotic pursuit, not far behind. Somehow he had to prevent them from simply mounting the coliyes and outrunning his tired celith.

Withdrawing his sword, he ran parallel with the sloppy line of logs the animals had been tied to, blade slicing each rope as he passed. With the shouting and general ruckus, the coliyes were already uneasy, and many took off. Yhkon returned to Eclipse, picking up a dropped whip on his way. By the time he had mounted, restraining a yell at the tearing pain brought on by the movement, there were mere seconds between him and the blades of the oncoming soldiers. Without prodding Eclipse bolted, the coliye with Yhkon's gear tied to him forced to follow. Yhkon directed the celith toward the coliyes that hadn't yet run off, snapping the whip down on their hindquarters and shouting, until almost all of them had scattered. As he kicked Eclipse into a gallop away from the camp, there were only a few Kaydorians that had managed to mount. They chased him for only a few minutes, before realizing that Eclipse and the stolen coliye still had enough speed to make it a long hunt, and that even if they did catch him...they'd be unlikely to survive the encounter.

It was a clean getaway. No pursuit, no likelihood of it.

Usually, he would have done his best to cover his tracks—no matter how slight the chance was that the beaten remainder of the lance should take up the trail later. This time he didn't bother. A few miles out he stopped just long enough to unpack his gear from the coliye and set the animal loose. After that, he simply set Eclipse headed west, and tried to stay awake.

It was long, dragging hours. Since it had taken nearly thirty-six hours of riding, most of it at a canter or gallop, to get as far away as he had, it would take at least forty-eight to get back, considering Eclipse was already tired, and the group would have been moving farther away in his absence.

Forty-eight unending hours. His canteen and provisions had not been on the coliye, meaning he had no food, and could not carry water with him, instead only able to drink as much as possible when he came to a reliable source. That only happened once. Hunger gnawed at his stomach mercilessly. For most of the trip, his throat felt like a sun-baked desert. And of course, the unrelenting pain that covered his back and shoulders. With dehydration and hunger came fatigue, dizziness, blurred vision. At one point when he stopped Eclipse, he woke up collapsed on the ground, unsure how he had gotten there.

After that, he determined not to stop again. He couldn't. He had to get back to the other Wardens and wards. Had to…In the periods of alertness, he tried to rationalize that he wanted to get there as quickly as possible, and that to delay was risky. During the stretches where his mind wandered, hazy and not quite fully conscious, all he knew was that he couldn't die out here, alone. He had to get back. To Grrake, to Talea, to all of them. He had to get back.

When he snapped awake after hours of drifting in and out of nightmarish semi-consciousness to see the glow of a fire ahead of him, it seemed impossible. A dream. Too good to be true. Surely the eternity couldn't have finally come to an end.

But it was true. A small fire, with three tents around it. A single person seated in the glow, on watch. Even from that distance, Yhkon felt sure it was Grrake.

And he was right. A strange tension crept into his aching muscles as they neared, Eclipse plodding along, nose nearly touching the grass in his exhaustion. Grrake was at his side the moment he stopped the wretched celith beside those of the other Wardens. Catching him when he weakly dismounted. Hand closing around one of his burned shoulders to steady him. Yhkon caught his breath on a groan without meaning to. Grrake retracted his hand instantly. "What is it? How are you hurt?"

Yhkon barely managed to rasp out a reply, and even then it wasn't complete. "Burn. I just need…" He made a vague gesture to the log Grrake had been sitting on. Even if he'd been doing nothing but sitting in a saddle for the last few days, he didn't think he could stand much longer. "To sit. And water."

Grrake took him by the arm instead, helping him to the

log. When Yhkon was seated, he fetched a canteen, which was empty in a few ravenous gulps. Once he was done, Grrake sat down in front of him. His eyes were an unnerving mixture of anxiety, despair, and anger. When Grrake was angry, things weren't good. "What happened, and where are you hurt?"

His throat still felt dry even after the entire canteen, and he wasn't sure if it was because he was still thirsty or because he didn't want to have this conversation. "My back."

It was only answer to one of the questions, but Grrake nodded and set to work, pulling Yhkon's shirt off and moving behind him. Yhkon could practically feel his friend's dismay and chagrin when he saw the burns. "What did you do?!"

"You think I did it?" the retort slipped out before he could stop it. He looked away. "They wanted information, I didn't give it, they boiled some water. Simple as that."

"Yhkon!" Grrake was in front of him again, giving him little choice except to make eye contact, and see just how upset the man was. "There's nothing *simple* about this. Don't try that on me."

Yhkon bit his tongue against another sarcastic reply. Grrake left and returned with medical supplies, sitting down behind him to tend the burns. If it looked at all as bad as it felt, no doubt it wasn't a pretty sight. The ointment Grrake was rubbing in only made it hurt worse, to the point where he had to wad up his shirt and squeeze the life out of it as distraction.

As if that wasn't bad enough, Grrake apparently wasn't ready to let the matter rest. "You can't keep doing this. What were you thinking, leaving to deal with that lance by yourself? Getting captured and—"

"I was thinking about the safety of the wards," he snapped. "If I hadn't drawn off the lance, they would have caught up to us, and caused a lot more trouble than just some burns on my back."

Grrake's slathered fingers quit their task. Yhkon didn't dare turn around. He didn't want to see whatever expression his friend wore, whether livid, desperate, or otherwise. But he could hear it in his voice. "We both know that's a lie. The safety of the wards was an afterthought. If that was all you cared about, you would have come back to get at least one or two others of us Wardens, and together we would have dealt with the lance. So stop hiding behind that lie and admit that you did it because you're reckless!"

Whenever possible, Yhkon avoided swearing around Grrake. He knew the man didn't approve, and he didn't take any particular pleasure in disappointing him. But in that moment he didn't care. In fact, he relished the vehement delivery of a curse just to spite him, before replying. "Tarol is reckless. Resh is reckless. Hell, Gustor and Haeric are reckless sometimes. But only *I* get this blasted lecture!"

"Yhkon…" Grrake's voice was losing its heat. When he moved forward again to face him as he spoke, his eyes had lost it too. They were only sad now. Sad, weary, forlorn. And that was worse than anger. "You know what the difference is. They're reckless just because they are, the normal bravado and daring of young men. But you…" He looked away, face contorted as if he were in pain. With a gesture to Yhkon's blistered back, he swallowed and continued, as if it took all the energy he had just to speak the words. "But you're reckless because you don't care. You don't care if they hurt you, or kill you."

Yhkon flinched.

"Please…" In the firelight, Grrake's eyes appeared to be glistening. "You have things to live for. I know that since, since Tessa—"

He balled his fists, squeezing until his knuckles were white. "Stop."

Grrake didn't stop, even if his voice quivered. "That since you lost her, you've felt like there's nothing left for you. I know that—"

"Leave me alone!" If he'd been any less exhausted, he would have stormed off. As it was, he felt unable to do anything but swear and snap and glare. They'd probably already woken up most of the other Wardens and the wards, why not finish the job. Let the lot of them hear the wretched business, let Grrake tell the world things he had no business speaking about. "Mention her again, and you'll lose all the confidence that you already take advantage of."

"Yhkon, you can't just keep—"

"I bloody well can!"

Grrake fell silent. Not for long. "I just...I can't let you keep trying to, to throw your life away. Please. Please don't do that to yourself, to Talea...to the Wardens and wards...or to me."

There was a tremble in his hands, no matter how tightly he clenched them. He couldn't bring himself to look Grrake in the eye, or speak, or even so much as straighten his hunched posture. The heat in his face wouldn't go away, yet a chill crawled down his spine like icy fingers.

Neither spoke. At first neither moved, until Grrake mutely returned to rubbing salve on Yhkon's back. Yhkon wished he wouldn't. It hardly made him feel any less...less...less of whatever he was feeling. If he could be engulfed by some black hole, some wonderfully empty void, he would. If there was any way to escape *this,* he would take it.

Except there was only one way he knew, and it was exactly what Grrake was pleading with him against.

He wondered how much of their conversation had been

heard by the others. The last part had been held in quieter tones, hopefully too quiet to be overheard. As for the rest...what did it matter. The other Wardens were perfectly aware of his *problems,* it was one of the reasons why they and everyone else disliked him. The wards might as well figure it out too. Though they were probably deeper sleepers.

What a wretched business. It was his responsibility as lead Warden that kept him going, yet it seemed to throw constant new miseries at him, too. In a way, it had taken Tessa from him.

His eyelids were growing heavy. A dull ache throbbed in his chest. Weary. He felt weary, the same feeling he'd seen in Grrake's eyes.

Perhaps he should have been consumed with his usual anger, or flaying Grrake for taking such liberties, or maybe even grieved and stricken. But he wasn't. He was sluggish. Remote. Passively listening in on his tormented thoughts, recalling the events that brought them on, knowing he couldn't do anything about it. He had no indignation toward Grrake anymore.

"There's not much more I can do for this tonight." Grrake's tone sounded much as Yhkon felt. "You should drink more water, then go to sleep."

His first thought was to agree. Sleep. It had been what, four days since he'd had anything more than dozing in the saddle? But that wasn't what left his mouth. "The sun will be up in an hour or two. I might as well—"

"Yhkon." He'd heard that tone before—it always made Grrake sound fatherly. "Go to sleep. We'll leave a couple hours later, and it will hardly be a setback." When Yhkon didn't immediately accept, he grabbed his arm to pull him to his feet. "Come on. You can sleep in my bed. You must be tired, just get some rest."

It would take too much energy to object. And he wouldn't be much good to anyone as sleep deprived as he was. So he limped his way to the Warden's tent, found the unoccupied bed, and let himself collapse into it.

12

Wards and Wardens

Talea woke early, thirsty and in need of an excursion to the woods. *Or...not early?* Sunlight was peeping through tears in the tarp. She took a swig from her canteen, dressed in her pants and shirt, put her boots on, and slipped out of the tent, managing to not wake Terindi or Kae.

Sure enough, the sun was up outside, the sky blue. It must have been nearing seven o'clock, yet the Wardens usually woke them for training at six. Only Grrake was in sight, having been the last one on shift.

There weren't any woods around, as it was, but the girls had designated a sheltered spot for the same purpose. It was a short walk from camp. As she was returning, Tarol ducked out from the Wardens' shelter, greeting Grrake cheerfully. "Say, Grrake, there's a bloody, shirtless, scraggly sort of fellow in our tent, in your bed no less. Starting on quite a beard, too. And so unfriendly that when I gave him a nudge he slapped my arm and said some very unkind words."

Her feet wavered in their path. Something was wrong with Grrake. His head hung low, eyes distant, not even the faintest of his usual smile or gentle expression. "Leave him be." His voice was even more tired than he looked. "He needs sleep. We'll leave a couple hours late."

Tarol sobered. Probably out of concern more for Grrake than for Yhkon. "Is he hurt? Other than those burns?"

"No, just..." Grrake trailed off, looking even more despondent than before.

Without further questions, Tarol simply sat down by the glowing embers of the previous night's fire. Talea continued walking, quieting her tread, more out of reverence for Grrake's affliction than everyone else's sleep. She sat down beside him. His grief was as tangible as if it were an ache in her own chest.

The other wards and the Wardens gradually began drifting out of their tents. The Wardens must have known the situation, probably having heard Yhkon return during the night or finding him in their tent in the morning, because none of them asked questions. The wards did, which she answered with the limited information she had. Grrake left not long after she woke, meandering away from the camp and out of sight. She noticed Larak frequently glancing the way he had gone, before eventually sighing and following him.

A breakfast of oatmeal and some dried fruit was made, eaten, and cleaned up as quietly as possible. Ahjul, Tarol, Resh, Haeric, and Gustor didn't seem entirely sure what to do with the wards in the absence of their three leaders. Eventually they decided to take them a ways off from the tent where Yhkon slept, and do some light training.

Grrake and Larak returned at nine o'clock, saying it was time to get going. Grrake was doing a better job of hiding his emotions, and took up his role as temporary leader. When instructions had been given, Talea moved to join Kae and Terindi in taking down their shelter, but Grrake's hand on her shoulder stopped her. "Talea, actually, would you go wake

Yhkon?"

The request sounded oddly similar to *"Would you go wake a hungry dragon?"* She squeezed her lower lip between her teeth, shooting a glance at the Warden's tent, the only one not yet being dismantled. "Okay, but why—"

"He and I argued last night," came the explanation, blunt, tired. "And he'll feel uncomfortable or uneasy with the other Wardens. Not with you."

It was probably supposed to be some sort of compliment, or privilege. *Talea the hungry dragon waker.* "Alright." She managed a small nod and smile for him and approached the dragon's lair.

Inside, Yhkon was something she'd never seen him: asleep. He had always woken at the slightest noise, or just been awake in the first place. Now, he was dead to the world. A blanket covered most of him, but his bare shoulders were exposed, allowing her to see the gruesomely blistered, fevered skin. Burns were somehow more upsetting than other wounds. If there hadn't been a knot in her stomach before, there was now.

She crouched next to him, trying to decide the best way to wake him. Verbally or by touch? *Oh just do it…* She said his name just above a whisper, her fingertips barely pressing on his arm. At a lack of response, she gave him a more substantial nudge.

He was sitting up and reaching for his sword before his eyes had even finished opening. "Wait, Yhkon, it's just me!" She gripped his arm even as she leaned backward instinctively.

His body relaxed, grimace slackening, and he more lethargically arranged himself in a sitting position to face her. He didn't look so different from Grrake, not only in their Sanonyan features but in countenance. Exhausted, tormented. His usually icy eyes were dull, looking more like an overcast sky, and bloodshot. Face haggard. It was still hard to believe he was only twenty-four, when he looked ten years older. A short beard, more facial hair than she'd ever seen on him, didn't help.

"You look beat," she said without thinking.

He didn't seem to mind. "I feel it."

"What…" She eyed his back. For some reason she felt nervous asking him how it happened. "Well, it's a little past nine, Grrake said we'd better get going."

Yhkon only nodded, rubbing a hand over his jaw, the beard making a scratchy sound. "I should have asked Grrake to wake me up in time to shave."

She flashed him a smirk. "Oh, you weren't just aiming for a caveman look?"

Her teasing earned the slightest of smiles. She stood up and, after a moment's hesitation, offered her hand. Rather to her surprise he accepted it, allowing her to help him to his feet. The movement made him wince. If the burns were even half as painful as they looked, it was no wonder. Not sure whether or not she should stay, Talea folded her hands behind her back and stood at the entrance of the tent while he painstakingly got into his shirt and gear. Before he did, she couldn't help noticing the collection of scars all over his upper body. One was large and gruesome on his stomach, maybe a stab wound. Others she suspected were from various sword fights. But some were strangely…orderly. In rows, or perfectly straight. How those would have occurred in a fight, she didn't know.

When he was ready, she held open the tarp flap for him with a smile. "We saved you some breakfast."

"Good," he put a hand to his midsection, though she couldn't tell if it was a display of hunger or if he was in pain, "I'm famished."

"Then hopefully it will taste better than it actually does. It's Larak's definition of oatmeal."

He peered at her sideways, one corner of his lips curling upward. "Mmhmm. Larak is actually a decent cook, as you know perfectly well…"

That was true. A playful reply that she knew was potentially risky was spilling off her tongue before she had time to mull it over. "Well, I was told you were being moody as a cold yuley this morning, and what have I got to defend myself but some humor?"

To her relief, his reaction was a smirk. "I believe a *lady* defends herself with her principles."

Talea feigned a sigh. "Too bad I'm no lady."

"Too bad indeed, considering I think I'm expected to bring you to Calcaria as one, yet I'm having no luck in getting you shaped up. Help me out, would you?"

She laughed, kneeling by the fire to dish out the rest of the oatmeal for him. He accepted the heaping bowl from her with a "thank you" and sat down to eat it, acting oblivious to the rest of the group that worked, or at least pretended to work, around them. It didn't take much observation to see that the wards and Wardens were giving their leader a wide berth until they were sure it was safe to approach.

Except Ahjul. Upon finishing what appeared to be a genuine task, he joined them, giving Yhkon a concerned smile. "I'm glad you're back! What happened? How'd you shake them? Tarol seemed to think you were injured."

"Nothing serious." Any merriment she had conjured up from him was dwindling. In its place, tension. *Even with Ahjul?* "I took down enough of the force and set loose their coliyes, so they couldn't chase me back."

Ahjul's head tilted slightly, eyebrows drawing together, as

if he were trying to see into Yhkon's mind to discover what was wrong. Clearly, whatever had happened at Yhkon's arrival during the night, Ahjul had not been involved. "Hey, I just wanted to say...I heard you and Grrake talking, some, when you got back. Not much, I just...well, you know he only wants—"

Or maybe he was involved.

Yhkon stood up, clutching the mostly empty bowl tightly. "Whatever you heard, I suggest you forget. Grrake had no business saying the things he did."

Talea cringed, seeing Grrake, only steps away, stop in his tracks. Yhkon must have sensed his presence, because he spun on his heel, as if ready to snap at the new prey—until he saw who it was. She thought there was a flash of regret. If there was, it was quickly swallowed by a hard frown, before he walked away to Eclipse.

~ ◆ ~

"Exactly how many times do I have to tell you that I *don't want to talk about it?*"

Talea recoiled from the rigid back of the man in front of her, brows drawing together and lips pursing. The rising frustration was what she wanted to respond with, but she spoke softly instead. "I just thought it might be a relief to, to, share it. Get it off your chest. I'm not trying to—"

"To what, pry into matters that don't concern you? Or oh, let me guess, you're just trying to help me. Fix me." He stopped a fidgety Eclipse without warning and dismounted, glaring up at her. "Here's some news for you: I don't want fixing, from you or anybody else. Everyone," he raised his already heated voice to address the rest of the group. "Get down, we're walking." He tossed Eclipse's reins in her lap and marched away, quickly pulling ahead of the others.

Talea remained in the saddle, motionless, watching him go. The wards and Wardens gradually passed her, some giving her questioning looks. Grrake looked at her for a long moment, expression strained, before hurrying to catch up with Yhkon.

Of course. Catch up with Yhkon. Cling to him like a loyal dog to an abusive owner.

Struggling to resist the hot stinging behind her eyes, she climbed down, taking the reins to lead Eclipse along at a plodding pace, at the back of the group. The group. Ki with Tarol, Kae with Haeric, Terindi with Ahjul, Rikky with Larak. Even Resh and Gustor walked together. The only ward without their Warden, was her.

It was then that she realized one person was missing. Wylan hadn't passed her. He was walking slightly back and to the side, head down and hands in pockets. *Me and Sir Secrecy. Though I suppose he's not the true secretive one around here.* He caught her watching him, and caught up to her. "Let me guess, he doesn't want to talk about it?"

The only response she could muster was a dry laugh. *Apparently someone has been observant.* They walked in silence. Mostly comfortable. Maybe she wished she were walking with her mother, or Brenly or Naylen, or her father, or Alili. But Wylan was a surprisingly good alternative.

Still, conversation might be better. "So have you heard anything about our soon-to-be newest recruit? Um, Skyve?"

A classic Sir Secrecy shrug. "That he's smart, has two little sisters, upper class."

That was all the more she'd learned of him either. Skyve Lagat, the seventh ward. Before she'd ruined his mood by so heinously invading his privacy with an unacceptable question about his childhood, Yhkon had told her they would be arriving at Skyve's city the next day. *Now I suppose I'll be lucky if he ever tells me anything again, after such an abominable intrusion...*Frowning to herself, she let her gaze return to Yhkon's distant figure. His irritated, brooding demeanor was still conspicuous. And Grrake, trailing a few paces behind him, broad shoulders drooping. How did the man have such an untiring patience? She knew he received much harsher retaliation from Yhkon than she did, and he'd been getting it for years, not just months. Yet he kept trying, and trying, never losing his temper. Grrake probably never, just for a moment, glared at the lead Warden's turned back and secretly thought that he was aloof, callous, even cruel, and undeserving of such compassion and support if he couldn't for one moment appreciate it, but rather spat in the faces of those who offered it.

She wanted to help him. She really did. But how could she? He resented it. The hostility it earned her wasn't something she could bear over and over again, for years, the way Grrake apparently could. Every time she thought they were making progress...every time she thought they were friends, that they could confide and trust in one another, he closed up and hurt her in the process.

Once, she'd thought that Yhkon reminded her of her father—both had a tendency to shut out the world, and not show their feelings, even to those closest to them. Now she realized that Loestin did so out of reserve. His distance had still hurt, but he'd never been harsh about it.

Yhkon, on the other hand, was brutal. He shut them all out, and attacked any attempt to help at the same time.

How could she possibly help him when he was so determined to remain unhappy? She couldn't think of a single time he'd smiled in the last week. Not since she'd woken him the morning after his return from the lance, and teased him. He had been sullen ever since and ignored all of her and Grrake's attempts to cheer him. And finally, when she'd asked simple, innocent questions about his childhood...he'd made it clear that they were not as good of friends as she'd imagined.

Wylan was her companion for the rest of the day's travels, joined intermittently by the other wards or Wardens. Yhkon kept to himself. When evening came and they all stopped to make camp, he was no longer angry that she could tell, just distant. Grrake kept trying to bridge the gap. She did not. She gave him as much space as possible.

Two days later, the lead Warden was finally relaxed, even pleasant. Especially toward her. As they neared Fesdor, Skyve's town, and it was acknowledged that she would be sent to talk to him first again, Yhkon even showed some sympathy and asked if she was alright with it.

In all, he seemed to be trying to make up to her.

Her first instinct was to accept it and forget about the previous conflict, and appreciate his efforts to put it right. Past experience, however, told her that as soon as she did that, he would just snap again.

They only rode for a few hours that day, before camping a few miles outside of Fesdor. From there, it was up to her, Resh, and Yhkon. The wards all wished her luck, Rikky with a grin that was somehow sweet and cocky at the same time. She climbed back into the saddle behind Yhkon, Resh riding beside them, and they set out at a trot.

Yhkon gave her instructions as they went. His tone was unusually, even unnaturally, bright and mild. *Still trying to make up.* Resh commented occasionally, usually with more specific details about Skyve or his circumstances.

"We would come into the town with you, but coming in Warden garb would make us too conspicuous, while coming without would be a risk since the Kaydorians may be on the look-out for me. You'll blend in a lot better. So," Yhkon concluded reluctantly, "it's up to you. But we'll be as close by as possible the entire time, just outside the city limits. Since Skyve's house is along the outskirts, we'll be within hearing distance, for the most part."

She wasn't sure whether or not that comforted her. All she did was nod, though Yhkon couldn't even see it.

"Alright," he stopped Eclipse, "this is as close as we can get."

They all three dismounted, the Wardens tying their mounts loosely enough that they could break free if needed. Yhkon faced her questioningly. Despite his neutral expression and light voice, she thought she could still see a shadow hiding in his eyes. "You ready? Clear on where to go?"

Another nod. When the remote answer seemed to trouble Yhkon, she swallowed and brightened her own expression. "Yeah. See you guys soon." Conscious of their lingering gazes, she walked away quickly, wishing she could be in the pants, shirt, and jacket that were so much warmer and more comfortable than a long-sleeve smock with only a shawl that had seen better days. It had been chilly all day, dreary, heavy gray clouds preventing even the soft warmth of sunshine.

A few minutes later, she was entering the outskirts of Fesdor. So far, it appeared to be a relaxed, gangly sort of town, not cramped and tight like Boroe or even Castown. Houses and shops were far apart, in no particular pattern, wooden or brick or stone or even sod, of all shapes and sizes. The people weren't much different. It was an Irlaish holiday that most of Zentyre celebrated, Emasvao, meaning almost everyone was home from work or school.

Large enough that a stranger could enter without suspicion, the town surprised her with a sense of hospitality. Passersby smiled or waved or tipped their hats. No one knew who she was, or what she was doing. To them she was just another person, a girl. Not Eun, Leader of the Eight. Just Talea.

A frown made her bite her tongue and duck her head. The eager whine of a dog caught her attention just before she saw a butcher's shop, with a sign outside that had "*Hasem's*" painted in fat letters. *Turn left at Hasem's butcher shop.* More than one stray dog hovered about the bloodstained shop. A small man with contrastingly large features, wearing a red-streaked apron with a knife in one hand and a slab of raw meat in the other, waved at her with the slab of meat. She smiled back despite herself, before lowering her head again and veering down the street to the left.

Skyve's house wasn't too deep into the city. Apparently upper class usually lived along the outskirts, where they could have more room and prettier views. By the time she recognized the neighborhood Resh had described, a light rain was falling from the laden clouds above. It dampened her thin clothing all too quickly.

Walking among grand houses, even mansions, of stone or brick, she felt more and more out of place. The only real experience she'd had with upper class and nobility was working as a maid in Lord Vissler's household.

Talea peered to either side of her, moving her head as little as possible. Were Yhkon and Resh watching her? The woods were in sight, but a long ways off. A tingling pressure on the nape of her neck remained all the same. *106. Just find the house, talk to Skyve, and get back. 106.* She focused her attention on the numbers painted on the doors of each towering house. *104, 105…106.* It was much like the others: big, luxurious. Intimidating. There weren't people out and about in the upper class neighborhood, like there were in the rest of Fesdor.

Lest the Wardens were watching her, she didn't allow herself any hesitation. Stepping up to the door, she knocked three times, and waited.

It opened moments later, to a young woman in a dress as simple as Talea's, topped with a clean apron. A maid. The apparel, the tired, expectant expression, the glimmer of restraint in her eyes—it was all uncomfortably familiar.

"Yes?" The maid's polite voice snapped her from her daze.

"Uh hi, I'm looking for Skyve Lagat?"

"Master Skyve is away with Miss Anber and Miss Glisi."

His little sisters, no doubt. "Where to, um, if I may? I need to speak to him."

The woman's eyes narrowed, but she replied courteously enough. "Shopping, for the misses. All I know is they were going to The Curled Dragon for lunch."

"Oh." Maybe she could still use the information. "The Curled Dragon…could you remind me where that is?"

"Innermost southern side, by the smithy."

"Thank you, I appreciate it." With a nod to the maid, Talea descended the porch steps and walked back the way she'd come. No doubt she was supposed to find Yhkon and Resh, relay the information, and they'd return later.

But her feet carried her deeper into the town, south as the maid had said. All the while telling herself it was foolish, she didn't even know what Skyve looked like. All the while wondering how upset Yhkon was, probably watching her as she walked away.

With the rain still falling, she was wet through by the time she found The Curled Dragon, with the help of more specific directions from a passerby. Keeping to the corners and walls, she entered the diner, scanning the customers. No teenage boy with two little girls.

Back in the rain, Talea inwardly lectured herself. She ought to go back. What good was it for her to wander around a strange town, cold and wet, looking for someone she wouldn't even be able to recognize?

Yet she kept going. She didn't want to go back.

A dress shop caught her attention, the fancy gowns in the window making it clear that it was upper class and nobility that shopped there. But Skyve was taking his little sisters shopping, wasn't he? Anyway, it would be shelter from the rain. Talea slipped inside, immediately intrigued by the vivid colors, sparkling jewels, and elegant lace that surrounded her. There wasn't a single dress anything like the sort she wore. They were all brighter, fancier, more flattering. What would it be like to wear such ornate finery every day? To walk into such a shop and buy whatever caught her fancy?

Well, according to Yhkon's idea of Calcaria and the status she would have there, one day she would know what it was like.

The excited squeal of a little girl came from somewhere else in the shop. "Oh, Anber, come see this one!"

Anber? Talea moved toward the voice, until she saw two girls admiring child-sized dresses fit for a queen. Dark hair, dark eyes, tan skin. They were Irlaish. As was the teenager who approached shortly after she did, eyes black and glinting, thin lips in a sort of impatient smirk. "Of course you two would like the most expensive shop best."

The older of the pair grinned at him. "Doesn't Mother say that you get what you pay for?"

Talea edged backward. Resh had said Skyve was mostly Irlaish, and looked the part. With two little sisters, by the names of Anber and Glisi. Could it be him?

She idled nearby, remaining discreet, until the boy wandered away from his sisters with no particular path, sighing. With a deep breath, she caught up to him. "Um, Skyve?"

He turned around. Those black eyes swept over her in a single, calculating glance that seemed to note every detail and analyze it. The conclusion his calculations came to didn't seem to be positive, based on his deepening frown. "Yes?"

As if the situation weren't awkward and daunting enough, without him glowering so critically at her. "Sorry, but you are Skyve Lagat?"

"I am." His head tilted slightly. Not curiously, not in an endearing way like Rikky. Rather, suspiciously. "Who are you?"

"I'm Talea." She swallowed. "I'm sorry about uh, this, but, well..." Unsure how else to proceed, she stuck out her hand for him to shake.

He looked at it, then at her, without saying anything or making any move to reciprocate. Finally, with a slow, lazy sort of blink, his expression lost its suspicion. "I'm assuming something *unique* will happen if I take your hand."

Hopefully she didn't look as stunned as she felt. "Um, well—"

"You're obviously a laborer. And you must know I'm upper class. There would be no other logical reason for you to so boldly introduce yourself, unless you were some form of mentally unstable, and while you're not exactly astounding me with your wit, it's fairly obvious you're sane. So my natural conclusion is that if I touch your hand," he abruptly grabbed her hand, observing the flurry of sparks with interest but no surprise, "something like this would happen."

After another moment of gawking at him, she narrowed her eyes, and snapped her mouth shut only to open it, tone nearly matching his with sarcasm. "Alright then, Mr. Upper Class." Probably better to be humored by his bluntness, and play along, than be offended. "I'm sure you know, then, that it's because I've got the ability too."

"Of course. Are there eight of us?"

How exactly did you pull that fact out of thin air? "Yes…" She shrugged in acceptance of his intuition. "They said you were smart." *Let me guess, "I assume 'they' are…"*

"I assume 'they' are some warriors, perhaps, assigned to protect us. Or maybe more generally, the—"

She jumped in. "No, your first guess was right. They're called the Wardens, they call us wards, there's one of them for each of us."

"I take it you're the *leader* of us wards, in some capacity."

Oh good, let's just jump straight into it. "Supposedly. You figured that, how…?"

"Well," he wasn't even looking at her anymore, "why else would they send you? Come on, let's get my sisters and go to my house, where we can talk privately."

Wow. She didn't let even a hint of indignation or hurt enter her appearance, lest he notice and take some cruel satisfaction from it. Then again, she had the feeling that his keen perception wouldn't necessarily extend towards the subtle mannerisms of human emotion. She could probably burst into tears and he would suspect a physical injury as the cause.

Anber and Glisi, upon being introduced to Talea and being told she was going home with them, had different reactions. Anber, the older, gave Skyve a sly look, and said, "So are you two *friends*…?" Skyve looked like he might literally gag at the insinuation.

Glisi, on the other hand, puckered her brow as she took in Talea's appearance. "Isn't she a laborer?"

Talea swallowed, breaking eye contact with the little girl.

Skyve's reply surprised her more than anything he had said thus far. "You say something that snobbish again, Glisi, and you'll get to try doing the maid's duties for a week. Talea is *not* a laborer, and even if she were that gives you no right to be so foolishly haughty. Understood?"

"Yeah," Glisi mumbled it under her breath.

"Speak up. And, you owe Ms. Talea an apology."

With a huff, Glisi lifted her chin and spoke clearly. "Yes, I understand. And I'm sorry, Ms. Talea, for my rudeness."

Talea cleared her throat, painfully aware of the wide gap between her etiquette and appearance, and theirs. "That's alright."

The four of them left the shop. The rain was heavier. Talea hunched her shoulders, prepared for the half mile long walk through the wet to their house, but Skyve didn't leave the shelter of the dress shop's canopy. Confused, she waited, not willing to ask what he was doing—the rain showed no signs of stopping anytime soon—lest it make her appear even more the ignorant laborer.

She didn't have long to wait for the explanation. A coliye drawn carriage across the street approached them. The driver jumped out, a large umbrella in hand, and held it over the heads of the girls as he helped them, then Skyve and Talea, into the carriage. She climbed inside hesitantly, hoping it wouldn't be too conspicuous by her fumbling or expression that she had never been in so much as a wagon, let alone a lavish vehicle such as this.

It took only a few minutes for them to arrive at the Lagat's stately home. It was even more impressive inside, not much different than Lord Vissler's mansion. Apparently upper class lived almost as royally as nobility.

The maid seemed rather uncertain about Talea's admittance when she was so clearly of the lower class, but she played her part with perfect courtesy. Skyve quickly dismissed her and the girls to leave them in private. Talea felt somehow less uncomfortable, once it was just the two of them. And the conversation was easier with him than it had been with the other wards—he asked the questions, many of which he already had an accurate guess as to the answer of. Nothing she said phased him, as if it was all as he'd expected. When she reluctantly breached the topic of Narone and prophecies, he nodded as if it were only natural that they should be prophesied by Narone, and when he noticed her skepticism, he looked at her like she was silly. Though she suspected he gave that look to a lot of people.

They only talked for ten minutes or so, before Skyve apparently found her knowledge inadequate and asked if they could go talk to the Wardens. With Anber and Glisi contentedly trying on their new clothes and playing, they left the house and made for the edge of the city. It was an awkward walk. Skyve trailed a few paces behind her for most of it, occasionally asking a question, but otherwise making it clear he'd rather they keep in their separate spaces. At least the rain had stopped.

As she'd hoped, Yhkon and Resh were waiting in the woods nearest them. She could tell almost at first glance that Yhkon was not pleased.

The two Wardens made their introductions. Skyve allowed time for the necessary formalities only, before launching into further interrogation, or just pondering aloud his suspicions and waiting for confirmation. Talea tried to remain involved in the conversation, tried to avoid Yhkon's penetrating gaze...it didn't work. "Skyve, please excuse us a moment. Talea, if you would come with me." Without waiting for acknowledgement, he was walking away, gait stiff. Gnawing her lower lip, she had little choice but to follow.

A stone's throw from Resh and Skyve, Yhkon whirled around to glare at her. "What were you doing back there?"

As tempting as it was to coyly pretend she didn't know what he meant, she just met his gaze as calmly as she could. "I asked the maid where Skyve was at, she gave me a general idea, I decided to see if I could find him."

"You were supposed to go to the house, and come back if he wasn't there. You know that perfectly well. We had no idea where you were going, or how long you'd be there. You could have been attacked and we never would have known." His icy eyes were more intense than usual.

Talea rubbed her thumb tightly against her fingers, taking a steadying breath. She should apologize. Admit it had been foolish of her. Push the conflict behind them. Instead her fists were clenching. "I can take care of myself, as *you* know perfectly well. And I found him, didn't I? I don't..." Another deep breath. "I don't think it's fair to act as though I—"

"As though you what?" His voice had abruptly gained volume and heat. "Had directly disobeyed me, and done something foolish? Well you did! I didn't expect such from *you*."

Her lips parted, throat constricting. A slap to the face wouldn't have hurt more. Cheeks flushing, hands trembling, she met his glare. "Because you've given me so much reason to obey your every word? Never bitten my head off over a simple question, never stormed off in a rage or done something reckless!" She let as much venom as she could muster taint the words. It was better than crying, which was what she wanted to do. "Forgive me for ever doing something on my own without consulting you first, oh, but maybe I don't consult you because I expect to be eaten alive if I do!"

His expression contorted with a mixture of indignation and confusion. "What does this have to do with me?! This is—"

She cut him off before she even knew what she was going to say, heart racing and blood hot. "It has everything to do with it! You're my *Warden,* well alright I get it—my bad for thinking we could be friends, or anything so foolish as that! Since all you do is shove me away and throw your temper tantrums and—"

He leaned forward, broad shoulders poised threateningly, his lip curled and eyes flashing with ridicule. "Oh, I see...you thought I was supposed to be your plaything, your perfect little guardian angel that did as you pleased and told you bedtime stories and bowed to your every wish."

The quiver in her hands had increased, as had the hot, stinging pressure in her eyes. *Don't you dare cry.* "That's not...I thought...I thought we could be friends." She hated how dejected she sounded. "At least I was willing to try. But you..." She balled her fists again, to keep them from shaking. "You clearly couldn't care less how I or anyone else feels, and you clearly don't value any level of friendship. I can't just...just pretend you've never snapped at me for no reason, or...or..." She trailed off, looking away, blinking rapidly against the gathering tears.

Some degree of remorse softened his glare. "Look..." He swallowed hard, his Adam's apple jerking up and down as he looked away too. "I do value your friendship. And I guess I shouldn't have said that. But..." He crossed his arms tightly over his chest, dissolving his previously threatening countenance. There was a long pause. "Can we just...forget all this? Move on?"

Talea lifted her head to stare at him. The urge to cry was rapidly fading. *Just move on?* She knew if she stayed, she'd say something she'd later regret. Biting her tongue and making herself glower at the ground instead of him, she spun and walked away, back toward the celiths.

"Talea?" At first, he sounded only perplexed. Then irritated. "Talea! Listen to me. Talea." She heard his footsteps, seconds before he grabbed her arm. Emotion surged like a tide from the rock in her stomach to a hot pain in her chest. With it came the familiar, tingling warmth in her veins. She felt herself reaching out to shove him off, felt the warmth gathering in her fingertips. Her mind stilled. *No.*

Her hand met his chest, just as she willfully forced the energy to recede. She could tell by the way he recoiled that there had still been a small shock. It couldn't have been too severe—there was more incredulity than pain in his expression. Perhaps it was for the best, since he didn't attempt to follow her again.

13
A Game of Two

Yhkon returned to where Resh and Skyve stood, muscles still rigid with frustration. He felt all too aware of Talea's presence, probably watching him, from where she was sulking by the celiths.

Looking up, he was surprised to find Resh rolling his eyes and Skyve frowning in Talea's direction. "'Move on'?" Resh gave him a disapproving sneer. "Really?"

"You heard all that?"

"Considering you were both shouting?" Skyve's expression was similar to Resh's. "Yes, we did."

"And *move on*? Seriously?" Resh repeated.

Yhkon crossed his arms. "Yes, so? I was trying to—"

Resh gave a dramatic sigh of exasperation, shaking his head. "No, no, no, and *no* some more. That ain't how it works, pal."

He scowled. "How what works? And what do you know about it?"

"More than you apparently." Resh quirked an eyebrow. "Women don't *move on*. They just don't. Better that you get that through your skull as soon as possible. They wanna talk about it, and accuse you of all sorts of terrible crimes against them, then graciously accept your apology, cry on your shoulder, eventually make a sniffling apology of their own, and probably end with a hug."

Skyve snorted with disgust. Yhkon realized a little too late that he had wrinkled his nose. Resh sighed even heavier and rolled his eyes heavenward. "I am standing in the company of two of the most ignorant men in Kameon, when it comes to women."

"Well," he exhaled heavily, "what's your suggestion, since you apparently know all there is to know?"

"I told you. You have to talk about it. Sentiment, chap." Resh gave him a clap on the shoulder. "Sentiment is the key. Women love it. Well," he gave a shrug, as if in an afterthought, "you might try not being a jerk, too."

Yhkon was about to make an indignant reply, only to be surprised by Skyve's voice. "You remember I'm still here? Maybe we should just arrange another meeting. My parents will probably want to hear all of this from your lips."

"Oh." Yhkon shook his head, as if he could as easily clear it of the puzzle that was his ward. "Right. Of course. And I'm sorry about all this, ah, drama. Tomorrow, perhaps?"

"Tomorrow would be fine. My parents are off work early tomorrow, at two."

"Then Talea will be at your house just past then."

Skyve nodded, before extending his hand first to Resh, then Yhkon. He looked Talea's direction, as if considering how obligated he was to make a similarly courteous farewell to her. Apparently distaste overruled obligation. "If you ask me," he said, already turned to leave, "women love sentiment a little too much. I don't see that it ever got anyone anywhere useful. I'm on your side," he said to Yhkon.

For some reason, Yhkon didn't find that particularly gratifying.

Resh swore with vexation. It seemed to disconcert Skyve—no doubt the upper class and nobility he was used to had better manners—but Resh only grumbled, "You're both blasted idiots. I never thought I of all men would be the one to sappily defend the virtue of a woman's tenderness. Be off with you, for goodness sake."

With nothing more than a skeptical frown, Skyve dipped his head to them and left. When he was gone, Yhkon found Resh glaring at him again. At his questioning look, Resh only muttered something inaudible and started toward the celiths.

Reluctantly, Yhkon followed, grasping for what to say to Talea when he got there. Sentiment? What was he supposed to do that was sentimental? He could apologize, for whatever it was he'd done, but she ought to as well. Maybe they both just needed a little space, before figuring it out. Or she needed space, anyway. He would have been happy to resolve the issue and leave it in the past earlier.

He arrived determined to make a vague apology and suggest they discuss it more later, but never got even the first word off his tongue.

Talea, not so much as glancing at him, walked straight up to Resh with a smile. "Resh, can I ride with you?"

At Resh's initial uncertainty, Yhkon thought the man was going to be helpful for once and turn her down. "But of course," he replied instead, with all the brazen charm that he was so good at. "I'm always happy to offer a ride to a fair maiden." When he winked, and Talea grinned in return, Yhkon was too furious to get an objection out of his mouth.

The ride back to camp in no way helped. Talea chattered and giggled and downright flirted, while of course Resh reciprocated happily—the scoundrel—the entire time. Neither of them so much as acknowledged his existence.

He knew, without a doubt, that Talea had no real interest in Resh's charm. If anything she was usually wary of him, as she ought to be. Which meant she was only putting on a show as revenge.

Well, if that was how she wanted it to be, then two could play at that game.

~◆~

The ride back to camp couldn't have ended soon enough. Bantering with Resh, when all she wanted to do was go into her room and lock the door, was exhausting. The hurt look Yhkon flashed her at the beginning of the ride nearly crumbled her bitterness, tempting her to stop the charade and give him another chance. His resolved glare that followed, however, only reaffirmed that another chance wouldn't do any good.

So, she bantered.

And when they arrived at camp, Talea accepted Resh's help getting down, before doing the next best thing to what she wanted: going into the girl's tent and sitting down on her bed. She caught a glimpse of Yhkon's retreating figure through the opening, Grrake starting to follow, until Yhkon said something that must have dissuaded him. She squeezed her eyes shut. *Don't come in here, don't come in here, don't come in here...*

"Talea?" It was Grrake.

Ignoring the urge to scream, she got up and ducked out from inside the shelter.

He searched her face with worry. "Did something happen?"

Subtle sarcasm dripped off her tongue unbidden. "Oh, well why didn't you ask Yhkon?"

By the immediate change in his countenance, the true feeling behind the words had not gone unnoticed. He moved closer, lowering his voice to allow for a more private exchange. "Did he...what happened?"

She inhaled deeply through her nose, not making eye contact. "I um...I'd rather not talk about it. I'm sorry." Escaping before he could respond, she went to where Ahjul and Terindi sat. They were whittling on chunks of wood. "What are you uh, making?" She resisted the temptation to look back and see if Grrake had followed. No footsteps.

"What are we making, or what are we *trying* to make?" Ahjul gave her a friendly smile. "A bird. I like whittling, but I can't claim I was ever very good at it."

He held up his project. It was nothing impressive, but it was perfectly recognizable as the shape of a bird. Terindi's a little less so. "Oh, well, I think it looks nice. Can I try?"

Ahjul obliged her with a knife and a piece of wood. She set at it with more vigor than necessary, too uptight to constrain her movements to delicate strokes. After a few minutes of silence save the rhythmic shaving of the wood, the tension began easing out of her muscles. Yhkon had vanished, no doubt to brood in the forest alone as was his custom. That was a relief. The other wards and Wardens were engaged in a variety of occupations, she didn't take the time to speculate on what. It was just Ahjul and Terindi beside her, perhaps some of the most pleasant, soothing company available. It wasn't home or her family, which was what she really wanted, but it was something.

All relaxation withered as she saw Grrake approaching in her peripheral vision. Her strokes became harsh and choppy again.

"Talea..." He sat down, slowly, beside her. "Please tell me

what happened. I want to help."

"I know you do." It came out more accusatory than it was meant to. There was no stopping the returning emotion now. "I know how much you want to help Yhkon. Or have me help him. But I..." Her voice cracked. She bit her lip until it hurt, finally meeting his anxious, hazel eyes. "I'm sorry, Grrake, but I can't."

His aging features sagged. "Are you sure..." He clasped and unclasped his hands. "I know he can be, well, difficult. Even...harsh. But maybe if..."

She stood up, dropping her brutalized block of wood. "I told you," she felt her nails digging into her palms, eyes stinging again, "I can't."

Grrake got up too, forehead creased with apparent grief. At first she thought he would try again, would ask her to just give Yhkon another chance...but he didn't. He only hung his head and walked away. That was almost worse.

When she tiredly sat back down and returned to whittling, wishing she could so easily make it appear as though nothing had happened, Ahjul tentatively asked if she was alright. All she could muster was an unconvincing nod. She could tell he almost asked what had happened, multiple times, but he never did. Terindi didn't say a word, though her pale eyes sought Talea's with empathy and concern. Talea hoped they knew she was grateful. They all went back to whittling, silent at first, before eventually Ahjul started some light and sporadic conversation, that required very little investment on her part and was simply calming.

The calm didn't last for long.

"Everyone up," came Yhkon's voice. "We're doing some training. Talea," he addressed her without so much as a glance, "you can begin the supper preparations. Also brush Eclipse, if you please."

Everyone looked to him, than her. It was all too blatant. He never refused the opportunity to train to one of the wards, and he almost never asked one of them to take on the task of supper without any assistance. Since he stood there waiting, however, none of them had any choice but to do as told or risk his wrath.

With sympathetic looks, Ahjul and Terindi left. Grrake went to Yhkon and whispered something to him. The mocking reply was not whispered. "Oh, were you elected to replace me as lead Warden in my absence? No? Then I think it's my word that stands."

Talea felt a new sort of heat in her blood. No tears. No remorse, no desire for amends. It had only been a few minutes ago that she had been wishing Grrake would leave her alone…but she would never so viciously abuse and humiliate him. None of them would. Only Yhkon would do that. And not even blink at the heartbroken flinch from the older Warden that resulted.

She stood up with fury hot in her cheeks. While everyone else began their training, Yhkon acting as an unnecessary supervisor, she set to her assigned chores. Gather wood, start a fire. Wrangle together the ingredients for a simple stew, all in a large pot to simmer over the flames. While it warmed, she found a comb and set to work on Eclipse's sleek hide, brushing until not a fleck of dirt remained, nor a single hair out of place. Since the stew still wasn't ready by the time she finished, she brushed Lenjeya, then Ahjul's celith.

The meal was a silent, awkward affair, with little said beyond Yhkon's declaration that they would continue training afterward. Since he didn't give Talea any separate orders, it was probably his intent to train with her, as well.

It was not her intent to train with him.

She did more than her fair share of cleaning up after dinner. But the moment the wards started dispersing to their Wardens, she practically darted to where Resh was sharpening a knife. "Resh, Ahjul says you're the best at hand-to-hand combat, of all the Wardens. Would you train with me tonight? I'm sure Yhkon won't mind."

Even if Resh made no particular display of it, they both knew that Yhkon *would* mind. Thankfully, though, he only grinned. "Ahjul tells the truth. Come on, let's find a spot with some room."

Letting Resh teach her hand-to-hand, with all the close-up interaction it required, would perhaps have been uncomfortable under different circumstances. As things were, she was happy to let him take her in a pretend choke hold, or guide her hands with his own through maneuvers, because seething jealousy was written all over Yhkon's face even as he pretended not to notice. Besides, Resh was a surprisingly pleasant and helpful teacher. More so than Yhkon, who was often too detached or moody to put in much effort.

By the time night had fallen and they all went to bed, it had been hours since she had even spoken to the lead Warden. The longer she could keep it that way, the better.

The Wardens let them sleep late the next morning. No one had anywhere to be until after noon, anyway. After breakfast had been cleared away, Talea knew it wouldn't be long before Yhkon ordered more training. Resh and Gustor were going hunting, meaning she would have no choice but to train with Yhkon.

She sprinted to catch up with the leaving Wardens. "Hey, um, could I tag along, maybe?"

After looking at her with raised eyebrows, they exchanged a thoughtful look between them. "Think he'll flay our hides for it?" Resh asked.

Gustor shrugged. "He can try," was all he said, before continuing into the forest. Taking that and Resh's smile as permission, she trailed behind them.

They stayed out for three hours. She suspected Gustor and Resh were keeping her—and themselves, for that matter—away from Yhkon as long as possible. She was no help to their hunting, having almost no practice with a bow, but she had at least mastered stealth well enough to not impede them. There was almost no conversation. It was a welcome silence.

When they finally returned to camp, Gustor and Resh sent her ahead with the game while they dealt with Yhkon. She could hear his angry voice, even if she couldn't make out the words. Gustor and Resh, as far as she could tell, didn't reply at all. They just let him rant.

He didn't say a word to Talea.

While he was saddling Eclipse for the imminent trip, Talea steeled herself and approached Grrake where he sat, doing nothing. His shoulders were stooped, movements sluggish. Seeing her, his eyes became all the more forlorn. "I'm sorry, Talea, for whatever he said or did. I really am."

Releasing the breath she'd been holding, she sat down next to him. "It's not your fault, and I'm sorry for how I acted yesterday. You didn't deserve that. But…I have a favor to ask."

He looked up, almost eagerly, waiting.

"I…I was hoping you might come with us." She rubbed her thumb up and down her index finger. "If he and I argue again, it won't be a good first impression for Skyve's parents, and anyway I…well, I can ride with Resh there but if Skyve comes back I couldn't…and I just…"

Grrake was nodding, almost with relief. "You're right. Of course. I'll come, and you can ride with me both ways. I'll go tell him."

Talea observed the encounter anxiously, far enough that she couldn't hear what was said. Yhkon's irritation was still evident. Why should it bother him? Surely he had no more desire to share a saddle with her than she had. It wasn't a long discussion, however. Grrake came back and said only that he was coming, and they'd best get ready.

Unlike that of the earlier hunting trip, the silence of the ride to Fesdor was unbearable. Though she hadn't even been given specific instructions, the moment the celiths were stopped, she dismounted and walked alone toward the town, unwilling to breach the silence and ask. Let alone ask Yhkon.

A light drizzle that had started shortly after they set out became a downpour as she reached Skyve's home. Picking a strand of wet hair from her cheek, she knocked on the door and waited, fidgeting. The maid answered, letting her in and leading her into the library.

There, three people awaited her. Skyve, standing tall, poised and proper, black eyes scrutinizing everything, just like the previous day. An intimidating man of even darker, more intent features than Skyve's, whose passive frown became more of a scowl when he saw her. And a small woman, with a blank stare. She was wearing cosmetics, something Talea had only seen on the Vissler ladies, but the dark powder on her eyelids was smudged, adding to her flagging appearance.

Skyve's parents. Mr. Lagat with his stern, permanent glare, Mrs. Lagat with the far-off, glassy look. Talea wished she could melt into the floor. She'd prefer to be in a cramped, dim haliop with dirt floors, among people of her own sort, than in these grand surroundings with people that looked at her as if she were a foreigner.

It was Mr. Lagat that finally spoke, hardly in a way that eased the tension. "You didn't say she was a laborer."

Talea's cheeks flushed.

Skyve, to his credit, smoothed matters as best he could. "Father, please, you mustn't be so rude. Talea was *born* among the lower class, and may be dressing the part now, but she is not a laborer. In Calcaria, she is one of the highest ranking among the San Quawr." He shot her a look that said she'd better fill the exaggerated picture he'd just painted of her.

If the frigid formality was a result of their class, Talea decided she was happy to miss out on all the luxuries. Middle class, perhaps, was the best of both worlds. Not starving but not so...*uppity*. Taking a deep breath, she thought of the way Grrake spoke, with his refinement and courtesy common to the Sanonyans, and did her best to imitate it. "I am sorry to be interrupting you in these circumstances, I know it's all rather peculiar."

The man's cynical air lessened, even if none of his general hardness did. "I see. Where are these *Wardens*, then?"

Oh, curse her laborer's dress, soaked hair, and simple looks. She knew it would take an elegant gown like Mrs. Lagat wore and flawlessly styled hair to truly convince them she was anything more than a peasant. *Not that I am anything more.* "They are waiting in the forest half a mile outside the city. We can go there, if you wish."

Mr. Lagat's frown deepened. "Walk out to the woods to meet them as if we were criminals exchanging stolen goods? Why do they not come here? They would be welcome," he added, with the slightest of nods to Talea. Probably the extent of the kindness she would receive from him.

"In this weather?" was Mrs. Lagat's only reply. Her face

was that of a woman aged beyond her years, tired, lined with worry, her eyes still holding that dazed quality.

Skyve's own black eyes sparked with irritation and impatience, but his voice remained as cool as ever. "As San Quawr and rebels toward Kaydor's imposed rule, coming into public is dangerous for them. It would be better to meet out of sight of prying eyes."

"Very well." Mr. Lagat fetched a coat for himself and a cloak for his wife. "We'll take the carriage to the outskirts of the city, and walk from there."

The carriage ride wasn't much better than the celith ride with the Wardens had been. At least there was some conversation—Mr. Lagat sporadically interrogated Talea, though he already knew a great deal about the situation, since Skyve had told them of his abilities years ago and since then of his various speculations, and then had conveyed to them everything she had told him.

There was also the matter of the weather. The rain had turned to snow, which perhaps would have been better, except she was already soaked. Even in the carriage she couldn't keep from shivering. When they got out to walk the rest of the way, her teeth were chattering, fingers and toes quickly growing numb.

By the time they reached the Wardens, she didn't have any more interaction in her. Leaving Resh to greet the Lagats, she went straight to Lenjeya, slipping her aching hands between the saddle blanket and the mare's warm hide. Her whole body shook with another chill, a slight breeze biting at the exposed skin of her face and neck.

Yhkon had left the group and was approaching her. Hesitantly, stopping every few paces, but still approaching. Dealing with him sounded about as pleasant as an ice bath.

She made eye contact, held it for just a moment, then purposely moved to Lenjeya's other side, putting the celith between them.

He took the hint. Retreating back to the Lagats and Wardens, he said something to Grrake, then reentered the discussion, while Grrake joined her instead.

"Your clothes are damp." He pinched her sleeve, giving her a sympathetic frown. "No wonder you're cold. Here," he dug around in his saddlebags, pulling out a cloak and draping it around her shoulders. It was far too big for her, considering Grrake's size compared to hers, but it was warm. "Can I see your hands?"

Talea reluctantly removed them from under the saddle blanket. Grrake took them in his own hands and rubbed them back and forth briskly, the friction easing some of the chill. "There you go, now put them back under." When she had thanked him and done so, he turned partially to look at the Lagats, Yhkon, and Resh. "How did it go?"

"Alright, I guess." She let her eyes drift shut, for just a moment, a sudden tiredness weighting every muscle in her body. If only she could be home, sitting on grass that sparkled with dew, enjoying the sunshine on a summer morning, listening to birds sing. Or curled up on the old sofa in their haliop, reading a book, talking with her mother. Even rushing about the tiny kitchen preparing a meager meal, to be eaten with her family all at the table. Together.

She cleared her throat. "They're not the most friendly people, especially to lower class."

Grrake's condoling frown returned. "I think they are kinder than they appear, but it's difficult to look past their arrogance and disdain for those they consider to be beneath them. I'm sorry you had to see it."

Oh, what of it? She could deal with haughty upper class turning their noses up at her much easier than contempt and cruelty from someone that was supposed to be her friend and mentor. So what if Skyve's parents thought her no better than a stray dog. It was Yhkon's enmity she couldn't stand.

And as far as she could tell, unless something drastically changed, she would have to stand it for some time to come.

14

Arrows

A sigh escaped Kaydor's lips as he drummed his fingers against his temple. "I think I must be missing something here. You had the man, tied and guarded. You were in the middle of torturing him for information. And he just…got away?"

Dejer's discomfort was tangible, even if he had more pride than the average soldier and kept his fear in check. "It was hardly that simple, but…yes. He's remarkably skilled, even if he is just an arrogant boy, and I can't exactly say that about most of the men in that lance."

Arrogant boy. No, unfortunately, there was nothing about him that was boyish or brazen, even if he was young. It was difficult to even blame Dejer for his escape, when Kaydor knew from personal experience how hard to beat the kid was. "Well. Did you get anything from him, for your efforts?"

"Only his name: Yhkon Tavker."

So that was the name of the boy, now a man, that in a way had haunted Kaydor for fifteen years. "Yhkon Tavker. I would demote you for such a failure, except I know for myself that the man is cunning." He rose slowly, hand lingering on the arm of his throne for a moment. "Instead I intend to give you all the resources you need to bring him and his companions before me in shackles. But if you fail me this time, I will hardly be so forgiving."

Dejer inclined forward in a bow. "Understood, Your Majesty. What would you like me to do?"

"Fetch my nephew, first."

"Excuse me?"

Kaydor eyed him sideways. "I wish for his input as we make our plans on apprehending these rebels. Is that a problem?"

Dejer made little effort to conceal his distaste. "No, I simply don't see the benefit of his presence. If I needed to know how to work at a sawmill perhaps—"

Silencing the man's impudent speech with a threatening glare was undeniably satisfying. "You will fetch my nephew, and you will never question an order of mine again."

Without another word, Dejer nodded and was gone. It didn't take him long to return, a curious Zoper in tow. Zoper was never far, now—Kaydor kept him training and learning as often as possible.

"Zoper." He spread his arm out in a welcoming gesture. "The band of rebels I've told you of—they've become a headache I'd like to be rid of. Their leader is a man named Yhkon Tavker, he's not much older than you but he's a powerful enemy. I sent Dejer with a lance of seventy men to capture them a few weeks ago, and despite catching Yhkon— briefly, anyway—he came back empty handed. What do you think we should do, to ensure that this time, the hunt is successful?"

He watched his nephew's face, seeing the initial confusion, followed by uncertainty, before Zoper shrugged and began working the problem. Someday, hopefully, there would be no uncertainty or nonchalance. For now it was good enough.

"Well…" And perhaps someday he could break his nephew of his habitual use of the word *well*. "I suppose if seventy wasn't enough to take down even the one guy, it's going to take quite a lot to take them all down. And the more you send the more likely your success. Since you have more than enough minions idling about getting drunk…"

Leave it to Zoper to never take anything seriously.

"Send a whole army. They'll have no chance against that. Their celiths are faster than most of ours, right? Then with a large enough force, we can box them in, to make sure they don't simply outrun us."

Kaydor smiled, clapping his nephew on the shoulder. "I knew you would make me proud. We'll do exactly as you've said. Dejer, take, oh…how about a thousand foot soldiers, and however many calvary you need?"

"A thousand?" Dejer looked at him like he was crazy.

He replied sharply. "What did I just say about not questioning my orders? Go and get it done." He returned to his throne, mindlessly rubbing his jaw. Yhkon Tavker would be hard pressed to get away this time.

~ ♦ ~

Skyve was welcomed into the group easily. He wasn't exactly friendly but he was polite enough and rather likeable for his straightforwardness. His interest was mostly in what sorts of things the other wards had learned to do with the electricity with practice, how being together seemed to increase their abilities. With the Wardens, he wanted to know all about Calcaria, from the economy, to the military, to the living conditions.

Talea had little to contribute, once Skyve's focus had been taken off their abilities. Before long, it was only Resh and Grrake he was talking to, leaving the rest of them as idle spectators. She had changed into dry clothes and was finally feeling warm again, sitting beside the fire, and even relaxed. Mr. Lagat had talked with the Wardens for almost an hour, then Skyve had come back with them to camp to meet the others. For the most part, she had been able to withdraw from the discussion.

It had been some time since she'd nervously scanned for Yhkon's whereabouts, or cringed when she heard his voice. Her mind had finally retreated, putting the conflict aside for a while, unwinding.

So it was with dread that she heard him address everyone that wasn't busy or talking with Skyve. "Let's do some archery practice."

How could she get out of it? Resh was occupied, Gustor wasn't around. Training with one of them instead wasn't an option. Yhkon was already waiting for her.

No escape. Fingers curled until her nails bit into her palms, she joined him, head down. All he did was hand her his bow and quiver, and point to the tree that was to be her target.

Other than taking a turn with her brother Naylen's homemade bow, almost two years ago, she had no knowledge of archery. Asking for guidance, however, was out of the question. She clumsily knocked an arrow to the string. Doing her best to picture and imitate Naylen's stance, she drew it back, surprised by how difficult it was, did her best to aim, and let it fly. It missed the tree by a couple feet.

"Your stance is wrong," was all Yhkon said. He proceeded to adjust her posture and grip, all wordlessly, while she bit her cheek and fumed. Satisfied, he stepped back, and she fired again. The improvement was minimal.

"No," he took the bow from her, "not like that. You aren't—"

"I was standing how you told me!"

Yhkon considered her cooly, almost mockingly, as he offered the bow back to her. "Oh, by all means, do show me. Since you're so knowledgeable about the craft."

Not only did he explode at a simple question, or shut her out for days. Not only did he disdain every attempt to help him. Not only did he spurn her trust and refuse to extend any of his own…he also treated her hurt and anger with contemptuous scorn.

Talea allowed herself one second to glare at him without restraint. But she didn't intend to be belittled by him, or let him continue belittling others. So her glare became soft, her head tilted to the side, mouth curving into a shy smile. No, that was too much. He would see through it. She let her gaze fall downward again, biting her lip. "Okay…you're right. Will you show me?"

There was still a glint of suspicion in his eyes, that faded into uncertainty, as he knocked an arrow and entered the "correct" stance. It didn't look much different than hers. As he became more focused on his aim, she retreated with all the stealth he himself had taught her. By the time he realized she had left a few seconds later, he couldn't yell after her without calling attention to the matter. She went straight to Resh and Skyve, cheerfully joining their conversation, ignoring the lead Warden's stare drilling into her back.

Skyve's stay tarried. Talea wasn't sure whether his presence made it easier or harder for her to avoid Yhkon. It seemed that as long as she was engaging with Skyve and Resh, Yhkon would leave her be. Racking her brain for questions and comments, she clung to the discussion, wondering at how unwanted her involvement was. At least Resh didn't mind.

It couldn't last forever. Eventually, Yhkon joined them as well, setting her teeth on edge. He soon recommended that Skyve practice with his lightning with the other wards. Skyve found the proposal an agreeable one. Talea did not.

Surprisingly, it was Yhkon who gave her a way out. "Talea. I'd like you to do a perimeter check."

No doubt he meant it as a punishment, "taking away" her chance to train with the other wards. Well let him think so—she'd infinitely prefer a solitary, peaceful ride in the woods. Away from him.

But then he spoke again. "Actually, nevermind. You'll trai—"

"What?" She didn't keep the challenge and derision out of her tone. "Do you think I'm going to ride off? Purposely hurt your celith? Set fire to the woods we stand in? Go flag Kaydor down?"

His eyes were as icy as ever, arms crossed, face hard and critical. "It had crossed my mind."

Talea tossed her braid over her shoulder and started toward the celiths. "I think I will do a perimeter check, thank you for the suggestion, *Silquije*."

He didn't speak again, though his anger was palpable. Since he probably didn't want her to take his celith without permission, that was exactly what she did, saddling and bridling the stallion under his venomous glower. Astride, she cued Eclipse into a canter. Away from the camp, away from her *mentor*.

The woods around Fesdor were thick and dark. There was a beauty to them, a mystery, the intrigue of shadowy alcoves and leaf-filtered sunshine, all on a mossy floor; but it was also heavy. Ominous.

Anything was better than the confines of their camp. With Yhkon prowling. How could things have gone so wrong, so quickly? Or, had it not been quickly? There had always been a tension. It had been evident from almost their first interactions that the lead Warden was reclusive, temperamental, volatile.

Still. A month ago, she had considered Yhkon her closest friend out of an entire group of people she appreciated, trusted, and considered to be a sort of second family. Now, she would prefer the company of any other individual in that group, infinitely.

What had happened, to cause such a rift? She couldn't look over the past few days and find any conclusive cause. Had she overreacted? Was the whole thing an exploded misunderstanding? She couldn't grasp any solid rationality on her part. She knew it dwelt somewhere in the fact that he wouldn't reciprocate her genuine interest and open friendship, or even accept it.

Other than that, all she knew was that just thinking about it brought on the urge to cry.

As she swallowed down the lump in her throat and blinked away the tears, she noticed Eclipse's gait was strange. Dismounting and leading him a few steps, she realized he was limping.

Panic snagged her breath. She had ridden off on the stallion without permission out of spite, now she would have to bring him back injured. When had he started limping? There was nothing visibly wrong with his leg. Could a celith sprain an ankle, or pull a muscle? Surely it was something simple?

Digging her nails into her thumb, Talea tightened her grip on the reins and kept going, on foot. She would at least save Eclipse the extra burden and walk the rest of the way. It wasn't far, less than a mile.

There was nothing else to do. She would take Eclipse back, tell Yhkon what had happened, and apologize, as was due. Beyond that...well...well she'd put aside their quarrel as best she could. At least she'd make it less personal. If he wasn't interested in friendship, if he preferred to remain in a more businesslike relationship, then...she could deal with that. It wasn't fair to everyone else to drag out this destructive struggle between them. It didn't need to be a consuming, inclusive affair, forcing itself on everyone around them. It didn't need to be a constant battle between her and him, either. She would not look past his cruelty toward those around him. She would stand up to him, when necessary, for their sake if not her own. But even so, the two of them could come to a straightforward and civil set of terms, in which they got along and respected one another as necessary, hopefully even reach a point of amiability.

She never got the chance to follow through.

Yhkon spotted Eclipse's limp the moment she returned, eyes already blazing and face flushed with anger. "What did you do?"

The accusation in his voice made her cringe. "Yhkon, I'm sorry. But I promise you I didn't do anything, it was just about a mile back that I noticed he was limping. He didn't trip or anything."

There was something savage in his demeanor as he looked at her, taking Eclipse's reins from her hands forcibly. "Oh I see. *Now* you're sorry."

"I didn't—"

"You *did*," he snapped, kneeling to inspect Eclipse's leg. "You rode off on him out of spite. If you hadn't, this wouldn't have happened. If you had just done as I said, but no," he drew out the word, mockingingly. "No, you're not going to take orders, you're not going to do what I say, because I hurt your feelings. I'm an emotional terrorist. I'm just so cruel, aren't I? And you're the sweet little angel, all you've ever wanted is to *help* me. You've—"

There were hot tears in her eyes and a tremble in her entire body. "Yhkon, I—"

"You've probably schemed with Grrake on how to *fix* me and my *problems*. He's probably implored you to just give me another chance, to try and get through to me. Well you know what?" He was on his feet again. She cowered, hand covering her mouth and vision blurred. "I am cruel! And you can't bloody fix it!"

Talea realized she was holding her breath, desperately holding in the pitiful sobs she knew were trying to escape. No matter how hard she tried to control herself, or how many times she swept roughly at the tears in her eyes, they kept coming. She didn't want to appear weak or pathetic to him. But that was how she felt.

He straightened out of his aggressive posture, expression losing some of its acrimony, becoming more dazed as he surveyed the campsite and discovered that they had a silent audience. Talea didn't know if they had heard what he'd said. Most likely they had, and they had certainly seen the entire thing.

She wasn't sure she wanted to see their reactions, whether pity for her, or anger at Yhkon. That wasn't what she wanted, for them to hate him, to stack on to his list of faults and push him farther and farther away…she didn't want any of this, anymore. She wanted to be back in Vissler Village, with her family and her friends—maybe relationships weren't perfect within her family, maybe they lived in poverty and servitude…but she was just so tired of *this*.

Anxiety increased the quiver in her hands as Yhkon looked back at Eclipse's leg, and the irritation started returning. Bringing red to his golden complexion, a rigidity to his shoulders. And that glinting light in his eyes. Like the harsh reflection of sunshine on an iron blade. He faced her again, voice lowered to avoid the ears of their spectators. "All I ask is that you do as I say. I could have fixed Eclipse's leg, but now its inflamed, thanks to you riding off without—"

"Yhkon." She hadn't realized Wylan had approached. His voice was steady. "Leave her alone."

There was a momentary twitch in Yhkon's expression, almost a grimace, or maybe just a flash of resentment. "This has nothing to do with you."

"No, it doesn't." Wylan moved forward, now between her and the Warden, like a shield. "But it doesn't have much to do with her, either. Eclipse's leg has no outer damage, which means it wasn't something she did. It would have happened even if you yourself had ridden him."

Yhkon's jaw clenched. As if half of him knew it was true and wanted to relent, while the other half wanted to unleash his mounting indignation. "That's not the only thing this is about, and in any case it doesn't involve you in the least, so if you would be so kind as to—"

Wylan's navy eyes flashed with a challenge. Yhkon fell silent. Taking it as victory, Wylan took Talea by the arm and led her away. She followed, rapidly wiping tears from her cheeks, feeling strangely torn between Wylan's calming protection and Yhkon's nearly tangible turmoil.

Wylan acted as her sentry. He let her go where she pleased, and remained within a few yards, taking up the mending of Ash's bridle. Without anything else to do, and not wanting to be the object of everyone's attention, she went into the girl's tent. There she sat, staring at nothing, lost in her thoughts. Only when someone came near the shelter did she start sewing up a tear in a shirt, or brushing her hair, or tidying her things. No one tried to talk to her. Not Grrake, or Ahjul, or Terindi. Whether that was because of Wylan's presence, or out of sensitivity to the fact that she might prefer to be alone, she didn't know. Either way, she was grateful.

The only person who tried to talk to her was Yhkon. She heard footsteps outside the tent that she recognized as his, making her grip the shirt she was mending tighter. But then Wylan's voice, cool, collected, even bland. "Leave her alone, Yhkon."

Yhkon's voice surprised her with its meekness. "I just want to—"

"No." Meek or not, she wasn't ready to face the Warden, and inwardly thanked Wylan. "Not right now."

~♦~

"Well, my dear," Resh took her hand and kissed it with a gallant flourish. "I suppose from now on you must be deprived of my company, when riding at least."

Talea smiled and played along with a slight curtsy. "How shall I ever bear the deprivation."

"Indeed," Resh took on a thoughtful mien, "how can anyone?"

With a grin, she shook her head at him and walked away, almost running into Skyve. He backed up and gave her a wide berth, as if he might catch a disease if he came too close. Rolling her eyes, she kept going. She liked Skyve, really, from what she knew of him after a few days' acquaintance. But he really was so finicky, and absolutely repulsed by the very idea of emotion.

One thing was for sure—she would not be sorry to leave behind Fesdor, Skyve's parents, and the campsite that had been like a prison. The sooner they continued their journey, the sooner it was over. Only one more ward to go.

She retrieved her pack and made her way along the perimeter of the camp to Gustor. He was busy saddling his celith, until he heard her approach and looked up.

Gustor's face was usually unreadable. He had the classic Sanonyan appearance, golden complexion, sharp features, light colored eyes and hair, matched with an intensity that made him look like Yhkon's older brother. In all, he was rather intimidating, though she had long since decided he was much kinder than he let on.

There was something readable in his expression this time, however. Reluctance.

She stopped a few paces away. "What is it?"

"You're going to ask if you can ride with me, I presume."

"Yeah..." Would he say no? He had been an ally of sorts during the last few days, taking her with him on hunting trips multiple times so that she could get away from camp. And while he never asked her about what had happened, or offered much verbal compassion, he seemed to understand and offer silent support.

Gustor finished cinching the saddle, then faced her with a frown. "I'm sorry. I would have had no objections, myself, but Yhkon already insisted against it."

Talea bit the inside of her cheek. Why, after almost two days of complete silence, did Yhkon see the need to drag them both back into the arena for another fight? She had, in the infrequent cases that interaction was necessary, made an effort to be courteous, even generous, in her behavior—if also to keep her distance. He had practically ignored her. Why force her to ride with him? "And I guess you'd be in trouble if you didn't listen," was all she mumbled.

He grunted. "I couldn't care less about that. But..." He shrugged a little. "I think he's ready to make amends. It would be better for everyone if he's allowed the opportunity." When she didn't answer, he added, "If he makes a mess of that opportunity...then you can ride with me as often as you please and I don't give a barbsit's tail what he says about it."

Well...maybe he was right. If she gave Yhkon one final chance, no one could accuse her of quitting too soon. She didn't think there was much likelihood of him taking the chance and actually trying to reconcile with her; it would probably be a miserable ride that ended in another fight. Then it would be over. After that she could ride with Gustor. In fact, she knew exactly what she could say, what topics to bring up, to practically guarantee that Yhkon flew into a rage and lost his window, and then the matter would be closed.

No, she couldn't do that. That wasn't fair. *Isn't it?*

After giving Gustor her thanks, Talea took a deep breath and approached Yhkon instead. He was waiting for her. "Are you sure I shouldn't just ride with Gustor?" she asked quietly, to keep the exchange private.

His only answer was to take her pack and secure it behind the saddle. Then he offered his hand, for her to climb up with. As sorely tempting as it was to haughtily ignore the gesture, she made herself accept the assistance.

With everything packed up, everyone mounted, Yhkon kicked Eclipse into a canter and they were off. Skyve's family had agreed almost immediately to the scheme, asking only a few days to tie things off and say goodbyes. If Skyve was sorry to be leaving his home and family behind, he didn't show it.

Talea thought that perhaps he would miss his sisters, and they him. For all his indifference and exasperation with them, she could tell he was a protective, loving older brother—perhaps especially so since it seemed that they looked to him for guidance and affection more than to their parents.

There was one ward left. Amilyne, the eighth, in Aydimor itself.

More pressing than that dilemma, however, was that of the man she shared a saddle with. As awkward as the silence was, she couldn't break it. As uncomfortable as it was to grip nothing but the back of the saddle, she couldn't make herself put her hands on his waist. The terrain was uneven, rocky and dry, with hills, cliffs, and ravines limiting the visibility.

He broke the silence. "Can we figure this out?"

Eclipse was far enough ahead of the group that they could talk privately. *Can we?* "I'm not sure yet."

"Well..." She couldn't see his expression, but she could see him kneading his thigh with white knuckles. "Can we try?"

"Alright..." *Give him a chance.* "Okay. Let's figure it out."

If her answer relieved him at all, he didn't show it. "I guess I'm not sure...how. I know you're upset that I'm not more open, but I don't see why I can't keep some things to myself."

Was that fair? Had she been asking too much? He clearly felt a need for privacy that she didn't, and maybe she should have accepted that earlier. "Okay...I mean, you can, I guess. I probably shouldn't have asked so much. But..." She closed her eyes, wishing she could unscramble her thoughts and feelings and coherently communicate them in words. "When I did ask, you got so angry. I thought we were friends but then you would snap at me and just..."

Yhkon's tension was visible, in his stiff posture and flexed muscles. "I don't like talking about my past."

As if I hadn't figured that out. "I know...and I'm sorry if I've been pushy...but don't you think it might be better to talk about it? Or at least to not—"

"Why would talking about it help, exactly?"

There it was. Icy acrimony, edging his characteristically cool tone. Talea curled her toes inside her boots, knowing the conversation was headed down the same path as all the others. Would it be better to just let him get mad, get through another fight, and then she could ride with Gustor? But then, she and Yhkon might never mend things, and would be stuck with each other for who knew how long.

The best she could do was try to soothe the situation and salvage the relationship, and if it didn't work, at least she had tried. "Well, if someone knew what it was that was wrong, they could better understand how...how you feel, I guess, and then you could just get it off your chest and not have to be stuck with it alone."

He inhaled ever so slowly. "So you think if you knew my life story, you might be able to fix me after all. Guess what. Grrake knows almost all of it. And his attempts haven't gotten him far, now have they?"

"Yhkon I'm not trying to *fix* you, but I would help, if you'd let me!"

"I..." The chill in his voice was gone. Instead it was lower than usual. "I don't think you, or anyone, can."

She didn't have time to react to the statement. Larak's thundering voice interrupted. "Yhkon, north!"

Yhkon's head jerked up, as did hers. Atop a hill north of them, the armor of several mounted Kaydorians glittered in the sunlight. He jerked the reins that direction, urging Eclipse into a gallop up the hill. *Right, 'cause running toward danger is always safest.* "Tarol, Resh, with me!"

Tarol and Resh fell in on either side of them as they charged toward the knights. Talea held tightly to Yhkon's waist, forgetting her earlier reluctance to do so, as Eclipse's powerful strides ate up the ground. The Kaydorians spurred their own celiths into a retreat, down the other side of the hill. Yhkon nearly elbowed her in the face as he reached back to get his bow. How he managed to stay astride without holding on, she didn't know. The knights were out of sight now, blocked from view by the hill, but she knew the Wardens' mounts would catch up easily enough soon. They crested the hill, and were met by a mass of glinting armor below them, and a volley of arrows.

15
Iron

Tarol's celith squealed in pain. Resh grunted. Arrows hissed through the air and embedded all around them. Talea ducked, making herself as small as possible behind Yhkon as he wheeled Eclipse around, away from the army below them and the archers it boasted. Tucked almost sideways against his shoulder, she caught a glimpse of the force as they turned away. Like a sea of iron. How many were there? Hundreds?

"Ki, up with me! Resh, take Tarol! Let's go!"

Yhkon's commanding voice honed her focus. She instinctively grabbed Ki's arm, helping him onto Eclipse's hindquarters behind her, where he had little to straddle and even less to hold, except for her. Tarol was up with Resh and Skyve, his own celith grounded, multiple arrows in its chest and neck.

They fled back the way they'd come. Grrake must have already guessed what was going on—he had steered the group away from the hill. Yhkon took Eclipse to the front and didn't slacken his pace.

Yhkon swore, seconds before Eclipse planted his hooves.

As she swayed from the jolt, Talea saw why: at least fifty Kaydorians on celiths ahead of them. The other Wardens had stopped as well, analyzing the force. Did they think they had a chance against them? *What if they...want us to use our lightning?* She was about to ask Yhkon what he was thinking, when Gustor called, between curses, "Yhkon, left and right, back! Better make a move!"

Talea whipped her head either direction. Sure enough, smaller, mounted forces of at least a couple dozen each were behind and to either side of them. Whichever way they tried to go, the Kaydorians would close in.

"What's the fuss!" Tarol was practically squirming behind Skyve. "It's a simple matter of deciding which idiots to attack first. Let's go!"

Yhkon ignored Tarol's outburst. She could tell he was trying to work something out, with his brow knit and eyes narrowed. "Why have the foot soldiers...if we're mounted..."

"Come on, Yhkon!" Tarol muttered. "All we need is your royal consent and we can deal with this!"

"Shut up, Tarol." Larak moved his celith closer to Eclipse. "I think it could be a trap."

"Exactly." Yhkon's frown deepened, as the three Kaydorian forces began advancing. "But it looks like we have no choice but to walk into it. Break through, west!"

The western force was the smallest, and hopefully easier to break through. Talea clung tightly to Yhkon and Ki clung tightly to her. Eclipse's muscles gathered and stretched beneath them with every powerful stride, the wind created by his speed whipping back her hair and bringing tears to her eyes. The glinting iron of the Kaydorians was a blur that raced toward them, brandished swords and armor that she could somehow still hear clinking, above the thunder of hooves that enveloped everything.

She knew they had reached the enemy when she felt Yhkon's body moving, swinging his sword. Everything happened too quickly to see. All she knew was that where his sword went, a spray of crimson followed. Celiths were snorting and squealing, men shouting, iron clashing...

And then it wasn't. The thunder of hooves dimmed until it was only that of their own mounts. Looking over her shoulder, she could see at least a dozen celiths and knights that had fallen. The rest were pursuing, but they didn't have the speed to overtake them.

There wasn't much time for relief at their escape. They had entered a canyon, jagged cliffs on either side, wide enough for about a hundred men to stand abreast. Within seconds, they rounded a corner, and found another army.

Yhkon swore, drawing Eclipse into such a sharp turn Talea had the sinking feeling of falling for a second. There wasn't time for discussion. With nearly a hundred cavalry charging them from behind, and an army ahead, they were hemmed in. Yhkon kept Eclipse facing the oncoming tide of celithmen. "Attack!" With a kick they were galloping again, straight toward the Kaydorians. With a hundred hoofbeats all around and the blood pounding in her ears, Talea barely heard Yhkon's second command. "Wards, lightning!" He grabbed her knee when she didn't respond. "Talea! Lightning, *now!*"

Lightning. Against the knights. To kill them.

Somehow she raised her hands and somehow she did as told, though she had hardly any idea what form the lightning would even take. It came as a series of bolts that struck like daggers into the cavalry. There was more than just hers, as the other wards did likewise. Screams sliced through the constant chaos wherever their lightning struck, making her grimace, even as she increased her efforts.

Until the chaos consumed them. The celiths and knights and swords were like a flood, crashing in on every side. She knew Yhkon was fighting, that the other Wardens were fighting, that lightning was still flashing around her, that some of it was even from her own fingertips. Hot pain flared in her thigh, and she realized with alarm that one of the Kaydorian's swords must have struck her. There wasn't time to worry about that. Something hit Eclipse. He staggered backward, a shudder running through his body that she could feel through the saddle. Yhkon was saying something, grabbing her arm... there was a jolt as another celith rammed into them. Eclipse went down, and they with him.

By the time Talea's mind caught up, Yhkon was pulling her to her feet, at the same time as he yanked her behind himself, engaging two knights. She saw light out of the corner of her eyes, that stayed instead of flashing. It was Ki. He swung a sword of electricity at any soldier that came within reach.

Sword. She could make a sword, too.

It came from her hands in an unsteady, imperfect rod rather than the dazzling and elegant blade she could usually make. But it would work just as well. The next time a Kaydorian came near, instead of ducking behind an already-occupied Yhkon, she made a reckless swing.

A sizzle. The Kaydorian's strangled shout of pain. The gleam of his iron, blackened. A tingling sensation crept from her fingertips into her core, taking with it the energy. She stood once more without a weapon, leaving Yhkon to defend her.

The soldier she had hit wasn't moving.

"Talea!" Yhkon's urgent voice snapped her from the daze. Three celiths were charging toward them, their riders whipping them to a mad gallop. She, Yhkon, and Ki would be trampled beneath those pounding hooves.

Talea stumbled backward, raising her arms. Warmth filled her veins and muscles while a chill crept over her skin, just before light spread like a miniature wave, traveling from her fingers toward the oncoming celiths. Their squeals and their riders' screams rang in her ears. All she could see was flesh and armor charred black where the lightning struck.

Something gripped her shoulders. Panicked, she wrenched herself away, energy surging to her hands. Just before she released it, her eyes met Yhkon's icy ones.

"Hey, Talea, it's me. It's alright. They're taken care of."

He was right. The entirety of the cavalry was down, a few soldiers crawling or writhing, a handful of celiths meandering, riderless. The rest lay perfectly still on bloodstained ground.

There wasn't time to feel relief that they had survived, or even to feel horror at the death and pain that surrounded her. "They're coming!"

Ahead and to either side of them were the infantry, advancing steadily like a slow-moving tide of liquid silver. Every Warden and ward was still standing, with nothing beyond minor injuries, but they had only two uninjured celiths.

"Archers! Haeric, take a celith and get to the outpost!" Yhkon grabbed her wrist and started running, the other Wardens and wards doing likewise. What archers? She twisted her neck to see the army as she ran, just able to pick out the soldiers with bows, behind the first two lines.

Larak's massive bulk caught up to them with surprising speed for his size. "We need cover!"

"No, really?!" Yhkon increased the pace, as if it hadn't already been hard enough to keep up with him. "Around the bend!"

She heard the *twang* of bows loosing their arrows just as

they reached the corner. The sound of whistling projectiles was next. Yhkon put an arm around her waist and practically flung her the rest of the way behind the cliff wall, at the same second as a hundred arrows pierced the ground where they had just been. She saw a streak of blood and a tear on his shirt where one had grazed him.

"Everyone keep going!" Taking her by the arm, he led them on, while Haeric mounted one of their two remaining celiths and galloped away.

Why had he sent Haeric to the outpost? Was there even one nearby? Not daring to ask aloud, she simply followed Yhkon with everyone else. He didn't leave her any choice, not releasing his grip on her arm.

Maybe the point of Haeric getting to the outpost was bringing back some spare celiths, and in the meantime the rest of them would just outrun the enemy that was slowed by numbers and armor. But as they started moving, she saw that Ahjul was carrying Terindi, whose pant leg was soaked in blood. That Resh and Rikky were limping. That outrunning the Kaydorians wouldn't be possible for long.

It was all they could do. Yhkon led them at as fast a pace as everyone could manage. When she tripped over a rock, he dragged her with him until she regained her footing, never stopping. The farther they went, the louder the noise of the pursuing army. They were catching up. All she could do was gasp for breath and will her body to keep going.

Rounding another bend, a new threat awaited them. A couple dozen warriors, in strange leather armor, with massive shields and spears aside from the usual swords and bows. They stood in formation atop a sharp rise in the canyon floor, about eight feet high.

But Yhkon didn't stop, or ready his sword to attack, or

even swear. Instead he ran straight up to the miniature wall, grabbed Talea by the waist, and hoisted her up toward the strangers. She had a terrifying moment of struggling to escape his, then their grasp, before recognition calmed her apprehension. The leather armor, in shades of navy and green...the San Quawr that had helped free her from the Asyjgon had worn it. They were Elikwai!

Sure enough, the men pulled her up and set her down behind them. They did the same with the other wards, before helping the Wardens up. Haeric was with them. When everyone was up, the Elikwai reformed their lines, stacking their large shields in front of them in such a way that it formed an almost solid barrier between them and the army that had just caught up.

The Kaydorians were forced to a stand-still by the small rise of rocks and the Elikwai that guarded it. Only a few of them could try to climb up at a time, and every one that did was struck down by an Elikwai's spear or sword through one of the gaps in the line of shields. Talea watched the first few. Saw glimpses of faces or chests between shields, the stabbing movement of a spear, and the bloody puncture left behind before the body fell backwards into the mass of men.

The rock in her stomach rose as bile to her throat. She staggered back, turning away from the horrible sight, covering her ears to try and shut out the groans and screams and the sound of weapons parting flesh.

"Talea." Yhkon appeared at her side. The last she'd seen him, he'd been firing arrows into the trapped army as quickly as he could string them, along with the other Wardens. "Talea, I need you to use your lightning. We have to take down as many as possible while the Elikwai hold them. Come on, you have to get up." He was pulling her up, forcing her to face the horror and mayhem again. "Lightning, Talea!"

She saw with surprise that Wylan was already taking down several soldiers at a time with a constant barrage of bolts. Rikky joined him without hesitation. The twins had a vacant look, Kae especially, but they did as told, almost mechanically. Talea swallowed the pressure in her throat and added more lightning bolts to the effort, as did Terindi, with Ahjul helping her stand, and Skyve too, once Resh somehow talked him out of a daze.

Each bolt could dispatch a handful of men at once. It was a familiar sensation, the pull between her glowing fingertips and the open space above the army, as she drew the energy from the air and directed it into one clump of Kaydorians after another. There was a constant strain, as if she were magnetized to the energy she was directing. Far more exhausting than the exertion was the repeated sight of electricity flashing, reflecting on the armor of its victims, before turning it black. Mixed with the nauseating smells of blood and death was burnt flesh.

She didn't know at what point a wave of dizziness made her fall back, vision reeling and peppered with black dots. There was a weakness in her muscles that made them feel slack and rubbery. Iron reflecting the bluish light of their electricity before it was scorched black was all she could see as she squeezed her eyes shut, wishing she could block out every terrible sight and sound that smothered her senses. Something touched her and she started to cry out, only to have it die on her tongue when she opened her eyes to see Wylan. He held her by either shoulder, searching her gaze for something. Whatever he found there made him push her back, behind him, while he kept up an onslaught of lightning.

She fumbled a few more steps until she could steady herself against a boulder. Rikky and Wylan were the only two wards still consistently fighting. Skyve would make a few attacks, before seeming to zone out, and only return when Resh called his name or shook him. Terindi and Kae were huddled together, Terindi holding a wad of fabric to her bleeding leg, Kae's eyes blank and staring. Ki kept going, sporadically, still looking as though he didn't even know what he was doing.

Talea's attention fell on Yhkon as he threw aside an empty quiver. Without meaning to, she let her gaze wander to the Elikwai, and watched in alarm as a Kaydorian managed to slip a sword through one of the gaps and thrust it into the abdomen of an Elikwai. The man fell backwards with a gurgled groan, dropping his hold on the shield. Just before the barrier would have been broken Yhkon dove forward, taking the man's place. Only seconds later another Elikwai had to be replaced by Haeric. How much longer could they hold?

As if on cue, the formation broke. Wylan grabbed her and threw them both away from the Kaydorians, off the incline into a valley of sorts on the other side. She didn't have time to so much as regain her balance before soldiers were flooding the valley. Wylan made an electrical blade in either hand and engaged, but she couldn't simply stand behind and let him do all the fighting. There were too many for that. Two men passed him and came at her with blades swinging. Instinct brought a burst of energy from her fingers that dispatched both of them. The tip of a sword sliced across her arm, drawing a cry of surprise and pain from her lips. She made a rod of electricity and swung it wildly in the direction of the attack, feeling more than seeing it go through armor and muscle. She knew she was moving, scrambling to get away. There was nowhere to go. With her back against the canyon wall she had no choice except to face the battle.

Wylan was gone. Blocked from view by the swarm of soldiers. But somewhere he was fighting, a sword of pure energy in either hand.

That was what she had to do. Yhkon had trained her everyday for months, trained her to fight.

Her hands trembled, but she poured energy out into the form of a blade that crackled and glowed with power, just in time to meet the attack of three soldiers. It took mere seconds to take them down, because almost any contact with her electricity killed them. But there was a constant supply. For every Kaydorian she took down, there was another. There were too many. Minimal muscle memory and instinct could only keep her alive against such odds for so long. Everywhere around her was chaos and death. Every nerve in her body was tense with fear, making her movements choppy and less efficient. Sweat made her clothes stick to her skin, along with blood.

"Talea! Where are you?"

It was Yhkon! "I'm here! Over here!" Where was he? All she could see was silver and red, blurred and moving all around her. Now that she was looking beyond her immediate foes, however, she could see the occasional flare of light. At least some of the other wards were alive.

Her distraction was an opportunity for the Kaydorians. Something solid hit her chest, sucking the air from her lungs and leaving an aching pressure in its place. She fell backwards against the rock, mind reeling, stuck on one thought: she would die. A sword would plunge through her heart at any moment. There was nothing she could do about it, stuck in this time bubble.

A sword did plunge toward her heart. But another blocked it, the iron ringing sharply. She caught a glimpse of eyes that held a savage intensity, contrasting their icy blue. Yhkon smoothly engaged all the nearest Kaydorians and maneuvered them a few steps away, giving her a moment to recover. It also gave her a moment to watch him fight. In training, his movements were precise and flowing, effortless. In real combat, they were still that…as well as ruthless. It was a frightening mixture of skill and brutality.

Most of the soldiers went to him, whether because they thought he was the real challenge, or thought he would be easier without magical abilities, she didn't know. Some still came after her. Yhkon positioned himself with his back to hers and her close to the wall, limiting how many men could reach her. Having him there, guarding her back and helping when she needed it, made it easier to focus. To let her mind rely on the training he had given her over the months. Parrying, dodging, striking. With the advantage of an electric weapon, it was enough to keep her going.

"Yhkon!" It sounded like Grrake, distant and smothered by the hectic din of the battle. "Ahjul needs help!"

Yhkon spoke just loud enough for her to hear, still fighting. "I need you to take down as many as possible. Can you do that?"

Can I? She nodded. He lunged at the nearest of their opponents, taking down three at once. It gave her the opening she needed to gather the energy in her core to her hands and release it, letting intuition determine its form. It traveled as a shimmering vertical wave several yards ahead of them before flattening, taking down almost two dozen men.

It took its toll. Where there had been a simmering power in her body, there was a drained weakness instead. Clumsily she followed Yhkon as he sprinted through the newly made path. They were just in time to see a sword leave a crimson trail along Wylan's midsection. He faltered with a groan of pain. Yhkon joined the fray before the Kaydorians could press the opportunity, while Talea helped Wylan to his feet.

"Yhkon!" This time it was Ahjul's voice, urgent.

Yhkon increased his efforts, taking down multiple of their adversaries, enough that he could briefly check that she and Wylan were alright, before starting to fight his way through the crowd toward Ahjul's voice. "Talea, Wylan, stay together!"

A scream from Terindi and an inarticulate yell from Ahjul rose above the pandemonium. The Kaydorian force had been thinned considerably, allowing Talea to see them: Terindi had collapsed, dead or unconscious. Ahjul stood over her body, surrounded by soldiers, fighting desperately.

"No, go with him," Wylan said between clenched teeth, stabbing a Kaydorian. She cringed, seeing again the reflection of electricity on iron, now burned black. "There's too many for only Yhkon. Go, I'm fine!"

Talea ran after Yhkon, forcing the terror that surrounded her out of her mind. Save Ahjul and Terindi. That was all she could let herself think about. Not the pain and weariness that dragged at her body, not the friends that were still fighting, maybe dying, not the hundreds of dead bodies.

Yhkon had carved a trail through the field, bleeding Kaydorians marking the path. She had almost caught up to him as he reached the base of a small knoll, near the top of which Ahjul fought. The youngest Warden groaned as a sword cut deep into his upper arm, nearly severing it entirely. Yhkon shouted something, increasing his already reckless drive, no longer taking the time to dispatch the soldiers in his way, just barreling through as quickly as possible.

That left them in her way.

Several of them charged her. Talea made another blade and engaged, but she could tell her movements were becoming more sluggish. Somewhere in the blur of iron and bodies one of them breached her defenses. Pressure squeezed her stomach. It throbbed into an ache, while a strange fear sent a tingle down her spine and pricked her consciousness. More energy traveled from her core, through her arms, into the open air as an explosion of sparks. All five of the men attacking her fell or staggered away, groaning, clutching at their faces or arms where the energy had burned them.

Thoughts hazy, Talea kept going. Had to help Ahjul. But her legs...they were shaking, muscles drained of strength. Her whole body felt like a sponge wrung dry. The ache in her stomach was throbbing, gaining intensity. Stumbling to a halt, she looked down. All she could see through misty vision was red.

Blood.

"Yhkon..." She put her palm against the ache, dimly feeling the hot, sticky blood as it coated her hand. The pain was becoming sharper.

Ahead of her he turned, somehow hearing her hoarse voice, and came rushing back. "Talea, you need to help me. I can't get through that many of them. You need to—"

She couldn't see his expression very well, but she knew he had noticed the blood soaking her stomach. Even without seeing, she could sense his dread. His voice, unsteady, not even swearing like he usually did under stress. "No...no, Talea, no, you're alright. Come on." He gripped her arms tightly, keeping her upright when her knees buckled. "You're going to be alright. Listen to me. Talea!"

His voice was losing its clarity, fading into the incessant hum of noise like everything else, drowned out by the pulsing in her ears. Rising above the hum was Ahjul's choked cry for help.

"No!" Yhkon dragged her a few steps. "I can't...he...you

have to, to stop them, Talea you have to…"

With his help she raised trembling hands. There was a soft glow in her veins, but she didn't feel the usual energy waiting to be used, the inner warmth and chill on her skin. Even before she released it she knew it wouldn't be enough. And it wasn't. A few lightning bolts that were too small and poorly aimed to make a difference.

Yhkon let her go, running forward. He wouldn't get there in time. She knew he wouldn't. He hacked down Kaydorians wildly, yelling as he fought, heedless of danger to himself or the futility of his mission.

The blood and strength seeping from her body allowed one mercy. It weighted her eyelids, drawing her mind toward oblivion. Slumped on the ground, eyes closed, she didn't see it. But she heard Yhkon scream Ahjul's name, and she knew it had happened. It was the last thing she knew.

16
Casualties and Candidates

Yhkon finally broke through the Kaydorian forces seconds after Ahjul had fallen with a sword through his chest. He took up position over Ahjul and Terindi's motionless bodies and fought any man dumb enough to attack him. His whole body was hot, heart racing, vision tinted with red. He knew he was abandoning strategy and cunning and instead letting anger drive his blade. It didn't matter. Anger was more powerful. It got the job done.

At some point he became the only person still standing upon the knoll. The other Wardens and wards were still battling throughout the valley, and in the back of his mind he recognized that they would win, sooner or later. With his help it could be sooner, but he didn't join them. He dropped his sword and knelt beside Ahjul.

Ahjul's chest was still heaving with ragged, feeble breaths. His eyes opened and landed on Yhkon. They were full of pain, and fear. "Y-Yhkon?"

He was supposed to offer comfort and hope. To say it was all going to be alright, that he could pull through, just hang on. What was the point, when none of it was true? "I'm here," was all he said.

Ahjul coughed, blood trickling from the corner of his mouth. "Terindi…"

Yhkon moved to Terindi's side, putting his fingers to her throat while scanning her body. She had lost a lot of blood, but her pulse was steady—she would recover. "She's alright."

"I'm n-not…ready…" His face contorted in a grimace, entire body clenching with a spasm of pain. "Terindi… my fami—" he broke into another coughing fit, groaning at the pain but unable to stop. Yhkon took Ahjul's hand, holding as tightly as he dared. This was a fellow warrior that had shown him respect and friendship he had never deserved. If Grrake were there, he would be doing all he could to give the young man some peace before he died.

Grrake was not there. Yhkon cleared his throat, knowing he had to do his best. All he felt was exhaustion, and a dull anger, but for Ahjul he knew he had to find some light. "You fought bravely. You hear me? You've…you're twice the man any of us are. No one could have fought better, Ahjul. You did well."

Ahjul tried to say something. Nothing would come, as he coughed on more blood. His grip on Yhkon's hand tightened. A convulsion made his muscles rigid, before they slackened. "I can't…please…don't—" His breath caught, head lulling to the side, eyes fixing on nothing.

Those eyes that had always been so full of light and kindness, were now dim.

Yhkon put Ahjul's hand down and stood. He lingered a moment, not quite able to pull himself away. Somehow he knew this would be the last time he could have the emptiness. That the next time he allowed himself to feel anything, it would be so much harder than nothing, than the hollow weariness.

It was Talea that made him leave. When he returned to where she'd collapsed, she was unconscious. Alive. But she wouldn't be for long. The sword had gone straight through her stomach, there was no surviving that. *Except...*

No. False hope would only make it worse. None of the "light" he'd faked for Ahjul was real. *Real* was Ahjul dead, Talea dying. Ahjul, one of the kindest, purest men he knew, one of his only friends, was dead, he who was the farthest from deserving it. Talea, his ward, the leader of the Eight...Narone was supposed to protect her. She was His chosen leader, as ridiculous as it was. Well, all the more proof of what Yhkon already knew: Narone was not the loving, involved Creator He was claimed to be.

Talea. Just fifteen years old, too young to be thrust into this violence and bloodshed, or the burdensome life she was supposed to be destined for. She was dying, and there was no use denying it.

Still, he tore off a strip from his shirt and wrapped it around her torso as a temporary bandage, to at least slow the bleeding. Part of him wanted to stay. To take her in his arms, to pretend she wasn't dying and do all he could to save her, to wait for her to wake up.

The other part of him wanted to kill every Kaydorian still standing.

The emptiness was not lasting as long as he'd hoped. Rage was already taking its place. At least that rage would accomplish something, it might keep the number of casualties to only Ahjul and Talea. So he picked up his sword, located the densest cluster of Kaydorians, and attacked.

He almost always felt a thrill in combat. This, however, was something else. It was the same wildness he'd felt when Talea had been captured by the Asyjgon. And when he'd lost Tessa.

It was consuming, numbing his mind to remorse or fear, numbing his body to pain or fatigue, fueling his movements and making every kill a satisfaction. His senses were heightened. A pulsing heat burned under his skin. Every sensation—his muscles contracting, the sharp clatter of iron, drafts of air from his movements, the resistance of armor and flesh against his blade, the fear or intensity on the faces of his opponents—all of it was vivid, distinct.

It was a feeling he knew, and the Kaydorians didn't stand a chance against it.

It ended too quickly. He thrust his final victim aside, all satisfaction lost now that the fight was over. The driving anger didn't abate. It only grew stronger, without an outlet to escape from. Because now…now he couldn't avoid the reality of Ahjul's lifeless body a stone's throw away, of the life slowly draining from Talea's.

When a hand landed on his shoulder he whirled, sword ready to hack it off, stopping at the last second as he caught sight of Grrake's nervous eyes. "It's alright, it's me. They're all taken care of. Tarol's leg is badly injured, everyone's hurt in some way, but they'll make it. Where's—"

Yhkon turned away, stabbing his sword into the dirt so that he could rake his hands through his hair. They caught on tangles of dried blood and dirt. Inwardly, he was screaming. Outwardly, he was doing his best not to do the same thing.

"Yhkon?" Grrake's voice was no longer just tired. It was worried. "Yhkon what's wrong? Where are—"

"Dead! That's where!" He faced him again, no longer bothering to control his countenance. His hand sought out a throbbing pain on his opposite wrist, where a sword had nicked him. Fingers pressing into the cut, he squeezed until the minor pain grew to something strong enough to occupy his thoughts. "Ahjul is dead. Talea is dying. Go ahead, tell me, Narone has a plan, right? Doesn't she need to be *alive* for that plan? Answer me that!"

Grrake couldn't answer at first, expression moving from shock to confusion, and finally to grief. "Are you...are you sure he's—"

"Sure he's dead? Yes, yes I'm sure." He could hear the bitterness in his voice, knew how it would only hurt Grrake, when it wasn't his fault. But he couldn't stop it. "Your God seems to take a particular pleasure in making me watch those closest to me die."

"That's..." Grrake was grimacing. Where Yhkon felt anger, Grrake felt sadness. Just like Ahjul. They were too soft hearted for this world, where nothing soft survived. "It's not like that, you know He doesn't...He—" He cut off, a new sorrow creasing his brow. "Your wrist."

Yhkon released his inflictive grip on the cut, lowering his gaze. "I need to get back to Talea," he mumbled, jogging back to where he'd left her. Grrake followed him.

She was still alive at least, even if blood had almost soaked through the makeshift bandage. Exhaustion beginning to replace his rage, he dropped to his knees beside her, instinctively beginning to get another bandage ready, but stopping. Should he even try to prolong her life a few hours by slowing the blood flow? She would die either way, and it would only be a few extra hours of pain and fear. So instead, he simply made a pillow of sorts with the bandage and gently lifted her head onto it.

Grrake knelt down. "We need to stop the bleeding. I'll go grab—"

"What's the point of keeping her alive for a little while longer, when she'll just be in pain?" He absentmindedly touched his stomach, where the gruesome scar was under his shirt. He could almost feel the constant, burning torment, like a hot coal scorching and eating away at the inside of his body.

"What's the point?!" Raising his voice was not something Grrake did often. It made Yhkon squirm when he did. "How can you give up on her so easily? You of all people? *You* survived the exact same injury. Why can't she?"

He rubbed at the scar, wincing. He could argue, but what was there to argue? Yes, an injury like Talea's was supposed to be impossible to survive. Yet, yes, he himself had been injured the same way—worse even, perhaps—four years ago, and had survived.

Taking silence as acceptance, Grrake left, returning shortly with a medical kit. "Here. Patch her up as best you can, and don't you dare say again that she's just going to die. You don't know that."

Yhkon took the kit, but not without a glare. "Fine, she *could* survive, like I did. Except I had the best possible care in Calcaria within a few days of the injury. Whereas it would take us at least a *month* to get her there. I can't give her the care she needs here. You know that."

"Alright, well," Grrake got up, pacing a couple steps, "we'll just get her there as quickly as we can, and we'll leave the rest up to Narone, regardless of how you feel about it."

He flinched without meaning to. Grrake didn't usually speak that sternly with him. Why he should be bothered by it, though, he didn't know. Yet he was. He used the scissors from the kit to cut open enough of her shirt for him to tend the wound. He had seen, and experienced, plenty of serious wounds in his life, but it was still never easy to look at a gaping, bloody puncture through the body of a friend and not feel a weight in his chest. Especially when that person was Talea.

Grrake cleared his throat, averting his gaze. He had always been rather squeamish around injuries. "I'll go check on Tarol. He may need to go with you to Calcaria, for the leg. Unless…you'd prefer I stay?"

A discreet way of asking if Yhkon could hold himself together on his own. "I'm fine." So long as one held a loose definition of the word.

When Grrake was gone, he focused all his attention on disinfecting the wound, cleaning up the blood, and finally doing what he could to sew it closed. The sutures probably wouldn't last long for such a deep puncture. But he did what he could, as Grrake had told him, all the while unable to share his friend's hope.

"Yhkon." Gustor was the first one brave enough to approach him. "Grrake told us…I think it's best Tarol does go with you, his leg is pretty bad. The good news is that it just so happens that the outpost those Elikwai came from has a couple dragons sitting about, from some emergency message to a scout or something. You should be able to get to Calcaria in six or seven days."

Just so happens. If it was Grrake delivering the news, he would give Yhkon a meaningful look, or even a gentle, humble version of "I told you so." He would credit it as Narone's providence.

Yhkon didn't care about crediting it to anything. If there was a chance of saving Talea, he would do all he could, even if the chance was a slim one. "Alright, get that dragons here and Tarol ready. And…"

Gustor's head was low; he must have understood Yhkon's unsaid request, to prepare Ahjul's body for the trip as well, so that he could have a proper burial in his home. "You just take care of Talea, we'll deal with the rest."

~ ◆ ~

As the dragon landed with a jolt just outside Calcaria's outpost building, Yhkon didn't dare trying to dismount with Talea in his arms. They had made the trip in record time, pushing the dragons—which were faster than lareers—as hard as they dared. The battle, Ahjul's death, it was seven...no, six days ago. Time had blurred. Six days of almost constant flying; of holding Talea's unconscious body; of keeping Tarol drugged into unconsciousness as much as possible to save him from the pain of a fractured, deeply lacerated leg; of wondering how long his ward would live; of being painfully aware of Ahjul's body in the dragon's belly netting.

Now, finally in Calcaria, he didn't know if his battered body could dismount while carrying Talea, and he didn't want to risk dropping her. She had woken only a few times to a semiconscious state, in severe pain, scared, and groggy. He had done his best to keep the wound clean, but it was becoming infected, and she was hot with a fever.

The outpost attendants came out, manner changing from casual to urgent when they saw the circumstances. One of them climbed up and took Talea from him, carrying her to a waiting carriage. Tarol was awake, mostly anyway, and was able to get down with the help of the Elikwai that had ridden with him. Yhkon stumbled in the dismount, legs unsteady after days of almost no sleep and limited food, not to mention lingering strain from the battle and minor wounds. While the Elikwai gave the outpost manager a brief explanation, Yhkon helped Tarol into the carriage, an attendant climbed into the driver's seat, and set the celiths toward the palace at a canter.

A man had ridden ahead of them, so that when they arrived, a medical team was waiting. Four of them had Talea on a stretcher and out of sight in seconds. Two more gave

Tarol their shoulders to lean on and helped him hobble away. The final two approached Yhkon hesitantly, no doubt able to see that he had injuries that had been ignored for too long, but also that he still had the strength to have a temper.

Most anyone that spent time in the palace was familiar with his temper.

He waved them off. "I need to report to the council, first. Are they waiting for me?"

"Yes, sir."

Reporting to the council was the last thing he felt like doing. As was climbing up the two flights of stairs to get there. He arrived with his legs even shakier than before, limbs clumsy with weariness. Forgoing formality, he entered the council room without knocking or announcing his presence.

"Yhkon." Bactah was already on his feet, surveying him. "We heard…are you alright? Talea? And…they said…"

"Yes." He wondered how humiliating it would be to take one of the extra chairs. "Ahjul was killed in combat. Talea was seriously wounded."

"How seriously?" Enisham's demeanor was less critical and calculating than usual.

The chair was too tempting to resist. He limped his way to the table and sat down. None of them made any comment. "Sword through the stomach. Same thing I survived four years ago, but that no one else I know of ever has."

There was a long pause. No one seemed to know what to say. Eventually, Enisham moved on. "Alright…what happened? Tell us about the battle."

He nodded, hoping they wouldn't pester him for too much information before letting him rest. "Kaydor decided to get rid of us once and for all. It was an ambush, involving a couple hundred cavalry and about a thousand infantry. Of course he didn't know about the wards' abilities. That and the assistance of a band of Elikwai is the only reason we won.

"No one got out uninjured, but Ahjul and the Elikwai were the only casualties. Talea and Tarol are the worst off, though I think it's safe to say that Tarol will be fine."

"But..." Juplay looked at him keenly. "Not safe to say the same of Talea?"

Yhkon put his head in his hands, rubbing his temples. If it weren't for the other circumstances, this would be almost refreshing, being so informal and straightforward with the council. As it was, Ahjul was dead. Talea probably dying. Not much could be refreshing. "I don't know. All I know is that if I hadn't survived the same thing, I wouldn't have the slightest hope. But I did. She's made it longer than I initially expected...but infection has set in." He let out his breath slowly. "We should know in a few days."

"Well," Enisham spoke after another pause, tone signaling that he was going to conclude the meeting. "You clearly need some rest yourself. We won't keep you. When you're feeling up to it, we can talk more about the situation of things in Zentyre, and about picking a new Warden."

Surprise made him jerk his head up. "A new Warden?"

Kwin spoke, soothingly. "It seems rather insensitive to discuss it so soon, and we certainly don't mean to suggest that anyone can replace Ahjul. But Terindi does need a Warden. Don't worry about it now. We'll have a Stitch sent up to your room."

With a tired nod, he dragged himself from the chair, out of the room, and up to his chamber. He sank onto the bed, sluggishly taking off his gear. Most of it was strewn about the floor by the time two medics, or "Stitches" as everyone called them, came in, already scrutinizing him for injury. He stretched out on the bed, putting his hand over his eyes. "Just knock me out, make it easier on everyone."

One of them mixed some powder into a glass of brandy and handed it to him. He gulped it down and relaxed, not having to wait long for the drugs to do their work.

~♦~

"Yhkon."

The Kaydorians were closing in. Yhkon was fighting, desperately, but there were too many of them.

"Yhkon!"

He groaned as another blade breached his defenses, leaving a bloody trail on his shoulder. They were overwhelming him. No! He had to protect Tessa, he had to—

A sharp poke to the rib jolted Yhkon awake, almost to his feet by the time he saw Bactah laughing at the foot of his bed. "Confound you, Bactah Falston!"

"Oh, but how would you ever have fun without me?" Bactah crossed his arms, giving Yhkon a skeptical look. "You look awful."

He lay back with a scowl. "Your mother would give you a tongue lashing for speaking like that, to me no less."

"Yep, which is why I didn't let her come in with me. But she is outside, quite frantic to have proof that you're still in one piece, living and breathing. Shall I let her in, satisfy her motherly concern? Even if you are rather terrifying. You've got on more bandages than clothing."

"Oh, shut up." Yhkon got up, wincing at stiff muscles and aching injuries. "Let me get dressed."

Bactah waited while he managed to fit a clean pair of trousers and a shirt over his various bandages. The medics had left him clothed, but they'd cut off the sleeves and a pant leg, and holes anywhere else they needed to access. When he was dressed, Bactah opened the door. Annyve Falston flew into the room, stopped long enough to make sure Yhkon wasn't missing any limbs, then hugged him tightly. "Yhkon! You have bandages everywhere...are you alright? Oh you look exhausted!"

Ann was the closest thing Yhkon had to a mother, and she wasn't far off, from what he knew of typical mothers. The only person she fussed about more was Bactah. Normally, Yhkon didn't like people fussing about him. In fact he preferred for most people to give him a wide berth, either out of fear or respect. With Ann, however, he didn't mind. Maybe it was nice to have a fussing, affectionate mother, just like anyone else.

She let him go, only to put one hand on his forehead and grab his arm with the other. "You have a fever!"

That explained why he felt chilled, muscles still shaky. That and the fact that he still hadn't eaten a proper meal in days.

"Oh, right." Bactah gave a dismissive wave. "The Stitch said you probably wouldn't be feeling so great. Infection. Something to do with leaving wounds unattended for days...?"

Yhkon gave him a frown. "I was otherwise occupied."

"Excuses, excuses. Anyway, they wanted you on bed rest for a few days. I told them sure, so long as you're willing to tie him down and risk death, and they seemed less convinced about it after that."

"Bactah," Ekirre, Bactah's father, entered the room with his steady smile and sleepy eyes, "sometimes I marvel that Yhkon hasn't repaid you for your constant insolence." He took Yhkon's hand and shook it. "Though I do have to agree with him—you've looked better. Maybe you should rest."

Yhkon rubbed his eyes. Apparently he looked as haggard as he felt. "Maybe I should, but I can't. I need to go see Talea.

And…" He moved his hand down, massaging his jaw. It needed shaving. "And find a new Warden."

Ekirre and Annyve frowned sympathetically. "Bactah told us, about Ahjul," Ekirre said. "I'm sorry. He was a fine lad."

"He was the best of us," was all Yhkon said. He picked up his belt and sword from where he'd deposited it on the floor and strapped it around his waist. "Bac, did someone already tell his family?"

"No, we weren't sure if you would want to."

How could he want to? But he owed it to Ahjul. "Yes, Tarol and I will. And I think we'd better go now." He noted Ann's sad, anxious eyes. "But I'll…maybe I could join you for supper, later."

She brightened some, taking his hand again. "You know we would love that, if you have time. And take it easy, please. You need to heal."

What was the point in his recovery, if his ward didn't make it? The chamber she'd been taken to was his first stop. He found Talea motionless in the bed, skin almost as white as the sheets, a grimace creasing her brow even in sleep. In that moment, she looked so much like Tessa that his breath caught in his throat.

The Stitch keeping an eye on her assured him that she was receiving the best possible care, and that her condition had at least not worsened. Beyond that, the man didn't say anything, but he wasn't as pessimistic about her chances as Yhkon would have expected. He should have ignored it. He should have been fine with some optimism.

He wasn't. "You do realize that it's a fatal injury?"

The Stitch made eye contact, and held it—something most strangers weren't willing to do with the reputedly temperamental Silquije Eun. "Four years ago I learned that if

Narone willed, this exact injury could in fact be survived."

Yhkon inwardly cursed. So the man was one of the medics that had witnessed his own *"miraculous"* recovery from the same injury. Which meant he was also likely one of the few people that knew the events leading up to and following that injury. He would rather no one knew. If that wasn't an option, he would rather not interact with those that did, with only a few exceptions, including Grrake. "I see. Do you suspect she might wake anytime soon?"

"Impossible to tell, but I don't think so."

"Then excuse me, I have other matters to attend. Please notify me if anything changes." He started for the door, but the Stitch spoke again.

"If I may, Silquije, I think you might do yourself a favor by having a little faith in the possibility of her recovery…and in other things."

Yhkon turned back to stare at the man. It wasn't every day a stranger—well, mostly a stranger—had the audacity to speak to him in that manner. That was usually something only Grrake did. Unfortunately for this man, Grrake wasn't around to restrain him with soft reprimands and disappointed looks. "You may *not,* actually. My faith or lack thereof is certainly not your concern." He walked out without waiting for a reply.

Still irritated when he reached Tarol's quarters, he didn't think to knock. His entrance interrupted Tarol and two Stitches all laughing. At what, he didn't know. And didn't care. They looked up at him, first surprised, quickly becoming nervous.

"I'm sorry," he glared at Tarol, "am I interrupting? Perhaps I should come back later to ask if you'd accompany me to the Rye'Shans' home, to tell them that their son and brother was killed last week?"

There wasn't the flash of indignation he had expected. Tarol lowered his head. "No, um, no, I'm coming." He started to get out of bed, but one of the Stitches stopped him.

"I'm sorry, Silquije, but you shouldn't be moving around so soon. Your leg—"

"Will survive a short trip. Grab me those crutches."

They reluctantly complied, watching silently as Tarol situated himself on the crutches and limped out of the room with Yhkon. They were almost out of the palace before he spoke, voice more remorseful than usual. Actually, more remorseful than *ever*. "Look, Yhkon, I was just—"

"Save it." Yhkon opened the door but didn't hold it, leaving Tarol to awkwardly prop it open with one crutch and hobble through on his own.

Tarol caught up to him, brown eyes hot with resentment. That was more characteristic. "Fine. Judge away, like you always do. But believe it or not some of us prefer not to mope about in a constant state of misery and drag others there with us."

Yhkon stopped and grabbed his arm, barely resisting the temptation to kick one of the crutches and let the impudent fool fall on his face. "Or maybe some of us have some respect, or even just the decency to show some solemnity, when a fellow warrior and friend has just died!"

Tarol shoved his hand off despite the crutches. "Would you shut up, for once?! As if I'm not mourning Ahjul. As if he weren't more my friend than yours—he would have been my brother-in-law! All you ever did was glare and snap at him, but oh, now he's dead so now he's your pal and you're heartbroken." Tarol kept walking, not so much as glancing over his shoulder. "Grrake may have you convinced that you're Calcaria's shining son, that you're a hero or a leader, or anything other than a fraud and a tyrant. But the rest of us know better. You're lucky Ahjul didn't."

Yhkon remained where he was. Unable to follow or respond even if he'd wanted to.

He eventually turned away. Let Tarol tell his fiance, Ahjul's sister, and her parents. Maybe he was obligated to be there too, maybe it was his duty as Ahjul's leader and even one of his trainers, but...he couldn't make himself go after Tarol.

His whole body felt overheated and weak. Annyve had said he had a fever. He made his way to the nearby Elikwai stable and sat down, leaning against the outside of the back wall, hoping it would be safe from spectators. Sitting down hardly relieved the exhaustion, and it certainly didn't offer any distraction from his nagging thoughts. From Tarol's words echoing in his mind.

"I didn't know you actually sat. I'm pretty sure I've only ever seen you standing."

The unexpected female voice would have made him jump to his feet, if he hadn't been so tired. Instead all he did was turn his head that direction, only to then clamber upright upon seeing who it was, distaste already making him set his feet away from her, ready to leave at the earliest opportunity.

She advanced and stuck out a hand for him to shake. "Jaylee Rhondel, maybe you remember, we—"

"I know." Of course he remembered—there were about five hundred Elikwai, but there was only one woman among them. He didn't take her hand. Grrake would give him a horrified look if he were there. "What do you want?"

If she was offended or intimidated by his bluntness, she didn't show it. In fact, her smile only grew. "The council sent me to talk to you. They didn't know you were going with Tarol to visit the Rye'Shans..." Finally her smile faded. "I was so sorry to hear about Ahjul. We were friends, and I always liked him. Of course, who didn't? He was a great guy."

Friends. Yes, that he knew too—Ahjul had courted this woman, for a brief time. Then again, almost every unmarried Elikwai under the age of thirty had. Yhkon crossed his arms. There was sincere sorrow in her face, at least. Still, it was Jaylee Rhondel. Some sadness over Ahjul's death couldn't make up for that. If her reputation as a flirt wasn't enough, she was also the stepdaughter of none other than Enisham. And she shouldn't be referring to the Wardens by their first names. "*Silquije Quoye* is telling the Rye'Shans by himself; what is it you need to speak to me about?"

She laughed a little. So much for genuine sorrow. "Yeah, after that little exchange of words you two had, I should think so."

Heat that wasn't from the fever flushed his cheeks. *Eavesdropping little tramp.* "To the point, please?"

She didn't react at all to his rudeness, which was somehow aggravating. "Simply put, you need a new Warden. More accurately, Terindi does. Since I scored the highest on the most recent Elikwai evaluation, I'm one of your candidates." She smiled sweetly. "That's the point."

He waited a couple seconds to make sure she wasn't playing a prank. All she did was keep smiling, head tilted slightly, her amber eyes sparkling in the sunshine.

It was perhaps the most ludicrous suggestion the council had ever made. He cleared his throat. "The council has actually not discussed this with me. Until they do I don't think there's anything for us to talk about."

He made it two steps before she spoke up again, "You're in a hurry to nowhere. The councilmen have gone their separate ways, I don't think they'll be available any time soon."

Confound this woman. "As I already told you, I can't think of anything for you and I to discuss at this time."

She laughed again. The fact that she was undeniably an attractive, charming young woman did not in the least improve the situation. He would rather deal with men that disliked him, or resented his authority, or were foolish, or even men that were trying to kill him, than...*this*. "Do you ever take a break from talking like a Sanonyan king?"

"You do realize that I *am* Sanonyan...?"

"Point proven. Of course I realize it—you've got that flawless golden complexion, it's a little obvious. See, you blush like one too."

His cheeks were flaming. Telling her it was due to a fever didn't seem like it would help much. "What is it you're so desperate to talk about?"

She grinned coyly at him. "Is me being desperate to talk to you wishful thinking on your part, an attempt at humor or flirting, or do you actually detect desperation in my address? See, I can talk Sanonyan too."

He realized a little late that he was staring dumbly at her. *Some Irlaish god, please smite me.* All he wanted was some peace and quiet, and Jaylee's company offered the exact opposite. Based on looks alone, it was no wonder she had been courted by almost every eligible man in the Elikwai barracks, but he did not understand how they could disregard everything else. Maybe if so many men hadn't reinforced the idea that she was a queen and every man her slave, she would have a little more humility and respect. "I would appreciate some propriety, if you can manage it, in our—"

"Silquije Eun!" A Stitch came running up to them, hastily bowing. "Arji Talereinna woke up. She's—"

He was already sprinting to the palace. Talea needed him.

17
Drifting

Yhkon arrived at Talea's room dizzy and breathing hard, forced to acknowledge that the medics had been justified in prescribing bed rest. That didn't matter. Talea's eyes were open, and terrified. She was squirming, clearly afraid of the Stitch trying to restrain her, and clearly made restless by the pain even as her movement made it worse. Tears shone on her cheeks. She groaned, clutching her heavily bandaged stomach.

He sat down on the bed next to her, taking her hands to keep her from moving so much. "Hey, Talea, it's me. You're safe." He caught the Stitch's eye and jerked his head towards the door. Understanding, the man left quietly.

Some of the confusion and fear drained from Talea's expression, as she looked at him. The pause didn't last long, a spasm of pain making her catch her breath and squeeze her eyes shut. "Yhkon it…it hurts…" She gripped his hand till her knuckles were white. "Wh-where are we?"

"We're in Calcaria." She was writhing again, with a whimper from the pain. Perspiration beaded her brow, yet her hands were clammy. "You have to hold still, Talea...I know it hurts, moving will make it worse." He pulled her against his chest, arms around her back, holding her close to stop her movement. Her skin was hot with fever, and she mumbled something inarticulate. "Shhh." He brushed her hair from her neck.

Gradually, she drifted out of consciousness. The fever must have been playing with her mind—she was groggy and even delirious after a few minutes. But she wasn't crying or moving anymore, and eventually her breathing steadied, telling him she was asleep. He didn't let her go, though, lest it disturb her. Gingerly he adjusted to a more comfortable position with his back against the headboard, and let himself relax. Or he would have, if he could control his mind. The image of Ahjul's lifeless body refused to leave, with Tarol's words playing over and over again. When he finally started to drift off, it was Tessa he saw, her eyes closed, skin ashen, a sword through her chest. It jerked him awake, briefly, before he dozed into a half-awake nightmare of Talea dying the same way Tessa had.

A soft knock on the door banished the dream. Bactah entered, anxiously surveying him and Talea. "Is she alright?"

Yhkon let his head fall back against the wall. "What does it look like?"

His friend frowned. "What about you?"

A convincing lie would be too much work. "Same answer."

Bactah swallowed and looked away. At length, he continued. "The council would like another meeting. As in Enisham. I would have told him to go chase a barbsit, but—"

"It's fine." Yhkon shook his head. "Let's get it over with." He gently set Talea on the bed and pulled the blankets up to her shoulders. Thankfully, she didn't wake.

The first flight of stairs was enough to make him dizzy and

hot, only to suddenly shiver with a chill. They were almost to the council room when a Stitch stopped them. It was one of the pair that had been taking care of Tarol. Fidgeting nervously, he bowed, before facing Yhkon. "Listen, sir…I just want you to know…Silquije Quoye seemed pretty low. We were just trying to distract him, cheer him up maybe. I just…well I thought you should know that I uh, I don't think he's taking Silquije Hyrru's death too, um, lightly."

Yhkon tried to form a reply. Nothing would come.

Bactah gave him a perplexed look, but addressed the Stitch. "Well, I don't know the details of the situation, but I'm sure Silquije Quoye mourns Ahjul's death just like all of us, I know they were good friends." Grabbing his arm, Bactah tried to keep moving, but Yhkon couldn't make himself simply follow, having said nothing.

He stopped beside the Stitch, not even sure what he was going to say yet. "Um, thank you for…for telling me." Pursing his lips, he followed Bactah.

He was almost surprised when they arrived at the council room, as if snapped from a daze, in which he'd forgotten that that was where they were going. He closed his eyes for a moment, both to recover from a wave of dizziness and to try and clear the fog that had taken over his thoughts.

The effects of his fever must have been visible, because Councilman Kwin got up with a worried look. "Good grief, are you alright? Come sit down."

Confused, he let Kwin and Bactah guide him to a chair. Only after he'd sat down and didn't feel so lightheaded did he bite his cheek in humiliation, wondering if he'd ever been quite so pathetic in front of the council. Bactah was explaining to them the infection-induced fever. Confound the whole situation. The last thing he wanted to appear as before these men was weak. They thought he was foolish, or arrogant, or belligerent, fine. But not *weak*.

He lifted his head, ignoring the chill that made him wish for his bed and some hot food. At what point would he be given ten minutes to himself, to eat a full meal? "I'm fine. Now would someone please tell me why your stepdaughter waltzed up to me and practically claimed herself as the new Warden, an hour ago?"

"She's not the new Warden," Enisham shrugged, "but she's going to be."

"Says you, the king of the Wardens? Last I checked, *I* was—"

"Yhkon, Enisham," Councilman Ilidyu interrupted him with an impatient gesture, "do we need to have a power struggle at every meeting? Jaylee scored the highest on the last Elikwai evaluation. Therefore she is the best qualified. But, that does not mean she is automatically the right choice, there are other things to be considered. We just want you to keep her as an option, along with the other highest scoring Elikwai."

Yhkon sighed, raking his fingers through his hair, flinching at a throbbing headache that seemed to be splitting his skull. If this day could get worse, he wasn't sure how. His friend was in a coffin…because *he* had failed. As if that wasn't enough, Talea might be joining him. And then there was Tarol, and Jaylee, and through it all he still had to be Silquije Eun. Without even Grrake around to back him up.

What he wouldn't give to crawl back into bed, shut out the world…and maybe just not wake up. "As if this isn't because she's your stepdaughter." He glowered at Enisham, and continued before he could answer. "So she scored high. But what about experience in the field? And…" He frowned. "Put bluntly, she's a woman."

"No, really?" Bactah rolled his eyes. "Do expound."

"You know what I mean."

"Actually," Juplay leaned forward, elbows on the table and fingers steepled, "I'm not sure that we do. Just because she's a woman doesn't mean she isn't capable. The battlefield might not be the traditional or even ideal place for a woman, but there can be exceptions. Before you argue, keep in mind that your ward, destined to be the captain of all Calcaria, is a fifteen-year-old girl."

Enisham nodded with an expression of smug satisfaction. "Precisely."

Funny, I seem to remember you disliking that the lead ward was female, back when Grrake told you. Being unable to come up with a reasonable argument was all the more frustrating. "Well, fine. But, having a woman on the team would be complicated for…other reasons. Do I even need to explain why?"

"No." Juplay nodded. "I understand that. But, again…" His golden eyes were keen. "Four female wards ought to involve the same complications."

What would it take to escape this blasted meeting? Months ago, at their last meeting, they'd practically threatened to replace him. Well, why shouldn't they? It wasn't as if he enjoyed this. As if he…as if he could handle the position.

"I don't see what the dilemma is." Enisham shrugged with uncharacteristic nonchalance. "Jay is the most qualified for the position. Talea is a girl, yet you hardly complained about her being your ward."

Reller was saying something, agreeing. So was one of the other councilmen. Yhkon closed his eyes, unable to follow their conversation, mind whirling as pain kept hammering his temples, the effects of the fever only increasing. Finally he stood up, having to grip the chair for balance. His action silenced the discussion as all eyes turned on him. "I...just...do whatever. Make her Warden. I don't..." He pinched the bridge of his nose. Trying to concentrate. To regain control. "Please excuse me."

Bactah and even Juplay moved to assist him as he started to leave, but he waved them off. Somehow, he made it to his quarters. The actual trip was hazy, he only came to full awareness sitting on the floor, back against his bed. He felt as though he were simply waiting for Grrake to appear. Grrake would see that he couldn't handle it anymore, and he would take over. He would fix things.

But Grrake wasn't there. It was just him, alone in the palace he had always hated, his dying ward a couple halls down. Everything was wrong. Everything had always been wrong...his family, Tessa, Ahjul, Talea. *He* was wrong, just like Tarol—among others—said. He didn't deserve his role as lead Warden, and he couldn't fill it. Talea and Ahjul were proof of that.

Yhkon let his eyes close, body relax. The list of things he should be doing didn't seem important. Nothing was. Not if Talea was dead. If he could just sleep...it was an escape, if only temporary. He could worry about permanent solutions later.

Even as exhausted as he was, deep, uninterrupted sleep wouldn't come. Instead it was drifting...drifting...nightmares, feverish haze...occasionally aware of his surroundings, even considering climbing into his bed, but never fully awake. Vaguely he felt the various aches and pains, coming and going with his thoughts.

18
Guilt

It was a knock at the door that woke Yhkon after the long, restless night. Sunlight was peeking through his shuttered window.

"Hello? Yh—oh my bad, not supposed to call you that, am I? I'm not calling you *Silquije Eun*...so, Mr. Tavker?"

Yhkon sat up, every muscle aching in protest, after spending the night on the floor. There was a hollow pain in his stomach, a reminder he'd hardly eaten. "Who..." Recognition of the voice dawned. *Blasted girl.* "Rhondel?"

"Yes, duh. Except actually my first name is Jaylee, if you forgot...you gonna let me in or what?"

"Um, no, actually." He let himself slouch against the bed again. The door was locked, and Jaylee Rhondel was certainly not among the few that possessed a key.

There was a scratching sound moments before the door swung open. He recoiled. "How'd you—"

"Picking a lock is not that difficult." Her brow furrowed as she looked at him. "Um, you look horrible."

He didn't feel up to challenging her further on having barged in. Standing up was enough challenge. "I'm fine. I'd be more fine if you left me alone."

Jaylee quirked an eyebrow. "I would beg to differ. Most people that are fine don't spend the night on the floor, with a perfectly good bed right next to them. I also get the distinct feeling that you haven't eaten a full meal in awhile. Finally…" She trailed off, head tilted slightly as she looked at him. Something about her expression made him think she was going to say something sentimental and make the whole situation twice as bad. Instead, she puckered her lips and finished, "I do believe you should take a bath and change those bandages and…shave."

His cheeks were flaming. If the council actually made her Warden with the delirious permission he'd given, he would be regretting it for the rest of his life. Some indignation and chastisement seemed the correct response, yet he only fumbled over the attempt, not even mustering enough energy to glare properly at her.

She smiled that beautiful, innocent…dangerous smile. "Good. I'm going to come back in half an hour, by which point I expect you to be cleaned up. I'll get some breakfast cooked up for you, and if need be I'll shovel it down your throat. Bye! You're welcome." Just like that, she was gone.

Leaving him still standing there, dumbfounded. He was still standing there when a servant came in with a bucket of hot water. With little other choice, and the steaming tub surprisingly appealing, he followed Jaylee's…*suggestions*. Telling himself he would have done it anyway, even without her interference.

It was undeniably refreshing. He still had a fever, he was still famished, but his body was less sore and the headache gone.

As promised, Jaylee returned, bearing two trays of food.

"There, see! You look better already. And I brought myself breakfast too, no one likes eating alone…well," she set the trays down at his table, "you might, being a recluse and all. But not today! Come on, eat up."

This was ridiculous. It was especially ridiculous that he was tolerating it. "You know, I don't usually tolerate—"

"Oh, shush, just eat." She smiled and set to work on her own tray.

Hunger was more powerful than dislike. He joined her, doing his best not to let on just how hungry he was.

"So," she pushed aside her mostly empty tray, "Enisham told me you agreed to my being the new Warden. I told him he might be hallucinating."

"I told him what he wanted to hear so he would stop talking and let me leave," he grumbled under his breath.

She smirked at him. "He hates you too, if you ever wondered."

"Ha. He never left much room for doubt."

"Alright, then are you looking into other candidates today? I could make some suggestions."

Yhkon got up and paced a few steps, the shaky feeling gone after a full meal. "I'm not looking today, actually. Or doing anything."

"Oh? Why not?"

"Simple, I don't want to."

"So…don't you need to pick a new Warden?"

No. He didn't. But he couldn't tell her that…he couldn't explain to anyone that if Talea was dead, there was no point. He shouldn't *have* to explain. How was it not obvious?

She continued. "Well, how about you go sit with your ward, then, until you feel like it. And before you object, it would be better for you than sitting in here alone, and she will certainly feel better with someone she knows around."

"She's asleep, my presence won't make much difference."

"No she's not." Jaylee said it as if it were common knowledge. "She woke up an hour ago."

He moved toward the door, scowling at her. "Why wasn't I told?"

"That was my other reason for visiting. I would have told you earlier, but I knew you'd rush out and you needed some food first. You wouldn't be any good to Talea if you passed out, now would you?" She waved him toward the door with a wink. "Go on, you can thank me later."

Rather than respond to her insolence, he left, navigating the palace at a jog. A Stitch was seated outside Talea's closed door. "She wanted to be alone," he said. "Didn't want to see her family yet. But she'll see you."

Inside, Talea was propped up with pillows, face still pale, but looking less pained and more awake than last time. The distant, dark look in her eyes was far more worrying. "Talea?" He sat down at the foot of the bed. "Are you feeling better?"

"Yeah," she said it without even looking at him. "Lots of drugs for the pain, I guess."

"Good, but," he waited for her to make eye contact, "that's not the only thing I was asking about." She didn't say anything, so he continued. "Why didn't you want to see your family?"

She shrugged, wincing a bit. "I don't know. Later, maybe."

"Is it the battle? You're awfully young to be in—"

She silenced him with four words. "It was my fault."

Yhkon cringed, knowing immediately what she meant. And he knew how she felt. Grrake, despite his best efforts, hadn't been able to convince him Tessa's death wasn't his fault after four years. How could he of all people convince Talea that Ahjul's death wasn't hers? "That's not true. You'd just taken a fatal injury. No one could expect you to keep fighting...I shouldn't have asked it of you, I was just, I was desperate. It was not your fault, okay? If anything it was mine."

"But..." She pressed her lips in a tight line. "If I hadn't...if—"

"Listen..." He hesitated. He knew how she felt, and he knew he should explain to her, to try and help...In the past, he'd never been willing to talk about Tessa, with her or anyone. But it seemed as though that unwillingness might have been the very beginning of their conflict. And how could he keep shutting her out? She had almost died. She still might. And if he could help her...well, whether she survived or not, he owed it to her. "You know...Tessa, who I wouldn't tell you about? Well...she was my fiance. It was just a few weeks before the wedding that Grrake and I had to make a trip to Zentyre. Tessa wanted to come...I told her I didn't think it was a good idea..." He balled his fists. Remembering her pleading look, the tender kiss that had melted his resolve. "But I gave in. She came. And on that cliff that overlooks the ocean, near Skoti's outpost? Kaydor attacked us with fifty men. And I..." He swallowed as the memory played in his mind. The explosion of pain in his stomach as Kaydor stabbed him, followed by Tessa's scream. "And I couldn't protect her. Kaydor gave me the same injury as you have now, and he killed Tessa."

Talea listened in perfect silence, eyes now soft with empathy. She took his hand.

He looked down at her small hand in his. "I've blamed myself for her death for four years. So maybe I'm not one to talk...but it wasn't your fault, Talea, and in any case it doesn't help anyone to think that way. I know I probably can't say anything to convince you...in the end only you can make the decision to forgive yourself, to accept it for what it is."

There were tears on her cheeks. "Thank you, for telling me." She took a deep breath. "I just...Ahjul was..." She was crying, trying to stop with a grimace and holding her bandaged torso, but unable to.

He did the only thing he knew to—put his arms around her and pull her into an embrace. When she stopped crying he let her go, wondering if he should have hugged her in the first place. But she seemed calmer, and smiled a little at him. "Thanks," was her hoarse whisper.

This was awkward, and entirely out of his element. But he felt it was right. "I should have just told you when you asked, I just...I don't like talking about it."

"Noticed that." There was a hint of mirth in her face, making him smile. "But, really...I shouldn't have pushed so hard. I'm sorry. You shouldn't have to talk about it if you don't want to..." It was a rather uncertain statement. He knew she did *want* that complete openness from him. Maybe he couldn't blame her for that, when she had been away from home and all her family, on such a crazy "mission," surrounded by danger, with him as one of her closest companions.

"Well." He cleared his throat and motioned toward her heavily bandaged torso. "The dressing needs changed...do you mind?"

"Kinda," she winced, "but go ahead."

He worked as quickly as possible, seeing her discomfort. To distract her he tried to keep up some conversation, and in so doing realized he needed to tell her about Jaylee.

She took it much as he had. Surprise, followed by reluctant acceptance. Terindi needed a Warden, it was as simple as that. "So...are you going to take Jaylee? Or try to get someone else?"

He sighed. "Unfortunately she scored the highest, and

she's Enisham's stepdaughter...I would need to conjure up a pretty good argument against it. I guess I'll..." If only Grrake, or one of the other Wardens were around. It wasn't a decision he liked to make by himself.

The thought made him frown. One of the other Wardens *was* around. And probably deserved an apology, that Yhkon was certainly not excited to give.

Talea was observing him inquisitively. "What is it?"

"Tarol and I argued about something...but I would like his opinion on the new Warden."

She nodded. "You should go talk to him. I'm alright. And...I guess I'd like to see my family, after all."

Now he had no excuse out of it. Promising to send them in, he gave her hand a squeeze and left. The moment he told her parents, Naylen, Alili, and Brenly that she was awake and wanted to see them, they rushed away with smiles and hasty *thank you's*. Watching them go, he found himself smiling ever so slightly as well. Talea wasn't going to die. Somehow it was the first moment he felt, with surprising certainty, that she would be okay. Logically he knew that while the infection had mostly been repressed, it could easily return and take her life. Yet he didn't feel the crushing conviction that she was going to die. Quite the opposite.

Any cheer he felt faded as he reached the Wardens' floor, Tarol's door a couple down from his. He could either go into his quarters, where he knew he would pace, sit with nothing to do, mentally lecture himself, or even end up breaking something. Or he could go talk to Tarol. Apologize. Apologies were bad enough...an apology to Tarol was another matter entirely.

Still, he ended up knocking on his door.

Tarol, not one to require identification before allowing

entrance, could be heard limping with his crutches across the room, before opening the door.

Anger, surprise, disdain, none of what Yhkon expected was there. Tarol just looked tired. "What do you want?"

"I…" Yhkon put his hands in his pockets, leaning against the doorway. "I guess to apologize."

Tarol nodded and frowned, almost disinterestedly. "Alright. Get in here." He hobbled inside his largely empty, but messy, apartment, sitting heavily on the bed. "I take it you have something to ask for, my opinion, a favor, something like that. Don't see any other reason you would have been willing to apologize."

Yhkon entered, crossing his arms. "I realized I was wrong and had been harsh. Can't that be why?"

"Sure you realized it," Tarol aimlessly spun one of the crutches a few times, "but you don't mind being in the wrong until it negatively affects you somehow. So you never would have apologized, until you wanted something from me."

Yhkon let his arms fall to his sides without even meaning to, unable to speak, or conjure up any idea of what he might say.

Tarol only shrugged. "Whatever. What does it matter. What do you need?"

"Well I just…" He cleared his throat, uncomfortably backing up a couple steps, angling himself away from Tarol. "I wanted your thoughts on a, a difficult matter…but I was also wondering, um, well how Ahjul's family is." As if he weren't humiliated enough, his tongue felt like a rock, refusing to communicate with his brain.

Perhaps that wasn't the best question to ask. Tarol stared at him dully. "How do you think? Just get to the point."

He should have gone to his quarters. Paced, broken a

chair—anything but this. Tarol was miserable enough as it was, now he was about to discuss replacing Ahjul, his friend and would-have-been brother-in-law. "I'm…I'm sorry, Tarol. I really am. Is Pear okay?"

Pear. Nicknamed so by Ahjul, which she didn't mind since she didn't like her real name, Perelei. She and Ahjul were the youngest of eight, not quite like any of their older siblings, so similar to each other. Both with the same kind, bright blue eyes. Yhkon couldn't claim an abundance of interaction with them together, but he knew they were as close as a brother and sister could be. Pear and Tarol had been engaged for months.

"She's…" He let out his breath wearily. "She'll be alright, I guess."

Yhkon slowly made his way to the door. "I think, maybe I should…ask my question later."

"No." Tarol stood up. "I already know it has to do with a new Warden. I just don't know who it is they've suggested."

"Someone tell you?"

"No, I figured it out. I'm not stupid."

Biting his lip, Yhkon nodded and turned back. "Jaylee Rhondel is the council's favorite candidate. She had the highest score, last Elikwai evaluation."

Tarol smirked a little. "Jaylee Rhondel. Shoulda known."

"How well do you know her?"

"Well enough to know that she's plenty capable, she likes cats, and she'll drive you insane."

"Already does," he muttered, arms crossed again. "So do you think she's a good choice? I'm not sure how her being…well…a woman, might…go."

Tarol laughed dryly. "It's gonna make everything different. But who's a better choice? Ol' Peck Wilwin? He has the next highest score, if I remember right, but he's only been in a real fight once, and I was there—he panicked, big time, barely kept himself alive for one minute without help. Egthenur does alright in a fight, but he's a clod otherwise. Dranin would be good...but the simple fact is that Jaylee could take him in a duel."

Barbsit tails. "Here I was hoping you would have some great reason for me not to accept her."

"Nope." Tarol shrugged. "Resh will be delighted."

Yhkon grunted his agreement. "Exactly. That's almost reason enough right there."

After a pause, Tarol put his hands on his knees, leaning forward. "Well, I imagine you have other errands to run...? Telling Jaylee the news, anyway."

A polite way of saying he was overstaying his welcome. *Fair.* "I suppose. Should I...can I have anything sent up to you, or, anything?"

"I'm good." Tarol just shook his head. Not exactly friendly or cheerful, but not bitter. At least they were in neutral territory, not at odds.

Neutral territory would have to be good enough. And mulling what Tarol had said would have to wait for later. For the time being, he had to confirm his agreement of Jaylee being Silquije Hyrru to the council. *Can't wait.*

They seemed anxious to see him, relieved to see that he was in better condition than the previous day. Pleased that he agreed. Or in Enisham's case, intolerably smug. Yhkon kept the meeting as brief as possible, announcing only his agreement and that Talea seemed to be improving, before leaving.

Bactah caught him in the hallway outside. "Feeling better? You were an absolute fright yesterday."

"Thanks," was all he said, dryly.

"You're so welcome. So. Supper was great last night…"

Yhkon looked at him. Supper. What was the—he sucked in his breath, remembering. "Oh. Blast. I'm sorry, I com—"

Bactah clapped him on the arm, walking at a leisurely pace down the hallway. "Well you better be sorry, but you're forgiven. I explained your pitiful condition to my parents."

He rolled his eyes. "You are such a—"

"Yeah well point is, think you'll be more up to it tonight? My parents would still like a more substantial visit with your sorry self. Why, I don't know. I suppose—"

"Oh stop talking." Grinning despite himself, he gave Bactah a shove. "Yes, I'll do my best to actually show up tonight. Or, better yet…are they available now? How about lunch?"

A nonchalant shrug. "Quite possibly. Let's go."

Usually Yhkon would borrow a celith for the trip, but Bactah hated riding. So for his sake, they made use of one of the palace carriages to travel the few miles to the Falston's home in the city.

Annyve was almost just as concerned for his condition as the day before, apparently quite upset by whatever Bactah told them as to why he didn't come. Again, Yhkon didn't mind her fretting. The only other person that so consistently and completely treated him as if he were their own son was…well, Grrake. And Grrake wasn't around. It was nice to have at least a few people who offered him care and guidance, instead of looking to him for it.

Heaven knew he rarely managed to give it as they needed.

Why was he here? Not Grrake? Grrake would make a better leader than him for a hundred different reasons, including that everyone—literally everyone, as far as he knew—liked and respected Grrake. Whereas almost everyone disliked Yhkon, and only grudgingly respected him, if even.

For good reason.

Ekirre watching him keenly made him realize he had gone silent, disconnected from his surroundings. Unfortunately, all of them had noticed. The usual chatter and banter and clicking forks was gone, three pairs of eyes trained on him. Waiting.

Yhkon leaned forward in a casual posture and shoveled another bite of food into his mouth.

Ann didn't fall for it. "Tell us what's wrong."

He hated that question. What was wrong? Most days, it would be so much faster to answer what *wasn't* wrong. Because that answer was short, perhaps nonexistent. *He* was wrong...so was it possible for anything in his life to be right? "Nothing, really. I'm just tired." Better give them something, or they would never believe it. "And...Ahjul, you know."

Her frown became all the more compassionate. "Of course. He was your friend, and such a sweet young man..."

When no one said anything for awhile, Ekirre changed the subject. "So how was it going? The trip, the mission, the wards...Bactah tells us some but not much."

Silently thanking Ekirre for offering him an escape, he took a sip of water and set his fork down to answer. "Alright, I suppose. We had just gotten Skyve...it was a bit of a rough patch for awhile, Talea and I weren't seeing eye to eye. That, at least, seems to have mended. Otherwise things were alright I think. I was hoping we would have longer before Kaydor figured out what we were up to. But we just have Amilyne left, before we can bring them here, and I fully admit that I look forward to that."

"We all do." Ann smiled. "I suppose you're too old now for me to say that I worry about and miss you, when you're gone."

He mustered a return smile. "It's good to have someone that misses me. Bactah can tell you that the council certainly doesn't."

They laughed. Good, the pleasant mood had been restored. *Now just keep it that way.* It didn't prove hard. The Falstons were amiable people, with whom he could usually relax.

He stayed for a few hours, partially for their sakes, partially because he didn't have anything else to do. The only other person in all of Calcaria he had any desire or reason to spend time with was Talea, and she was with her family.

Yet he couldn't keep himself at leisure in their living room for too long. Three hours pushed the limit of how long he could keep his mind occupied with casual, light conversation, or stay seated without anything to do, or keep his thoughts from wandering to the dark, murky places they always tried to go.

So he made excuses. Hugged Annyve, shook Ekirre's hand, punched Bactah's shoulder, and left the peace of their company and home. Without any destination or task. With time he didn't want on his hands. A lifetime. He would wander aimlessly, train, pace in his room. All the usual. By himself.

But there was nothing new about any of that. That was his life.

19
Tessa

"When do you go back?"

Hearing Alili's voice, small and raspy but her voice all the same, always made Talea want to smile. The question, however, was a bit more conflicting. She took the little girl's hand. "I'm not sure. When I get better, I guess. But then we just have one more ward to get, and I'll be back."

Alili studied her with those huge, expressive brown eyes. They never sparkled with mirth, or glowed with energy. Almost no matter the situation, they were the same—wistful, observant, appearing to hold far greater wisdom and experience than a seven-year-old ought to have.

Seles caught up to them, her own expression much as it often was—concerned. "Are you sure you're okay to go back at all? Couldn't you stay, and the rest of the group could get Amilyne?"

Okay to go back...In regards to the injury, as Seles was asking, probably, given a couple more weeks. But otherwise? Not as easy to answer. As happy as she was to be with her family again, and to be in Calcaria, where she was *safe,* where she could simply rest...she missed everyone. And she missed getting up every morning with a mission, a purpose.

But then, there was the battle. There was the fact that she was going back to a hostile region, even if it was her home, where she could find herself in another conflict at any time. Where she could lose another friend...

"You okay?" Brenly, like Alili, watched her intently, perhaps having noticed her grimace at the memories.

"Yeah." She flashed a smile. "Yeah, I think I'll be okay, going back. The Stitches said two more weeks should be enough for this to be healed, at least well enough for me to ride and do a little walking."

"But you can't even laugh without doubling over," Naylen said with a contradictory mix of teasing and worry.

"Well," Yhkon's voice behind them made her turn, surprised, "fortunately, someone once told me laughter ought to be considered a medicine."

Her family made room for him to walk beside her and Alili. They were giving her a tour of the palace gardens, now that she was able to walk. "Who told you that? Grrake?"

"No, though it does sound like something he would say. It was...well his name is Mahzin. You'll meet him someday." He glanced sideways, toward her bandage-distended waist. "How are you feeling today?"

She let her hand fall to her torso, to the ever-present ache of the scar. "Pretty good. What are you up to? Haven't seen you a lot, lately."

Part of him shrugged. The other part did a poor job of covering his discomfort. "Just busy."

Busy my foot. Upon being presented to the council yesterday—it had been slightly less of a nightmare than she'd expected—she had immediately liked Yhkon's friend, Bactah. Later when it was just the two of them, she'd asked him what

Yhkon was doing each day. The answer had been, "Nothing, really."

She was convinced that Yhkon wasn't upset with her. So why did he stay away? Maybe just to give her time with her family?

"I was hoping to have your company for something today, though."

Forcing the question from her mind, Talea looked up at him. "What sort of something?"

He took a deep breath. *Uh-oh.* "I have to talk to Jaylee. Thought you should be introduced...and maybe could make it a hair less horrible than if I were by myself."

She smiled. "A hair less, huh? Well I am quite curious to meet this Jaylee...when are we going?"

"Whenever you're free."

Do I look particularly swamped to you? True, her family was there. But she'd spent almost every waking moment with one or all of them in the past week. They could spare her for awhile. As it was...she wanted to have some time with Yhkon. For all their fighting only a few weeks ago before the battle, she had been missing him in his many and long absences these days. And she missed the rest of the group, the wards, the Wardens, each of them a friend in their own way. Tarol had visited her a couple days before. They had laughed, reminisced, and in her case choked on tears—about all their friends and the adventures they'd been on, but mostly about Ahjul.

She felt Yhkon must need that. He had opened up to her about Tessa...for all of five minutes. And then he'd gone back into his shell and acted as though it hadn't happened. He hadn't gone back to giving her the cold shoulder or snapping, to her he was generally caring, but he wasn't...he wasn't recovering. He was dwelling in the same place he'd already been, and in Ahjul's death. And as far as she knew, he had no one to help him bear the pain. Grrake wasn't there. Bactah's family seemed to have practically adopted him, but even they, she could see, were kept at a safe distance.

Well, best make their trip to see Jaylee count, then. "I'm free now. Mom, Dad, I'm going to go with Yhkon to meet the new Warden." She smiled at her family and Brenly, giving Alili a hug. "I'll see you guys later."

When her family had left, Yhkon led her out of the gardens, around the palace. The building was huge. *How long before I don't get lost...* "She lives in the Elikwai barracks. Are you alright walking that far, or should we get a carriage?"

She could see the barracks from the window of her bedroom, which Yhkon told her wasn't nearly as nice as the quarters she'd have when they were actually living in Calcaria. It seemed plenty nice to her. "I think I'm okay walking." They were already a quarter of the way there, anyway. "So what is it you need to talk to her about? I assume it's not just because you love her company so much..."

He gave her a look making it very clear that that was not the reason. "For some reason *I* have to be the one to tell her how to get outfitted for her new gear. And since she's now a Warden, I guess I'm supposed to give her a report of sorts on where things stand in Zentyre." He sighed. "Really I think Bactah just convinced the council to tell me to do it, because he thinks we should be," he wrinkled his nose, "friends."

Unable to help herself, she grinned sideways at him. "I dunno, Tarol told me she's not bad looking, and quite endearing."

Yhkon groaned on an oath, almost making her laugh with his utter disgust. "Please not you too."

Gulping down the giggle, she shook her head and smiled.

"No, I wouldn't dare. But Bactah might have a point...if she's going to be a Warden, part of our group, the closer we are to friends the better. And I imagine you're going to have the hardest time out of all of us making that happen."

His only response was a grunt.

It was only half a mile to the barracks, in weather that Yhkon said was uncharacteristically mild, though she still thought it a little too cold and windy to qualify as *mild*. The building was about the same size as the palace, but that was where the similarities ended. The palace was grand, marble and stone, designed for royalty. It was quiet, with a relatively small number of occupants, who all seemed to abide by an unspoken rule of tranquility. The barracks, on the other hand, were mostly wood, some brick, with the simplest architecture possible.

And brimming with loud, lively residents.

The advantage to that was that their entrance went unnoticed. In the palace, it was difficult to go anywhere without being recognized, and probably bowed to. Here, she ducked her head and stayed behind Yhkon, letting him shoulder a path through the crowd of laughing, talking, horseplaying men. Even without knowing she was in the Elikwai barracks, she could have guessed. She felt dwarfed in the sea of warriors.

It didn't take long to notice that first, Yhkon was well known among the Elikwai. And second...not necessarily well liked. Most, upon seeing him, either stepped hastily out of the way, frowned and mumbled something to their companions, or even glared at him the moment he had passed. Yhkon didn't give any of them so much as a glance. Yet she knew he was perfectly aware of their reactions.

Out of the crowded mess hall, Yhkon led her through a

couple hallways, eventually stopping at one of the closed doors that lined either side and knocking.

"Who is it?" a female voice called from inside, sounding as though she were moving around.

Yhkon was already scowling, as if offended she hadn't automatically opened the door. "Yhkon Tavker. I have—"

"Oh, then get in here, silly!"

A tormented look flashed across Yhkon's face as he opened the door. Talea was pretty sure she already liked this woman.

It was confirmed when they entered the room to find a young, beautiful, brightly smiling woman busily rearranging the furniture and decorations. Her eyes sparkled as she blew a strand of hair from her cheek and faced them, a stack of books propped on one hip. "I never thought the day would come that the mighty Silquije Eun would condescend to step foot in my lowly Elikwai chamber." She winked at him, brushing past before he could reply and extending a hand and a warm smile to Talea. "I've always hoped I might get to meet you, but I never thought I'd get to be a Warden and get to know you! You can call me Jay. What would you like me to call you?"

Dazed but smiling, Talea shook her hand, grateful she hadn't bowed or called her *arji*. "Just Talea. Nice to meet you."

Jay pressed her lips together before grinning, as if excited. "You probably get so sick of this sort of thing, but can I see it? Your lightning?"

Yhkon rolled his eyes. Funny, since he usually seemed to enjoy showing her ability off to other San Quawr. Talea happily obliged Jay's curiosity, enjoying the woman's obvious delight.

Jaylee dove straight into a cheerful conversation without so much as an uncertain pause. She wanted to know all about Talea, her childhood, about the other wards, what were laborer's villages like. Talea was trapped between enjoying the conversation and wanting to get to know Jaylee, but practically feeling Yhkon's mounting impatience. It was as if just being in the same room as the new Warden vexed him.

She was wondering how she might go about soothing the situation, when Jaylee—to both Talea's horror and amusement—poked his arm and gave him a playfully chiding look. "And aren't you being an unfriendly recluse! Would it kill you to speak to me?"

His lip curled with distaste, while he looked down at her with discomfiture, apparently uncomfortable with her being within arm's reach. "Why do you think I came here? You haven't given me a chance to say a thing."

"Ohhh." She leaned back with raised eyebrows, giving Talea a knowing smirk. "Am I seeing some jealousy over your ward, Silquije?"

"What?" He wrinkled his nose, brow knit, as if she were ridiculous.

Talea wasn't sure if she should try to intervene, or enjoy the show at Yhkon's expense.

"Well," Jaylee shrugged and pushed her hair behind her ear, "anyway. Say away, Tavker. I presume you and I are not on a first-name basis yet."

At first he just looked confused. Then, still irritated, but resigned. "I'm supposed to give you instructions for getting outfitted for your Warden gear, and a report on how things are going in Zentyre."

"Reports have always been my least favorite part of being an Elikwai." She flopped onto her bed, putting her hands on the mattress behind her so she could lean back. "Care to sit, Mr. Warden? Talea?"

Talea accepted the invitation, her torso beginning to ache

from all the standing. Yhkon did not, and only looked all the more uncomfortable as the only one one his feet. He looked entirely out of place, a tall, weapon-clad man, who was visibly tense, in the middle of a small room that was brightly, femininely decorated. While Jaylee listened with surprising diligence, he rattled out his directions and information with as little eye contact and expression as possible.

When he finished, Jaylee nodded once, asked one question, before returning to more pleasant topics with Talea. She occasionally made a subtle effort to include Yhkon, but never seemed surprised or deterred when he ignored it to the best of his ability.

As far as Talea could tell, there was very little that could be done to improve his mood or involvement. She'd work on that when they left. In the meantime, she found Jaylee more and more likeable. Fun, easy to talk to, and she showed sincere interest and understanding. In a way, she hardly seemed like Warden material…except there was something to be said for her feisty spunk, that might be just as fierce under the right circumstances as Yhkon's drive and tenacity.

The visit was interrupted after awhile by a knock at the door. Yhkon's head jerked up instantly. Jaylee invited the caller to come in.

It was an Elikwai. He smiled at Jaylee, with what appeared to be more than courtesy, looked with confusion at Talea, and eventually eyed Yhkon nervously. "Silquije Eun, there's someone to see you, waiting in the office."

Yhkon was already moving to the door. "Excuse me Miss Rhondel."

Eager to escape, aren't you? Talea watched him go, as did Jaylee, before they both looked at each other and laughed. Jay shook her head. "I have my work cut out for me, don't I?"

She hummed her agreement. "When it comes to Yhkon...we all do."

~♦~

Yhkon let a breath of relief escape his lungs as soon as he was out of Jaylee's room. Confound that woman and her uncanny ability to fluster him. The fact that she was *flirting*...that just made it all the more appalling.

The Elikwai acting as messenger had left, since Yhkon hadn't even bothered to ask anything about who was waiting for him. Probably one of the Falstons. Not many others would have a reason to visit him, and anyone who did would probably choose to have the message delivered by someone else and save themselves the trouble.

He reached the door to the office, knocked once to announce his presence, and entered without another thought.

But it was not one of the Falstons that stood up to face him. It was a middle-aged woman, black hair, soft blue eyes, a narrow face. Dia Zalders.

Tessa's mother.

His tongue felt like a rock and his brain had gone blank, yet he was speaking anyway. Simply saying her name, voice hollow with shock and anxiety. "Dia?"

She didn't look much different than he remembered. A little older, more melancholy than she had been when he'd courted Tessa. But a far cry from how he'd last seen her, four years ago—haggard, sobbing, face red with rage as she'd screamed that he'd taken her daughter from her.

Her eyes glistened slightly as she lowered her head, taking a tentative step closer. He resisted the urge to back away. To open the door and flee. Irritation with Jaylee, that was hardly consequential now. It was vague and fleeting compared to the squeezing ache he could already feel in his chest.

Why resist, though? They hadn't spoken since that night he'd practically crawled onto her porch, still weak and feverish from the gruesome wound in his stomach. As far as he could tell, they had mutually agreed that with Tessa gone, with him guilty of her death, any affinity they shared had gone to the grave with her. What was the point of reawakening old anguish? He couldn't do this. Not now.

Yhkon turned for the door. She said something he didn't hear and didn't heed. Her hand tight on his wrist, refusing to let go, was the only thing that stopped him. "Yhkon, please."

He faced her again, wishing he didn't feel the stinging in his eyes, the weight in the pit of his stomach, the unavoidable, painful feeling of loss, of something missing. "Please what? Why now? Nothing's changed. She's still gone. I don't want to—"

"Things have changed." Dia gripped his arm even tighter, her fingers like a claw. "Or they should. What I said to you that night...how I felt...." She pursed her lips, looking away for a moment. "*That's* changed." She raised sorrowful, somehow peaceful eyes to him. No more accusation, or bitterness, or raw heartbreak. Yet he still felt accused. Still felt the raw heartbreak. "I need to apologize to you. It wasn't your fault, and I hate myself for ever having blamed you...I was just so..."

His need to escape this room, this conversation, was only growing. Tension tightened every fiber in his body, the muscles around his eyes twitching as he fought to regain composure. "Yes it was."

Her gaze became a strange mixture of stern and sympathetic. "No it wasn't. It was Kaydor. He killed her."

Yhkon let his eyes wander the room, settling on anything but her. If only she would let go of his arm so that he could leave without having to forcibly break her grip.

She did not let go. She kept her hold, and drew him deeper into the room, sitting down in one of the chairs and giving him little choice except to sit down next to her. "I never realized just how much you loved her." He knew she was looking at him, but he didn't dare so much as glance in return. "I knew she was absolutely infatuated with you, that she was happy with you...but you were, well, you were *Silquije Eun*. Quiet and withdrawn and for as little as you talked, obviously in pain. I always thought that..." Her voice held a tremor. "That if it had been reversed, and you had died, it would have hurt Tessa more than it hurt you when she died."

Without meaning to, he looked at her, grimacing.

The tears in her eyes were brimming, ready to spill over at any moment. "Now I know how wrong I was."

He tore his gaze away again, gritting his teeth.

"But Yhkon..." She softened her grasp on his wrist, then wrapped both her small hands around his clenched fist. "You have to let yourself keep living. Everyone, yourself most of all, seems to forget that you are still so young. You still have your whole life ahead of you. Live it. Enjoy it. You know she would want you to." She squeezed his hand. "Let yourself be *happy*."

Yhkon got to his feet, forcing her to release her grip. He was at the door before she had the opportunity to react. Only there did he finally face her again. "I was probably happy with my family in Sanonyn, before my mother died and my father left us. I was relatively happy in Zentyre with my siblings and my aunt, barely having enough food to eat, before Kaydor took all of them from me. And I was happy with Tessa, before he killed her." There was a strange heat traveling up his spine, tightening his muscles and hardening his expression into a glare he knew she didn't deserve. "Happiness has only ever been short lived for me, and always ended in greater pain than the last time. So explain to me, why I should even bother?" Without waiting for a reply, he flung the door open and left.

He heard hurried footsteps seconds before she caught up to him in the hallway, pushing something small and metallic into his hand. It was the ring he had given Tessa as an engagement gift. Delicate bands of silver, with a sparkling amethyst jewel carved in the likeness of her favorite Zentyren flower, the seeds of which had been his very first gift to her, before they'd started courting. The ring had cost him all the money he'd had at the time, as well as a little from Grrake. Her reaction had been worth every cent.

Dia closed his fingers around the ring. "You should bother because you deserve it, and whether or not you believe me, one day you'll have it. Tessa loved you. Honor that by trying to find and share the joy she so desperately wanted to share with you."

She gave him a final, compassionate smile, and left.

~ ♦ ~

Talea followed Jaylee through the barracks towards the office Yhkon's visitor had been waiting in. When he hadn't returned after a few minutes and the herb for pain Talea was on started wearing off, Jay had suggested they find him, so he could take her back to the palace.

They entered the hallway leading to the office just in time to see a middle-aged woman put something in his hand, smile at him sadly, and walk away. He stood statue still.

Confused and with a sense of worry, Talea moved a little closer, surprised he hadn't heard their approach. "Yhkon?"

He jumped, spinning to face them. There was something vacant about his demeanor. And pain in his eyes. "I…" He flinched, gaze drifting and locking into a blank stare at nothing for a long moment. Then he just shook his head and started to back away, glancing at Jaylee without actually making eye contact. "Would you take her back, please? I have to..." He shook his head again. "I have to go."

Talea's mind told her to catch up to him, to see what was wrong, but her feet remained rooted in place as he rounded a corner and was gone. She was surprised by the pity she saw in Jaylee's face as the young woman took her arm and started walking at an easy pace. "Let's get you back," was all she said.

Did she know something? "Do you know who that was?"

Jay frowned. "It was his fiance's mother." She looked up at the spot Yhkon had been a moment ago. "It might be a few days before either of us see much of him."

20
Miracles and Nightmares

Talea's head jerked up after the alarming sensation of falling, as she'd started to doze off in the saddle. Resettling herself, she tapped her fingers against her thigh in an attempt to keep herself awake. It didn't help much, her eyes still losing focus as their lids slid downward, mind drifting…

"We're almost there. Then you can get some real sleep." Yhkon's voice snapped her awake again. If he had difficulty staying awake as the trip had dragged them into the night and early morning, he didn't show it. Which was hardly fair, since she knew that between the two of them, he got far less sleep as a general rule.

Then there was Jaylee. She did show her sleep deprivation—it took the form of her being even more energetic and playful than usual, which had long since left Yhkon tongue-tied with seething frustration. Jaylee had finally stopped pestering him, since he wasn't making it very fun. Instead she and Tarol bantered on and off.

Fortunately, Yhkon was right—they arrived at the outpost within minutes. There was a single candle within, visible from the window. Otherwise, it was pitch black. A shiver traveled down her spine. Logically, it made sense that everyone would be inside, asleep. She knew it was entirely irrational to feel anxious at the silence.

Stopping their borrowed mount at the rail the other celiths were tied to—those that had survived the battle, at least, which included Eclipse—Yhkon dismounted and helped her down. Getting in and out of the saddle still brought a spasm of pain.

The four of them entered the outpost as quietly as possible. Someone was waiting for them, sitting in the main room with his elbows on his knees, hands clasped. Though his face was too shadowed to recognize, it looked like Grrake. Sure enough, he stood and moved closer, already starting to smile. He took Talea's hand. "I can't tell you how glad I am to see you. How are you feeling?"

She returned the smile, inwardly realizing how glad she was to see him, too. "Not too bad."

After a friendly greeting to Tarol, he looked to Yhkon, and to her surprise as well as Yhkon's, embraced him. Without saying anything, he turned to Jaylee. "Jaylee. Good to see you again, and good to have you with us." He surprised Talea again, with the warmth of his greeting. Yhkon had sent a message weeks ago, of when approximately they would be returning and who their new Warden was. And naturally, it made sense that Grrake would have known Jaylee previously, as Yhkon had. By his manner, Grrake knew her better. "Come on." He started toward the hallway, waving for them to follow. "You must be exhausted." He led them down the hallway, opening one of the doors and gesturing Jay and Talea in. Inside, Terindi and Kae were asleep on the floor, with two extra beds beside them. "Sleep well," he whispered, shutting the door behind them.

Talea swallowed, a twinge in her gut at the sight of her friends. She hadn't even seen Kae during the battle. Yhkon had told her, of course, that everyone had survived. Everyone except Ahjul. Yet somehow…somehow it had been hard to believe him. Hard not to expect more death when she got back. And Terindi…well, the last she'd seen her, she had been lying on the ground, with Ahjul fighting desperately over her.

Jay's hand on her shoulder made her jump. They silently crawled into the two beds waiting for them, managing to not wake even Terindi, who had always been a light sleeper. Talea's body, stiff from long hours in the saddle and sleeping on the ground the last few nights, gradually relaxed. The ache in her stomach, a minor but ever-present reminder of the battle and its horrors, faded some. As exhausted as she was, though, her mind remained alert. To the slight creaking from Yhkon and Grrake's footsteps, elsewhere in the building. The inaudible hum of their whispered conversation. Terindi and Kae's steady breathing beside her, Jaylee's quicker, apparently she hadn't fallen asleep either.

What about everyone else? The other wards, and the Wardens? Yhkon said they were alright…they had received a message from Grrake while they were in Calcaria saying the same thing. They were alright. They were. She would wake up in the morning and find them all eating breakfast, perfectly well.

She closed her eyes and forced them to stay that way, even as memories from the battle came like waking nightmares, gradually becoming more and more indistinct, fogged by drowsiness. Ahjul's scream echoed in her mind, just as it had echoed in the canyon…the flash of iron just before pain flared in her torso…

Talea woke to Terindi and Kae knelt over her, saying her name.

Kae grinned. "We were beginning to think you had died after all." The moment Talea started to sit up, Kae hugged her.

Terindi was next. "We were so worried about you. Are you alright?"

Talea held her close for a long moment. She didn't feel like the one that deserved worry. "I'm fine…" How could she say it? It didn't seem right, even to ask if Terindi was alright. It didn't seem right not to. She could only hope that her friend saw the question and sympathy in her eyes.

Terindi must have, because she bit her lip and looked away.

Silence. Painful, meaningful silence. None of them knew how to acknowledge what they were all thinking, and none of them could bear not to.

Talea pushed her hair out of her eyes and said the only thing she could think of. "Have you guys, um, met Jaylee already?"

"No." Terindi took a deep breath through her nose, as if thankful for the topic, even if it was another reminder of the other topic they wouldn't address. "Yhkon said she went for a ride before the rest of us woke up."

Well what was he doing awake? She nodded and got up. The weeks in Calcaria and the trip back to Zentyre had confirmed her previous observations that Yhkon almost never slept.

Terindi and Kae waited as she got dressed. Without even thinking, Talea turned away as she removed her clothes, hiding the hideous scar on her midsection, even if there was still a lesser scar to be seen on her back. It would always be there, not as gruesome as it was now, but there all the same. She had seen Yhkon's, plenty noticeable still, the morning she'd woken him after his return from drawing the Kaydorian lance away.

Ready, she followed Terindi and Kae out of the bedroom. Down the hallway that, just last night, had made her shudder with its shadowy corners and closed doors. Now the doors were open, the rooms empty. In the main room, there they all were. All the wards, all the Wardens...except one.

A lump rose in her throat but she gulped it down, giving a small smile as everyone noticed her. A pause. Another painful, awkward silence.

Though the timing of his humor was questionable, she was grateful when Ki grinned and said, "So ya ain't dead after all!"

With the silence broken, the uncertainty and tension abated, replaced by relieved smiles and greetings. Each of them welcoming her back in their own way. Everyone with a smile. Haeric with a hand on her shoulder; Gustor with an insightful look that caught her off guard; Skyve a mumbled "Glad you're alright,"; Rikky a hasty hug that was both sweet and awkward; Larak scanned her up and down and remarked that she looked well; Resh gave her a grin. And then there was Wylan. He didn't so much as look at her until everyone else had made their greetings. Only then did he stand up from his chair, walk up to her, and hold her gaze for a long moment. "I'm sorry," was all he said. No explanation. No follow-up. He lowered his head and walked away.

It was at that moment that the door opened, and there stood Jaylee. In her new Warden gear, she looked all the more the spunky, feminine warrior that she was: golden brown hair in a loose ponytail, eyes bright, cheeks flushed, a smile curling her lips. It was no surprise when Resh approached her with a strut in his gait. "If it isn't the famous Jaylee Rhondel." He cracked another grin, entirely more authentic in its flirtatious interest than the one he'd given Talea. "Missed me?"

Jay lowered her chin, looking at him coyly from the corner of her eyes. "Don't all the young ladies?"

Resh was going to say something else, but Yhkon

practically shoved him out of the way as he, rather brusquely, took Jaylee by the arm and led her toward Terindi. "Terindi, this is Jaylee. Rhondel, this is Terindi."

Jay flashed a smirk Yhkon's way that suggested she wanted to comment on his refusal to call her by her first name again. Instead, her expression softened into the kind, empathetic smile that made her so easy to befriend—for everyone but Yhkon. She took Terindi's hand in hers. "Terindi…it's my absolute honor to meet you. And I want to meet the rest of you, too," she cast the smile briefly about the room, before returning it to her new ward, "but I was hoping you and I could get to know each other a bit, first. Would you mind walking with me?"

Terindi glanced at Yhkon, as if for permission. When he neither gave nor declined it, she nodded to Jay, and they left the bunker.

"Well," Tarol slapped his knee, "dunno 'bout the rest of you, but I think it's past breakfast time."

Yhkon appeared at Talea's side, leaning in enough to speak quietly to her. "You feeling alright?"

"Not bad." She eyed him sideways. He looked sleep-deprived as usual. Haggard, maybe even gaunt. She wanted to talk to him—what about she wasn't even sure. They had hardly spoken anything more than necessary information and questions in weeks. He had, as Jaylee had predicted, secluded himself as much as possible while they'd been in Calcaria. But now, with everyone else around, a conversation wasn't exactly possible either.

And, having given her a single nod as his acknowledgement, he was already walking away, mumbling something about not being hungry and leaving the bunkhouse as everyone else turned to breakfast preparations.

~ ♦ ~

Stepping out into the chilly morning air, Yhkon closed the door behind him as softly as possible, hoping for his departure to go unnoticed. Seeing Jaylee and Terindi walking to his left, he went right, wandering with no destination in mind. It was mere seconds before he heard footsteps catching up to him. Talea, maybe, since he'd left rather abruptly. Or Grrake. *Probably Grrake.*

And it was. "You alright?"

Don't I look it? "Yes. Why?"

Grrake closed the rest of the distance between them, standing in front of him with that gentle, concerned expression that he so constantly wore. "As if I don't know you better than that." A pause. "Did something happen, in Calcaria?"

Well, at least he hadn't brought up the fact that Talea had survived, in the *miraculous* fashion Grrake had predicted. Yhkon paced a few steps, hugging his arms to his chest. Did something happen? No, just the usual. Dia's visit wasn't usual, but everything else...everything else was the reason Grrake had wanted to come with him, and had seemed worried when he had declined. "No. Not really."

His friend frowned, clearly not convinced. "How is Ahjul's family?"

Yhkon squeezed his tongue between his teeth, shaking his head as he paced back the way he had come. *As if I don't know you better than that.* It was Grrake's subtle attempt to find whatever it was that was bothering him. "I know what you're doing. So fine. Something *did* happen—I realized that I..." He stopped pacing. "I shouldn't be lead Warden."

Grrake moved forward. "That's not true. Are you saying that because of Ahjul's death?"

"It is true!" He clenched his fists until his fingernails dug into his palms. "You saying otherwise doesn't change that. And I'm saying it for lots of reasons, with Ahjul being at the top of the ever growing list." He quickly moved out of reach, expecting Grrake to put a hand on his shoulder or some other soothing gesture.

"Ahjul's death...it wasn't your fault. It wasn't any of ours." Grrake tilted his head, as if with a different angle he could get a better perspective on Yhkon's thoughts. "And I think you know that. So tell me the real reason."

The real reason. He faced his friend, his mentor, the man that had practically raised him. "You *know* the real reason. I'm not..." he forced the word past gritted teeth, "*right*. I can't do this. I'm more likely to get the wards killed than protect them, more likely to push Talea away than be her...her friend! Come on, Grrake." He swallowed the rising pressure in his throat, feeling desperation twist his expression. "You know this. You know that I'm...that since..."

Grrake grabbed him by either shoulder before he could move away. "Yhkon, look at me." He didn't speak until Yhkon did. His gaze was pained, maybe even moist. "You're right. I know you better than anyone—and that's why I know that you *can* do this. All your pain...it's made you stronger than anybody else I know. You—"

"I'm not a leader, Grrake!" He shrugged out of the older Warden's grip. "The other men...they practically despise me. Ahjul was the one exception to that. He thought I was...he thought I was what *you* think I am...but I'm," he raked a hand through his hair, only to fling it down, "I'm not!"

Grrake didn't say anything for a long moment. An unendurable moment, where Yhkon thought that even Grrake, who had been by his side, who had believed in him every step of the way, was coming to the same conclusion Tarol had. But eventually, his friend just shook his head. When he spoke, it was quietly, but resolute. "That's not true. They don't despise you. Tarol is jealous of you, Resh doesn't want to admit that he respects you, the others sometimes question your judgement. But they don't despise you." He went on without wavering. "And that's because you *are* what I, and Ahjul, think you are. You don't have to be perfect to be our leader."

Yhkon went back to pacing. Unwilling to agree, unsure how or why to argue further. He wasn't what Ahjul had thought he was, on that at least Grrake was wrong.

Grrake started again, when he didn't say anything. "If you feel you failed Ahjul as a leader...by not being who he thought you were, or who Talea needed...then there's no point in tormenting yourself over it. Just...try to improve. Earn the admiration Ahjul had for you. And the friendship that Talea wants to give you." He smiled a little. "Just keep at it. You'll get there."

~◆~

Talea stuffed the last of her things into the bag, hefting it over her shoulder and carrying it outside. Yhkon took it from her with the faintest of smiles, rather a miracle from him, these days. Leaving him to secure it to the back of Eclipse's saddle, she went back inside to make sure the other girls didn't need help.

Everyone was doing something, most of them packing, as they prepared to leave the outpost and go to Aydimor, the capital city. Other than herself, Yhkon, Tarol, and Jaylee, everyone else had spent the better part of a month at the station, and had become more settled than they did when only camping in a spot for one night, meaning there was more to pack.

Jaylee nearly bumped into her in the doorway of the girls' bedroom. "Sorry!" She flashed one of her bright, energetic smiles. She was never in short supply of those. It faded, however, as her forehead puckered with concern. "You look tired, though. Did you not sleep well last night?"

Talea curled her toes inside of her boots. Short answer or long answer? The long answer was that she often didn't sleep well, restless with nightmares, most of them about the battle. They had remained at the outpost a few days, Yhkon saying he wanted her to have a little more recovery time after the long trip from Calcaria, before they went back to traveling. She hadn't made it through a single night without a nightmare. It seemed worse, being back in Zentyre. *Short answer.* "Not really, but I'm okay."

That didn't ease Jay's concern. "Terindi hasn't been sleeping well either…" She lowered her voice. "Are you having nightmares? From the battle?"

"Sorta." There wasn't much point hiding it from Jay. And if she'd already guessed anyway, why not tell her? "It got worse, since we got back to Zentyre. I'm okay though."

Jaylee started to say something, probably to disagree, but Resh and Haeric interrupted. Resh immediately gave Jay a cocky smirk. "Just checking if you ladies had this room cleared out."

"Sure do." Jaylee's dazzling smile was back.

The four of them went back outside, leaving the bunkhouse empty, except for the manager that lived there.

"Your Highness." Jay approached Yhkon, throwing a pack at him the moment he turned around. He barely caught it, giving her a confused frown. Grrake, nearby, cleared his throat and walked away, perhaps to give them space. "What?" She simpered at Yhkon. "You don't want to go by first names, you don't like it when I call you Mr. Tavker…what's a girl to do?"

His frown became a scowl. "I told you that Yhkon was fine."

"Yes, yes." She raised an eyebrow, clearly amused and enjoying herself. "But you glower at me so fearsomely when I say it, I was hardly convinced it was actually *fine*."

He was on the verge of glowering again. "I do not—"

She was laughing. "You're doing it now!"

His cheeks flushed, as he visibly tried to neutralize his countenance. "Just…" He exhaled sharply. "Yhkon is fine."

She wasn't going to let him go so easily. "Then are you going to start calling me Jaylee…?"

Yhkon sighed again and faced her more squarely. "Yes, *Jaylee,* I am. Now would you please get Terindi and get on your bloody celith?"

Jay faked a gasp. "Is my celith bloody?!" She beckoned to Terindi and sauntered to her celith, winking at a seething Yhkon.

Talea tried to conceal her entertainment as she mounted behind him. As soon as the group was moving, he pulled Eclipse to the head and put a comfortable gap between them and the others. He often did so, but she suspected he was all the more eager, with Jaylee around. His shoulders were still tense from her teasing. "So…you and Jay…" She didn't bother hiding her smile anymore, since he couldn't see it. "Following my advice about being friends with her, I see."

His reply came as a snarl, only serving to increase her humor. "*I'm* not the one being as…as *annoying* as possible every—"

She interrupted him with a laugh. "I'm kidding, I'm kidding. But you *do* realize she's actually flirting with you…" *Though that probably isn't going to make you any less irritable.*

"I'm all too aware," he spat out, confirming her thoughts. "I'd much rather she save her flirting for someone else."

"Well," she just grinned, "if it makes you feel better, I'm pretty sure you are not the only one who gets it."

All he did was grumble something she didn't catch.

They didn't talk much after that, just riding. While being back in Zentyre with the group had made Ahjul's absence more blatant, and made her own lingering fear from the battle more prevalent...it was peaceful, back in the saddle with Yhkon, everyone else close behind. She'd missed it more than she would have expected.

Aydimor was a week's ride away. They traveled as quickly as possible, hoping to get Amilyne and get out of Zentyre before Kaydor made another, stronger attempt to take them down.

By the end of the first day, Talea felt exhausted, body aching, her stomach especially. Yhkon noticed her grimace as she climbed out of the saddle and ordered her to sit and rest, not even letting her help set up camp as she usually would. The only concession he made was that she could help Terindi prepare supper, if she stayed sitting. Since it was mostly a matter of stirring a pot of simmering stew, she had plenty of time to watch the rest of her companions, busy around the developing camp.

Her attention shifted to Yhkon's voice. "Tarol." Yhkon caught up to the limping Warden, taking his armful of firewood. "I thought I, and Larak, *and* Grrake told you to take it easy on the leg."

Something about it struck her as unusual. Maybe Tarol thought so too, because he gave Yhkon a raised eyebrow before shrugging and hobbling away to a more stationary task.

Yhkon deposited the wood next to her and the fire with something akin to an unprompted smile. *Wow. The second miracle today.* He went on to join Gustor and Haeric in setting up one of the tents. Then he helped Grrake, Resh, and Jaylee with another.

A few seconds in and he was snapping at Resh.

But, only when all the jobs that required multiple people were done, did he withdraw to the outskirts of the camp, to attend to his more solitary matters of caring for Eclipse and checking all of his tack. He finished faster than usual and rather than lingering or finding something else to occupy himself, he joined her and most of the others at the fire to wait on supper.

It was one of the few times she'd known him to willingly join them when he could reasonably stay away. Or to actually help with the group tasks, when there were individual roles that could be filled. Sure, he'd been quiet and kept to himself as he'd done it, he'd snapped at Resh…but he'd done it.

As small as it was, it made her feel hopeful, that maybe real improvement was on its way. Their stay in Calcaria had been tense at times, he had been exceptionally withdrawn since, yet somehow she still felt that, in a subtle way, he was less…distant. And less angry. *And,* she watched with a discreet smile as Jaylee chattered on with Yhkon, faking oblivion to his helpless, vexed demeanor. *Jaylee clearly will do everything possible to speed the process along.*

21
Infiltration

"Alright, let's get ready and get this over with."

Talea moved closer, along with everyone else, so that Yhkon could give instructions. Not much had been said about their upcoming trip into Aydimor, Zentyre's capital, to get the final ward. So she'd assumed that it would involve her, as it had the previous times.

When everyone had gathered around, he continued. "Myself, Talea, and Gustor are going in to get Amilyne. And," he thought for a second, "two volunteers too, just in case anything goes wrong."

It took Jay all of two seconds to pipe up. "I'd like to come."

Yhkon didn't quite manage to hide a flash of reluctance. "Fine." Wylan volunteered next, and was accepted without the look of resignation. "Now, the trick is going to be getting *in* to the city. The—"

Skyve lifted his hand to interrupt. "But you wouldn't come into Fesdor with Talea to get me, for fear of being recognized. Isn't that still a risk?"

"It is," Yhkon admitted, "but it's an unavoidable one. Fesdor, though large, was small enough that I could give Talea directions and she could find you on her own. Aydimor is huge. There's no way we can send any of you in alone. Very few Kaydorians actually know what any of us look like—it's a risk, but a reasonable one."

He waited to see if there were any further questions, then continued. "Anyway. Getting in is our first problem. The wall is about fifteen feet high and goes all the way around. Anyone coming through the main entrance will be checked and expected to have some proof of identity and purpose...which we probably can't forge. So we're going to have to find a way over the wall and past the guards." He started to continue, probably to offer an idea, only to bite his lip and instead ask, "Any suggestions?"

"Well how 'bout a good old fashioned distraction?" Resh crossed his arms, leaned back in a nonchalant posture. "Myself and Daddy-Grrake, say, pretend to be trying to get over the wall in one spot, drawing the guards' attention while you kids get over somewhere else. And then, of course," he shrugged, "we'll just escape. Shouldn't be difficult, from a bunch of Kaydorian metal heads."

Gustor's lip curled, as if with distaste. "If they're kids, does that make me the uncle?"

"Oh it's perfect!" Tarol's brown eyes sparkled with mirth as he slapped Grrake and Gustor on the shoulder, grinning at Yhkon. "The three of you golden boys: Daddy-G, Uncle-G, and Baby-Y!"

Yhkon started to say something that she guessed would end with a profanity, only to walk a few steps away with an exasperated scowl. When he came back, it was with a deep breath and an impatient expression. "Are we all clear on the plan and can get on with this?"

"Crystal, Baby-Y." Resh winked.

Yhkon jabbed a finger his direction with a glare. "Call me that again and I'll skin you. Let's go get ready."

Resh only grinned, especially when Jaylee laughed. Yhkon, looking a little red, muttered instructions for everyone that was going into Aydimor to wash up and change into the nicest clothing they had, escaping the group at his earliest opportunity to follow his own orders.

Talea went with Jaylee to the nearby stream where they could bathe and change into dresses. Jay in a pale pink dress that flattered her slim figure and complimented her complexion was quite different than Jay in trousers and armor with a dozen weapons about her person. Yet both versions had the energetic sparkle in her eyes and a playful smile. When they returned to the group, Talea could have sworn she caught Yhkon glancing away, swallowing hard, only to look back when Jaylee wasn't paying attention. He himself was in more normal clothing, probably what most men in middle class would wear: trousers, a simple shirt, and a vest. Not a single weapon. Even when he was sleeping, he always had at least one knife on him. Still, she'd be surprised if he hadn't tucked a dagger somewhere inconspicuous.

With everyone ready, they set out. The city was about two miles from where they'd camped. Grrake and Resh walked with them for the first few minutes, before breaking off to create the distraction elsewhere at the wall.

Talea ended up walking beside Wylan, the three Wardens ahead of them discussing details of how to get over the wall and how to go unnoticed once in the city. She glanced sideways at him. He looked like his usual self—head down, posture straight, thumbs hooked in pockets, expression almost blank in its composure. She, meanwhile, felt less like a San Quawr fugitive and more like a simple laborer in a well-worn frock.

Behold, the great Eun and her Marshal. And what were they doing? Breaking into Aydimor, the capital of Zentyre…one of the largest cities in the region, and one she had never dreamed of ever seeing. She glanced sideways at Wylan. "Ever picture yourself infiltrating the capital city?"

"Nope." He smirked, which for him was hardly more than an upward twitch of his lips. "Definitely never thought I'd do it with you."

Talea returned his smirk. "I do believe that was an insult. Why am I not surprised?"

"Not an insult, exactly," he shrugged, "just saying you weren't much of a…city infiltrator, when I first met you."

Fair point, Sir Secrecy. "Well I never thought I'd hold an actual conversation with you. Oh no worries, not an insult, exactly," she mimicked his shrug, "just saying you weren't much for…human interaction, when I first met you."

Wylan quirked an eyebrow. No grin, no reply, but there was amusement in his eyes and that was enough to make her smile.

The nerves didn't come on until the stone wall of Aydimor was looming over them, while they hid in the trees from the guards that patrolled the top. She caught up to Yhkon. "Um…explain the part to me again about how we get over that? Not sure if you know this but I can't fly…"

"But this boy can." Gustor gave Yhkon's shoulder a pat. "He jumps like a rabid barbsit."

Yhkon gave him a good-natured glare, before answering her. "I'm going to get up there first, and pull the rest of you up. Just waiting for the distraction."

They didn't have to wait long. One of the guards turned, watching something a moment, before shouting and gesturing to his companions as he ran that direction. Yhkon was on his feet. "That's our window. Once I'm up there, I want all of you up as fast as possible. Jay first, Wylan, Talea, and Gustor last. Ready?" Without giving them time to answer, he eyed the wall briefly, took a deep breath, and charged.

Talea watched, somewhat in disbelief, as he covered the distance in a handful of powerful strides, and using a boulder at the base of the wall for extra height, propelled himself from it with one foot. For that split second he was sailing through the air…surely he wasn't going to make it. But he did. He caught hold of the edge with both hands, and next thing she knew, he was on top.

Jaylee was already running at the wall. She jumped from the rock and clearly wasn't going to be high enough, but Yhkon caught her wrist and pulled her up with surprising ease. He did the same for Wylan.

Oh barbsit tails.

Steeling herself, Talea sprinted forward, inwardly just praying she wouldn't trip and pitifully fail. Two more strides…step on the rock…jump…Yhkon's fingers closing around her arm. And suddenly she was up, Wylan's hands on her shoulders to help her find her balance.

It was as Gustor got up that another guard saw them and raised the alarm.

Yhkon was already grabbing her and pushing her toward the opposite edge of the wall. "Go!"

Wylan didn't hesitate. He hopped off, landing in a squat and turning to gesture her down. It looked unnervingly far away, that patch of grass at the base of the wall…but, the swords of the guards rushing toward them also looked unnervingly sharp. "Come on!" Jaylee grabbed her wrist and jumped, giving Talea little choice except to jump with her. The patch of grass rushed to meet her in a terrifying blur of warped time, before her feet made contact, her knees bending to absorb the impact. A slight sense of relief was undone by the clash of steel above them.

Yhkon and Gustor were engaged against five Kaydorians. They had only moments to fight, however, before a hooded figure appeared and cut down two of them with the element of surprise.

"Thanks, Daddy-G," Gustor said with a smirk as he and Yhkon swiftly finished off the other three. He jumped down to join Talea, Jaylee, and Wylan. Grrake gave Yhkon a pat on the back and said something she didn't hear, Yhkon answered quietly, Grrake nodded a little, and he was gone.

Yhkon came down, waving for them to follow as he sprinted into the tightly packed, small, wooden houses that made up the outskirts of the city. Lower class housing, he'd told her. In big cities like Aydimor, laborers rarely lived in haliops. Looking at the miniscule houses in various degrees of disrepair, Talea wasn't so sure they were any better.

A short way into the houses, with no sign of pursuit, Yhkon let them stop in an alleyway. "Everyone good?"

Nods all around. Jaylee looked at him with a curve to her lips and a sparkle in her eye. "That was quite the jump, Tavker."

He looked back at her for a long moment of indecision, as if wavering between his usual indifference and what appeared to be some satisfaction that she was impressed. The slight smile and the way he averted his gaze, almost bashfully, said that the latter had won. All he said was, "Alright, let's keep going."

They did so, moving quickly and keeping to alleys as much as possible. There were no civilians around to see them, it was late morning and almost all of the lower class would be at work or school.

Only when they were past the lower class housing and about to enter the heart of the city did Yhkon abandon the stealth and direct them to split up and act as normal as possible. Talea would have stayed with Yhkon, but he indicated for her to join Gustor and Wylan. Perhaps because Gustor could pass as their father, while Yhkon and Jaylee, being the same age, would just look like a couple. *Which I'm sure delights you...* She peered at them from the corner of her eyes, not missing Yhkon's subtle signs of discomfort. Those signs became significantly less subtle when, as they passed a band of knights, Jaylee grabbed his hand and giggled as if he'd made a joke. She seemed to be enjoying the charade, even going so far as to kiss him on the cheek at one point. Talea had to struggle against a grin at the way he reddened.

Gustor chuckled, low enough that Yhkon and Jaylee wouldn't hear from where they walked a stone's throw away. "That girl. She has her work cut out for her, but she's certainly giving it her all."

Talea moved closer to make conversation easier. *Probably blend in better as a family talking as they walk...you know, a family of three different ethnicities.* "You mean flustering him as much as possible, or what?"

"I mean at making him fall for her. You two have only known her for a few weeks, but in Calcaria, she's quite proud of her reputation as having courted all the most eligible Elikwai, or being able to court them at any time she pleases. Yhkon is, in many ways, the most eligible man of all—in his twenties, not bad looking, he has fame, power, even some wealth. Yet I doubt if a single young woman has gotten so much as a smile from him in years. As such," he smirked, "he'd be her greatest catch yet."

Wylan scrunched up his face, as if somewhere between

confused and cynical. "How many *catches* does she need to make before she just picks one?"

"That is the question." Gustor shook his head slowly, musing. "That is the question."

They'd been walking for what Talea estimated was an hour before she looked up from her observation of the increasingly strange citizens around her, and realized that the top of a castle was rising above the horizon of houses, shops, and mansions. Aydimor was officially unlike anything she'd ever seen. Even Calcaria, or at least the small part of it she'd seen, wasn't so…opulent. And big. The cities were probably of similar size and population, yet somehow Calcaria held on to a feeling of simplicity, or rusticism. Aydimor, on the other hand, went far beyond the scope of every outlandish tale she'd heard of it as a child.

After leaving the lower class neighborhoods, it had been mostly middle class. Now, there was some middle, but mostly upper class, and nobility. Their houses weren't houses at all—they were mansions, even palaces. Some were nearly as big as the one in Calcaria. Yet if she understood it right, even the enormous ones like that were the homes of only one family each. *The word "ridiculous" comes to mind…*She laughed a little to herself. *So does "awesome."*

The citizens of Aydimor were foreign to her, as well. She was used to lower class, a little middle class, and a sparse handful of upper class. That sparse handful, made up mostly of Skyve and his family, were a few levels of crazy below these people. As far as she could tell, not a single one of them had a job, or any sort of chores to do. Music and delicious smells drifted from the open doors of mansions, where laughter and chatter inside spoke of large parties. Ladies with tiny waists contrasted by large hoop skirts, their gowns in brilliant colors

Talea hadn't even thought possible for fabric, bejeweled so that they sparkled in the sun and heavily perfumed, walked in pairs or groups, or sat in the shade of umbrellas held by servants, chatting without an apparent care in the world save what the latest gossip was. Men wore such perfectly unwrinkled coats, such shiny silk shirts and polished boots, that she could only wonder how much that single outfit cost them. Probably more money than her parents made in a month as laborers.

And finally, the castle. It was towering above them now. Made mostly of stone, with marble accents, she couldn't tell if it was beautiful, or formidable, or both. It seemed to be larger than the entirety of Vissler Village, and she could only see a portion of it.

Gustor stopped for a moment, squinting up at the castle. "Behold the grand Fortress of Aydimor, or Zentyre's Palace, whichever you prefer."

"So..." Wylan's eyes traveled the massive building thoughtfully. "How did he manage to make himself king, when Zentyre hasn't had royalty in decades?"

"That *is* how," Yhkon said, catching up to them with Jaylee. "The Leadership was a failed attempt at a new type of government. There were too many of them, with too many conflicting ideas, and not enough brains to make it work. They weren't getting the job done. People were beginning to feel that it would be better to go back to the traditional way—a king. Kaydor played his cards just right and got himself the throne."

"You say that as if the majority of Zentyre knew of and approved a change in government," Wylan said distantly, as if he were simply thinking out loud.

No kidding. "I didn't even know the name of a single person in the Leadership until I met you guys," Talea agreed.

Yhkon nodded. "That's because lower class, and often

middle class, are overlooked when making decisions or assessing general sentiment. Trust me, I know; I grew up in a haliop just like you," he directed it at Talea. After all, Wylan had been middle class before his parents died, Jaylee had been raised in Calcaria where there was no such thing as laborers, Gustor had been born in Sanonyn, where the social system was apparently set up differently.

But if Yhkon had been born in Sanonyn as well…at what point had he become a laborer in Zentyre?

It would have to be a question for later. He had already continued walking, still toward the castle.

Talea caught up to him. "Okay remind me why we're um, going to the big, scary castle?"

"We're not, thank Narone," he muttered. "But the orphanage is inconveniently placed right next to it. Kaydor likes to make people think that he actually has a heart and cares about orphans."

They traveled toward the left side of the castle, where there were less sprawling manors and more simple, practical homes, probably those of middle class. Finally, they came to a larger building, not shaped right to be either a house or a shop. A sign over the door read *"Orphanage."*

It was strangely quiet.

"Oh, gsorvi." Gustor frowned. "If it's this quiet, they've taken the kids on some sort of outing."

Yhkon sighed. "And I suppose there's really no way of us knowing *where.*"

Gustor shook his head in confirmation, but Jaylee spoke up, without concern. "Well sure there is. We ask. Excuse me, gentlemen." Yhkon tried to grab her arm to stop her, but she had already darted out of sight. They ran after her, stopping when they saw her casually approaching a band of Kaydorian knights.

Talea glanced at Yhkon's expression of both outrage and horror, and curled her toes inside her boots. This could be interesting.

~ ♦ ~

Yhkon walked as calmly as he could manage toward Jay and the knights, fighting the glare that wanted to replace his casual demeanor. Confound it all. What was she thinking!?

She was just greeting the knights with a bright smile as he caught up. The fact that she was a beautiful young woman with far more charm than good sense would be either their doom or their deliverance. He hardly liked relying on Jaylee's abilities as a flirt to get them out of the situation that *she* had put them into. "Hello, gentlemen!" She cast that dazzling smile about the group. "Sorry to bother you, but my sister is one of the caregivers at the orphanage, I was hoping to see her but apparently they've taken the children on an outing. I don't suppose any of you would know where?" Letting her smile become even sweeter, she took Yhkon's arm and pulled him close. "My beau and I would really appreciate it."

Of all the nerve...he wasn't actually sure if he was grimacing or smiling. Whatever expression he wore, it was the best he could muster, with Jaylee snug against his side, having had the audacity to drag him into her performance as her *suitor*. If he'd had half a brain, he would have accepted Grrake's offer to come in his place. Or sent Resh. Resh would have no difficulty pretending to be this conniving, bewitching little scamp's lovesick squire.

Disappointment crossed more than one of the younger soldiers' faces. *You should just be grateful for your escape.* The man appearing to be their leader, probably in his thirties, gave her the friendly smile of a man who was probably married but was still susceptible to a pretty smile and innocent gaze. "They've gone to that ice cream shop on Kenton's Street, on the north side. A couple of my boys could escort you, if you'd like."

"Oh, no," it was no wonder they were all so easily played, when she kept flashing that smile of hers, "you've been so much help already! I think I know the one you're talking about. Thank you so much!" With a slight curtsy, she tightened her grip on Yhkon's arm, as they walked away leisurely.

Until they were back with the group and out of sight of the soldiers. Then Yhkon broke her grasp and instead took her by the wrist. "Excuse us a moment," he said without even looking at the others, before hauling her around the corner for a more private...discussion. "Alright, *Jay*." He pushed her against the wall, leaning in to block any chance of escape. "If you're so desperate to be a Warden and gain my respect, you might start by *earning* it. Not by being reckless and disregarding my..." The thought drifted off. He was blank. "My uh...authority." It was a feeble finish...because it was at that moment that he realized the position he'd put them into. Her against the wall. Him leaning over her, hands on the wall on either side of her head, enclosing her with his arms. Her face only inches from his.

No intimidation, no resentment in her countenance. That would have made it easy for him to simply back up and continue the conversation with a more appropriate distance between them. But instead, she was smiling. Not with her flirtatious charm or playfulness or pretend innocence...she looked eager. Those soft lips were slightly parted, those beautiful amber eyes fell as if magnetized to his mouth.

And he was left somewhere between inner terror and an overwhelming desire to kiss her.

If only she would look away, or flinch, or try to get past

him. If only she would, in even the slightest of ways, discourage it. But she was inviting him in. Her hand touched his arm, sliding up to his shoulder. Clearly any resistance would have to come from him. Yet…he wasn't sure he wanted to resist. He was leaning in, closing the gap between them. He could feel the warmth of her breath. The tingle of heat when her fingers found their way to his neck. The desire to move the final inches and kiss those waiting lips only grew, blocking out every other thought, making his heart pound against his ribs and warmth flush beneath his skin.

Only one thought managed to creep through, just before he would have given in: that four years ago, it had been Tessa's blue eyes first gazing deep into his, before closing as they'd kissed.

Jaylee finally lifted her eyes back to his, a slight crease between her brows. "Yhkon," she whispered, her tone imploring.

"No." He started to pull away.

Her hand tightened on his shoulder as she tried to prevent him. "Why not?" She didn't wait for a reply, continuing. "Because of Tessa? I know you loved her, I know you must miss her…but do you really think that means you can't let yourself try for even a little happiness? Or let yourself get close to anyone?"

Yhkon shrugged out of her grip, putting a few feet of distance between them, forcing his expression to harden. So she knew about Tessa. Well, she didn't know as much as she thought. "As if it were that simple. You probably see me as some challenge to be conquered. What, am I the last single man in Calcaria that hasn't courted you?" He turned away, crossing his arms. Hating himself for the cringe, the hurt in her expression, that was surely coming.

Except it didn't come. No cringe. She squared her shoulders and held his gaze, the amber of her eyes that had been so soft only moments ago now bright and fiery. "No, what you are is a man who seems to think that everyone is either only pretending to care about him, or will someday betray him. Who thinks that by being a recluse and abusing his friends, he's being strong. Yhkon," her voice became more gentle, as her head tilted, "can't you even give me, or anyone for that matter, the *chance* to care about you? Do you really think there's no possibility that you could ever be happy, if you would just…just, allow it to happen?"

He wanted to keep his rigid posture, his indifferent frown. To keep her out. But her words felt like a physical weight on his shoulders, straining the muscles and making it exhausting just to keep his head up. Because he'd been here before. He knew he could listen to what she was saying, he could open up and let her "help" him…and it probably would help, for awhile. Maybe he would be happy. He had been happy with Tessa for almost two years, and he had been *whole*.

But then she'd been taken from him.

"No," he said again. Shook his head, without even realizing he was doing it. "I could, but I'm not going to. Let's…let's just go." He started walking away. "We need to—"

Jaylee caught his hand before he made it far, forcing him to stop. "Yhkon! You can't just turn everyone away. As far as I can tell, you've let one, maybe two people get close to you. Grrake and Talea. And don't you think you're better off for their friendship? Why can't you give me that chance?"

He shoved her hand off with an oath. "Maybe because I know we'd probably be together for all of two weeks before you got bored with me and instead spent your charms on Resh, or some handsome Kaydorian!"

"Ouch," she said dully, sounding more impatient than upset. "Alright, you know what, fine." She gestured for him to continue walking. "Go ahead. Push me away too. But know two things. One, I am not going down easily. And two…" She narrowed her eyes, somehow one of the fiercest women he'd met, and still the beautiful, kind girl that had been so eager to kiss him. "If you want to pretend otherwise to me and everyone else, go ahead, but deep down you better know that it is not *my* problems preventing anything between you and me, it's yours."

She walked away. He had thought she would be the one left standing there, the one flinching at his words, the one finding it difficult to keep her head up. Somehow, the roles had been entirely reversed.

He followed mechanically, almost surprised to see Gustor, Talea, and Wylan waiting. He'd rather forgotten they were there. Gustor raised an eyebrow at him, stepping closer to say quietly, "I take it she won this round."

Yhkon opened his mouth to reply, but changed his mind. Yes, she'd won. So he didn't answer.

Gustor just nodded. "The sooner a man learns that he can never win an argument with a woman, the better."

Jaylee stood with hands on hips and a relaxed smile, as if nothing had happened. "So, to this ice cream shop? I'm assuming you know where it is," she directed it at Yhkon.

Of course. Because we wouldn't want the day to get any easier. He *should* know where it was, he *should* know as much of Aydimor as possible, from visits there over the years to check on Amilyne, with extracting her someday in mind. The other Wardens did. They all had become as familiar as possible with every ward's circumstances, not just their own.

But he hadn't been in Aydimor for four years.

Every time they had come to check on Amilyne, Grrake had helped him find a way to avoid going into the city. He had offered to do the same this time, to go in his place. *I should have let him.*

Thankfully, Gustor saved him from having to answer. "We've seen it in passing. Let's go."

Not so thankfully, Jaylee still gave Yhkon a look that suggested she knew there had to be a reason why he hadn't answered for himself. Well, let her mull it and figure it out and have more reasons to think he was in desperate need of her pity and love, let her try all the harder to *fix* him. There wasn't much he could do to stop her. Might as well let her sympathy run its course. She would eventually realize she was wasting her time.

He kept pace with Gustor, both because if they were both leading it would look like he knew where they were going, and because he seemed the safest option to walk with.

Gustor kept his voice low but still returned to the topic Yhkon was hoping he would drop. "Going to give her a chance?"

"Um, *no.*" He glared sideways at him. Of all the Wardens, Gustor was usually the one that didn't cause trouble or frequently annoy him. Except for his occasional sarcastic moods when he applied his greater knowledge of Yhkon's personal life to amuse himself. "As you ought to know perfectly well."

A shrug. "You could do worse."

There wasn't much argument against that. *This is the point where we let this subject die.* "Well I can tell you that next time, *you* get to pretend to be her man."

Gustor smirked, shrugged again, and didn't say anything more.

Yhkon briefly listened to Jaylee talking to Talea, long enough to convince himself that he wasn't the topic, before tuning it out, forcing himself to focus. No more worrying about Jay or her fantastical ideas of romance. *Get Amilyne, and get out of this blasted place.*

22

Kings and Orphans

"I can't believe I'm doing this."

Talea wondered if anyone else was finding their new companion as vexing as she was. At the same time, she couldn't help wondering if a large part of the reason the girl was vexing was because she was possibly the most gorgeous fifteen-year-old alive, and she knew it.

Amilyne, who apparently preferred Ami, had been the hardest ward to convince. Terindi had taken it calmly, as she took everything. Rikky had been eager at the prospect of being a hero and starting a new life. Skyve had already known a great deal of what was going on, and practically been expecting the rest. But Ami…it had taken three seconds to assess that she did not like or trust Talea. And only three more seconds to determine that she had spent far more time worrying about hiding her ability, than wondering if there was a reason for it or others that shared it.

And then, when she'd finally agreed to meet the Wardens and Wylan, it had taken three seconds into that introduction to conclude that she and Jaylee had something in common—flirting. Gustor was old enough to be exempt, but Yhkon and

Wylan were not.

Now, with Ami at least mostly convinced, they were returning to the orphanage to gather her few belongings. For Yhkon and Wylan she had only angelic smiles, for the rest of them only complaints and suspicious frowns.

"So." Ami was almost jogging to keep up with Yhkon's long strides. He clearly didn't want to be kept up with. "What is it that us...what do you say? Wards? What is it that us wards are supposed to, um, do? With our abilities and the San Quawr and everything?"

"End the Eradication." Gustor answered.

"More specifically," Yhkon didn't slow his pace to accommodate her at all, or even turn to look at her, "defeat Kaydor."

Ami's step faltered. "Defeat as in...kill him?"

Yhkon stopped and turned around after all. "Yes..." His tone was questioning.

Her perfect eyebrows drew together as she crossed her arms. No more angelic smiles. "He's a good king. He's been funding the entire orphanage from his own pocket for years, and comes to visit us. And while everyone else sees us as nothing but worthless orphans, to be made into laborers as soon as possible, where we'll be slaves...well not only is he trying to improve the conditions of lower class, he's also trying to make it so that orphans can move into middle class. He—"

"*He* is a tyrant," Yhkon interrupted, his expression stone cold. "You think he cares about you, or the other orphans? You have no idea the type of man he is. It's all a front."

She was intimidated, as she ought to be. Yhkon was still frightening even to Talea when he was in one of his moods, let alone to a girl that had just met him. But Ami stood her ground. "What proof do you have? Zentyre is improving under his rule, isn't it?!"

Yhkon swore under his breath. "How would you know if it was improving? Have you ever even left the city? Even if it was improving—no king that wants to *murder* an entire race that has committed no crime can be considered anything near *good*," he spat out the final word, spinning and continuing with an even faster, angrier gait. Jaylee stayed on his heels.

Amilyne was left both flinching and glaring after him. She had more fortitude than Talea would have given her credit for. Gustor watched Yhkon go with something like an impatient sigh, before walking beside his ward and explaining quietly. "You have to understand, Ami, that Kaydor is the one who instigated the Eradication in Zentyre years ago, and now has brought it back. He is killing and enslaving innocent men, women, and children simply because of their race."

She sucked in her breath through flared nostrils. "Well…couldn't there be a misunderstanding? I've met Kaydor, unlike *him*," she glowered at Yhkon's back, "who's just judging him without even knowing him!"

Talea bit her lip, feeling resentment at Ami's unfair accusation and wanting to set the record straight. But Yhkon was extremely particular about who knew his life story, and probably wouldn't appreciate it even if it was in his defense.

Gustor, however, apparently wasn't going to let it go uncorrected. "Which is exactly what you are doing, to Yhkon." He stopped her. "Kaydor personally killed Yhkon's family and his fiance."

That erased the glare from Ami's exotic gold eyes, and softened her jaw into a distressed frown.

Without further discussion, they kept going. Talea trailed the group beside Wylan. "Did you know that?" she whispered. "I mean, about Kaydor supposedly trying to improve conditions for lower class? Had you heard it before?"

He didn't answer right away. "Yes," he said at length. "Grrake said that he raised the base wage lords can pay their laborers, and now requires that every village be provided with a school, whether the lords like it or not."

It probably should have been heartening. The people she had grown up with, still in Vissler Village, weren't starving for lack of money to buy food with, as they often had. Children in other villages were getting the education that might have otherwise been denied them. Yet...it was Kaydor behind the progress. Kaydor, who they intended to wage a war on.

But it wasn't just him. They would be entering a war against *Zentyre*. She'd never been in a war, but she'd been taught enough history to know that there were always consequences. That it wasn't just the soldiers fighting who suffered.

What if they didn't start a rebellion as they'd supposedly been destined to do? If Kaydor were left to rule Zentyre, undisturbed...would the region be better off? Wouldn't their war actually harm the innocent lives they were trying to protect?

Their arrival at the orphanage didn't give her time to find answers, if there were any. "Gustor," Yhkon held open the door, "take Ami and get what she needs, we'll keep watch."

Gustor nodded and gestured Ami in ahead of him, but she paused before entering, looking at Yhkon timidly. "Yhkon...I'm sorry." She lowered her gaze and disappeared inside before he could react.

He looked confused briefly, before frowning at Gustor, no doubt realizing that he must have told her something, to bring about such a change of heart. Displeasure was plain enough in his demeanor. Still, he only jerked his head for him to go in. Not so long ago, Talea felt sure he would have shown his irritation much more vividly. It was still visible…but he wasn't acting on it.

They waited in silence, Yhkon pacing, claiming he just wanted to keep an eye on all sides of the building. Jaylee was watching him with a contemplative frown, as if she were trying to work out a problem in her head.

It was just as Gustor and Ami came back out, her bag slung over Gustor's shoulder, that two sounds made them all freeze. One, from the direction they'd recently come from, the voices of a large group of children. The other, from the direction of the castle, clinking armor.

Yhkon didn't curse like she might have expected. He just sighed. "Knew we couldn't get out of here without trouble." More loudly for them to hear, "Let's go! Keep it tight."

Ami looked a little dazed but she followed the rest of them. Talea kept close behind Yhkon, not wanting a repeat of what had happened in the last big city she'd been in, when they'd been separated. He started to his right, probably hoping to sneak out between the two oncoming groups.

No such luck.

Instead, they rounded a corner and found themselves faced with glinting iron. Ten soldiers. At their lead, a man not in the usual armor, but in much fancier black leather and light chainmail, with a maroon cape matching the Kaydorian insignia on his chest.

More notably, there was a crown on his head.

Talea could sense as well as see the tension that seized Yhkon, making his whole body as taut as a bowstring. His eyes narrowed and glared at the man with a more icy hatred than she'd ever seen from him.

Between Yhkon's reaction and the crown, it wasn't too hard to guess that she was looking at Kaydor Veserron himself.

The man was powerfully built, probably in his forties, beginning to show his age but still attractive, with deep-set gray eyes and dark hair framed with silver. He eyed Yhkon for what felt like a long moment, only briefly scanning the rest of them. "I was wondering when I'd see you again," he said at last. His voice was low and gravelly, seeming to vibrate through his chest.

Yhkon only lifted his head. No reply.

Kaydor's attention shifted to Amilyne. "Ami? Why are you with them?"

She looked like a barbsit caught in a trap. Paralyzed.

"Yhkon," Gustor spoke under his breath. "We need to go."

No reply to him, either.

He tentatively put his hand on Yhkon's shoulder. "This is not the time or place."

Kaydor's passive expression was hardening. "I heard that you had some teenagers with you, that supposedly can perform some sort of witchcraft. I suppose these are them. Let me guess, you're going to use them to try and kill me?"

Yhkon balled his fists. "Unfortunately, not today. Gustor, go!"

Gustor grabbed Talea and Ami's wrists and called Wylan as he took off at a sprint, away from the Kaydorians. Yhkon and Jaylee brought up the rear. The all-too familiar sound of iron grating iron and heavy footfalls told her that the soldiers weren't going to give them an easy escape.

Gustor navigated them deftly between buildings and down alleys, managing to throw the Kaydorians of their trail. *For awhile.* They stopped in an alleyway. She could still hear them searching the nearby streets. It could be mere seconds before they were found.

Ami's flawless features were contorted with fear and confusion. "No, this isn't right...I shouldn't...I don't want to go with you! Let me go back!"

"Hey, shh." Gustor put a hand on either of her shoulders. His tone was half impatient, half gentle. "You're going to be fine. We'll get out of this."

"I don't *want* to get out!" She looked back the way they'd come. "I was fine there. The other kids...they need me. I can't just—"

"Listen!" Gustor tightened his grip, giving her a slight shake so that she fell silent. "There is no going back. Even if you did, Kaydor knows that you were with us. He knows we have some reason for taking you. He'd never just let you go back to the orphanage. You have to trust me, Ami."

She was panting, cringing as if pained. Yhkon moved closer and spoke quickly at a whisper. "We don't have much time. Gustor, Jay, you get them out of here. I'll draw their attention and catch up with you. If you have a chance to get out of the city, take it."

Gustor had a reluctant look, though he didn't say anything. Jaylee did. "Um, no. You're not staying here by yourself. Both of us can draw their attention while Gustor gets the wards out."

Yhkon looked at her like she was crazy. "*Um, no.* Just—"

Gustor cleared his throat. "Enough bickering, just go! They're almost here." He gave Yhkon a shove in one direction, and tugged Ami the other. "Go!"

Talea hesitated as Gustor took off with Amilyne, Yhkon and Jaylee preparing to meet the soldiers. Just the two of them? At least if she was there, she could use her ability if they got into an impossible situation. "Yhkon—"

He didn't give her a chance to argue. "We'll be fine. I

promise. You and Wylan go." He indicated for them to follow Gustor. Wylan took her by the elbow, and they left Yhkon and Jay in the alleyway, catching up to Gustor and Ami.

"Alright." Gustor crouched beside a wooden fence, and they did likewise. "We move quick and quiet. No talking, you just stay as close to me as you can. Got it?" He looked younger, with energy flushing his cheeks and lighting his eyes. As if the prospect of a dangerous escape from a giant city, chased by soldiers, was exciting. *Well I suppose if you're an ex-assassin, maybe it is.* Personally, she just felt out of breath.

But he was already helping her and Ami over the fence. From behind them, where they'd left Yhkon and Jaylee, she heard shouts and clashing steel.

~ ♦ ~

Yhkon watched until the wards and Gustor were out of sight, before turning to Jaylee. Stubborn girl. He wasn't sure she would be a help so much as a distraction. "Here's the plan. We take down a few, then run. We're not trying to take them all, alright?"

"Right." He had never seen her in combat, and had vaguely worried she would be frightened. She looked calm and ready.

He untucked his shirt from his belt and reached behind to grab the hilt of the short cutlass he'd strapped against his bare back. "I'll take the first one down and get you his sword."

"You think I can't handle myself without a sword?" She wore a confident smirk. Which he found far more attractive than he should have.

"I'm sure you can, Rhondel." He found himself smirking back at her. "But it's rather hard to penetrate armor with nothing but one's fists."

The Kaydorians came clattering around the corner seconds

later, with only a moment of hesitation before advancing. Yhkon attacked the nearest one with the quickest, most efficient sequence of strikes he knew, dispatching the man and catching his sword. He threw it to Jay just in time for them to engage the rest of the knights together.

There were a dozen that he'd counted. One of them had been dealt with. Yhkon was skirmishing with two more and knew he could easily take them down with a few more seconds, but Jaylee was up against three with the other six pressing in around them. If they wanted to avoid injury, they had to end the fight. "Time to go!" Cutting down one of his opponents he engaged another of Jay's, just long enough to give her the opportunity to retreat. He spun and sprinted after her, narrowly missing a blade through his spine.

Now was when it would have been advantageous to be familiar with the city. As it was, he could only run blindly and hope they didn't find themselves at a dead end. The soldiers were hard on their heels, there was no time to stop and plan or to hesitate at turns. Down the alley, left turn, between two houses, left turn, right turn—

Dead end.

They were trapped between three buildings, with no more than four seconds before Kaydorians would have them completely surrounded. Breathing hard, heart pounding, Yhkon grabbed Jaylee by the waist without another thought and threw her as high as he could. It was enough elevation for her to climb onto the roof above them. He jumped up after her, barely grabbing hold of the edge, pulling himself up just before a sword would have taken off his foot. Jaylee was already pulling at his arm, helping him to his feet on the slanted surface. "Did you have to *throw* me, Tavker?"

He took her hand, running up the incline to the peak of

the roof. "Did you want to die, Rhondel?"

She grinned at him. Her grin faded as the sound of bow strings being drawn came from below them.

Instinct made him wrap his arms around her and fling them both down and forward, bringing them to the opposite side of the peak, just as arrows whistled through the air where they'd just been. But they were sliding rapidly down the roof toward the edge. He kept one arm around Jay and grasped for something to hold with the other, his fingers and palm being scraped raw by the shingles but finding no purchase. His stomach jumped to his throat. That edge and the empty space beneath it, followed by a cobblestone street, were rushing toward them and there was nothing he could do to stop it. All he could do was feel the surge of fear, helpless at the time warp that made the moment so long and so short at the same time.

Jay.

He tightened his grip, pulling her closer to his chest. The lip of the gutter at the edge snagged him slightly. Not enough to prevent them from slipping off.

Nothing but empty space. Falling. The cobblestone racing to meet them. Yhkon twisted himself as best he could in the air, putting as much of himself between Jaylee and the ground as he could. Dimly he knew to hold her with one hand, and bend his free arm behind his head to keep it from cracking against the street.

For a fraction of a second, he knew, more than felt, that he had hit the ground. For the next fraction of a second he felt pain. Then he was blinking away black dots from his vision, trying to breathe, his lungs wrung free of air like a rag of water. There was a noise trying to penetrate the pounding in his ears and behind his eyes. Something was on top of him.

"Yhkon!" The noise became a voice. Jay's voice.

The pounding became a throbbing ache. An ache that spread throughout every muscle and bone, centralizing in his upper back. A raspy groan squeezed it's way past his constricted throat. His lungs refused to do their job, burning as they begged for breath.

Whatever was on top of him shifted. "Yhkon, hey, hey, breathe!"

He gasped, the air filling his chest painfully at first. The black dots faded away, allowing him to see Jaylee's face. Right above his. A worried crease between her eyes, and her mouth open slightly, as if she'd been holding her breath with him.

Her weight abruptly lifted as she got to her feet and ran out of his view. Alarm sparked in his mind. Where was she...iron *clanged* nearby, followed by a moan and a scream. He tried to sit up. Stopped at the wave of pain it sent radiating through his back and shoulders.

The clamor ended. Silence.

Then she was back, knelt over him with that concerned frown. "Please tell me you're alright."

He stared back at her blankly a second. "Um..." He sat up the rest of the way, managing it with a wince. "I'm fine."

"Good." Her frown lifted into a relieved smile. "Because we'll have company any minute and I'd rather not have to carry you out of here."

"Not my preference either." He gave her a lopsided smile, fighting another wince as she helped him to his feet.

Running footsteps were growing louder from their left. "Come on." Still holding his hand, she tugged him into a sprint. His body was stiff and achy, but he found his stride and was able to keep up with her slightly slower pace. They had just enough of a head start to get away unseen. Now just to find their way out of the city, and hope Gustor and the wards had been able to do the same.

It wasn't difficult. They simply got away from the castle, then began retracing their steps as much as possible until they reached the outskirts. Since Gustor and the wards weren't at any of the locations they'd stopped at earlier, which was where Yhkon knew Gustor would have waited if he was going to, he assumed they had already gotten out of the city. He and Jay just had to do the same. They had the advantage of it being just the two of them, but the disadvantage of Yhkon's back becoming more and more immobile.

Jaylee's simple solution to the problem was to leave him on the street without a word while she charged the guards on the wall nearest them, and attacked. By the time he realized what she was doing and ran to catch up, she'd taken them both down and was waiting for him. Yhkon reached her just as another guard noticed. While he shouted to his companions, they jumped off the wall to the other side, and fled.

Yhkon grit his teeth and made sore muscles move as fast as possible, inwardly thinking of all the ways he ought to lecture Jaylee on once again doing something reckless without so much as telling him before she did it, let alone asking for permission. And this time, he wasn't sure they would so easily get out of the mess she'd made—the guards atop the wall were shouting back and forth, several of them were probably in pursuit.

The drumming of hooves, however, solved the problem. Two hooded figures flashed by on celiths, one easily identifiable as Larak by his size. The other Yhkon knew was Grrake. He and Jaylee ran on, allowing themselves into an easier pace, knowing that the two Wardens would be dealing with any pursuing Kaydorians.

After a few minutes, Yhkon called for Jay to slow down,

so he could take the lead. "This way." He angled to the left. As he'd suspected, Grrake had left his and Jaylee's celiths at the location the Wardens had often used as a rendezvous over the years. Grrake and Larak returned shortly and dismounted.

Grrake took one look at Yhkon, bent over and walking stiffly, and frowned with concern. "What did you get yourself into this time?"

Jaylee smiled as she made Yhkon sit down on a log. He only scowled, half at Grrake, half because of the pain that was squeezing his muscles and bones like a claw. "Don't be too hard on him." She let her hand linger on his shoulder. Maybe he had made a mistake in letting her help him as much as she had in Aydimor…she didn't seem to realize those liberties were over now. "We ended up falling off a rooftop, and he took the brunt of it."

Grrake's frown softened. Larak, inspecting with his massive arms crossed, remained critical. "I won't even ask how you ended up on a rooftop or why you had to fall off of it. You may have broken some ribs."

Yhkon waved his hand dismissively. He'd had plenty of broken ribs before—besides, he didn't think they were broken, this time. Just bruised. "They'll mend. Gustor and the wards get back okay?" No doubt they had, if they'd sent Grrake and Larak to help.

"Yes, they're all back at camp." Grrake nodded. "Do you want to rest a while, or go back now?"

"I'm fine." The sooner they left, the sooner Jaylee would have to give him his personal space back. "Let's go." She moved to help him up and to his celith, but he, somewhat politely, told her he was alright by himself. They all mounted and rode away from Aydimor. *Good riddance.*

"One thing, though." Grrake brought his mare, Lenjeya,

beside Yhkon as they rode. "An Elikwai found us while you were gone. The rest of his team was captured a few days ago, they're being held prisoner in a town a week's ride from here. It's on our way. He was looking for more Elikwai to help him get them out, but I told him we would do it."

Yhkon inwardly sighed, wanting little more than to be back in Calcaria. Out of this blasted region. "Right. Still some daylight left, so we'll leave straight from camp." A simple mission, hardly even a delay. Nothing to worry about.

23
Grrake

Talea arched her back into a stretch, arms behind her, thinking how nice it would be to be in Calcaria where she didn't have to spend the majority of each day in a saddle. Yhkon must have felt her movement and guessed its cause, because he glanced at her over his shoulder. "We should be getting close." Then louder, to Grrake, "Right? There's an outpost a few miles from that town, isn't there?"

"There is," the older Warden confirmed. That was the end of the conversation, until suddenly Grrake straightened. "Who's running that outpost now, remind me?"

Yhkon shrugged that he didn't know. Tarol thought a moment. "I dunno, some Sanonyan chap."

Talea could have sworn she saw fear flood Grrake's demeanor, before it became a more mild look of uncertainty. "Yhkon..." He brought Lenjeya closer to them. "Maybe we should, um, reconsider staying at that outpost."

Since Ash had died in the battle, Wylan rode with Grrake. Talea saw her confusion mirrored in his frown.

Yhkon on the other hand seemed distracted. "Why?" was all he said, not even looking up.

"Just…" Grrake's distinctly refined, Sanonyan accent had faded into a more casual dialect. For most people, that would probably demonstrate relaxation. For Grrake, it did the opposite. "If it's the man I think it is…we have some, well, unpleasant history."

Yhkon finally looked at him, briefly. "Oh. Well he ought to know better than to cause you any trouble, if need be I'll remind him. But it's the most convenient place to stay, everyone could use a break from sleeping in tents."

Grrake's ability to hide his apprehension was slipping. "But—"

"There it is," Yhkon interrupted, nodding toward the bunkhouse and barn at the base of the hill they'd just crested. "Besides, maybe it's not him that runs it. Come on." He kicked Eclipse into a trot the rest of the way, effectively silencing any further argument Grrake could make.

Talea felt an ambiguous sense of trepidation, perplexed by Grrake's strange behavior, as they trotted into the yard. The low rumble of thirty-two hooves was enough to bring the outpost manager out of the bunkhouse. After an initial moment of surprise, his round cheeks bunched with a smile as he waved them a welcome.

"Yhkon!" Grrake whispered through gritted teeth, face contorted with anxiety as he eyed the manager. "Can we please—"

Yhkon gave him a questioning frown, already dismounting and approaching the man. By his posture and narrowed eyes, he was prepared to end any show of disrespect toward Grrake. "I'm Yhkon Tavker. You are?"

The manager gave a hasty version of the bow that all San Quawr greeted Yhkon with, smiling curiously. "I was wondering if you all would show up here, one day! Grrake!

How've you been, my friend? Boy it's been a long time!" He moved past Yhkon to clap Grrake on the shoulder.

Grrake, meanwhile, barely managed even a ghost of a smile. He cleared his throat. "Um, Lentli, good to see you…we should, well, maybe we could catch up, before—"

"Ah, yes." Lentli looked back to Yhkon. "There is some catching up to do. I mean, look at you! Last time I saw you, you were this high." He leveled his hand a couple feet off the ground with a chuckle.

Yhkon frowned. "I don't understand…"

"Oh," the man's smile became apologetic, "s'pose you don't know me, can't blame you that, you were only four! I'm Lentli. Your family and mine were neighbors, back in Sanonyn."

A pause. Yhkon still looked confused, and perhaps uncomfortable. "I see," was all he said. "And how do you know Grrake?"

Grrake started to say something. Lentli didn't notice, and spoke before he could, with a quizzical smile. "Well, the same way I know you, obviously. Why is it you've been going by Tavker, anyway?" He laughed a little when Yhkon's brow furrowed. "Are you pulling my leg, lad? Come on, why don't we head inside." He started toward the bunkhouse.

Yhkon grabbed his arm, stopping him, with irritated bafflement creasing his forehead. "What on Kameon are you talking about?"

"Well what do you mean?" Lentli laughed again, but it sounded nervous.

Both the irritation and the bafflement in Yhkon's demeanor grew. He didn't release his grip on Lentli's arm. Feeling a knot growing in her stomach, Talea looked to Grrake for his reaction. She had never seen him so pale. So terrified.

"Yhkon...could I speak to you, it's—"

"No." He didn't take his focus off of Lentli, who's amiable grin had turned downward, consternation shadowing his eyes. "Tell me what you meant."

"Well..." Lentli recoiled slightly, as if shocked that Yhkon didn't understand. He looked at Grrake. "In Sanonyn, when you were just a toddler...your family and mine were neighbors. That's how I know you and your father." When everyone only stared at him in shocked silence, he looked at Grrake again. He sputtered out a weak attempt at another chuckle. "Is this some joke?" Silence. Lentli's uneasy smile died altogether. "What's going on, Grrake?"

Grrake tried to speak, but couldn't seem to get the words off his tongue. His gaze shifted to Yhkon, who was watching him expectantly, and spoke in an undertone. "What is he talking about?"

Lentli took the opportunity of Yhkon's distraction to escape his grip, retreating a few steps, the befuddlement on his face starting to look more like horror.

No one moved or said a word. After a long moment Larak stepped toward Yhkon, trying to take his arm. "Yhkon, I think Lentli is confused, let's—"

"No!" he snapped, shrugging Larak's hand off. His eyes were ice cold as he glared at Grrake. "What the hell is he talking about?"

Grrake swallowed hard, grimacing so much Talea thought he might be in physical pain. He still didn't say anything.

Yhkon whirled back to Lentli, grabbing his arm again, posture threatening. "Then *you* tell me, or I swear I'll—"

Larak tried to intervene again. "Yhkon! Listen to me. Let him go. Give—"

"Shut up." Yhkon glowered at him next. His face was red

with anger, jaw clenched. Talea resisted the urge to flinch. "Unless *you* want to tell me. No?" He faced Lentli again, expression savage. "Then it's up to you." His grip tightened, making the man wince. "Tell me!"

Larak was moving forward to get between Yhkon and the terrified Lentli. Lentli apparently didn't trust him to get there in time, because he sent Grrake a frightened, apologetic look, before meeting Yhkon's furious gaze. "Well...I don't know why you don't...well, you're Grrake's son, aren't you?"

~♦~

Yhkon picked up the clear glass between his thumb and index finger, spinning it a little. The amber liquid inside swirled, foam clinging to the rim. He sat alone at a table beside three empty chairs. It would probably stay that way—when a man clad with armor and weaponry entered a tavern, any other occupants tended to steer clear, in case he drank more than he ought.

Hearing the door to the tavern open and quiet footsteps approach, he took a sip without looking up, even as the newcomer sat down at his table. "Hello, *Dad.*"

Grrake's anxiety was tangible. He leaned forward, glancing over both shoulders. "Yhkon what are you doing! You can't go into public like this, in all your gear without—"

"Oh, how thoughtless of me," Yhkon interrupted the chastisement with a flippant smile. "I should get you a drink. Hold that thought." He got up, ignoring Grrake's whispered objection, and returned to the counter. "A beer for my *father*, please," he made sure it was loud enough for Grrake to hear.

When he sat back down, setting the glass at Grrake's elbow, he smiled again, leaning back in his chair nonchalantly. "Now, where were we? I believe you were in the middle of lecturing me, like any good father. Do continue."

Grrake just looked at him for a long moment. There was a deep sadness in his eyes...not enough to give Yhkon any sense of regret or sympathy. "Yhkon...I'm sorry."

"Mmm, you might have to specify...what for? Lying to me ever since you just *took me in*, fourteen years ago? Abandoning us? Or is there something else I don't know about yet?"

His gaze lowered, as he clasped his hands tightly. "All three."

"Ah." Yhkon smiled triumphantly. "So there is more!" He made his posture even more relaxed. "Alright, let's hear it. This grand tale of how you abandoned your children to nearly starve, probably so you could run off to your lover who just happened to be the queen of Sanonyn; and then came back but chose to never tell me you were my father."

Grrake's expression became almost skeptical. "Of course I didn't go to her, she's married now. I'm going to tell you everything, Yhkon...but I think we should do it somewhere else, and sometime when you're sober."

He laughed. Surprisingly, it wasn't hard to laugh. "I see...you think I'm drunk. Well, you'll be glad to hear..." He took another sip. The glass was still mostly full. "This is my first."

Whatever twisted amusement had fueled him so far left in the space of a couple seconds. He leaned forward over the table, head cocked slightly and a sneer curling his lip. "I'm not drunk. What I am, is *done*. With you. Maybe with everything. I haven't decided yet. In any case, I don't care about your explanations or apologies." He shoved his seat back, standing up. "You can go tell it all to Jaik's grave."

Yhkon left the tavern without another word or glance. At first he thought he'd struck a hard enough blow that Grrake would leave him alone, but he soon heard him catching up.

"Yhkon, Yhkon! Please wait."

He kept walking.

Grrake caught hold of his wrist, forcing him to stop. "Please, just give me the chance to at least explain...it was to protect you. If anyone knew you were my son, they would have tried to kill you. I didn't—"

Yhkon flung his hand off, glaring at him. Not caring that there were tears in the man's eyes. "I don't care! I don't care what your reason was. I trusted you. *Only* you. You *knew* that, and you lied. And now..." He clenched his teeth. "It's over. I'm done." He kept walking.

"Yhkon—"

"Enough!" he spat over his shoulder, quickening his pace.

Once again, Grrake grabbed his arm to stop him. Blind rage launched Yhkon's fist before he even knew he was doing it, slamming it hard into Grrake's jaw. Unsuspecting, Grrake lost his hold and stumbled back. For the briefest of moments, something in Yhkon told him he should regret striking his closest friend, his mentor, and apparently his father.

The moment was gone instantly. Somehow he felt confident that Grrake would not follow him again. And he was right. No more footsteps. Instead, three words spoken quietly. "I love you."

Those words echoed in his mind as he left the town behind, returning to where he'd tied Eclipse in the woods. He didn't even remember untying the stallion and mounting, he just found himself on a galloping celith. His knees and heels were tight against Eclipse's ribs, a command for more speed, which the animal was trying to obey despite the treacherous terrain of the forest.

It took a surprisingly long time for Yhkon to realize that his mount could easily break a leg—he never galloped a celith in woods like this, for that reason. He slowed Eclipse to a walk. It felt unbearably slow. As if something were pursuing him and he needed to escape it.

All the while, the simple words Grrake had last spoken haunted him.

Because he knew they were true. He knew Grrake loved him. He'd known it before, he'd just assumed that Grrake loved him *like* a son, not *as* one. And to be loved *like* a son had been a comfort. It had been from someone he respected and perhaps even loved like a father, in return.

But now it was from his actual father. Who he hated.

Maybe he should allow Grrake to explain why he'd done what he had. Maybe…maybe he really did have a reason, a reason that would…would somehow make it okay.

Or maybe it couldn't be *okay*. What reason could possibly make it acceptable for a father to abandon his children, then lie to one of them for fourteen years? He'd been only four when Grrake had left them, after uprooting them from Sanonyn and leaving them with their aunt in Zentyre. If Grrake hadn't left them…maybe his brother and aunt wouldn't have been murdered by Kaydor. Maybe his sisters wouldn't have been taken as slaves. At least they wouldn't have spent the prior years living in utter poverty, spending so many days hungry or cold. Yhkon wouldn't have been left an orphan, alone, wandering the streets and surviving on the rare kindness of a stranger, before the Falstons found him.

No. There was no reason that could excuse it. That being the case, he felt no need to hear whatever the reason was. He felt no need to ever speak to the man again.

Yhkon realized Eclipse wasn't even moving anymore. He had no idea where he was, but he could probably retrace his steps. The question was…should he? Did he want to go back?

Could he continue as lead Warden? It was Grrake that had convinced him to become a Warden. Grrake had trained him. Grrake had persuaded the council to make him the leader. Grrake had been the only reason Yhkon had become a warrior and joined the San Quawr's cause at all. Now, maybe Grrake was the reason he would finally quit.

The hours passed. Backtracking when he'd been paying no attention to where he was going wasn't easy. The only reason he was going back at all was to grab his pack. But he was finding it difficult to keep his eyes open, exhaustion weighing his limbs and clouding his mind. Besides, he should rest Eclipse for a night, make sure no inflammation was going to show up from the reckless gallop.

By the time he'd picked his way back to the outpost, it was dark. Everyone would be inside, asleep. Good. He and Eclipse could get a few hours of sleep in the barn and slip away in the morning unnoticed. Where to, he didn't know.

Dully he remembered that the whole reason they'd come was to free a band of Elikwai from the nearby village. There. That was it, then. He would free them by himself. And if in doing so, he was captured, so be it. Maybe it would give him the opportunity to assassinate Kaydor. Or, if he was killed...so be it.

He dismounted outside the barn and led Eclipse in.

It was already occupied.

Jaylee was grooming her celith, though the mare looked perfectly clean. She looked up as he entered. Her usual smile and energy, but also a softness in her countenance that somehow made him relax. "I was hoping you'd come back."

"Thought I wouldn't?" He took Eclipse into the stall next to hers and began removing his tack.

She gave him a meaningful look, "Are you planning to stay?"

Finished with Eclipse, he closed the stall and sank onto a hay bale. "I don't know."

She sat down next to him. He didn't have it in him to care that she was closer than he usually would like. "Do you want to talk about it?"

"No."

With a nod, she didn't say anything else. They just sat. He felt empty, unable to think, unable to feel anything distinguishable. Just weary. His body begging for sleep, his mind dimly telling him it was useless, what was the point? It was only a temporary escape. After awhile Jaylee lay down, and he did the same, his tired body overruling his mind's resistance. What was the point of resisting? Asleep, awake, it didn't matter. Nothing did. With any luck, he wouldn't wake up.

It was one of the last thoughts he had before sinking quickly into sleep.

He woke with a start. There was a blanket over him that hadn't been there when he'd fallen asleep, and another on Jaylee, sleeping beside him. Light came from the window overhead.

He inwardly swore at himself as he got up. Not only had he slept later than he'd meant to, he'd let himself fall asleep on a hay bale with Jay. It was entirely inappropriate. And, it meant he couldn't get Eclipse out of the barn without waking her—hooves on a wooden floor made too much noise. She would never let him go to the town to free the Elikwai by himself.

She looked peaceful, breathing steadily, a piece of straw poking out of her hair. Impulsively, he pulled the blanket up over her shoulders gingerly. She shifted a little but didn't wake.

After checking Eclipse's legs and confirming that there was no strain, Yhkon resigned himself to going to the town on foot. Depending on how it went, he could come back for Eclipse and then leave for good.

Outside, it was cold and overcast. The yard of the outpost was completely quiet, completely still. Empty…except for a lone figure hunched over, sitting on the porch. Yhkon didn't even take the time to see who it was, he just ran. He already knew it was Grrake. He ran as quickly and quietly as possible, hoping for his departure to go unnoticed. If Grrake saw him leave, it wouldn't take him long to figure out where Yhkon was going and why. His eyes stung. He told himself it was because of the wind.

Once out of earshot he slowed to a jog that he could maintain for the rest of the trip. It was almost four miles to the village. Distance running had never agreed with him. But he'd been forced to do it and build up stamina for years…by none other than Grrake. Almost everything he knew, every skill he possessed, all his training, it had been under Grrake's tutelage.

He balled his fists and ran harder.

Half an hour later, he was there. Most of the adult villagers were at their jobs. Most of the children, at school. The village was tranquil. Good. He'd rather not have spectators.

It was large for a village, no doubt owned by an exceptionally wealthy lord. The only place he was familiar with was the tavern he'd gone to the previous day, but it wasn't hard to pick out the building that served as the headquarters for the Kaydorians, and as a prison. That was where the Elikwai would be. The one that had escaped to find help had said there were about thirty Kaydorian soldiers currently stationed in the village.

If those thirty were mostly drafted infantry, with nothing

but a sword and a month's training, the task would be fairly easy. If those thirty had a few brains among them, or a captain with experience, it could be a suicide mission.

He was confident that he could get the Elikwai the chance they needed to escape, and that was good enough for him. What happened after that was of little concern. What was a concern was the possibility that this day would play out much as a similar night had, four years ago. That night he'd been up against far greater odds. The only reason he'd survived was because Grrake and a team of volunteers had rescued him.

The last thing he wanted was for the same scenario today. He would either get the job done and not require any rescuing, or he would make sure they killed or captured him quickly, before the Wardens could stop them. It was time to go.

~♦~

Jaylee woke gradually, stretching a little and curling deeper into the bed. Until something poked her nose. She opened her eyes and crossed them to see a piece of golden straw. *Hay bale. Yhkon. Blanket?* She sat up, contemplating the blanket that covered her. It hadn't been there when she fell asleep. Yhkon, who *had* been there, no longer was, another blanket crumpled in his place. He certainly would not have woken up, gotten them blankets, and returned to the hay bale. If he'd woken up he would have been mortified and left.

Grrake.

Yawning and rubbing bleary eyes, she stood. Eclipse was still in his stall. Where had Yhkon gone? She left the barn, rubbing her arms against the chill. It was morning, probably seven o'clock. She surveyed the yard, and saw Grrake sitting on the porch, head in his hands. Sympathy twinged in her stomach as she approached.

When he looked up, he was more haggard and bedraggled than she'd ever seen him. Usually, he looked less than his fifty years. Today, he looked far more. Anxiety lit his previously dull eyes. "Where's Yhkon?"

"I don't know." She sat down next to him. "He was gone when I woke up."

At first, there was no reaction, as if he hadn't even grasped what she'd said. Then he jumped to his feet, expression taut with fear. "He went to the village. To free those Elikwai…by himself…" He started pacing, grabbing handfuls of his hair and gripping it with white knuckles. "Not again…"

Her waking mind caught up. Four years ago, after Tessa died, he'd snuck out of Calcaria and tried to infiltrate Aydimor by himself, she assumed to assassinate Kaydor. Now he was going to take on thirty knights by himself. Under the right circumstances, she knew he could win…but who was to say if the circumstances would be right?

Grrake was already running toward the barn. "Wait!" She caught up, making him stop. "Wait. He'll be furious if you show up to help him. Really he'll be furious if any of us do, but less so if it's me. I'll go."

He must have known that she was right. Still, he looked frantic. "But—"

She put her hand on his arm. "Trust me. If we're not back in two hours, send a couple of the men."

Swallowing, Grrake finally nodded. Giving him a reassuring smile, she continued to the barn to get her celith. Without knowing when Yhkon had left, she had no idea if she could even get there in time to help him.

24

The Village

Yhkon strode calmly toward the Kaydorian station. Knocked twice. Waited. When the door opened, he grabbed it and thrust it into the soldier on the other side, simultaneously bashing the man's head against the wall. He fell limp to the floor. Lazily, Yhkon stepped over him and entered the office, smiling at the stares of the five occupants.

There was the dangling rope of a bell to his right. If he moved now, he could reach it before they did, and keep any of them from ringing it. Instead, he held his ground and crossed his arms. "I'm here for the San Quawr prisoners. Let them go, and I let you live."

Their stares became glares. One of them went for the bell, the other four came for him. He was ready.

Duck the first fist, planting his elbow into the gut of one, yanking the man's head down and into his rising knee. Another had grabbed him by the shoulders. He jumped, flipping and hooking him with a kick on the way down, before crashing into one of the others. They went down in a writhing heap. A few fists and elbows landed blows that he hardly felt. He broke the knee of one man, silencing his scream with a hit to the head.

The final of the four had been joined by the one that rang the bell, and managed to get Yhkon into a stranglehold, while the other punched him in the stomach. The pain only made hot anger pulse through his veins. He got a grip of the man holding him and used brute strength to yank him up and off, shoving him into the other. As they scrambled to regain their balance, he kneed the skull of one, and threw the other against the wall.

The clamor of the bell ended at almost the same moment. Yhkon pulled the ring of keys from the nearby cabinet and took the stairs to the lower level, lit only by a single torch. The flame was reflected on vertical iron bars. The nine Elikwai must have heard the commotion of the fight, because they were waiting expectantly. Grins lit their dirty, bruised faces. He jammed keys into the lock until one worked, then led them up and out.

They spilled out of the building just as soldiers began appearing from various parts of the village. "Go." Yhkon faced the hesitating soldiers, flexing his hands. "Get out of here. I'll take care of them."

Though most of them were visibly injured, the Elikwai were all forming up on either side of him. "No way." Their leader shook his head. "We can take them."

Yhkon glared at him. "I said *go*." The man only shook his head again, seeming confused by the refusal. Clearly Yhkon couldn't intimidate them into obeying his order. *Fine.* He lowered his voice. "The other Wardens are hiding. I have all the help I need. You men have done enough, I want you to get to the outpost. Go."

Though reluctant, they eventually all turned and retreated toward the forest, at the same time as the Kaydorians charged. Hopefully, none of the Elikwai would bother to look back and notice the absence of any hiding Wardens coming to his aid.

He waited motionlessly as the soldiers charged, only taking out his sword at the last moment. Their attack was disorganized, some rashly engaging without any form of strategy, others with a bit more intelligence trying to circle around and surround him. Those few with some wit would be the challenge. Yhkon met the flying swords with his own and kept on a steady backpedal, preventing them from getting behind him. With at least seven men fighting him at once, he could only parry and dodge, making it impossible to take any of them down. No doubt more soldiers were still rushing in from around the village—soon, he would have a lot more than seven to deal with.

Well aware that the move exposed his back, he gave up the defensive and instead pushed back, raining down blows. Hacking, cutting, stabbing. Letting the pulsing, boiling rage that fueled his muscles and tinged his vision red control him. Why resist it? Iron, flesh, and bone all gave way to the edge of his blade. He was soon stepping over bodies, mercilessly driving into the Kaydorians like a wedge being beaten into wood, steadily cutting down their numbers even as more poured in to join the fight.

The only problem was that the handful with a brain could now encircle him.

He knew they'd taken the opportunity when he felt the tip of a sword rip a gash down the back of his shirt, barely missing his skin. With a snarled oath, he whirled and focused his rage on them instead. The brief seconds he had before the rest of the knights caught up was enough for him to dispatch two of the cleverer opponents. Knowing that in so doing, he had allowed them to fully ensnare him.

Then the snare was sprung.

They rushed him from all sides. For one, terrifying

moment, he knew they would cut him down.

But they didn't. They attacked him with the pommels of their weapons instead of the blades, beating him to the ground and tearing his sword from grip. Multiple pairs of hands grabbed his shoulders and arms, restraining him. So they wanted him alive.

The men that weren't holding him parted, allowing a single knight to advance. The captain. He had the weathered face of a man with plenty of military experience, and the smirk of a man satisfied to defeat a worthy foe. After considering Yhkon a brief moment, he slugged him in the gut, hard. The squeezing pain and the way all the air slipped out of his lungs told Yhkon that he was also a man who knew where to hit, and probably who knew how to handle himself in a fight. "So. You freed the San Quawr." The captain shrugged. "No matter, I think you are the better catch. After all," he leaned forward, eyes glinting, "the king has offered quite the reward for whoever brings in the Sanonyan rebel, Yhkon Tavker."

Yhkon wore a smirk of his own. He decided that he would never give Kaydor the pleasure of capturing him. These men would either have to kill him, or he would win and go kill their king on his own terms. With a heave, he swung his legs up and into the captain's chest. A few of the men holding him lost their grip, the others released theirs with screams when he threw his forearms up, the fin-like blades on his gauntlets stabbing or slicing those closest. Not bothering to regain his sword, Yhkon attacked the first to move with nothing but his fists and gauntlets.

It wasn't the most efficient form of combat, but perhaps the most gratifying. They stood no chance against him. Fear was evident in their eyes, in their movements. All he felt was rage. Power. And satisfaction every time a body fell.

Until, there were no more bodies to fall.

Yhkon stood over the last man he'd struck down, rooted to the spot. Looking at the bodies strewn about him. The village that had been so serene before he'd entered was again silent, but the dusty paths were bloodstained, the sun glaring against the iron armor and weapons. The smell of death, of blood and sweat, surrounded him. It was a scent he was familiar with, yet he found it difficult to breathe.

All the anger was gone. The raw strength ignited by adrenaline, gone. The thrill…gone. The only thought or feeling he could grasp in the strange emptiness was that he wished it was him lying lifeless on the ground, not them.

"Yhkon?"

The voice sent a shiver down his spine. It was Jaylee, watching him from a few yards away. Her gaze swept over the corpses at their feet. He felt sick.

Why had this never bothered him before?

She pressed her lips together, walking the rest of the way to him and taking his arm. "Are you okay?"

He knew she was looking him over for injury. He knew the question deserved a reply. But he didn't have one to give.

Jay sighed and tugged him away from the havoc he'd wrought, making him sit down on the ground a little way off. He didn't resist—he was exhausted. And for a short time at least, there was no danger. It would take a while for the village's lord to learn of the incident and send for more Kaydorians. So he let himself sit, and she settled down beside him. "Talk to me," she whispered.

"About what."

"Anything."

He eyed a beetle crawling slowly toward his boot. "Did the Elikwai get to the outpost alright?"

Another sigh. "Yes, I passed them on my way. Why did you come to free them by yourself?"

"Because I wasn't sure I wanted to win." He put his hands on the back of his head, elbows on his knees. Why he'd admitted that to her, he didn't know. He shouldn't even be having the conversation with her in the first place. He should be...doing something. Figuring it out.

Except...what else was there to do? He had freed the Elikwai. He had defeated the Kaydorians. There were no more goals to accomplish. All that was left was to decide whether he would go back to that outpost.

She nodded slowly. "Okay. So you did. What do you want to do now?"

Nothing. "I don't know. I'm not sure if I can go back to the way things were."

"Because of Grrake. Did he have an explanation?"

He frowned at the beetle as it climbed up the side of his foot. "I don't care what the explanation is," was all he muttered.

"I don't think that's true." She was looking at him, even though he wouldn't look back. "I understand why you would feel that way, but in the end, I don't think you'll be able to come to terms with the matter one way or another if you don't know the full story. I'm not saying there's justification for what he did...but maybe there's at least a reason that would make it less of a betrayal."

His muscles tightened. "He abandoned us. Four children, left with our aunt in a village, when she had no way to provide for us all. And then he lied to me for fourteen years. You know," he laughed darkly, "it's ironic, really. The one person I fully trusted, since I was ten years old, and turns out he was lying to me the whole time."

She set her hand on his gently. "Then if nothing else, you deserve to know why. If you know...there's no loose ends. If things have to end, then they end with clarity."

Yhkon left his scrutiny of the beetle to instead look at her hand, lightly holding his. Distantly he realized that it should irritate him, or at least make him uncomfortable. It certainly shouldn't be making him wish for something more, for her to move closer, or to interlock their fingers.

No. He shook his head. Pulled his hand out from under hers. "I don't care about his explanation. And I don't—" he stopped. *What was that?* Creaking leather?

The captain. He hadn't seen him among those he'd killed.

Jaylee looked behind him. He had a split second to see her eyes widen and mouth open, a split second for panic to flare in his chest, before a knife pierced skin and muscle to slide between his ribs at the same moment as something slammed into his head.

Everything went dark, as if a blanket had been draped over him. He sensed rather than felt himself falling, his palms in the dirt as he scrambled to get away from the invisible threat. Reeling. His body moving forward, his mind spinning backward. A fire in his ribcage. Something gripping his skull, squeezing, crushing it with excruciating pain. Jaylee screamed his name and her voice rang in his ears again and again. He sensed a struggle behind him. Her voice still echoing, the only thing he could hear over his racing heartbeat that seemed to fill his whole body, he lunged at the attacker. Grabbed his ankle and yanked him away from her. His eyes saw, allowing him to react and respond, but his mind didn't register any of it. The man was grappling with him, throwing punches. Yhkon felt each blow as if it were dealt by a sledgehammer. He grabbed the captain by the shoulders and threw his weight to the side, sending them both rolling. A single hit was all he managed before the man ended up on top. Yhkon had a momentary glimpse of the descending fist before fresh pain exploded in his temples.

Everything was black.

Thump. Thump. Thump. Thump. Thump. His heartbeat was the only sound.

He couldn't move. Trapped inside of his body, no longer in control.

Something touched his chest, then throat. "Yhkon!" Jay's voice woke his senses, alerting him to his surroundings again. The slight breeze. The warm stickiness of blood on his head and neck. "Yhkon, please wake up! Say something!" He could hear her breathing, rapid and uneven, hitching in her throat.

He forced heavy eyelids to open. All he saw was blurred colors and shapes, one of them a tan oval above him.

"Thank Narone! Can you hear me? Yhkon?" She brushed his cheek with her fingers. "Please, please can you hear me?"

His vision began to clear, a distraught Jaylee only inches above him coming into focus. "Yes," the word was barely audible. His tongue and jaw didn't feel right.

Tears pooled in her eyes as she cupped his face with her hands. "I thought…I thought he killed you," she whispered, her lower lip quivering. "Are you okay?"

He was surprised to feel his hand lifting, his thumb wiping away a tear from her cheek. "I'm…" The word wouldn't come. *I'm what?* "I don't…know. C-captain?"

She nodded shakily. "I took care of him. Okay. Do you want to try and sit up?"

Yhkon blinked his assent, wrapping his arm around her back while she slowly pulled him up. Pain flared in his head with an intensity that took his breath away, a groan escaping his lungs. Jaylee stopped, instead putting her arms around him and leaning into his chest.

She was hugging him.

The pain was making it impossible to think, but he didn't mind at all. He held her as best he could, trying to steady his breathing, hoping it would ease the strange burning sensation in his side. "Jay..." He pulled her closer, fear bringing a lump into his throat. "Some-something's...wrong."

"Shh, it's okay," she pulled away enough to look at him. He squinted, trying to keep his focus on her. Then he ended up blinking, as blood began trickling into his eyes. "We just need to get you out of here. Do you think you can stand?"

Stand? Where did they need to get out of? He got his legs under him and gripped her arm as she stood up, drawing him with her. His vision dimmed as his whole head throbbed with pain. Sensation left his limbs, only enough remaining for him to feel his knees buckle. Jaylee kept him upright until the strength returned to his legs, enough for him to stand. The pain only receded slightly. "I can't...my h..." What was the word? "My...head. I can't..."

She kept an arm around his waist but rotated to face forward. "We'll take it slow. Alright? Just one step at a time...there you go. I've got you. We just need to get out of the village." It would have been more reassuring if she didn't sound so scared. He made his feet move, leaning on her heavily. Out of the village. Just out of the village. He still couldn't see normally, and kept his head down to alleviate the pain some, trusting Jaylee to guide him.

His thoughts refused to stay in order. He kept trying to remember why they were in a village, and what had happened to his head, why his face and neck were slick with blood, or why his ribs burned. Briefly, he would recall. Then his thoughts would scramble again and he would know that he knew, but he just couldn't remember. He didn't know why they were walking. All he wanted to do was lie down and rest, yet they were walking. He stopped. Jaylee made him keep going. "Come on, we can't stop yet. Almost. Please, stay with me!"

Yhkon instinctively obeyed. "Where are we...getting?" That wasn't right. "Where...going?"

"Just a safe distance, alright? Not much farther."

The captain. He had snuck up on them. But why? What had happened?

"Yhkon? Hey, come on, we have to keep going."

He kept walking. Everything started spinning. A queasiness twinged in his gut, only to become a wave of nausea. He stumbled, the ground and the sky mixing and swirling, pressure rising in his throat. Doubling over, he gagged, but there was nothing in his stomach to come out. Looking at the ground, he watched a few drops of his blood hit the dirt. *Have to keep going.* He straightened up again. Increased pain made him cry out.

Jaylee's hands tightened around his torso. He sensed her fear. He felt it tight and smothering in his own chest. "Alright, um, okay, this is far enough. Come on, just over here." She led him to the side, helping him sit down with his back against a tree. The process jarred his sensitive head more, but after a few seconds of sitting the ache subsided some. She crouched next to him, scrutinizing his ribcage. "I should probably pull that knife out."

The knife. That was the reason behind the inferno in his side. The idea of her removing it made him cringe.

She had already wadded up a strip off of his shirt and held it ready with one hand, cautiously grabbing the handle of the knife with the other. Even that tiny disturbance of the blade he felt. Without giving him more time to dread it, she smoothly retracted the dagger and immediately pressed the wad of fabric against the wound. He sucked in his breath through gritted teeth. Her gaze lifted to his face, worried. "Are you okay?"

Once again, he wasn't sure how to answer. Something was wrong. He didn't feel normal…yet he didn't know how he should feel, or why he should think that what he felt was wrong. He must have nodded, because she returned her attention to stopping the bleeding. His attention, meanwhile, stayed on her. It was hard not to look at her, at the sun in her hair, the way she bit her lip in concern.

She was stunning.

Yhkon swallowed and forced himself to look away. Somehow he ended up watching her again. Feeling a strange tug…like he wanted to move closer to her, or hear her voice again. He was fidgeting, restless from the pain in his side and his head, trying to make himself stop.

He spoke without thinking. "Jay?"

She looked up. First expectantly, then curiously. Her head tilted slightly when he didn't say anything more. "What is it?"

Blast. What had been his plan? Cheeks flushed, he lowered his eyes. But he'd already put his hand on her arm, also without thinking. He told himself he should let go. All he wanted to do was instead pull her closer.

"Yhkon?" she asked, when he still didn't reply.

"Sorry…I don't know…" Yhkon shook his head, as another wave of pain made him squirm, arching his back…that just made the knifewound burn hotter.

"Shh." Jaylee gave him a soft smile that made her even more beautiful, something he hadn't thought possible. "You need to hold still." She leaned toward him, her hand settled on his collarbone, her sparkling eyes caught his and refused to let go. He wasn't sure what the strange tug was that he'd felt, but it was getting stronger. For some reason he was fighting it...why? Everything hurt, everything felt wrong...he bit his tongue and broke her gaze.

But then she simply closed the final inches between them and kissed him. His mind went blank. Instinctively he slid his hand from her waist to her back and pulled her closer, deepening the kiss.

It was a long moment before they separated, but not long enough. "There. Now stop squirming," she whispered.

A frightening chill contrasted the warmth that filled his core. He tightened his grip without meaning to, keeping her close. She would leave. Like everyone did. He caressed a strand of hair from her cheek, knowing by the way she frowned that he was not concealing the inexplicable fear he couldn't displace. "Don't leave."

Her brow creased. "I won't. I promise."

Something told him that she would. That he should have resisted the tug he'd felt.

"Just relax," she murmured, coming close again to rest her head on his shoulder. One hand she kept pressed against the wound on his ribcage, the other she interlaced with his. "Once the bleeding slows, we'll figure out what to do. Until then, you need to rest."

Feeling calmed by her soft voice, Yhkon let his head fall back against the tree, and closed his eyes. The pain had been dimmed by the warm contentment of Jaylee tucked snugly against him. Drowsiness eased any lingering tension in his muscles. Her hair tickled his neck, her steady breathing relaxed his own, her hand was soft and comforting in his. A peaceful void beckoned him. Gently fogging his mind, drawing him out of consciousness.

The local lord.

Yhkon straightened, the grogginess temporarily fleeing. The local lord…he knew it meant something. It had come to him for a reason. "The local lord…"

Jaylee sat up, her hand on his upper arm, soothing. "It's alright."

"No…" He grimaced, pinching the bridge of his nose, as if by doing so he could squeeze out the haze that obscured his perception. "The local lord. He'll had…" That didn't sound right. "Have, um, more kn-knights." He looked at her, holding her hand tightly. "You have to go. Get…" Blackness invaded his peripheral vision, traveling inward, eating up his senses as it went.

"Yhkon." She shook his shoulder gently, jarring him back to alertness. "Hey, I'm not leaving you, okay? We'll be fine, I'm going to figure it out. Just—"

"No," he said again. Shook his head. It didn't hurt anymore, but it was heavy and fuzzy. "I think I'm…going to, to pass out." Another wave of dizziness confirmed the notion. "You need to g-get…" He clenched his jaw, unable to find or speak the words. Exhaustion made it hard just to keep his eyes open, let alone focused.

She rubbed his arm gently, nodding. "Shh. I'll worry about that. You just rest. Alright? Come on, let's get you lying down."

He was too tired to resist as she pulled his shoulders down, making him lie down in the grass. Any desire he might have had to resist faded when she curled up beside him, her head on his chest and arm resting over his torso. She murmured something he couldn't grasp as his mind dimmed. His senses retreated, until only a flicker of his consciousness remained. The last thing he felt was her kiss on his forehead.

~ ♦ ~

Jaylee listened as Yhkon's breathing soon slowed, until it was steady, if a little shallow. His body relaxed. She brushed his hair from his face and kissed his forehead where it wasn't covered in blood, noting how hot his skin was. A few more minutes and she was sure he was unconscious.

All the anxiety she'd kept under wraps for his benefit now put a tremble in her hands and made it hard to breathe. He was injured and she was scared to think to what extent. For those few minutes before and after they'd kissed, he'd seemed like himself. At least, an unusually open and tender version of himself. He'd seemed *there*. But the rest of the time…

She moved behind him and sat with her legs bent under her, carefully lifting his head onto her lap so she could see where the Kaydorian captain had struck him, the blasted man and his blasted brass knuckles. Blood had matted Yhkon's hair and covered his face and neck. It made getting through his hair almost impossible. She could barely see where his scalp was torn but she couldn't tell how deeply. At least the bleeding had mostly stopped from the knifewound.

Setting his head back down, she got up and paced, grinding her teeth against her fingernails. It had been what, an hour since she'd left the outpost to get him? Hour and a half? Hopefully almost two, so that Grrake would send some of the other Wardens out after them. Her celith was nearby but she didn't think she could get Yhkon into the saddle. She could ride back to the outpost and get help, it would only take fifteen minutes to get there and back…but she couldn't leave him. Not when more Kaydorians could be looking for them, and could so easily follow a trail of flattened grass and the occasional drop of blood.

The only thing to do was wait for the Wardens to arrive, and hope it was before any Kaydorians did.

She alternated between pacing and sitting beside Yhkon, wishing the time would move faster. Yet it was all too soon that she heard voices and movement, from the direction of the village, not the outpost. She crouched and watched from behind the tall grass, all that lay between her and the men she could just see coming through the trees. Iron caught the sunlight and glimmered as they moved. *Kaydorians.* There were ten, following the trail they'd left. Few enough that she could win in a fight. Too many for her to guard Yhkon at the same time.

Fear quickened her breathing and heart rate. If she ran and attacked them instead of waiting for them to arrive, maybe they wouldn't think to circle around her and look for Yhkon, and she could defeat them before they even knew he was there.

Or, they would see him, lying there defenseless. She squeezed her eyes shut, desperately trying to find a solution that didn't risk his life.

Hoofbeats.

Wardens! Jay looked over her shoulder, barely able to see the two celithmen coming their way. One of them was easily identifiable by his size, even from a distance. This was her chance.

She stood. "Larak!" was all she yelled, before charging the Kaydorians.

Over the clash of steel as she engaged as many of them as possible, the thunder of hooves. *Thank Narone.* The other Warden, Resh, arrived in time to attack the rest of the knights before they could get past her. Larak didn't appear. She glanced over her shoulder, to see him picking Yhkon up and putting him on his celith.

With Resh's help and the advantage of him being mounted, it took mere seconds to defeat the knights. As soon as her last opponent had fallen, she whistled for her celith, spun, and ran back, just as Larak was mounting behind Yhkon. Larak held one arm around Yhkon, keeping him secure. He was already cueing his massive celith into a canter back to the outpost. Apparently, he didn't need to be told that Yhkon was seriously injured.

Her celith came running. She mounted and followed, catching up and slowing to the same pace Larak kept. It only took a few minutes to get to the outpost, but it felt too long. The moment they were in the yard Larak dismounted, carrying Yhkon. Jaylee kept on his heels. Resh followed more loosely. Grrake, still sitting on the porch, was on his feet and walking with them to Lentli's cabin in an instant. Seeing him so worried made guilt and sympathy squeeze her chest. None of it was her fault…but somehow it felt like it. If only she had verified that all the Kaydorians in the village were dead before letting down her guard, the captain wouldn't have been able to jump them.

"What happened?" Grrake looked Yhkon over, terrified. Jaylee couldn't blame him—Yhkon's head and shoulders were covered in blood. It was almost hard to look at him, yet impossible not to. "What happened?!" he said again.

Larak was looking at Jaylee expectantly. Her rapid panting and the nerves that made her whole body quiver made it difficult to reply. "He had defeated all of them when I got there…or I thought…but we were talking and," she took a deep breath, "one of them snuck up behind us, he stabbed Yhkon and hit him in the head, he was wearing brass knuckles."

The explanation didn't lessen the fear in Grrake's eyes at all.

Larak's heavy brow was drawn, thinking. "How long ago was it?"

"Maybe...half an hour? Forty-five minutes?"

"Did Yhkon pass out then?"

"No, he sort of fell and was dazed but then he tried to pull the man away from me a few seconds later, they ended up fighting, and he hit him in the head again. Then I think he might have passed out, for a few seconds."

They were almost to the cabin. Larak asked for a couple more details as they entered, barging past a shocked Lentli to lay Yhkon down on the sofa. The cabin was quiet and unoccupied save Lentli, probably the reason Larak had gone there instead of the bunkhouse. "Lentli, get me medical supplies. Resh, go tell everyone what happened, and keep them out of here." While the two men left to do as bidden he scrutinized the back of Yhkon's head as best he could through his matted hair, then the knife wound in his ribcage. "What was he like, after the hit? Confused?"

She gripped the back of a chair to steady herself. "He was in a lot of pain, um, some nausea and dizziness, he was having trouble talking, he didn't seem all...*there*, some of the time."

Grrake's expression was becoming more tormented. He looked to Larak. "What does that mean?"

"Nothing good," was the only reply.

Lentli returned with the supplies, and Larak set to work. He patched up the stab wound between Yhkon's ribs first, then cleaned and bandaged his head. The whole process took several minutes. Grrake hovered, barely staying out of the way, watching every move.

Larak had just finished and started to back away when Yhkon drew in a deep breath, stirred, and opened his eyes.

Grrake knelt beside the couch, a hand on his son's shoulder. "Yhkon?"

Yhkon looked at him. Then closed his eyes again in a

grimace. "Where...wh-what..." He coughed a little. "Jay?"

She smiled without meaning to, and joined Grrake at his side. "I'm right here."

Grrake nodded, even though Yhkon wouldn't see it. "We're at the outpost. You're safe. Everyone's fine."

The tension in Yhkon's jaw and forehead slackened visibly. For awhile she thought he wouldn't say anything more, but he did. "What...happened?"

"What do you remember?" Larak asked.

He thought for a moment. "Jay and I were...outside the vil...the ver...the village." She was rather relieved that was all he specified about their time "outside the village." His struggle to find the word, however, was far from relieving.

Grrake managed a tight lipped smile. "Larak and Resh went looking for you two when you didn't come back in time. But you're here now. Everything's taken care of."

Yhkon opened his eyes to look at him. For a long moment, he just looked puzzled. "Where were you?"

Jaylee sucked in her breath, and saw Grrake do the same. Yhkon may have forgotten the recent revelation of Grrake being his father, but he was about to rediscover it. They exchanged a look with Larak. He moved closer. "Grrake stayed here, to keep an eye on things, while Resh and I went."

"But..." Yhkon exhaled and wrinkled his nose, as if frustrated, or unable to solve a problem. This one time, she wished the hit to the head would keep him from figuring it out. It didn't. His expression went from vulnerable and confused to stone cold. "Get out."

Fresh pain lined Grrake's face. "Yhkon, I—"

"Get out!" He tried to sit up, swearing in a slurred voice, groaning in pain even as he tried to get off the couch. Grrake attempted to calm him, or at least keep him down, but Yhkon shoved his hands off with surprising strength, face red with anger.

Larak, however, grabbed Yhkon by both shoulders and pushed him back onto the sofa without hesitation. "Calm down. He's your father, he's worried about you, he gets to stay. Got it?"

Yhkon stopped struggling, but he didn't look any less savage. "He is *not* my father," he said slowly, without a slur.

Larak just crossed his arms and gave him a stern, impatient frown. "Actually, like it or not, he is. Now lie down and rest."

Jaylee inwardly cringed, knowing Larak's words and tone would only add fuel to the fire. Yhkon was on his feet before anyone could stop him, still almost a head shorter than Larak but far less defenseless looking than he'd been lying on a couch. "You don't get to t-t..." Unable to finish the sentence, he snarled out a string of inarticulate oaths instead. "To tell my-m-me what to do!" He flung a hand in the general direction of the door. "So you g-give out too!"

She wasn't sure how Larak would respond, and she didn't wait to find out. "Yhkon." She moved closer, and put a hand on his arm. "You do need rest, to recover. Please?"

His glare fixed on her.

Suddenly he wasn't just handsome and powerful, with that aloof mystery she'd found enticing. He was frightening. He was damaged, unpredictable. His bicep flexed beneath her hand and for a moment, she expected him to wrench free of her grip and strike her.

Then disorientation erased the anger. He grimaced, taking a step back as if he'd lost his balance. When she drew him toward the couch, trying to ignore her pounding heart, he didn't resist, sitting down with her clumsily. Larak remained poised, ready to act, but Yhkon only mumbled something inaudible, closing his eyes and relaxing into the seat. She focused on easing the tension in her muscles and her quickened breathing.

Larak let down his guard and retreated a few steps, sighing. "Well, he just needs rest for now. You two stay with him and keep him on that couch, let me know if anything changes." He set a hand on Grrake's shoulder briefly, before leaving the cabin.

At some point Yhkon's arm had ended up around her waist, and now tightened, pulling her closer. It almost made her flinch. But the brutal, frightening man of a few minutes ago was gone. So she adjusted accordingly and kissed his cheek, hoping he would stay docile and fall back to sleep. He did, within minutes, his expression so tranquil compared to how furious it had been only a short time ago.

She had almost forgotten about Grrake sitting at the other side of the room, until he spoke in an undertone. "Did that happen before or after he got the concussion?"

No doubt by "*that*" he meant the affection between her and Yhkon. That he would remark on it didn't bother her. It was easy to share things with Grrake, there was little chance of criticism—and besides, in this case, there was nothing to be ashamed of. Yet the question still bothered her. "After, I guess." She wanted to say that it had *started* earlier, that it had almost come to life in Aydimor. But she couldn't. She knew why he had asked, and she knew...he was probably right.

He nodded, slowly, inspecting his hands without seeming to see them. There was something so...broken, about his posture, the weariness in his eyes. It made her wonder what all those years of being Yhkon's father without him knowing had been like. *Not easy.* "I'm glad for both of you, if it works out," he said finally. "Just...be careful, Jay."

She fidgeted. "What do you mean?" Why she bothered asking, she didn't know. It was clear enough without him saying it.

Grrake still didn't look up. It wasn't like him, to not make eye contact as he spoke. "When he recovers, he might not feel the same way about it." He clasped his hands together, so tightly it looked painful. "Everyone who loves Yhkon either hurts him or gets hurt by him."

~ ♦ ~

Jaylee woke confused. Something had happened…

Yhkon's shoulder was her pillow. His arm around her was lax as he slept, so still that she straightened. Was he breathing? She put the finger of one hand lightly against his throat, the other she put just under his nose. A feeble pulse. His breath was so shallow she could barely feel it. Still, it was there.

The flare of panic she'd felt faded, letting grogginess return. She relaxed. Dimly, she felt like something was about to happen. Like she was missing something. But all was peaceful—Yhkon asleep, his skin hot where their arms touched, Grrake also having dozed off in the chair across the room. The cabin entirely silent.

Movement. Yhkon's arm tightened around her. At first she thought he'd woken and was simply pulling her closer. But his arm continued to tighten painfully, compressing her ribs and stomach, making her suck in her breath. "Yhkon—" She still felt him moving against her, and fell silent as she looked. His eyes were rolled back, only the whites showing. Every muscle was rigid as his whole body spasmed.

She cried out in alarm, resisting the pressure of his arm to get upright and grab his shoulders. "Yhkon! Yhkon wake up!" No response. His body continued to jerk, the veins in his neck and forehead bulging, face flushed and glistening with perspiration. With effort, she got out from his hold. "Grrake!"

He had already woken and come to her side, shouting Yhkon's name and trying to hold him still. He wrapped both arms around his son and held him, but the writhing didn't stop. "Go get Larak!"

Jay scrambled for the door. She'd made it three strides toward the bunkhouse when Larak came out. "I was just coming to—" he cut off and moved faster when he saw her face. "What's wrong?"

"He's…he's…" She gripped his arm without thinking, chest so tight it was hard to breathe. "A seizure…" was all she got out before they were back in the cabin.

Larak took only a glance and went to Grrake, taking his arm to make him loosen his grip on Yhkon. "Give him a second. He'll wake up."

Grrake backed up slightly but didn't appear to relax. Jaylee couldn't so easily assuage her own anxiety either, standing close to Grrake, hoping to comfort both him and herself. It felt far longer than it was before the seizure finally stopped, Yhkon's body going slack. He stirred slightly and mumbled something, and didn't open his eyes. Larak frowned. "He should wake up, at least for a few minutes…"

Grrake took it as an order. He first nudged, then shook Yhkon's shoulder, calling his name. Yhkon's brow creased and he shifted a little. Another moment, and his eyes opened. Jaylee could see the confusion in his eyes instantly. And the fear, something she was not accustomed to seeing in him. It made any relief turn into concern. He backed as far into the couch as he could, gaze darting around the room, eventually landing on their faces. "What…" He trailed off, looking around the room again, gripping the edge of the seat with white knuckles.

With a pained look, Grrake leaned forward as if to calm him. Yhkon recoiled, wincing, eyeing him suspiciously.

While Grrake retreated, Jaylee slid into the seat next to Yhkon, taking his hand. "Yhkon?" She gave a squeeze. "It's alright. You're fine." He stared at her. The blankness, the lack of recognition…it unnerved her. Did he even know it was her?

"That is not a good sign," Larak whispered to himself.

She wet her lips. Surely something could snap him out of it. Maybe…maybe something to trigger a memory. She decided to act on the first idea that came to mind, despite Grrake and Larak's presence. Ignoring the way Yhkon flinched, she leaned in and kissed him. His mouth was hot against hers, hotter than it should have been. For a split second he was kissing her back. Then he stopped, completely unresponsive, and after another moment pushed her away.

She should have been surprised, but she wasn't. Just disappointed.

The comprehension and awareness gradually returned to his eyes. He looked at her for a long time, with a new sort of void. She held his gaze, willing herself to see something else. There wasn't anything else. There wasn't anything. Just indifference. His attention moved to Grrake, passing over Larak disinterestedly. No rage. No irrational, erratic anger. Instead, it was controlled. It was cold. Aloof.

None of them got out a word before he silently lay down and turned his back to them.

25
Queens and Questions

Dunk, scrub, swish, hand over. Dunk, scrub, swish—the plate clanked against another when she went to hand it over. Talea looked up. Rikky was watching her with mirthful blue eyes, as he held out the plate she'd last given him. "You missed a spot."

Giving him a mock scowl, she took the plate back and scrubbed it again, then handed both to him to rinse. "There."

Grinning, he dunked both and set to work drying them while she continued washing. "So." He added the two plates to the growing stack of washed, dried dishes. "Do you know what happened with Yhkon and Jay?"

Not that hard to guess... "No, not really."

"Hmm. Think he'll..." Rikky scrunched up one side of his face and clicked his tongue. "Improve? You know, not verbally murder anyone in sight?"

She laughed despite herself. "*Verbally murder*, I guess that's a good way of putting it, if a *little* exaggerated. And of course he'll improve." She scrubbed vigorously at a stubborn stain. *Who am I trying to convince?*

Still, Rikky only nodded. They continued working in

silence. Only as they finished did he decide to splash her with the cold water from the rinsing basin, then glance away with a whistle as if it had been an accident. She gave a hum of disapproval, scooped up a handful of the frothy bubbles lining her own basin, and slathered them onto his cheek. They were both laughing as they cleaned up the water and put the dishes away.

It was refreshing. Laughter wasn't easy to come by, in the week since Yhkon had gotten the concussion.

With the task done, they went their separate ways. Rikky probably in search of Ki or Skyve or one of the Wardens who was still fun to be around. Talea hesitated in the kitchen doorway, not sure where to go. She could follow the same idea, and go find one of the other girls. Or even Wylan, or a Warden.

Or, she could go find her Warden. The one who didn't want to be found.

Yet, as was often the case, she decided to try anyway. If she didn't, who would? Most of them weren't brave enough to try, or didn't want to. The rest he would curse out the door. So she went. The stable was the first place she checked, since it was where he stayed most often. Today was no exception. He was pacing. Pacing, always pacing. Talea knew he would have heard her open the door, but he didn't look up. "Hey. Want some company?"

Yhkon's only indication of having heard her was a twitch in his frown. *I'll take that as a yes.* She closed the door behind her and went the rest of the way in. "Where's Larak?" *The better question: who chased him out this time, you or himself?*

He gave a dry laugh. "Done with me, and me with h-him, that's wh-when...where."

No progress, I see. Or hear. "Any progress?"

As if he could hear her thoughts, he gave her a glare that

very clearly said, "Seriously?"

She put her hands up. "My bad. Well...why don't we try?"

Yhkon exhaled heavily and finally faced her fully, arms crossed. "Sure, let's. You kno-kn-knot I'd love to dwell on the f-fact that I can-n't talk."

"No," she drew out the word, sitting down on a hay bale. "I know you would love to *practice* so that you can improve. You can talk. If you go slower, I think it will be easier."

With another impatient huff, he replied, slower. "That's what Larak says, and la-look where it got us."

"See!" She smiled. "That was better. Come on, Your Highness the Stubborn One, you can no longer say that we haven't made progress. If you slow down, it's much better."

He had softened, ever so slightly, and only in posture. His tone remained the same. "What's the point? Who am I g-g-gone to take to, my *dad*?" Just like that, his shoulders were rigid again.

Talea sighed, tapping her finger on her thigh. She was the only person that, in the last week, could talk to Yhkon without receiving a hearty dose of his heightened temper. But even if he wasn't angry at her directly, he was always angry. Usually at Grrake. "Okay. Can we talk about that, though? You have every right to hate him, from what I know of the situation, but don't you think just at least knowing *why* would be better? Not so you can forgive him or something." *If only.* "But just so you'll understand."

He was back to pacing. "I'm not g-going to hal-ha-half a set-si...si-"

"Slow down," she whispered.

Jaw visibly tight, he stopped and continued, controlled. "A sit-down ch-chat with him. I don't want to see him."

They'd done a good job of avoiding each other. Grrake

hadn't wanted to, at first...well, she knew he still didn't, but it had eventually gotten to the point where even he knew it was better to stay away. "Alright...well...what if I talked to him? Found out the story? Or, you do realize that Larak probably already knows it. Maybe he'll just tell you." *Not that you two are best buds either...*Larak had the medical knowledge to try and help Yhkon recuperate from the lasting effects of the concussion, but he did not have the patience or tact also needed. She hadn't seen them spend more than twenty minutes in the same room without shouting.

Yhkon didn't reply. It was probably as close to permission as she was going to get. "Alright, then that's our plan. I'll talk to him, okay? See what the story is, and then if you're willing, I can tell it to you." She stood up, and put a hand on his arm. At least he didn't flinch. "I'll be back in however long it takes him to explain. You just..." She extended her hand to indicate the rest of the barn. "Hang tight and don't have too much fun without me."

He glowered at her, but she could tell there wasn't any actual disdain in it. "I would mention that I don't l-like being tee-tr-treated like a child, but it seems painless."

"Pointless," she smiled, "and yes it is." Leaving the barn, she walked toward Lentli's cabin. That was where Grrake stayed, mostly. Lentli had been horrified upon realizing the disaster he'd accidentally caused, and had been especially obliging to both Grrake and Yhkon in anything they wanted since, though Yhkon gave Lentli no more grace than he gave the rest of them. So the barn had become Yhkon's haven, the cabin Grrake's.

Inside, Grrake sat alone, staring at the floor. She could almost never look at him anymore without sympathy wrenching her heart. It just wasn't right. Both he and Yhkon were in so much pain, caused by one another, when only a week ago they had been each other's closest and most trusted friends. She knew Grrake loved Yhkon, perhaps more than any other father she'd ever met. So she had to believe that there was some explanation for what he'd done. "Grrake?"

He glanced up enough to see who it was, and made a pitiful attempt at a smile that only made her feel worse for him.

"Hi." She moved closer to sit down next to him. He leaned forward, elbows on knees, hands loosely clasped. A pose she'd seen Yhkon in so many times. Now that she knew they were father and son, it sometimes surprised her she hadn't guessed it long ago. They looked alike, talked alike, shared so many mannerisms...even if in personality, they were such opposites. "So, I was just talking to Yhkon."

He immediately became more attentive. "Is he alright?"

How am I supposed to answer that? "He's his usual...anyway, well, I tried to tell him I thought he should let you explain things."

Grrake's interest faded into discouragement. "He won't."

His voice was so hopeless. She mustered some reassurance. "No, he won't, but I offered to get the explanation instead then relay it to him, and he mostly agreed." She watched for his reaction, realizing she hadn't even thought about whether or not Grrake would be willing to tell her. "Would that work...?"

He sat back in the chair, rubbing his hands over his knees. There was a strange mixture of the hope that had just been so absent, and reluctance in his expression. "Of course I'll tell you," he said finally. "It's just...I keep telling myself that if he only knew, he might at least hate me less...but honestly I'm not sure if he will."

Talea cringed. She didn't even know what the explanation would be, yet she'd wondered the same thing. Yhkon was so angry and hurt...was there any explanation that would be good enough for him? "Well...only one way to find out." *And he deserves to know.*

"I know." He nodded. "But he's not going to take it well. Are you sure you want to be the one to tell him?"

Ha. What an excellent question. "I'm not sure he'll take it at all, from anyone else. And if there's a chance it will help...then yes."

Grrake gave her the slightest of appreciative smiles, quickly replaced by a pained frown as he continued. "Alright. Tell him...that his mother's name wasn't Mayra. She was the mother of his siblings, but she died almost four years before he was born. His mother's name was..." He bit his lip, so hard she thought it would bleed. "Shanteya Ken'd'Valsem. And if her father had known Yhkon was still alive after his siblings died in Zentyre...he would have killed him. That's why I didn't tell him, or anyone, who he was."

"Shanteya Ken'd'Valsem," she echoed. "Why does that name sound familiar? And why would her father want to kill his own grandson?"

He grimaced. "Yhkon will know. Just tell him, I'm sure he'll send you back for more details."

Uncertain, she stood up, hesitating. When he still offered nothing more, she left. As she returned to the barn she mulled the explanation that, as far as she could tell, hadn't explained much. And if it was such a secret, why did Yhkon's mother's name sound so familiar?

Yhkon was pacing when she entered but stopped. He watched her approach. Expectant.

Why, again, did I agree to get into the middle of this? "Okay. So..." She couldn't decide if standing or sitting would be better. *Sitting.* Settling onto the edge of the hay bale, she took a deep breath. *Just say it fast.* "He says your mother's name wasn't Mayra. That was your siblings' mother, but she died four years before you were born. Your real mother's name was Shanteya Ken'd'Valsem and her father would have tried to kill you—"

Yhkon went from standing passively a few feet away, to right in front of her in less than a second. "*What?*"

His icy, infuriated eyes were so close and drilling so fiercely into hers that it took her a moment to regain her voice. "Um…that's what he said. I thought the name sounded familiar…do you know her? Why would her father—"

He turned on his heel, snarling out profanities as he stormed out of the barn.

Talea remained seated, dazed. She had expected anger, confusion, maybe annoyance…not contempt. And where was he going? She jumped up and ran after him, catching up just as he reached the cabin. *Oh dear.* "Wait, uh, Yhkon!"

He didn't wait. He ripped the door open so violently she thought it would fly off the hinges and smack her in the face. She scrambled inside after him, not entirely sure that she wouldn't have to get in the middle of the mess *physically*.

Grrake stood up as Yhkon came in. He didn't appear particularly excited for the encounter—not surprised, either.

Yhkon was so red-faced he looked like he could burst. "If you're g-gone to lay-lie to me, fine, bet don't th-tha-thank I'm so stupa-pid as to believe that—" He ended up on another string of oaths.

Grrake looked like he would rather melt into a crack between the floorboards, but he managed not to recoil, despite Yhkon's aggressive words and posture. "I know it sounds crazy, but it's true."

"Really?" Yhkon gave a scornful laugh. "Shanteya K-Ken'd'Valsem." He had remembered to slow down, making his speech impediment less noticeable. "Queen of Sa-n-nonyn. You didn't just c-court her, you *slept* with her and—"

Queen? It clicked. Shanteya Ken'd'Valsem. That was the name of the queen of Sanonyn.

Talea could hardly blame Yhkon for his reaction.

Grrake was still standing firm. "That is not what happened. We eloped, we didn't—"

"Oh!" Yhkon smirked. It was one thing when he was just angry. When he was sarcastic and mocking, it was even harder to watch. "So you're now cla-climbing to be *married* to the queen of Sanonyn. Funny then that she already has a husb-band and t-two children."

"We divorced!" Grrake was losing his composure, becoming desperate. "When you were four, her father found out about you, and wanted to kill both of us, to remove us as contenders for the throne. So I took you and your siblings to Zentyre. I only left you with Karren so I could throw the king's men off your trail, but then the Eradication came and I couldn't get back to you…" He paused, as if expecting another outburst. Yhkon was completely silent. Almost mumbling, Grrake continued. "When it finally ended…they found me as I was coming back to Zentyre to you and your siblings. So I told them you had been killed, and I agreed to divorce Shanteya. Obviously you hadn't," he seemed surprised Yhkon was still letting him talk, "but I knew the king didn't trust me and would be waiting for the first sign that you were still alive. No one could know that you were my son, or he would have found out and killed you, as he considered you an illegitimate heir."

Yhkon was still silent. Grrake started to seem hopeful, until Yhkon finally did speak. Slowly and clearly. "Fourteen years aga-ago I would have believed you." He stood so still. His voice, his demeanor, he had it all under control. Somehow that was more frightening. "But th-there hasn't been a day since then that you haven't lied to me, so I don't think I will now."

"Yhkon, wait, I—" Grrake started to move forward, but Yhkon was already out the door.

Talea stayed, to see the older Warden's shoulders slump and his brow knit, facial muscles strained, fighting to keep his emotions on the inside. His eyes still glistened as he looked at her. "I guess the explanation won't help, after all."

She wasn't sure what to do. Or say. "I'm so sorry, Grrake..." she whispered. "Maybe...do you have some sort of proof? That would convince him?"

"Yes, Larak and three of the council members know the whole story, and," his voice cracked, "Shanteya's letters. She wrote to me, and to Yhkon, for when I told him."

"You stayed in contact?" She didn't finish the question with what she was thinking. *Even after you divorced and she remarried?*

He might as well have heard her thoughts. "We only divorced because we had to. Her father wanted her to marry a duke, to have proper heirs." He looked away. "But that doesn't mean I don't love her. She found someone trustworthy to carry letters back and forth without anyone finding out."

Talea hated the feeling of seeing him so tormented and not being able to do anything to help. It had always been obvious to her that Grrake had lost people, that he'd faced hardship. He'd always had a quiet sadness, under his gentle smile and dependability. But she'd never known how much he'd been through.

Grrake swallowed and hugged his arms to his chest, gaze imploring as he faced her. "Would you talk to him? Maybe...with some more time, he'll come to terms with it."

"Of course I will." She wet her lips. "But, were you planning to tell him? At some point?"

"I was supposed to tell him as soon as he was eighteen." He shook his head slowly. "I didn't...because by that time, I knew *this* would happen."

Talea left and made her way back to the barn feeling heavy. It was difficult to blame Grrake for acting as he had, first to protect Yhkon, and then to protect their relationship. It was equally difficult to blame Yhkon for being so hurt and bitter. How they would reconcile...how she could possibly help the situation...she didn't know. All she could do was try. And be there for both of them.

When she entered the barn, Yhkon wasn't pacing. He was sitting, head down, hands buried in his hair, allowing her to see that his knuckles were bleeding. She touched his arm, gently pulling his hand out toward her. Sympathy knotted her stomach. "Which wall wronged you?"

"If only it were a wall," he said, barely audible.

"So I take it that the explanation didn't make you feel any better. That you don't believe him."

"Belive-be...lieve him, not believe him." He shrugged wearily. "What does it matter."

She let go of his hand and went to the stalls, looking for a first-aid kit among the Wardens' tack. "Well, if you do believe it, then at least you know he did have a reason. He was trying to protect you."

"He could have told me."

No arguing that...She found the kit and returned with it. "He said he was going to when you turned eighteen. But he didn't...because he didn't want this to happen."

Yhkon only nodded. He didn't object as she took his hand to rub ointment on the scrapes. "Or he m-made it up. What are the cha-chances—"

"Actually, I asked," she carefully wrapped his hand with a small strip of bandage, "and he has proof. Larak and three councilmen can confirm the story, and…he has letters. From Shanteya."

"Great." He apparently didn't have the energy for his scornful cynicism of before. "Shanteya. Queen of Sanonyn…my m-mother."

Unsure what to say, she took his other hand to dress it. He watched the process blankly for a long moment before speaking. "You know, it was always Grrake that pi-patched me up when I did somewh…someth-thing stupid."

That he had required patching up for this sort of thing before didn't surprise her. "He does love you," she murmured without thinking.

He got up, turning away to pace. "Never understood why."

She opened her mouth to reply. Nothing came. What could she possibly say? She just put away the medical supplies while he paced, inwardly searching for what she could say or do to help. Eventually she decided just to give him something else to occupy his mind. "Well, if you're secluded to the barn, there's still no reason you can't train me. I'm hardly a professional, you know, and that's what you promised all those months ago at the beginning of this craziness."

Yhkon only gave her a dull look, lifting one of his hands. It quivered slightly. "How about the h-hu-hit to the hea…h-head as m-my…" he muttered something she didn't hear and didn't bother finishing.

The speech impediment was the most prominent consequence of his concussion, but he had also lost some hand-eye coordination, and there was a tremble in his hands. "Well," she said again. "Maybe it can be training for both of us. It might help, for your hands to do one of the things they're best at. Come on." She gave him a smile. "No matter how bad you are, you'll still be plenty good to train me."

Clearly not as optimistic, he assented by going to Eclipse's stall to get his sword. He unceremoniously put it into her hands and proceeded to use as few words as possible in directing her through a few new maneuvers. The longer they went, however, the more she smiled and laughed at her mistakes, the more he relaxed. Eventually he was earnest about the training instead of merely obliging. Immersed to the point of seeming to not notice when his hands fumbled.

Practicing a particularly complex move, he even smiled a bit, amused as she failed at it yet again. He went behind her and put his arms around her, hands over hers on the grip of the sword, to physically guide her through the movements. In such close contact, she could feel the way his whole body tensed when the barn door opened and Jaylee entered.

She stopped in the doorway. Yhkon moved away from Talea, turning his back to both of them. "What are y-you doing here," he muttered, without so much as looking at her.

Jay's frown deepened. "Getting my celith. Sorry to interrupt."

Yhkon scowled as if she'd made some overbearing demand, and waved his arm in the direction of her celith. Talea could see the hurt in Jay's expression. Yet another person she wished she could help.

Jay went quickly to the stall and began saddling the mare. Talea thought maybe that was as many words as would be exchanged, until Jaylee spoke unexpectedly. "You know you could at least be civil to me, for everyone's sake. I'm not asking for anything else."

His glare made Talea cringe. "Aren't you?"

Jaylee's gaze darkened, less hurt and more offended. "No, I'm not. I gave you the companionship *you* wanted when you were hurt, and tried to offer some comfort. Now I'm offering for us to go back to…to a platonic, business relationship, and you're acting like I'm some manipulative, conniving—"

"Just get out," he said it only loud enough to cut her off.

"You know what," she threw her free hand up as she led the celith out of its stall, "fine. You want to lead me on for a day, then treat me like the dirt on your boots, go ahead. But I'm done feeling sorry for you. I'll leave that to Grrake," she glared at him, "who I'm surprised has managed it as long as he has." She stomped out, a nervous celith in tow.

Talea took one look at the torment on Yhkon's face, and felt a weight settle in the pit of her stomach. Empathy and desperation to offer comfort gnawed at her gut. "She doesn't mean that."

He sat down on the hay bale. "Yes she does. And she's rate. R-right."

"No, she's not." She sat down beside him. "She's upset and I think she probably does have reason to be. But first off, she does care about you, whether she admits it or not. And second, Grrake hasn't *managed* anything." She paused, not sure if returning to the topic of Grrake was a good idea. Too late now. "He cares about you and always will, even if he didn't always get things right."

It was impossible to read his expression. All she could discern for sure was that he was exhausted and in pain. Probably physically, as well as mentally. She tentatively slipped a hand onto his shoulder. Sometimes she had to remind herself that a couple months ago, she had been sure they would never be friends, certainly never reach a point where she was the person he trusted most. "Larak would probably tell you that you need rest. If I left you to get some sleep, would you do it? I could tuck you in if it helped."

His lips twitched in what was supposed to be a smile. For her benefit. It was all too obvious that mirth was not a possibility. A nod was his only answer.

"Alright." She got up. "I'll make sure no one bothers you, save in the event of, say, a fire." He just nodded again, staring at nothing. Biting her lip, Talea hastily sat back down and hugged him, pulling away again before he would have to react. "Get some rest," she said quietly, and left the barn.

As promised, she went to the bunkhouse and informed everyone present that the barn was off limits, though that was nothing new. Everyone stayed away as much as possible anyway. Kae and Gustor both asked her how he was, and she answered the only way she knew how—a shrug and a sad smile. Wylan hadn't even made eye contact when she'd told him not to go in the barn, but when she left the bunkhouse she heard his quiet tread after her. He joined her in his usual manner. Head down, hands in pockets, expression steady and reserved. "You doing alright?"

Talea let out her breath slowly, giving him the same sad smile she'd given Kae and Gustor. "Been better. I wish I could help him. And Grrake and Jay."

He nodded. After a thoughtful pause, "I don't know that any of us except Yhkon can help Grrake, and I don't know about Jay. But I'm pretty sure that for now at least, you're the only one who's managing to help Yhkon." The straightforward comment made her breath snag in her throat. Thankfully he must not have expected a reply, because he continued. "Just wanted to make sure you were doing okay. Want some company, or time alone?"

If anyone else had asked, she probably would have gently

asked for the latter. "If you don't mind…company would be great."

Another nod, his favorite form of communication, and they started walking at a leisurely pace.

26

Handler

Talea hefted a bag over her shoulder, carried it out to Haeric to be loaded onto a celith, and returned to the bunkhouse for another. She grabbed the strap of one and tugged to discover that it was heavier than she expected. *Who packed this, Ami? Probably has the name of every guy she's ever mooned over, etched in stone...* She was about to put more effort into picking it up, when it lifted all on its own. Wylan's eyes briefly met hers before he was gone, bag in hand.

Larak appeared—she never understood how he managed to be so stealthy, when he was so huge—and waved her off of picking up more luggage. "We've got this, if you would go check on the other girls, see if they're ready." Just as she was about to do as told, he spoke again. "And if they are, would you go track down Yhkon?"

Nodding, she left. Another request that made her feel like she was somehow the lead Warden's *handler*. At least that was what everyone else seemed to think—that he needed a handler and that she was the best fit. Not that she blamed them for thinking so. Nor did she mind...not really, anyway. It just got a little lonely, sometimes.

She found Terindi, Kae, and Ami in one of the bedrooms. They had been tasked with cleaning up the bunkhouse, and by the looks of it, they were finished. "You guys need any help?"

"No." Ami set a hand on her hip, surveying the room. "Everything is clean." Terindi and Kae affirmed silently.

"Alright, then I think we're about to leave." She left the bedroom and they followed. "I just need to go tell Yhkon." *Yep. Handler.* "I'll be back in a few minutes."

Outside the bunkhouse, all the celiths were loaded and ready. A quick scan found at least most of the group present. Yhkon, of course, an expected exception. Not only did he avoid interaction with the rest of them whenever possible, Larak also kept him strictly off duty. No chores, no work, no training...no need for Larak to know that Talea trained with him privately every day. At first she had been concerned that Larak was right and the activity might inhibit Yhkon's recovery, but it seemed to be the only time when he could relax, set aside his problems, and not be miserable. And as far as she could tell, his coordination and strength were improving. Besides, she had decided that at least half the reason Larak kept him so sternly away from activity was actually to keep him away from the other Wardens and wards. Maybe for Yhkon's sake...more likely for theirs.

Not finding him in the barn, she set out into the woods behind it. Larak had told Yhkon that other than the bunkhouse, he could only go to the barn or a short distance into the woods behind. Before the concussion and everything that came with it, she knew Yhkon would never have listened. As it was, he did. As long as Larak left him alone, he did as told.

Sure enough, he stood with arms crossed, watching nothing in particular as she arrived. Talea went to his side and stopped.

"Time to go?" he asked at length.

"Yeah." She folded her hands behind her back, rocking between her heels and the balls of her feet. "You ready?" *To be confined to a saddle, surrounded by everyone else, again? To not be able to hide away and be left alone by everyone but me?*

"Since it's the only we-way to get out of this blasted re-regain, yes."

"Region."

"Region," he repeated. Two weeks since the concussion, and technically there was little improvement in his speech, except that he finally accepted her help without frustration. And at least when he was talking to Talea, he was calm and controlled enough to go slow.

She mustered a smile and took a step back toward the outpost. "Then let's go."

As they joined the group, she could feel the instant increase in unease. The celiths caught on and pawed the ground or sidestepped anxiously. Most of the other Wardens and wards had already mounted, those that hadn't did at the same time as she and Yhkon. Only when she was in the saddle behind him did she realize that usually, this was the point where Yhkon would be the first to move, to set the pace and take the head of the group.

He didn't.

After a second of uncertainty, Larak kicked his celith into a trot, and they all fell in behind him. Yhkon took Eclipse to the very back. The rhythmic motion of the stallion's gait, the saddle creaking softly, dozens of hooves drumming the ground beneath them. It was all so familiar. It had been almost every day of her life for the past five months. Yet it felt different now. They weren't travelling to get the next ward, they were travelling to Calcaria, every ward present. The mission was complete. At least, the very beginning of it. Supposedly, the majority of it still lay ahead. In Calcaria, they had to become the Eight as they had been prophesied, not just eight teenagers with an ability they barely knew how to use. And once they were ready, they would lead the war to end the Eradication.

It was easy to forget all of that. It had been such a constant, large presence in her mind for months, but in the last two weeks it had faded. Replaced by a more immediate need. Yhkon. Grrake, Jay…the whole group. Or, more accurately, keeping the group whole.

Except it was too late for that. The unity of the Wardens and wards may have been questionable before. Since the day they all found out Grrake's secret, it had rapidly disintegrated altogether. It was strangely difficult to imagine a day when they would all work together to fight a war.

The day passed slowly. She had spent enough time out of the saddle to feel stiff and sore as the hours ticked by. There was little conversation, even when they were moving slow enough to make it easy. Or, any conversation that did take place, was too far ahead or too quiet for her to hear. She and Yhkon spoke little. There wasn't much to speak about, and she didn't think he would be comfortable talking with other people around.

She was happy to get out of the saddle by the time they stopped for the day, but already worried about what conflict might arise once they were all stuck in the same camp. Everyone dismounted and spread to their usual responsibilities. Everyone except her and Yhkon. She didn't like doing nothing while everyone else was working, but she couldn't simply abandon Yhkon.

He, however, apparently wasn't going to stand by and watch. After tying Eclipse he strode to where Resh and Haeric were setting up a tent, and started to help. Unsure of what else to do, Talea did the same, though she knew she was hardly much use to them.

Larak interrupted within seconds. "Yhkon, I told you, no—"

"I'm f-fine and you knot it." He kept working. His teeth were already clenched. *This isn't going to go well.*

"Oh really?" Larak just frowned and crossed his massive arms. "You don't sound fine. Hit to the head, remember?"

Yhkon stopped the job to glare at him, answering as slowly and clearly as possible. "A speech impedi-di-ment does not mean I can't set up a bloody tent."

Talea would have been gratified by how well he'd controlled his speech, except Larak's frown didn't lighten. "Fine. Then you can go help set up *that* tent." He tilted his head to where Grrake and Wylan were constructing another.

She winced. Yhkon's glare kindled, and she knew her apprehension had been right. Then he took a deep breath and lowered his voice, moving closer to limit the conversation to only her and Larak's ears. "There's no reas-son I can't help without wa-working with him or Jay."

Larak didn't relent. "And there's also no reason you shouldn't work with them."

She'd never thought the day would come when she would be tempted to slap the giant, usually rational man before her...yet it had.

Yhkon's patience, already stronger than she'd expected it to be, had run out. "*You* are n-not the ladder here, so I suggga-gest that you stop th-thinking you can-"

"Neither are you." Larak's thundering voice could cut him short even when he was angry. "You were hardly a leader before, and you certainly aren't one now. If you want that position back, I suggest that you get over your issues and your bitterness and handle problems like a man."

Talea stared at him. Shock silenced anything she might have said. Yhkon was speechless with either surprise or fury, which one she didn't know. And she didn't want to wait to find out. Anything he did say to defend himself would probably come out a mess, so she would do it. She moved between him and Larak, putting a hand on Yhkon's arm just in case he was furious enough to become aggressive. But before she could say a word, Yhkon spun and walked away.

They both watched him go. Larak, with something like a sense of accomplishment. Talea with mounting indignation on Yhkon's behalf. "What in Kameon are you doing?" She glared up at him. "That was *progress*, and you completely ruined it! He—"

"He needs a little more correction and a lot less coddling," he interrupted impatiently.

"Correction?" She recoiled. "What is he, a misbehaving celith? Can you honestly blame—"

Larak spoke over her again. "He's been like this for over a decade and I've been there the whole time, so don't—"

"Enough!" Grrake's voice surprised them both. He stood by, demeanor both pained and firm. "Larak," he looked him squarely in the eye and held it, "he is my son, he is an adult, and he has every right to hate me. I appreciate everything you've done, but you do not get to discipline him."

That was clearly not what Larak had expected to hear. Or wanted to hear. "We have done nothing but coddle him all these years," he snapped. "Don't you think if that was going to work, it would have by now? He needs to learn to move on! Call it tough love if you want. And what about Jaylee? She certainly doesn't deserve that sort of treatment."

Grrake's hazel eyes hardened with more sternness than she had perhaps ever seen from him. "You know what he's been through. Can you blame him for pushing her away because he doesn't want to lose someone he cares about again? Don't you dare act like he's some cowardly, spoiled child." Larak started to say something. Grrake didn't give him the chance. "He's recovered as much as he will from the concussion and does not need you medically, so I ask that if this is how you feel, you leave him alone."

Larak hardly looked pleased. Still, he nodded after a moment. "You know where I stand. But I won't intervene again." He walked away without another word.

Talea turned to see where Yhkon had gone. He was with Eclipse...not very far away. Had he been able to hear them? Grrake must have thought so, because he drew Talea further away and spoke quietly. "I've been wanting to thank you, for…" He didn't seem to know what word to use. "For sticking with him, in all this."

She blinked. "I'm with you too, you know."

A small smile. "I know. And thank you for that, also." He set a hand on her shoulder, and left.

With the familiar knot in her stomach, she did what she always did—left the group behind, and went to Yhkon. He was on his knees, checking Eclipse's hooves for rocks. "Hey," was all she could say.

No reply. He sat back, eyes losing focus. She sat down next to him, and after a few moments of silence, leaned her head on his shoulder. It allowed her to hear his whisper, barely audible. "I don't hate him."

The knot in her gut twinged. "I know."

He swallowed, hard enough for her to hear. "And I didn't want to hurt Jay."

"I know," she said again. "And eventually you'll have to deal with it, with both of them. But maybe for now, you just need time."

Yhkon's gaze fell. His eyes had always reminded her of ice, and now, that ice looked like it was shattered and melting. "I don't know wh-what I'm doing."

"You don't have to." She pursed her lips, thinking. "For now...let's just get to Calcaria. You don't have to have it all figured out right now. You can take it bit by bit."

The savory smell of the supper the other girls had put together drifted across the campsite. Her stomach had been growling for an hour, and she'd heard Yhkon's doing the same. "How about some food?" Not giving him the chance to say he wasn't hungry, she got up and went to the fire. As had often been the case, everyone made way for her to go first, getting a serving for herself and Yhkon. Like always, she gave them all a smile, and left again. They would eat their supper around the fire. She would eat hers with Yhkon. Most of them would treat her differently, just like they treated him differently, the rest would try not to exclude her, but still had to keep their distance for Yhkon's sake. So be it.

She was just sitting back down beside him, when she heard footsteps. Wylan, Kae, Gustor, and Ami stood, bowls in hand, looking to Yhkon for his reaction.

Except Gustor. He shrugged, smirked, and gave Yhkon's shoulder a whack as he sat down. "Forget this. Since when do I need your permission for where I sit or don't sit?" He arranged himself nonchalantly. "Besides, Tarol was about to drive me back to my assassinating days."

A hint of a grin tried to work its way out of Yhkon's grimace. "Fine." It was all he said, but she still found herself smiling.

~ ♦ ~

"I'm just saying." Tarol slapped a hand to his chest, the other he outstretched as if he were displaying himself as some trophy. "You would have died ten times over by now if it weren't for me."

Gustor's reply was muttered under his breath. "Speak again and I may kill you ten times over."

Talea smiled to herself. She'd missed the casual banter that was finally returning, as they all adjusted to the changed dynamics of the group.

"No no, I'm serious!" Tarol moved his hands in front of him to count on his fingers. "There was the time with the Zentyren patrol, when we were all asleep and they found our campsite. Then—"

Haeric coughed into his fist, smiling. "I recall Gustor saving you, by kicking you out of the way when a soldier was going to cleave you in two."

Tarol waved his hand dismissively and continued. "Then the time that the dragon picked you up, and I—"

"No," Haeric shook his head, "it picked both of you up, and Gustor stabbed its foot so it dropped you."

"Irrelevant!" Tarol sucked in a deep breath to add to the list, only to have Gustor hook his arm around his neck in a chokehold, then kick his feet out from under him.

"There." Gustor smirked down at him, offering a hand to help him back up. "Now I saved you, from me, because if you keep talking there's no saying what I might do." He pulled Tarol to his feet and they kept walking, Tarol grinning and soon claiming that Gustor's one save didn't make up for his ten.

Talea glanced sideways at Yhkon to see if he was at all enjoying their antics. He walked with his head down, brow knit, apparently not having been listening at all. Then again, that was no surprise. It was rare for him to show any sign of amusement with everyone around anyway. Let alone when they were approaching the hill where Tessa had died.

She surveyed the scenery. Or what could be seen of it, with the fog that shrouded everything. It was a cold, bleak day all around. There wouldn't be a breathtaking view over the ocean when they reached the top this time. That was probably good—for Yhkon's sake, she didn't want them to dawdle. They were within an hour of the seaside outpost, from which they would take lareers the rest of the way to Calcaria.

Three long weeks since they had left Lentli's outpost outside the village where Yhkon had freed the Elikwai. Five weeks since he'd found out about Grrake and gotten the concussion. In that time, a lot had changed, and a lot hadn't.

At least Yhkon, and Talea as his closest companion, weren't so isolated from the others anymore. As far as she knew, he had not spoken to either Grrake or Jaylee since leaving the outpost. He did interact somewhat with the rest of them, not more than he had to and rarely with any enthusiasm, but it was improvement. And even if he wouldn't speak to them, he would tolerate Grrake and Jay's presence. No more eating supper on the fringe of the campsite, or always keeping Eclipse as far back as possible.

Jay, meanwhile, had kept to her word—if she was sympathetic toward him, she didn't show it. She didn't speak to him either, or if she did, it wasn't pleasantly.

Little had changed in Grrake's case. He had tried once

more to talk to Yhkon. It had lasted mere seconds before Yhkon simply walked away, and later asked Talea to tell Grrake not to push his luck. Though she'd phrased it differently, she'd done so, and Grrake had accepted that for the time being, he had to stay away.

Now, finally, they were almost done. Almost to Calcaria. The flight would take four or five days, and then it would be over. She didn't know what would come then. *Deal with that later.*

Her attention snapped back to Yhkon when he abruptly stopped. "Something wrong?"

He cocked his head, as if listening for something, then just shook it and kept going. The celiths were spent from the weeks of traveling, so Larak had decided they might as well give them a break and walk the remaining few miles that morning.

Inexplicably jittery all the sudden, Talea kept close to Yhkon. After a few seconds she let herself tune back in to the various conversations around her. Tarol, not surprisingly, was still talking, though now to Resh and Ki. Skyve was trying to explain something scientific-sounding to Rikky, who hardly appeared to be listening. Ami and Kae giggled as they walked with Gustor and Haeric. Terindi and Jaylee walked together; if they were talking, it was too quietly for Talea to hear. Grrake and Larak were at the lead, Wylan trailing them, all three walking silently. The disagreement at the beginning of the trip over Yhkon had not damaged their friendship in any way she could see. And, as promised, Larak had limited his interaction with Yhkon and had kept it civil.

Her jitters had just abated when Yhkon brought them back by stopping again, straining to hear something. Eclipse snorted and stamped a hoof, probably impatient to get to the outpost like the rest of them. She waited quietly, caressing the stallion's neck to calm him, watching Yhkon expectantly. The intent furrow in his brow deepened as his eyes narrowed. He lifted his head and called in a loud whisper, "Larak!"

Larak turned, the whole group coming to a halt. "What?"

Yhkon scanned the woods. There wasn't anything to see except trees and fog. "I had something."

Larak scrunched up his face. "What?" he said again, confused.

"Heard," Talea said for him.

The Warden only sighed. "Of course you did. There's sixteen of us and just as many celiths making a racket, that one especially." He pointed at Tarol with a chastising glower. "Come on, it's—"

"No." Yhkon shook his head, backing up a step. The muscles in his neck and jaw were rigid. "We n-need to get ou-t-out of here."

Larak's lack of concern became annoyance. "Listen, I get that considering our location, you would be uneasy, but that doesn't mean there's any real threat."

Yhkon swore. "I said I ha-heard something!" He had grabbed Talea's wrist, as if ready to flee with her at any moment. Her heartbeat quickened.

Grrake's expression had all the concern Larak's was missing. "Alright. Let's go." When Larak opened his mouth to object, Grrake silenced him with a hard stare. He left Larak scowling and joined her and Yhkon.

Yhkon tightened his grip on her wrist and caught Grrake's eye, jerking his head toward Eclipse. She didn't understand, but Grrake did. He raised his voice to address all of them. "Everyone mount up!"

She had only gotten one foot in the stirrup when the sound of footsteps and rustling underbrush enveloped them.

There wasn't time to mount. She stepped down and instead took Eclipse's reins as Yhkon withdrew his sword and ran to meet the attackers. But there weren't simply a few that the Wardens could take down while she and the other wards kept the celiths from bolting. There were dozens, coming from all sides.

Her heart hammered against her ribs. The clash of iron, shouts, grunts, movement everywhere, all of it overwhelmed her senses. Making it impossible to comprehend everything that was happening around her. All she saw was four of the attackers coming straight at her. Pale skin. Long hair in dreadlocks. Heavily built, wearing rusty armor.

Asyjgon.

One of them was Farve. The man that had first seen her ability when she defended herself against them, all those months ago, and had then informed Captain Lerrip so that they could capture her. The sight of him made her throat tighten until it was hard to breathe.

He slowed his approach, smiling at her wickedly. "Hello, Talea. You should have known better than to cross through our territory again."

She stared at him. He lunged. Heat raced down her arm into her fingertips, forming an electric blade that she swung at him as he neared. Perhaps not expecting a trained reaction, he didn't see it in time to dodge. It sliced across his torso, burning through armor, clothing, and flesh as it went. He stumbled back with a scream, but the other three men had caught up. The first sword she ducked. The second she parried with her own, the electricity traveling through the Asyjgon's blade and shocking him. The third she didn't see in time. She twisted away, the tip still leaving a trail of fiery pain down her arm. Off balance, she turned back just in time to see a sword descending toward her head.

There was a flash of light, and the man swinging it crumpled to the ground. Kae stood a few yards away, eyes wide with terror, body poised for action. She ran to Talea's side as three more Asyjgon charged them. One engaged Talea, two Kae. Instinct and muscle memory took over, directing her through the maneuvers Yhkon had drilled her on, parrying, dodging, striking. Her electrical blade plunged toward the Asyjgon's stomach and through. There wasn't time to feel the horror she knew was coming—another man had body-slammed Kae. She staggered into Talea and they both fell. Her hands landed in a pool of warm, red liquid. Nausea brought black dots to her vision even as she grabbed Kae's arm and scrambled away from their assailants. She sensed rather than saw one of them advancing, about to hack down on them. Energy sprayed from her hand in a diagonal wave. She made the mistake of looking up to see the result—his arm hit the ground, then the rest of him. The other man had already collapsed.

They had just gotten to their feet when Kae screamed, at the same time as both Yhkon and Wylan shouted Talea's name. She started to turn. There was a moment that she saw a club swinging toward her head. Impact. Everything blurred. Then black.

~♦~

Yhkon watched Talea hit the ground, her body slack. He wanted to shout, to swear or call her name or anything, but his jaw was as immobile as a rock. He was already running full-out. The man that had struck her down was about to finish the job, two other Asyjgon having occupied Kae. Instead, he heard Yhkon coming at the last second, and didn't even have time for fear before he was dead.

Yhkon dropped to his knees, putting his fingers to Talea's neck. There was a pulse. She would have some bruises and an awful headache, possibly a concussion, but she would live. Back on his feet, he readied his sword to guard her from the next onslaught.

Until he heard Jaylee call for help.

The adrenaline that felt like fire in his veins gave way to a chilling dread. He couldn't see her in the chaotic battlefield swathed in mist. Her cry, however, rang in his ears.

Unable to swallow with his throat so constricted, he took a few tentative steps toward her voice. Anyone would probably take one look at Talea's unconscious form and think her dead, meaning she was safe...unless the Asyjgon intended to capture her again, as they had last time.

Jaylee called again, her voice strained with fear.

Yhkon grit his teeth and sprinted in that direction. Wylan was fighting nearby, he would keep an eye on Talea. Jay needed him.

He was forced to take down two Asyjgon before he was finally close enough to see her. She was engaged with four men. One of her arms was bleeding heavily, dangling uselessly at her side. "Jay!" Somehow it got past his locked jaw, as he kept running. Only two strides in and movement came rushing into his peripheral vision. He swung wildly at them and kicked one down, but didn't take the time to dispatch them. Jay was—

Pain erupted in his leg. His feet left the ground and his body hit it instead. He was already moving to regain position...except he couldn't. His leg wouldn't move. A glimpse of blood and a misshapen lump where there shouldn't have been one confirmed that the limb wouldn't be usable anytime soon.

Jay cried out in pain.

Desperation drove him on, all rationale lost. He hacked at the ankles of the nearest Asyjgon, wildly attacking anything he could reach even as he tried to get onto his good leg, aware of his movements but unable to discern them. He had to reach her. He had to save her. Some inarticulate yell of frustration or pain or fear left his gasping lungs. He was standing, hobbling to her...only to be tackled by another opponent.

Everything slowed. He watched as Jaylee's foes knocked her down. As one of their clubs lifted. Its descent was inevitable, no matter how he struggled.

A blurred figure came into view. It happened in mere seconds, too fast to understand. One moment it was Jaylee's name he screamed, the next it was Grrake's. One moment it was Jaylee under the diving mace...the next it was Grrake.

Yhkon grabbed the man grappling with him by the shoulders and heaved his weight to the side. They rolled, punching and elbowing where they could...despite his effort Yhkon ended up underneath. The Asyjgon was larger, and he didn't have a broken leg. But he also wasn't fueled by rage. The man pulled a knife. Yhkon wrenched an arm free and grabbed it just before it would have been stuck in his chest. Yanking his knee up between the man's legs, he used the moment's distraction to take the knife and plunge it into his neck. A spray of blood, a gurgled cry, and the Asyjgon became dead weight.

Shoving the body off, Yhkon got himself upright and limped as fast as his one leg could carry him, ignoring the pain of dragging the other behind carelessly. There was one more Asyjgon that Jaylee was barely managing to fend off. He took a dagger from his belt, praying the shake in his hands wouldn't ruin his aim. It didn't. The blade embedded into the man's chest, and he fell.

Yhkon's good leg gave out a few feet from Grrake and Jay. He half-crawled, half-dragged himself the rest of the way. Jaylee was on her knees. Grrake was on his back. Blood soaked his shirt where the spiked mace had hit the left side of his chest and shoulder. Yhkon's hands fumbled as he searched for a pulse...waiting...it was there. Feeble. He couldn't tell if Grrake was conscious, but his eyes were closed, and he was struggling for each hoarse, weak breath. He might just be dazed or knocked out from the impact...or, if the spikes had punctured a lung...lack of oxygen.

Pressure rose from Yhkon's stomach to his throat and lodged there. His eyes stung, vision blurring. He clumsily tore off part of his shirt to use as a bandage against Grrake's chest. Inwardly pleaded that the pauldron he wore had been enough to protect his friend from lethal damage. Jaylee was covered in blood. Her eyelids fluttered, eyes glazed, as her body slowly collapsed. Yhkon caught her, propping her against his shoulder and wrapping his arm around her, pressing his lips to her hair. Blinking didn't keep the moisture off his cheeks. *Please no...not again...* It was all he could think. Hold them close and squeeze his eyes shut, feeling his own body gradually shutting down, was all he could do.

27

Letters and Doors

Bob her knee, up and down, up and down. Rub her bleary eyes. Yawn and shove her hair from her face, wishing she'd braided it to get it out of the way.

Yhkon remained comatose, entirely unaware. That was Larak's doing. Apparently he'd been nigh on delirious anyway when the fight had ended, so Larak had drugged him. When he'd woken part way through the flight he'd been even more delirious and impossible to soothe, so Larak had gotten him some food and water then put him under again.

Now it was time for him to wake up, and he was taking his sweet time.

Talea flopped backward into the chair, able to peer into a mirror across the room from that angle. Half her face was still red and purple with bruises from the club an Asyjgon had tried to kill her with. Larak said she must have managed to duck and avoid the full brunt of the blow, saving herself from a potentially fatal injury. Or even a serious concussion, like what had given Yhkon a speech impediment. Yhkon, meanwhile, had come away with a broken leg. After some initial doubt, the medics had said it would heal fine. That had been a relief. She could only imagine how insane he might go if a permanent limp was added to his physical impediments.

Though there weren't as many of those anymore. Larak had been surprised by how well he had fought and had asked her about it. She had admitted that they had been training, expecting him to disapprove. Instead he'd given her a nod and said she'd done well, and that it had apparently been just what Yhkon needed to regain the majority of his coordination and capacity for fine movements with his hands.

There was a knock at the door. "Come in." She kept her voice low instinctively, even though Yhkon couldn't hear her anyway and even if he could, she *wanted* to wake him up.

Wylan entered. A brief scan of Yhkon. "That answers my question."

"No change. But I want to be here, when he wakes up." *So he doesn't freak out and kill some poor Stitch, or go berserk because he can't talk and they can't understand him.*

A nod. "And how are you feeling?"

"Little sore." She gingerly poked her bruised cheek. "How's everyone else?"

"Him, Grrake, and Jay got it the worst," he answered with a shrug. "And Kae. She won't be able to walk much for a few days but they say she'll mend. Haeric about had his arm taken off. But just scrapes and bruises otherwise."

Another relief. Everything had been so rushed and hectic...she had seen everyone at one point or another, either during the flight or since they landed that morning, but not close enough to know whether or not any of them were seriously injured. She knew without looking that they were all glad to be out of Asyjgon territory, out of Kaydorian territory...in Calcaria, where frigid temperatures would be their greatest worry. Ami had still seemed reluctant and nervous about coming a week ago. After the battle, however, she'd had a different perspective. The twins had been ecstatic, after hearing tales of Calcaria since they were eight years old and finally seeing it for themselves. Wylan had once again been reunited with his little sister, Nakelsie. And Talea with her family.

It had revealed a different side of the Wardens, too. She'd known that Larak and Haeric had families, that Resh had a brother he was close to. Yet those facts had been somehow extraneous, all those months in Zentyre. Seeing those family members with tears in their eyes as they hugged loved ones they hadn't seen in all that time had made the Wardens seem less like Wardens...and more like any other men with families and homes and lives.

Her attention returned to the present when Yhkon stirred.

Wylan's hand went to the doorknob. "I'll let you deal with that."

Unlike some of the others of the group, she knew he wasn't simply avoiding a potential flare of temper or awkward interaction. He just knew that Yhkon was more relaxed with only her around. She smiled a farewell as he left. Yhkon mumbled something, expression going from slack to disoriented as his eyes opened. She moved from the chair to the bed, sitting down on the edge as he jerked upright, looking ready to jump out from under the covers and attack some adversary. "It's alright." She caught his anxious eyes and smiled. "We're in Calcaria. No more Asyjgon. Or Kaydorians, for that matter."

His tension abated, focus shifting to her bruises. "Are you...alright?" Before she even answered, all the apprehension returned as he started moving again. "Grrake, an-d-d Jay, they—"

"No, it's okay! They're okay." She put a hand on his shoulder before he tried to get up and painfully rediscovered that his leg was broken. "Both of them. They're going to be just fine. Everyone is."

He relaxed, falling back against the pillows and letting out his breath. She could have sworn his eyes were moist. But he only nodded unevenly and swallowed. "Okay," was all he said. Then after a moment, "I'd like to...see him."

Her smile grew. "I was hoping you would. The Stitch said I need to get you some food and water as soon as you woke up, but after that, I have a pair of crutches here that ought to get you down the hallway."

Yhkon nodded, wincing. From physical pain or something more mental, she didn't know. Talea fetched a breakfast tray for him. He ate, but he was unusually subdued, even for him. So she talked while he ate, telling him how everyone was doing, about the flight, about the wards' reactions to Calcaria. He listened, smiled a couple times, asked specifically how she was doing at one point, but as soon as he had finished the tray, he sat up. "I need to talk to him."

"Okay." She bit her lip. "Just, if you don't mind me asking...is this a talk that ends with hugs and tears, or with slammed doors?"

He cracked a bit of a grin. "Hopefully neither," was all he said. His tone and countenance, however, were reassurance enough.

"Too manly for that stuff, right?" she teased, sliding off the bed and getting the crutches for him. He propped one under either arm and stood, keeping his casted leg off the floor. Talea opened the door so he could hobble over and through, down the hallway a few yards to Grrake's closed door. She paused with her hand resting on the knob. "This is where I wish you luck and give you a hug whether you like it or not."

Another smile. For as quiet and withdrawn as he seemed to be...he wasn't his usual unhappy. Just solemn. "Why do you act like I'm such a hatless, cruel creature all the time?"

"Well," she simpered, "most of the time you *are* hatless..."

He rolled his eyes. "Heartless."

~ ♦ ~

Yhkon opened the door, entered, and closed it behind him all without allowing himself to make eye contact with the man in the bed on the other side of the room. He hadn't been looking forward to the conversation from the beginning, now it was altogether ghastly. As if it weren't going to be uncomfortable enough, throw in that he couldn't talk properly, especially when he was uptight.

For a second he considered opening the door again and escaping.

It was too late for that. He released his grip on the knob and turned to face the interior of the room. Grrake was watching him with that familiar look, of concern, of remorse, of desperation. "Are you alright?" he asked, just as Yhkon asked him the same question. They both looked away.

Yhkon spoke again. "I didn't know if you..." *were going to survive.* Now he did know. That time when he hadn't, however, was the reason he was finally ready to have this conversation. He suspected that Grrake knew that. Grrake knew the way he thought and could surmise how he felt or what he planned to do better than anyone. Yet another thing that made him kick himself sometimes, for never realizing that the man was more than just an attentive friend and mentor.

"I'm alright," Grrake said, with a hint of a reassuring smile. "Can we...talk?"

Not a skill of mine. He couldn't bring himself to say yes. Limping the rest of the way in and sitting on the foot of the bed had to be confirmation enough. Grrake, though, got up almost the moment he sat down, crossing over to his dresser and opening one of the bottom drawers. Yhkon realized he had never seen him take anything out of that drawer. Now he took out two bundles of envelopes, and brought them back. He set one of them in Yhkon's hands as he sat down beside him.

All of them had his name written in a flowing hand on the front.

"They're from your mother," Grrake said. "Shanteya. She wrote one for each of your birthdays, and just when she felt like it. Not being able to be a part of your life..." He paused. "She made a lot of hard sacrifices, but I know that was the hardest."

Yhkon could only stare at the dozens of envelopes. He finally undid the string that held them so that he could open one. Not allowing himself to read the letter itself, he only looked at the bottom of the page. At the last three words. *"I love you."*

Rustling paper forced him to refocus. Grrake was unfolding a letter from his own bundle. He turned it for Yhkon to see and pointed to the signature at the end:

With all my love,

Shanteya

He knew Grrake was watching him closely, and he had already known that Shanteya had written to him...yet he couldn't take his eyes from the signature. "Do you believe me?" came the tentative question. When he didn't answer, Grrake continued. "Enisham, Ilidyu, and Juplay all know the story. Now that you know, they can confirm it for you."

Yhkon slowly folded the letter he had opened and returned it to its envelope. "Why did-didn't you tell me when I was eighn-t-teen, like you were s-supposed to?"

Grrake grimaced. "I was going to. But that day something had upset you and…" A pause. "Because I didn't want to lose you. I knew you hated me…not me as just Grrake, but me as your father. I thought if I told you…I would lose the relationship I had with you, and I couldn't stand that."

"Didn't she," he lifted the letter to indicate who he meant, "want you to? Tell me?"

"Yes." He sighed. "She reminded me that you would eventually have to find out, and when you did it would only be worse. So did Larak. But I just…" He shook his head. "They were right. I should have told you. I'm so sorry."

Yhkon met his gaze briefly. Looked away again. "Why did you l-live us in Zentyre?"

Grrake rubbed his palms over his thighs. "It was only supposed to be for a few months. I spent some time throwing your grandfather's men off your scent, leaving a false trail for them to follow, then I went to Calcaria both to lie low while they searched and because a friend here had asked me to help train the beginning of their military. But a few weeks before I was planning to come back and get you and your siblings…Kaydor started the Eradication. They wouldn't let anyone leave Calcaria. I tried, but they closed off every form of transportation."

Yhkon didn't say anything. It was becoming impossible not to believe the story. It was becoming more difficult to blame Grrake for hiding it. And it was becoming painful to be in the same room as him.

He stood up, clutching the bundle of letters tightly. He started for the door.

"Yhkon!" Grrake was up and blocking his way in an instant. "Please. I know there's no reason you should forgive me...but I am so sorry. I betrayed you. But...I have always loved you, nothing is more important to me and I just—"

"You shouldn't!" He hadn't intended to say it. There it was.

Grrake fell silent for a long moment. "What do you mean?"

He clenched his teeth, hating himself, wishing Grrake would hate him too. "I mean...Kinzie."

Understanding, and grief, softened the furrow in Grrake's brow and the anxiety in his eyes. "I don't blame you for that. I never have." He moved closer, hesitated, and put a hand on Yhkon's shoulder. "I love you and nothing can change that. Kinzie's death wasn't your fault."

Yes it was.

Grrake unexpectedly hugged him. "Please don't carry that on your shoulders."

Yhkon didn't pull away from the embrace, even if it was awkward...it was comforting, too. Grrake was still Grrake. His friend. The only friend, really, that had seen him at his very worst, had known him his whole life, and been there without fail. Who never gave up on him. He was also his biological father, whom he had hated as an abstract figure, for leaving him, Jaik, Kinzie, and Lanissa when they needed him, and then for lying to him. But he was still Grrake. And maybe that made up for everything else. *Especially since...* He pulled away and sat back down. Grrake did too, waiting. Except Yhkon didn't say anything. Couldn't. Everything he'd done over the years, the things he'd said, all the ways he'd returned Grrake's loyalty and care with abuse...

Eventually Grrake looked away. "I understand if you still hate me, for leaving, for lying..."

"No," Yhkon said it more quickly than he'd meant to. "I

mean…" He shrugged a little. It was time to let it go. "I'm ticked, and the-this is weird, but I don't hate you."

Grrake slowly grinned. "I can take that."

Coughing and smiling a little despite himself, Yhkon got up again. "I'm going to l-leave be-before it gets any weirder."

"If you don't mind me saying…I think you should talk to Jaylee."

Oh blast. "You can say it but I'm not sure I'm going to lis-s-en."

Grrake gave him the head-tilted, meaningful, somewhat chiding look. *Definitely my dad.* "I'm not saying you need to go in there and propose. I'm not even saying you need to…to reopen a relationship. But she does deserve an apology. And for everyone's sake it would be best if the two of you could work it out and at least be friends."

"Glad a pr-proposal is at least off the list," he muttered, adjusting one crutch under his arm. A sigh escaped his lungs. "I'm going," was all he said.

Grrake's grin returned. "That's a good lad."

Yhkon glared at him. "I should hit you with a clutch for that."

"Crutch," Grrake's grin only grew, "and thank you for not acting on that impulse. I have enough broken ribs as it is. Go on, then."

Once he was out of Grrake's room, there was only about seven feet between him and the ominous door to Jaylee's apartment, once Ahjul's. Not much time to come up with what he should say, or better yet, a way out of it altogether. As if anything he said would come out the way it was supposed to anyway. He'd end up stuttering, or saying something he didn't mean to, or completely tongue-tied. She'd had that effect on him even before the concussion.

Unfortunately, there was no reasonable way out of it. It had to be done. He gulped down the already rising pressure in his throat and rapped his knuckles against the door.

"Who is it?" Her voice sounded tired. She had lost a lot of blood, and was probably still suffering the consequences.

He barely managed to keep from stuttering on his own name.

There was a long pause. Eventually, "Come in."

He opened the door. She was in bed, paler than usual, eyes drowsy. They narrowed as she scrutinized him. He missed the energy she had always had. Even the first few days after he'd ended things, she'd still had it. But after that...she'd just been closed off. "You okay?"

Jay concluded her inspection of him. "I'm alright, thanks to Grrake. You?"

He glanced down at his leg. It wasn't his first broken limb, and he doubted it would be the last. "Fine. I..." His jaw tightened. Gulping again only slightly eased it. "Can I sit?"

A slight dip of her head was the only answer.

Setting himself on the very edge of the bed, only enough to take the weight off his legs, he took a deep breath. "I came to ap-apol...to say I'm sorry."

By the way her expression twitched without softening, he expected her to make him clarify what for, even though she must have known. She nodded instead. "And what now?"

That was easier than expected. Though she hadn't exactly accepted the apology, only acknowledged it. "Well," he rubbed the nape of his neck, "maybe we can j-just be...friends."

Still no sign of warming up. "If that was all you wanted, why were you so tempted to be more before the concussion, and so willing during?"

Should have known it wouldn't be that easy. Knowing if he lied or tried to edge around the truth she would catch it, and that she probably already knew the answer, he resigned himself to honesty. It took effort to speak slowly. "Yes, I was tempted, and then d-during I...enjoyed it." There was no going back now. "But I can't have anoth-ther uh, relationship, like that." He briefly made eye contact. "And I think you know...why."

"I know why you think that. But I don't necessarily agree."

It sounded like something Grrake had probably said at some point. "Still," was all he mumbled.

Jay sighed. "Yhkon...I care about you. And I think you care about me. Am I wrong?"

Unfortunately, "No."

"Then I don't think you should refuse to give us a chance. I understand that after losing Tessa, you're, well, nervous...but who says you're going to lose me?"

He squeezed his lower lip between his teeth. "Who says I won't."

"So you're just going to keep everyone at arm's length, because of that possibility? How is that better?"

Why do you have to be so impossible? Yhkon frowned at her. "Jay." He cleared his throat. "Just friends."

She huffed and squinted at him, as if he were an obstacle to surmount. And to her, he probably was. It was simultaneously endearing and vexing. "Fine." The smile he'd missed more than he cared to admit curved her lips. "On one condition. You take me out to dinner, just once."

It was his turn to squint at her. *It's a trap.* "Why w-would I do that?"

"Because you owe me."

"For what?"

"Being a jerk."

"But why—"

"Yhkon," she crossed her arms, staring sternly at him even as she simpered, "just dinner."

Absolutely impossible. And somehow irresistible. "One dinner."

Her grin became triumphant, and all the more beautiful. "Done. Next Werday. You can continue your grovelling then, and perhaps by that time I'll be ready to forgive you." She made a shooing motion. "Now I'm tired. Don't press your luck on my hospitality."

He shook his head, unable to keep from a bit of a smile. Just as he was getting up to leave, she spoke again. "What are those?"

The letters. "Ap-parently they're from my moth-ther."

"I heard something about your royal lineage…read any of them?"

"Not yet."

Her head tilted as she looked at him. "So I take it you talked to Grrake? Maybe mended some things?"

He answered with a nod.

"I'm glad." She smiled. "Now off with you, go meet your mom the queen of Sanonyn."

As told, he hobbled his way back to his quarters, happy to sit down and set the crutches aside. The packet of letters was becoming damp where he gripped it with a perspiring hand. Part of him was curious. The other part, vaguely terrified and reluctant.

There was no reason to put it off. He'd spent two decades thinking his mother had died when he was a toddler, now he knew she was very much alive, and had the proof in his hands. He took a deep breath and opened the first letter.

28

Captain

The shimmering, teal satin gown was one of the most comfortable things Talea had ever worn, the fabric unbelievably soft against her skin. The corset underneath, however, was far from comfortable. She sucked in as deep a breath as she could, her ribs squished against the cage-like garment. Her feet, meanwhile, had to be pinched into gorgeous shoes that seemed entirely inappropriate for walking.

A knock at the door. Hiking up her skirt even though it wasn't necessary, Talea crossed from her bedroom to the main room of her apartment. A whole apartment. In a palace. *So crazy.* She flung open the door, nearly startling Yhkon. "Yhkon! I feel ridiculous in this…this…well, *this*. I'm not a princess! And why do we need a whole ceremony? I mean really. Whose idea—"

"Talea." He put his hands on her upper arms and smiled patiently. "Breathing between sentences is recollected."

"Recommended," she corrected out of habit, flopping onto the sofa. Her sofa. *Still crazy.* "And you're avoiding the subject. Why do I have to—"

He silenced her again as he sat down next to her, setting

his crutches aside. "Because, you are Talereinna, the Aysa of C-Calcaria. And it's not just you, it's the other wards too. It won't be nearly as bad as you think. And," he smiled at her again, "you look beautiful, not ri-d-diculous."

She smiled without meaning too. "Fine then. Just butter me up. You know…" she looked sideways at him, "I saw the dress Jaylee is wearing, and she's going to look beautiful too…"

He rolled his eyes. "We've been over this. *Friends.*"

"Ah come on! You're no fun."

He ignored her teasing. "You remember what we reheard? What to do?"

"Rehearsed, and yes, and I don't want to." She picked up a pillow and tossed it at him.

He easily caught it and used it as an armrest, shrugging. "Too bad. An inescapable retirement of Aysa-dom."

"Requirement, and thanks a lot."

Yhkon snarled out what was probably an inarticulate oath. "If the man that deci-ided to hit me in the had wasn't alr-ready dead I would—"

She laughed. "Calm down now, you only make it worse when you're mad." In truth, he'd improved drastically in the week since they'd arrived in Calcaria. Probably because *he* had improved. He and Grrake were working things out, not without hiccups but steadily. He and Jay had, as far as Yhkon was concerned, worked it out. Talea knew that Jaylee still had her hopes set for more.

"Anyway," he grabbed his crutches, "we should go. Wouldn't want to be late for your own ce-ceremony."

Talea groaned. He was already up, balancing with one crutch so that he could grab her wrist and drag her to her feet. Mirea, her maid—*perhaps the craziest thing of all*—had left out a necklace for her. She put it on, the metal chain cold around her throat. Mirea had also done her hair and cosmetics, something Talea had never expected to wear.

Yhkon held the door open for her and they left the safety of her apartment behind. An altogether-too-short trip through the palace and they were at a set of double doors, where the other wards and Wardens were all gathering.

"All make way!" Tarol dramatically flung his arms wide and shoved Ki and Resh out of Yhkon's path. "The prince of Sanonyn has arrived!"

If looks could kill, Tarol would be in the grave. "Who told—"

Grrake approached with a sheepish smile. "They've all been pestering me…and I didn't think there was any reason that just our small circle couldn't know…"

Talea was grinning. Yhkon, glowering. "That doesn't m-mean—"

"Come now!" Resh put an arm around his shoulders. Talea was rather surprised Yhkon didn't strangle him then and there. "You should be pleased! Maybe Tarol will finally listen to you now. Actually, no, he won't. But hey, at least we now know why Enisham has always despised you—you're royalty and he isn't."

"I am not—"

"Save it, Highness." Gustor clapped him on the back. "I believe our grand entrance is due."

Still scowling, Yhkon went to the doors, waiting for Talea to join him. Unfortunately, she for some irrational reason was the first ward and had to go in first. She could already hear the muffled hum of the crowd on the other side.

"Ready?" Yhkon whispered. He didn't actually wait for her to reply, he just opened the door and gave her a nudge.

People. Lots of people. They immediately burst into

applause as she reluctantly entered the throng, following the path that was cleared for them. Yhkon was beside her. Wylan just behind, and everyone in their order behind him. The hundreds, perhaps thousands, of clapping hands were deafening. And terrifying. Still, the applause was moderated. Polite, not necessarily excited.

It died down as they reached the stage at the front of the crowd. Lining the back of the stage was the council, while Enisham and another man waited at the center. She had never seen the other man. Yhkon had told her his name was Mahzin, and he was the first person that Narone had apparently told about the Eight, a couple decades ago. She'd been expecting an old, wizened looking man. Instead, he was perhaps in his mid-thirties, with an eager, outgoing, sort of awkward look about him. Behind the two of them was a rack holding eight swords.

She and the other wards and Wardens lined up beside the stage. For this part, at least, she didn't have to go first. Enisham took a step forward to address the crowd. "People of Calcaria!" His voice carried surprisingly well. "I know that not all of us expected to ever see this day. When Grrake and Mahzin conveyed the message they'd been given by Narone to us, I found it impossible to believe at first, too."

Same here, she thought with a silent laugh.

"But now, standing before you, here they are: the Eight! To prove to you that they really are what Narone promised," he smiled, "a brief demonstration. Wards?"

The demonstration. The Wardens all backed a few paces away as she and the rest of the wards lifted their hands. At least with it being dark, only torches lighting the assembly, no one would be able to see how terrified she was. She felt like a dog doing tricks for everyone's amusement. Yhkon had assured her that he understood, but that the demonstration was necessary—at least half of the San Quawr in Calcaria had never accepted the idea of eight teenagers with such a crazy ability, chosen by Narone to lead the war. But once they saw it with their own eyes, they would have to believe.

So, she let aqua light glow in her hands, counted to five, and brought twin lightning bolts from the sky into her palms, at the same time as the other wards. Despite the thunderclap and sizzling of the electricity, she could hear the gasps and whispers from the crowd.

Then silence. Clearly no one knew quite how to respond.

Enisham spoke again. "Now that they're here, let us all be united in a common belief in Narone's provision and power."

Sappier than I would have expected from you, Enisham. But it was enough to pull the crowd from their shocked silence. The applause started slowly at first, growing into a far more deafening, more zealous thunder than before.

As it quieted, Enisham looked their way. "Ami, please come forward."

Ami, downright breathtaking in a maroon gown, her already beautiful features accentuated by cosmetics, could have been a depiction of an Irlaish goddess as she walked up onto the stage. Still, Talea knew what the eagerly watching crowd didn't—the poor girl was still reluctant, and homesick. Even so, she performed flawlessly, going to one knee, facing the assembled San Quawr, as Enisham began.

"Amilyne Elireth Firreyl. Do you accept the responsibilities as Lavess of the Eight, Caretaker, to fight for and serve your people and your Creator?"

Managing to look resolved even if she wasn't, Ami nodded ever so slightly and spoke clearly. "I do."

Mahzin took one of the swords down from the rack and

put it into Ami's hands as Enisham finished: "Then rise, Caretaker of the San Quawr."

Ami returned to her place beside Gustor.

The process repeated with Skyve. "Skyve Ferderick Lagat. Do you accept the responsibilities as Xen of the Eight, Advisor, to fight for and serve your people and your Creator?"

When Skyve came back with his brilliant sword, it was Rikky's turn. "Rikayis Del Iserwood. Do you accept the responsibilities as Shive of the Eight, Soldier, to fight for and serve your people and your Creator?"

It kept going. Kae, Orrah of the Eight, Friend. Ki, Quoye of the Eight, Mediator. Terindi, Hyrru of the Eight, Supporter. Finally, Wylan, Werrin of the Eight, Marshal. Until she was the only one without a sword, still glued to her spot beside Yhkon, trying not to cling to his crutch the way she wanted to.

"Talea, please step forward."

She must have obeyed, because she found herself on the stage facing the crowd, standing rather than kneeling, as Yhkon had told her. A sea of unfamiliar faces stared back at her, countless pairs of eyes watching her every move.

Except, not all the faces were unfamiliar. She could pick out her family—tears in Seles' eyes, Loestin holding her hand, Naylen's arm around Brenly; apparently they were courting now. Alili with a small smile, observing everything with those big brown eyes that held depth and understanding beyond her years. There were the Wardens' families. The Falstons, Yhkon's adopted parents of sorts.

And there was Ahjul's family. She had only ever met his sister Pear, but she knew the five men with her and the middle-aged couple must be his older brothers and his parents. His mother was crying.

He should be here. Talea bit the inside of her cheek as

Enisham started. "Talereinna Gen Andul. Narone has chosen you for a very special purpose. It is not to be taken lightly, nor as something you have earned. This is an honor. You must use it to serve your people, not to lord over them."

Her head bobbed in terrified agreement.

"Then do you accept the responsibilities of Eun, Aysa of the San Quawr?"

At first she thought she'd already answered, and the blood pulsing in her ears had just drowned it out. Yet he was still looking expectantly at her. Talea cleared her throat and licked her dry lips, cast a quick glance over her shoulder at Yhkon. *This is for Ahjul, for Yhkon's family, for Wylan's.* "I do."

Mahzin picked up the final shimmering sword from the rack and offered it to her. Kneeling, she took it carefully, hoping her trembling wasn't conspicuous. The weapon was beautiful, similar to Yhkon's, except with foreign words engraved along the blade. Heart pounding, she lifted her gaze back to Mahzin as he smiled at her and gestured for her to rise. "Rise, Aysa of the San Quawr." His brown eyes held hers for a long moment, and he added in an undertone, "And lead us to peace."

~♦~

Kaydor stood at the fence of the arena, observing the duel taking place within. Neither the trainer nor the trainee had noticed him, but that was fine. It might affect their performance if they knew their king was present.

The older of the two, a lean man with a harsh and permanent scowl, was experienced. There would be no reckless swings or poorly calculated moves from him. The younger was far from experienced. But he was something else, something better...he was a *natural*. His movements were fluid. This wasn't a strenuous chore for him, it was a dance. Yet his strength was just as obvious as his agility.

Mere months of training, and the lad would be a worthy opponent for any warrior.

The duel eventually ended without a winner, simply practice. Only then did Kaydor make his presence known. "Zoper! Come walk with me."

Spotting him with a smile, Zoper set aside his practice sword, and jogged to the fence, smoothly sliding over to join him. "Zoper," Kaydor put a hand on his nephew's shoulder as they started walking, "do you remember that elite band of warriors I told you about, that I'm putting together? The Tarragon?"

Zoper yawned, in a typical demonstration of his perpetual nonchalance. "Vaguely. Doesn't *tarragon* mean 'dragon', in...well...in some language?"

"Yes, in old Zentyren. The Tarragon will be an aerial unit when necessary, and I want them to symbolize the throne, too...to be the face of Zentyre's power, you might say."

"Mm-hmm." Not really paying attention, as usual.

Kaydor hid his sigh. There was a long way to go in correcting Zoper's passiveness. That he had been right, and the boy was a born fighter, however, had already been proven. It had been six months since Zoper and his siblings had come to live in the castle, and he was already excelling remarkably in his training. Which was good—that was what Kaydor needed. There had been no sign of the San Quawr rebels for weeks, and he suspected they'd returned to their secret hideaway. But that just meant they would be preparing.

When they returned, he would be equally prepared. "As such...I want you to be their captain."

Now he had Zoper's attention. Those lazy blue eyes

snapped to his. "Umm...I've only been training a few months."

"And you've already advanced much faster than most. I'm not saying you have to lead a battle tomorrow." He gave his nephew a smile and a pat on the shoulder. "Some of the men I'm choosing for the Tarragon are more experienced, yes, but others are young and new like you. You're all going to train together. I won't officially make you captain until you've had the opportunity to prove yourself to them...but I have every confidence in you."

Zoper wrinkled his nose. "I suppose that should be flattering."

Rolling his eyes, Kaydor whacked his arm. "Yes, it should be. Now listen. This is important. You and the Tarragon will be the best in Zentyre, and my right-arm in the war."

"Uhh...war?"

"Yes." He stopped walking, to look Zoper in the eye. "The San Quawr rebels will be back, and there will be a war. When that happens, *you* will be the one to defeat them."

ABOUT THE AUTHOR

Anna Kate is a college student living in South Dakota, constantly on the run between the real world and the one in her head. In the real world, she's studying for a degree in communications and working in retail. In her head, she's probably flying on the back of a dragon. Her favorite things in reality are books, coffee, and her spoiled corgi. She has loved writing YA through her teen years as much as she's enjoyed reading it, and hopes to bring a fresh perspective to the genre with the advantage of being one of its members.

javadragonbooks.com

THE STORY WILL CONTINUE…

HEIR OF THE DRAGON

Available on Amazon. Visit javadragonbooks.com for more information.

Made in the USA
Monee, IL
23 January 2021